MERGEWORLD

BOOK ONE

MERGEWORLD

BOOK ONE

Mason Elliott
&
Garan R. R. Faraday

High Mark Publishing

High Mark Publishing
www.highmarkpublishing.com

Seattle & Portland, Chicago, London

Mergeworld

Book One
by
Mason Elliott & Garan R. R. Faraday

Trade Paperback Edition
© 2014 by Mason Elliott. All rights reserved.
Published by High Mark Publishing
ISBN 978-1-930451-10-0
Watch for other titles by these authors in the future.

Cover Art by
Frank Miller
frankmillerdesign.com

Edition Notes
If you do not see this edition note here in this spot on the copyright page and on the very last page of your ebook or print version of this title, then you are not getting the final, polished version of this novel that the publisher, editors, and authors intended for you to receive. Please contact either the publisher or the authors via their emails or websites if you do not see the following update code:

High Mark Publishing Update Code K2428E

1

David Pritchard woke up gasping from one nightmare and went straight into another. A terrible agony tore through him as if the universe twisted him inside out.

Then he snapped back again.

What in damnation had just happened? Something…was very wrong.

Startled, groggy, it only took an instant for his bleary mind to figure it out.

Flames engulfed the front of his college apartment building. The stench of smoke, and the sounds of screams and breaking glass outside, only confirmed it.

He felt dazed, and blinked his scratchy eyes. The first thing he instinctively reached out for was the framed picture of his dead parents.

That was the last picture he had of them, taken a few years back, right after he started college in South Bend.

They hugged and smiled at each other in medieval garb at the Bristol Renaissance Faire up in Wisconsin. The picture froze both of them happily in time, retired in their forties. Unlike many parents that age, they weren't divorced and they still loved one another. One of their Ren-Faire pals had taken that picture for them on their digital camera.

The same camera retrieved from the car accident on the Illinois highway on their way back home from Bristol. A tractor-trailer jackknifed in the heavy rain and took them away.

The same weekend David begged off going with them.

He had blown that picture up in Photoshop, printed out an 8 x 10, and bought a nice oak frame for it. He kept it with him wherever he went. He'd die before he'd part with it, fire or no.

All that history and pain flashed through David as he clutched their picture close to him in the dark. He didn't even have to see it, just cling to it in his hands. That picture always sat prominently behind his small alarm clock on his night stand with his smart phone and wallet while he slept. That was how he found it, even in the semi-dark. He also grabbed his phone and wallet.

His clock normally flashed bright green. Power outage, probably from the fire. And the backup battery must have gone dead. Light switches? Nothing, of course, due to the fire.

The growing reek of smoke triggered his desire for self-preservation. Once he got out, he could call his friend Mason Tyler, who lived in a duplex over on Allen Street. His buddy Mace would help him.

Somewhat more awake now, David struggled not to panic. He staggered out of his room like a robot. His lanky, five-eleven frame stumbled down the hall toward his front door. He stubbed his little toe hard in the darkness. A second later, he grunted and cursed the sudden blinding spread of pain, but kept moving.

Oh, hell. No way out the front.

Dangerous ribbons of smoke curled violently through the metal front door frame and snaked up across the ceiling like an upside-down waterfall. The paint of the metal fire door already bubbled and blistered. David choked and swallowed hard.

If that door had been wood, his entire apartment might have already been completely engulfed. He might not have even come to. He saw no sense in touching the steaming door knob.

The apartment building stairs acted like a natural chimney, funneling the fire and heat straight up.

A window—climb out a window. He was only on the second floor.

His three richer roomies were already off on spring break for the next week, to the Bahamas or some such. Their parents could afford such junkets. David could not.

He suddenly realized two very important things. First, the fire hadn't spread to the back part of the apartment building yet.

Next, he was only wearing navy boxers and a gray T-shirt over his shaking frame.

Early April in South Bend, Indiana, could be any weather from sun and sixties to a flippin' blizzard.

Clothes. Only seconds to throw some on. Even in the dim, flickering orange light spilling out of the thick curtains, he spotted his laundry basket on the couch.

The smoke in the living room grew thicker. He put his precious picture, smartphone, and wallet down for only a few moments.

Jeans. On. Socks. On. He snatched up his thick blue, gold, and green hoodie from the back of the old couch where he usually left it, and pulled into its soft, warm comfort. Stocking cap. Popped on his head. Wool scarf. Around the neck. He sat down and jammed on his old gray Nike running shoes, feeling a pair of thin gloves and keys in his hoodie pockets still when he bent over.

Ready to ride, or, at least, climb out the back window to escape burning to death.

He stuffed his folks' picture, wallet, and smartphone into his dark green Jansport backpack with his pad, gel pens, and a few books. He zipped it all up.

To the back window. He pulled the curtains aside and yanked the big panel open.

He jumped slightly at the sight of some guy who had already climbed down the back of the building from the third floor. Their eyes locked, only a window screen between them in the dim, pre-dawn light and the cold morning air.

The guy looked utterly terrified.

"Watch out!" he warned, trying to keep his voice low. "Those things are killing people. They're everywhere!"

"What things?" What was this guy freaking out about?

The guy jolted, wide-eyed, and then choked.

A bloody iron arrowhead jutted out the front of his throat. In the time it took them both to blink, another arrow punched through the front of his chest, out of his T-shirt. The poor guy's mouth gaped and worked. Then his eyes rolled up white. He fell backwards, head down.

David grabbed for him but missed, his hands blocked by the barrier of the screen. He tore it away and stuck his head out the window.

He spotted strange movement down in the darkness.

Two dark, twisted, hunched-over figures loped in on bandy legs and clawed feet wrapped in fur and rags. They were smaller than humans, about four to five feet tall, and very skinny and wiry.

Whatever they were, they were definitely not human.

One of them slit the dead guy's throat from ear to ear with a long, wicked-looking rusty knife.

Blood spurted bright black in the night.

The other creature sniffed the air and snarled up at David with a greenish-black, twisted, inhuman face. Long pointed ears stuck out of holes in its ragged hood. It had a big warty nose, and gleaming green eyes. It gave full draw to the same kind of short, black bow of jagged horn that the other one carried.

The creature took dead aim at David.

And fired.

2

Twenty-year-old Mason Tyler felt a sickening crunch of pain. An intense explosion blasted his off-campus duplex apartment building to shreds all around him.

The strange destructive burst flung him out of bed to slam into the buckling ceiling, wall, and floor. It was a wonder he wasn't smashed to death as the exploding house was demolished. He awoke in confused terror, panic, and pain—hurtling through the air.

And from a nice cozy dream where he had been canoodling very pleasantly with his cute, towny girlfriend, Tori Nelson. Only the most kissable nineteen-year-old, redheaded beauty on the planet. He had been staring into Tori's gorgeous brown eyes, when—

Ka-wham!

The next thing he knew, his duplex house toppled over and went to pieces in a rush of flying fragments, as if it were being swept away by a cyclone. He and his personal belongings from his college room and closet spilled violently into the open air.

The next instant, they all toppled into what appeared to be a glowing lake of strange water that seemed to have appeared out of nowhere. As if by magic.

Terror paralyzed him.

Why was the water glowing in such a weird way? Was he still dreaming? Had he somehow gone into a bizarre nightmare?

The glowing water exploded as he, his belongings, and the house debris crashed into it in a sweeping wave. The water surged forward in a blinding spray of light and liquid.

What in the holy hell?

Mason couldn't believe it. None of it made sense.

A lake, on Allen Street, in the middle of South Bend?

No way.

Lakes just didn't appear out of nowhere.

Yet this one had.

And the blast or whatever it was had just smeared him, his room, and all of his possessions over that lake—the same way a gigantic knife might smear butter across the surface of a huge pancake.

All of this flashed through his mind as it instantly unfolded.

Mason sank beneath the surface of that eerie, glowing body of water, stunned and gasping in pain. Multicolored flares and flashes of light lit up everything around him.

Hell, he thought he saw flashes of light ignite within him, in his arms, legs, and hips. He felt energies burst inside himself, filling him further with fear and wild, queasy sensations. Feelings that would have completely freaked him out if he hadn't been so stupefied from the initial blast.

What was this? Was he on drugs somehow? Had someone slipped him something freaky before he went to sleep? Acid or something like that? His mind was racing. Was the glowing water real? Was he going to drown?

Mason's fears ran rampant, flooding his mind with dread and doubt.

What happened if you died in a dream? Did you also die in real life?

All of this had to be a nightmare, and a really weird one at that.

Yet at the same time, it all seemed so frighteningly real.

Mason watched his antique wooden gun box—filled with all of his single-action, cowboy-era competition shooting gear—sink slowly along with him.

The strange, colored light show passed through all of his gear at the same time that it passed through him.

Where in the hell would he have gotten acid?

What was happening? He felt so odd. Mason held his right hand up before his face under the water. His own flesh and bones pulsed with the suffused, strange lights that permeated them.

Perhaps he was dying. Oh, hell…maybe he was already dead.

6

Deep sudden regrets took him.

It was selfish, but all he could think of was his beloved Tori.

He'd never kiss her again or taste her mouth. Or see her smile up at him and then veil her pretty brown eyes.

He'd never get to ask her to marry him the way he wanted to, someday. Everything else in Mason's world was secondary to his beloved.

He didn't sink down far—only seven or eight feet. His box of shooting gear hit lake bottom. He bumped into it, still stunned

Mason would miss the single-action, black powder, fast-draw pistol events he loved competing in. He'd miss his local Civil War reenactor's unit. He'd miss his best friend, David Pritchard, another reenactor, but a medieval nut. His goofy roommates. Other people in college.

He didn't want to give up and die, but he seemed frozen with fear. How could he make himself move? What could he do to force himself to live? What could possibly make the strange colored lights, the weird lake—all of this odd nightmare go away?

Tori.

If he could just hold her again and tell her what she meant to him and his life. If he could tell her how much he loved her with all his heart and everything that he was and ever would be.

If he could just have the chance to do all of that before he died.

The strange lights all suddenly winked out, as if someone had thrown a switch.

Mason gasped, feeling the cold, dark water and its stifling pressure close in about him. He tried to breathe, but he only drew in water. The pressure felt as if rhinos crushed down on his chest.

That much of his ordeal was real.

He lay over the top of his shooting gear box. His feet and hands scrabbled, sinking into the slimy marl and silt that he stirred up on the shallow lake bottom.

Frantic, he pushed off the box with his hands and feet and shot back up toward the dim, morning twilight shimmering above the weird lake's surface. He clawed his way up toward air and life. It seemed so far away, lit by dim, glittering light, but still lit.

Just when he thought his heaving chest and head would explode, he breached the surface. At first he treaded water, coughed up some, and gulped in the cold air of an early, midwestern April morning.

Then he shook the water from his eyes and made for the nearest shore. In moments he touched bottom and could stumble out the rest of the way, water streaming from his soaked clothing. Here, the lake wasn't really that deep at all. Perhaps just five or six feet, at most.

Still deep enough to drown in.

Mason looked around and tried to get his bearings, but he continued to stare at more insanity.

Most of Allen Street was, in fact, now submerged in the new lake that had somehow appeared. More houses from down the street stretched out in their normal line. Only now, they led right into the water. Some of their shingled roofs were just above or below the water itself.

Yet something else wasn't right. In the ebbing twilight, Mason saw fires raging in the distance in every direction, as if dozens of homes were somehow on fire. How could there be so many? Had South Bend been hit by some kind of massive bomb? Perhaps by a chain reaction of numerous, out-of-control gas explosions?

Then his hearing clicked back in, returning abruptly. In the distance and even close by, everything sound like chaos. So many bizarre sounds. People shouting and screaming. Other weird noises, like some kind of animals or even monsters roaring and snarling. What sounded like people and the monsters clashing and fighting together for their lives.

Breaking glass. The sound of breaking glass seemed to come from every direction.

In his shock, Mason grew more worried. Had he died? Was he dead? Had he somehow woken up into some kind of hell?

Even more disconcerting, when he looked back at them—at the Allen Street houses that extended out into the lake—at some point they did not continue on. They ended. Some of them were only partials, as if sheared in half. What could do that?

Where did the other halves of those houses go? There wasn't any wreckage or debris.

And beyond them... Nothing but a dense, thick forest of large, dark trees. Trees like nothing he had ever seen before.

He glimpsed more fires and heard more screams and breaking glass extending far off into the distance and beyond.

Mason staggered back up out of the cold water and collapsed again at its edge, still gasping. Everything around him threatened his sanity. None of it made any sense.

How long before hypothermia killed him?

Then he tripped over a dark body in the poor light at the water's edge.

He knelt down to check it. At least it was another person and not some demon or some such.

Please, don't be dead...don't be dead.

Mason very suddenly had no wish to be alone.

The cold night air closed in around them both. But at least it wasn't raining or snowing—yet.

Gosh, he couldn't tell if he was shaking more with the cold, or from raw fright.

He struggled to focus on the body at his feet. It still felt warm. He grabbed the outstretched arms and tried to drag it further from the water's edge. Mason had taken some first aid and medic training in ROTC. He needed to get it together and check for a pulse and breathing, to see if this person was injured, and if there was anything he could do to help.

It was a young guy, college age, like himself, about twenty-one or so. They shared the same build: tall, thin, and wiry. Mason was six-foot-two. This guy was maybe slightly shorter, about six-foot-one. But there the comparison stopped. This guy had shaggy golden-blond hair. Mason's own hair was short, straight, and black. He was due for a haircut. Mason checked Blondie's black eyes. This guy wasn't dead—just knocked out.

His patient's breathing was shallow, but Mason found a steady pulse at Blondie's wrist and neck. He quickly checked him over for any sign of serious injury: bleeding wounds, broken bones, any major trauma. There could still be internal injuries that he might not notice right away. Mason struggled to drag Blondie to a safe, dry place, make him comfortable, and elevate his feet.

There was something very odd about the guy, however. At first Mason's dazed, shivering mind couldn't place it. Faded navy hoodie, black T-shirt, jeans. No phone, wallet, or ID—but maybe Blondie hadn't been carrying them at the time all of this happened…whatever all of this was.

His boots.

That was it, exactly.

Blondie had him some strange leather boots. Mason pulled up one pant leg to examine them closer.

The boots were, in fact, extremely odd. Hand-tooled, black leather boots with intricate images of writhing people and monsters fighting to the death. Most guys would not wear such flashy boots on campus, or anywhere for that matter. Even his best friend David, the medieval buff, didn't have such boots. Although Dave did own several other pairs of period-style boots, just as Mason himself had several pairs of western-style boots for his six-gun competitions.

All right, perhaps Blondie's boots weren't that weird, but they still seemed out of place somehow, and they looked very expensive. Maybe the guy was a medieval nut like Dave, or some kind of gamer geek, or super, *LOTR* fanboy.

9

Being soaked to the skin on an early April morning in South Bend, Indiana, was not the greatest situation for either of them. Being cold and afraid was a double whammy. And if Mason continued to shiver and suffer in the nippy air, then he was certain that his new friend Blondie would also.

For just a moment, as he stood there in his own wet underwear, gray cotton sweatpants, navy long-sleeved T-shirt, and bare feet, Mason seriously considered taking Blondie's hoodie and boots for himself. But that wouldn't be right. Wet cotton didn't keep anyone that warm, in any case. And those odd boots were just…freaky.

He suddenly spotted and chased after a section of burgundy window curtain that tumbled past on the wind. At least he could cover up with that. It sure looked thick and dry. He needed anything to stay warm with and get warmer. Pride wasn't even a consideration at that point.

By the time he returned with his new curtain wrapped nicely around his shoulders, Blondie was sitting up on a shattered dresser. He held his head bent down into both hands and groaned. He trembled with cold.

Mason sighed, walked up, and reluctantly wrapped the warm curtain around Blondie's shoulders and tucked it in around him. Blondie tried to look up at him with a startled expression, but he was still too weak and too cold to do even that very quickly.

Blondie continued to shiver, and tugged the warm curtain even tighter around him.

"You okay, dude?" Mason asked. "What's your name?"

Blondie's mouth fell open; he blinked and then shook his head. "Ahh…I feel terrible. I don't know. I can't…remember anything."

"Great, you must have hit your head," Mason muttered. "I find one other guy, and he's got amnesia!"

"What's that?"

"It means you can't remember anything–your past, who you are. I checked you for a wallet. Nada. No phone, either."

"What's a wallet…what's a phone?"

"Skip it for now. You don't have them. Just take it easy, recover your strength, and try to remember something. My name's Mason. Mason Tyler. Until you remember or we find out who you are, I'm gonna call you Blondie."

"Why?"

Mason pointed. "You've got blond hair, and you just look like a Blondie to me."

Blondie gasped and blinked, still in clearly in disbelief. "I'm Blondie?"

"Yep. Don't wear it out."

"Huh, why would I do that?"

Mason tilted his head, unable to wait any longer. "Nice boots, dude. You a gamer geek, an Otaku?"

"Your words are strange. What are boots?"

Mason frowned. This guy had it bad; he didn't know anything. "Skip that, too, I guess."

Noises came from one of the houses nearby. It sounded like something inside had been knocked over or had fallen. Everything else was relatively quiet around them, so the noise nearby was quite alarming.

Mason and Blondie both stared at the house with the noises inside, for a moment, unable to move.

What now?

An old man in his late sixties staggered out the front door and left it open behind him. Both Mason and Blondie breathed a sigh of relief.

But the old guy did have a shiny Colt revolver tucked in the elastic belt of his blue and green flannel pajamas and a dark, bloody golf club clutched in one hand–some kind of iron.

And the dark blood was a bit off-putting, too.

The old guy stumbled toward them, stammering and muttering as if he were also in shock. "G-g-guns don't work. Nothing's working. You have to fight the monsters hand-to-hand."

Now all three of them were confused.

Mason at least went over to help the old guy, who kept staring straight ahead. But he offered Mason his trembling, wrinkled hand.

"Howard Kazinsky," he muttered.

"Mason Tyler; my friends call me Mace. Do you know what's going on, Howard?" He walked Howard over and sat him down next to Blondie on the toppled dresser.

"I dunno," Howard said. "I woke up and everything was strange. Then the monsters appeared and started breaking windows, setting fires, and attacking and killing people. My dog was barking like crazy. I clubbed one of the smaller monsters in the head a few times with my nine iron."

Mason reached over calmly and pulled the loaded Colt Python revolver out of Howard's waistband and checked it. A .357 magnum, all six rounds live, none fired. "This is a nice piece," Mason said, well-versed in firearms. "Why didn't you shoot that monster with it? You didn't have time?"

"I tried. I keep telling you, kid. Guns don't work. No electricity. The cars don't work anymore, either. Nothing works. I'm lucky I had this golf club, or that thing would have carved me up like a turkey. I saw more of those creatures coming, so I ran out the back door and got away. My neighbors weren't so lucky. I could hear them screaming as I ran."

The old guy had to be off his rocker. Perhaps he wasn't just in shock. Maybe he suffered from dementia, Alzheimer's, or some such.

But what if Howard was telling the truth?

Come to think of it, Mason didn't hear any cars, and no sirens or fire trucks—or gunshots. If monsters were attacking people, there would certainly be gunshots.

He lifted the revolver in the air and pulled the trigger.

Click.

He tried to fire all six shots, but the action kept clicking. He examined the firing pin and then the rounds themselves. Everything looked fine. Why wouldn't the bullets go off? He put the Colt back down next to Howard.

The light grew slightly in the distant sky. A ruined bed lay in the water just at the edge of the lake, off to one side.

It was Mason's bed.

Two of his blankets were wool. Even wet, they'd still be warm. Mason and his friends were shivering. He retrieved his blankets and did his best to wring them dry before spreading them out on the relatively dry ground. The mattress and shattered box frame and wooden bed frame were obviously ruined.

Then he spotted his black leather, double-holster, quick-draw rig, still hanging on the splintered post of the crushed headboard. His .36 caliber Spiller & Burr black powder revolvers were still strapped down in his custom holsters. He had cleaned and reloaded them the night before and hung them on his bedpost. His first instinct was to get them out of the water.

Of course, they were waterlogged. But if he could retrieve his gearbox from the lake and get to his sealed containers, he could reload them. He currently didn't have much else to do. His weakened, disoriented friends weren't going anywhere, and they seemed relatively safe where they were.

First he retrieved his rig and the Spillers. He started everything drying on the blankets in the crisp early morning air.

The next part would be the hardest, but there was nothing for it.

Mason had to go back under that cold water and retrieve his gear box. He was still half-soaked and shivering as it was. But if he was going to do it, he needed to do it now, before he grew weaker or changed his mind.

Once all that was accomplished, he definitely needed to find some warm, dry clothing for himself and his new friends.

For being half-frozen and scared almost witless, he commended himself for at least staying practical. The main thing was not to freeze up, or curl up in a ball of fear and do nothing. Keep moving, keep busy doing things.

If he could load his guns up and get them working, then he wouldn't feel so scared and defenseless.

Mason shucked off his damp T-shirt and sweat pants, spreading them out next to the wool blankets. His clothes were half dry by now. No sense getting them soaked again.

He went into the water in nothing but his boxers, rubbing his arms, wincing, his teeth chattering as he cursed. He took a deep breath and dove under the lake's surface near the same point he had stumbled out.

The sky was a bit lighter above him, but it still took him time to find the gear box underwater, mostly by feel.

He came up for a few breaths of air as needed, and went back down.

He grabbed the rope handle of the antique gun box and dragged it toward the edge of the lake. Mason had to repeat the process four times before he could keep his head above water, and then finally tug the heavy box out of the lake.

He rolled onto one of the wet blankets, shivering and recovering.

Once he could move again, he took his wet boxers off, dried off with the other damp blanket, and put his damp clothes back on. It was better than nothing.

He opened the latch on the crate. Of course, everything inside was wet, but his gunpowders and some of his gear were in sealed containers. He had several other black powder, single-action pistols of various types and sizes. Mason spread his arsenal out to dry on the blankets.

He retrieved more powder and shot, more bullet-making supplies, and two gems: his 1858-style carbine, and his Howdah Hunter, 20-gauge, double-barreled, black powder shotgun pistol.

Then he spotted his Civil War replica cavalry saber, emptied the water out of the scabbard, and strapped it to his side for good measure. If Howard wasn't delusional, and there were monsters about, the saber would help.

He wasn't as good with swords as his good buddy, David Pritchard, the medieval maven. But Mason had practiced fencing with the saber enough to know how to handle the weapon—even on horseback.

When Mason checked on his friends, Howard and Blondie were slumped against each other and the dresser with the curtain pulled around them. The buggers were sleeping quite pleasantly.

Lucky bastards.

He put a plumed, black cavalry hat with braids on Blondie's head. It just worked somehow.

All three of them jumped when something else crashed inside another house up the dark street, making a huge racket.

Mason studied his two shivering comrades. Neither of them looked up to doing much of anything. "You two guys stay here and look after each other. I'm going to go check out that noise. It might be someone else who needs help. They might be hurt." He drew his saber and clutched it tight in his right hand.

Keep busy, keep moving. Don't let the fear take hold.

Mason picked his way over to the house quietly. It was just a regular old brownstone from the forties or so.

When he got close enough, he saw that the front door to the house stood half open. Not a good sign. He slipped in, trying to be quiet, fearful of broken glass with his bare feet.

He remained still and listened for a while. Nothing seemed to move or make noise. Perhaps something had just fallen down.

It took him a few minutes more to work up the gumption to actually go further inside.

Once he was already in the house, he checked for any other survivors or victims.

Mason went through some dressers and closets. He felt some relief at finding extra blankets, dry clothing, hats, and three jackets. He even found socks and tennis shoes for him and Howard. The man of the house apparently had feet that were only half a size larger than Mason's. That was much better than bare feet.

Something else might kill them, but they weren't going to freeze to death.

He wrapped his bounty up in a blanket and hauled it all back out to his friends like a jolly burglar. Outside, his new friends—those bums—were sleeping again.

Once Howard and Blondie were awake, they all changed into dry clothing and felt much better and warmer with their borrowed jackets, baseball caps, and shoes and socks on.

Mason went down to the lake edge to check on his drying gear. He strapped on his double holster rig and took up his Spiller & Burrs, twirling them deftly in his hands without thinking. Now he could reload them and see if they worked.

He called back to his friends. "Once it gets light out, we'll walk out of here and see what's happened to the rest of the city."

"Mace!" Howard shouted, his voice shaking with fear.

Howard and Blondie retreated toward him and the edge of the lake. Howard clutched his bloodstained golf club. Blondie ran up beside Mason and drew the saber and held it out in front of himself without even asking.

Both of them were shaking so bad they could hardly stand.

From out of the trees, a horde of about forty of Howard's monsters emerged from the trees, as big as life.

14

Monsters. That was the only way to describe them. Humanoid monsters of all sizes, some hairy, some furry, some with scales. Various, snarling, monster faces. Some wore pieces of rusty armor or battered helmets, and carried clubs, jagged axes, swords, and spears.

The horde spotted the three humans and charged, shrieking and roaring.

Mason's mouth hung open in shock, petrified with horror. He instinctively drew both of his pistols. Blondie lifted his saber on the right. Howard lifted his nine iron on the left.

They barely had time to do that.

"Guns don't work," the old man muttered.

3

Only half a second to react.

David pitched back into the hallway. The black-feathered arrow barely missed his face, zipping into the ceiling like an angry hornet. He lay there for a moment, gulping air.

He stared up at the arrow stuck in the crown molding, trying to process all the weirdness—resisting his urge to vomit.

He checked himself and glared at his shaking hands. He was still real. His burning college apartment—still real.

Still very much on fire.

Coarse laughter from down below. The things that had just killed that poor guy? They were also now horribly real.

David flipped over on the floor.

He crawled into his room, gasping hard.

Those things weren't human. No way in hell. Where did they come from?

He peeked out his curtains down at them from another window so that they wouldn't spot him.

Their armor looked to be layered bands of leather and hide, studded with metal and spikes—like something out of a fantasy movie or a video game.

But they butchered the college kid's body right where it lay, hacking off the leg and arm muscles away from the bones first and then ripping open the belly. They devoured the gory meat, skin, and entrails raw, with gusto.

Flames crackled in the living room by that time. If he didn't get out, he'd die in the fire.

David thought of that poor dead guy. That could have easily been him down there.

He clenched his fists.

To hell with those creatures down below. Better to take his chances with them than the fire.

A life with Medieval Historical Society parents taught him both swordfighting and archery. He had weapons, and he knew how to use them.

He reached under his bed, dragged out his crossbow and a covered hip quiver full of bolts. Then his sword belt with with his scabbarded longsword, competition tomahawks, and fighting dagger.

The rest of his medieval garb and gear was still down in the trunk of his old car in the apartment parking lot. He'd just been to an event two weeks before and never bothered to unpack.

That included his own personal suit of armor.

But for now, these weapons would need to be enough.

He loaded his crossbow, went back into the hallway window, and shot the first monster through the goddam neck. Screw those murdering bastards, whatever the hell they were. David's anger flared.

The creature fell to one side, gurgling and clawing at its death wound as David efficiently reloaded.

The second monster scrambled to shoot back.

David's next shot passed right through its ugly, gore-stained face and out the back of its head. Dark black blood pooled around both of the dead creatures.

Good. To hell with those ugly buggers. They wouldn't hurt anyone else ever again.

With them dead, David dropped his backpack to the ground, and then his crossbow on top of that. Then he quickly climbed out the window, hung from the sill, and jumped to the cold hard ground.

He rolled to one side and back up to his feet. His breath came out of his mouth and nose like white smoke. Frost coated everything like white dust.

He checked the bodies of the creatures and their weapons quickly. Nothing but pitted iron crap. His gear was far superior, but theirs could still kill.

Geez, they reeked. Their bodies already seemed to putrefied. They smelled like two-week-old roadkill in a hot summer.

David gagged while he retrieved his bolts and wiped off the black monster goo from them. What in the hell was he in for next?

He had to ask.

Something even bigger and uglier loped around the corner of the building. It was seven feet tall with huge dangling arms, its body covered in some kind of tough hide or carapace, with gray-green patches of hair or barbs. The huge head and maw were a terrifying mass of horns and teeth, with two mismated eyes.

It dragged the bloody, headless corpse of a college girl still wearing a pink bathrobe. The monster ripped an arm off the body and gnashed into the flesh. Then it spotted David.

Damnation.

It dropped its meat, roared, and charged at him.

David shot it right in the chest with his crossbow.

The towering thing broke the bolt off like a stinging insect and kept coming.

Screw this.

David ran for his life.

The lumbering thing only chased him a short distance before turning back. David had covered a little distance by then. He knew the area well near Angela and 23 from walking, biking, and driving back and forth to school. He dodged in among the other apartment buildings—through Clover Village and around Ivy Court.

Finally he crouched down out of sight in the cold darkness and the growing twilight and shuddered, trying to catch his breath.

In the distance, all over town, fires and more screaming raged, along with the sounds of breaking glass.

How many of these murderous things were out there on the loose? Where did they come from? None of it made any sense.

He dug his phone out of his backpack with shaking hands. Dead. It wouldn't even power up.

Then he noticed something else. Power was still out everywhere. No lights. No cars or trucks moved on any of the streets. No police or sirens, ambulances, or even fire trucks.

Something else very strange.

No gunshots. Very weird. With these monsters attacking the city at random, there ought to be pockets of gunfire all over the place.

But there wasn't—in the most heavily armed nation on Earth.

Then he heard feet pounding, people running.

People of all ages ran here and there in breathless panic. He watched from where he hid.

Some of the monsters roared and cackled, attacking the routed humans, cutting some down, dragging others away as captives. Screaming and shrieking erupted everywhere.

The heavy stench of the invaders wafted on the cold, light April winds.

David spotted a man in his thirties running from one of the monsters hot on his heels. Both of them stepped into a puddle of strange shimmering water. It was strange because when they stepped into it, the water flashed bright with a weird, yellow-green energy.

Both the man and the monster shrieked and turned to dust.

Dust that scattered and faded on the wind.

David gawked, shot to his feet, and struggled to stop shaking. What had he just witnessed? It didn't make any sense, but he just watched it happen.

He ran. Note to self: get the hell out of there and don't step in any glowing water.

What he needed was some kind of plan. Whatever these things were, they weren't going to take him down. He needed to get somewhere safe—away from all of this craziness.

He slung his crossbow behind him and secured it with a metal clasp on the sling strap. He drew his longsword and picked his way among the buildings, moving away from the sounds of the spreading terror. He crouched down and quickly ran across open areas.

A larger version of the first two creatures, man-high, suddenly charged at him from some brush. Without thinking, David cut it down with a wide, sweeping arc of his long, sharp blade. It fell back in two pieces.

David kept moving. He darted down Twyckenham, then Angela. He spotted the basketball arena in the distance, but tall shadows like weird trees obscured what should have been the football stadium complex. Half of the campus appeared to be missing, replaced by dark trees. More insanity.

He made it across the street and ducked behind the hotel.

After a mile he made it past Notre Dame Avenue and the Eddy Street Commons, heading west towards 933. The latter was one of the main drags through South Bend, what some of the locals still called Michigan or 31 from back in the day.

He jogged left on St. Louis, skirting any sounds of trouble. He came around a dark brick brownstone near Hill Street.

A middle-aged guy in a winter coat and black slippers aimed a shotgun at him point-blank and pulled the trigger. David jumped. Oh, hell.

The trigger only clicked.

The man paled.

"Gun's don't work!" he stammered. "How do we protect ourselves?"

David hefted his sword. "The old-fashioned way. Get a club, an ax, make a spear. These things can bleed and die. I've killed a couple of the bastards, already. Good luck, Mister."

He kept running. The guy called after him to come back, but the sounds of chaos and fighting still seemed to rage on David's heels.

He didn't know what to do. But just running scared was going to get old, and fast. He needed to get somewhere. Find someone he knew.

He had a couple of good friends on the northwest side. Mason Tyler and Mace's girlfriend, Tori. Dirk and Belinda Blackwood, from the local MHS, medieval reenactment group. They'd help him.

He jogged past Lawrence, still making for 933. Monster stink was very heavy on the wind.

More screams, very close, down Stanfield Street. A woman and some kids by the sound.

He had to do something.

Even as he went forward, three kids rushed past him in terror, still in their pajamas. The youngest about eight.

"Get to a house," he told them. "Bang on the door. Get in and hide!"

The woman around the corner still shouted, her tone both angry and scared. But her words were...strange. They didn't make sense.

Some kind of weird language.

David poked his head around low.

Four of the monsters circled an odd young woman with her back to him.

Three of the smaller creatures had hatchets. The other larger one a jagged sword. Bastards.

But the girl was really something. She wore medieval garb of high quality.

Midnight blue wool robes, the long skirt split down the middle for walking or riding. Ornate embroidery. Long athletic legs in hosen matched the rest of her.

She squared off against the creatures, wielding a carved wooden staff banded with metal.

She moved as if she knew how to use it.

They snarled at her in some other weird language.

She spat back something. It sounded like a curse.

20

David smiled.

One of the smaller things charged in from her left.

She spun and shouted a quick spurt of weird words. She thrust her staff at the thing, as if she actually expected something was supposed to happen. For an instant, both of them hesitated.

The creature snarled and grinned.

She spun the end around and jabbed it hard into the monster's face. It grunted and dropped.

David rushed in as the other three closed with her. She caught another one in the groin before they yanked her staff away and tossed it aside.

He cleaved one monster head open with his sword stroke, bashed the other with the pommel.

The leader backed away, trying to hold his sword to the girl's neck as they struggled. Her jet black hair drooped down over her glorious face. Luscious red lips parted, breathing hard—pretty porcelain skin.

The lead monster snarled at him.

David ignored it and chopped the brute clutching its groin in the face, before it could snatch up the knife it reached for.

Then he faced off again with the leader.

The leader tried to back away, and moved to cut the girl's throat.

David grinned and advanced, sweeping his sword down. He cleanly severed the monster's arm holding the sword. It flopped to the ground, the hand still around the pommel. Another precise cut took off the other arm.

The young woman dropped to her hands and knees and whirled out of the way. Smart girl.

The leader stumbled and turned around. David smote him to the ground with one stroke.

Applause broke out from the window of a nearby house.

Four drunken street punks laughed and cheered, watching the whole fight from their safe vantage point. David felt his anger well up.

"Why didn't you come help us!" he yelled.

The girl scrambled to retrieve her staff.

The punks just laughed and slammed the windows shut. David made sure that all of the creatures were dead.

By then the odd girl was already hoofing it down Stanfield and then left down Howard. He couldn't take his eyes off her.

David ran after her, wiping the weird black blood off his sword onto a rag. They passed Niles Avenue, where Howard turned into Northshore. He didn't know her name—nor had he completely seen her face.

"Hey! Hey you...Miss!" What in the heck could he call her? Hot girl in wizard garb? That's exactly what she looked like—a cute D&D wizard.

She glanced back and then squared off with him just as she had with the monsters, staff ready to fight, brilliant violet eyes blazing.

Whoa.

David took in a breath when he caught a glance of her stunning face. His knees buckled slightly. Huge violet eyes, ivory skin, a soft upturned nose. Her red lips spread over set white teeth. Even ready for a fight she looked amazing.

"Shosta dere!" she commanded. "Coma nasa klisser." She wore a dark blue gem on her forehead on a silver circlet—but the gemstone was clearly cracked.

David sheathed his longsword and held up both hands empty as a token of non-violence. They kept walking, slowly. She maintained the distance between them, eyeing him suspiciously.

She seemed very intrigued by his weapons.

"I don't want to fight you. I just want to talk," he told her.

"Jaessa dakko?"

"Uh, yeah. What you said."

She halted and leaned wearily on her staff, glaring at him with narrowed violet eyes.

By the Powers themselves—this girl was so hot, it was a wonder she didn't burst into flames right before his eyes.

Okay, time for a break. Definitely. David sat down on the same side as her, giving her space, by the curb of Northshore and Leeper Streets. He put his shaking hands together. He was still very freaked out. His heart still pumped from the brief fight, and chasing after the pretty wizard girl with the strange language.

The sky lightened in the east.

Strange. He looked around them and listened. The attacks sounded as if they had stopped. He didn't see or smell any more monsters. But fires still burned, and people yelled and shouted in the distance all around town.

"Dey dasna laggo daz zahn," she said. She touched the cracked gem on her forehead and frowned.

Did that damn gemstone suddenly flash and fizzle in a strange way?

Then David suddenly figured out what she was trying to say. "They don't like the sun?" he repeated.

She nodded.

Every time she spoke, her speech got closer to something he could understand. How in the heck was she managing that? He knew a little bit of several languages, but was fluent in none, including Latin and Japanese, the latter from his Kendo days.

22

Wizard girl was definitely *not* from the Midwest.

"Who are you?" he asked.

"I aza Jerriel," she said. "Asha yoo?"

"David."

"Daeved."

Close enough. "Where are you from, Jerriel?"

She looked around and then back at him with those killer violet eyes.

"Natta yoor vorld."

4

Mason instinctively pulled the triggers on his Spillers even as the monsters bore down upon them, lifting weapons to overwhelm and slaughter the three humans.

His guns had been in the lake water. He winced and fully expected to hear dead clicks, right before they all died.

Instead–the entire world went blinding, white-hot directly in front of them.

In that instant, his Spillers went off and the resulting explosions were catastrophic. They stupefied and shocked everyone present, including the charging horde of monsters.

When the nova of light faded and Mason's scorched vision returned...the pack of monsters that had been about to annihilate them was gone–almost completely vaporized. Right along with two wide, fan-shaped swaths of the new dark forest.

If Mason had been stupefied before, he was flabbergasted now.

Burning monster feet, crude shoes, and charred bones in scorched boots and leg wraps peppered the ground where the horde had been, directly in front of smoldering, glowing orange stumps left behind at the same level–about a foot or less off the ground–in the wake of the two blasts. The upper parts of the severed trees fell back and crashed down.

Mason, Blondie, and Howard just stood there staring with their slack, dry mouths drooping wide open like a trio of deranged imbeciles.

"What the hell was that?" Howard stammered in fear.

"What did you just do?" Blondie asked him.

Mason stared and check his pistols, just as shocked as they were. Two chambers had fired.

"I don't have a clue," Mason told them, still shaking. "But if more of those things come around…I've got five shots left in each cylinder."

Blondie pointed at the Spillers. "What are those devices?"

"Watch where you point those damn things," Howard whined. "They're dangerous."

Mason shook his head in disbelief and examined both revolvers more closely. "This doesn't make any sense. After being in the water, they shouldn't have worked at all. Not like that, at least."

"You can say that again," Howard said. "Nobody else can get their guns to work, and yours work like something crazy."

Mason just shook his head.

"Do you have any more of those devices, and can you show us how to use them?" Blondie asked. "If there are more of those creatures around, we might need them."

Mason nodded and led them back to his blankets and gear to the right, near the lake edge. "I've got a whole box of guns and gear. We'll load up and try them out."

"Get me one of those cannons, too," Howard said.

While Mason sat down, and carefully loaded each of his weapons, Howard and Blondie raided another nearby house and garage. They brought back a little food to snack on and a two-wheeled cart to load their supplies in.

Once they were loaded up and, ready to move out, Mason gave them pistols and holsters, and set up an impromptu practice range in front of the same devastated area as the backdrop. He used various cans and bottles for targets.

After several attempts, they learned very quickly that none of Mason's guns would go off for either Blondie or Howard. To them, all of the pistols were inert and useless.

But whenever Mason fired any of those same weapons–then stand the hell back out of the way. He unleashed a blast that vaporized anything directly in front of him.

Crazier still—even when he dry-fired the *empty* pistols—a spurt of destructive, red-orange energy of some kind shot out of the barrel and blasted precise holes in trees and buildings. It was a lesser effect, but at least his guns still worked, even with the chambers empty. That was a neat trick in itself. None of it made any damn sense.

"It's you, Mace," Howard said. "Something about you and them guns allows them to function in this crazy way. They won't work for anyone else. How did this happen? Do you remember anything?"

Mason sat down and struggled to think.

He told them everything he could remember. He described waking up in the midst of the explosion and being flung into the glowing lake that had just appeared along with the weird forests.

He explained how he had nearly drowned, and about the strange lights all around in the glowing water that seemed to pass through him and his gun box.

"It's all something more than just you and your guns," Howard said at last. "That's all just a little part of it. Take these trees, for instance. Anyone who lived on this street for the past year knows that these strange trees weren't here before. And this lake. Something big has happened to change everything this much. That's why nothing works. No planes, cars, phones, guns, electricity. All of the technology that our world relies on has suddenly stopped working."

"I wouldn't think anything like that could happen accidentally," Blondie noted.

Mason sneered. "How would you know? You've got amnesia. You don't know anything."

Blondie turned around, waving his arms. "Howard's right. Look around. Important changes have in fact occurred. The trees. This lake. The very lay of the land has been changed. Everything has changed. There's no denying it. While you now possess some kind of sorcerous power."

Mason clenched both of his fists in anger and frustration. "I don't know what has happened, but it's morning now, and the sun is up behind those spotty clouds. Those monsters don't seem to be around any more."

"Maybe they can't stand the sunlight," Howard suggested.

"Maybe they can't," Mason said. "But whatever it is, things are definitely quieting down. I'm still cold, and now I'm hungry and thirsty." The small amount of food they had snacked on seemed to have gone right through him, and his throat was dry with thirst.

"You're right," Blondie said. "We can't stay here until something worse happens to us. We need to find out what's going on."

"Right," Mason said. "At the very least, we need to find some more food, and a safe place to stay tonight." They made their way through the thick

26

trees and forest, away from Allen Street, the lake, and toward what he thought was Portage Road and north toward Angela Boulevard.

The many fires had done heavy damage to that part of town. Scattered sparsely among the patches of forest, entire blocks of homes still smoldered or had been reduced to piles of smoking ruin, scorched down to their concrete foundations. The stench of smoke seemed to be everywhere.

But the dead bodies were the worst.

Lots of dead bodies, everywhere. Too many to begin to count. All ages, too. No exceptions, from the very old right down to the very young. Mason saw dead kids and even infants and babies for the first time in his young life.

Grim, disgusting, and terrible; there was no describing it. He didn't want to look. He never wanted to see anything like that ever again, but it was everywhere at random, wherever they turned. Like a slap in the face.

Most of the bodies looked as if they had been hacked or cut up, or had the bones and heads crushed and beat in. Some had been shot with nasty-looking black arrows.

Their guts were torn open, muscles sliced off their bones.

Even worse, many of the bodies had been…eaten. By the looks on some of those twisted faces, some of them had been partially devoured…while they still lived.

Howard was right, of course. People had tried to defend themselves with guns at first. And many of them had perished not far from from their loaded, but useless weapons. Many guns were still clutched in cold, dead hands.

Mason tried several of the weapons, all still fully loaded. Not a single one of them worked. Especially not like his.

He looked around at all of the madness and swallowed hard. "Within a day or so, all of this part of town is going to stink to high heaven—like a hunter's gut pile left out in the sun."

Then they came across bodies of the monsters, mixed in among the dead. People had resorted to hand weapons and taken some of the attackers down with them.

Looking at the corpses of those monsters drove Mason's mind to the edge of his sanity once more. Big ones, little ones, and others in between. There seemed to be several different kinds or variations. But they were all vicious-looking brutes.

It became very tough not to let his fears take hold.

An insane fantasy novel had exploded into real life. But what was real anymore? He was basically staring at dead goblins, hobgoblins, orcs, trolls, and ogres. There was no other way to describe the horrific monsters. They were hairy, furry, scaly, with snouts and wide maws filled with vicious teeth. Their hands and feet ended in claws. They wore medieval-style tunics of hide and rusty pieces of armor, patched together here and there.

They wielded dangerous weapons of rusty, jagged iron. Spears, swords, maces, war clubs, hammers, and knives. A few had short bows with quivers of the lethal black arrows barbed with metal.

Blondie picked among them and found himself a working short bow and three quivers of arrows.

"Do you know how to shoot a bow?" Mason asked his new friend.

Mason had practiced archery with his good buddy Dave, and could still barely shoot one. It took hours of training to shoot a bow effectively.

Blondie grinned. "I think so. How hard can it be?"

"Harder than you might think. Getting good at shooting anything takes lots of practice."

"Well, at least now I have something to practice with."

Howard suddenly took a breather and began to rub his chest with a very worried look on his face. "My house burned down. Everything must be gone. What'll I do? What'll I do for my medicine?"

"What's your medicine for, Howard?"

"My heart."

Mason frowned. Just great. Something else to worry about now. "That's not good, Howard. There's a CVS up the street by the Portage Martin's. Let's go there and see if they can give you something. Let's go, just take it easy."

Big sections of Portage Road were gone, including the part with the turnabout near the bridge over the St. Joe River. The river was there, still, but no bridge. They'd have to go a ways either way to find a way across.

There were bodies leading down to the river and floating in it. They spotted even more bodies as well, in the strange patches of forest punctuating the riverbank and among the remaining houses along the river.

There were dark, forested hills north of town, and even the far distant shadow of mountains—actual mountains—way off to the west.

Indiana never had mountains like that.

Mason spoke out loud, noting all of the changes as they tried to pick their way toward what they hoped would be the drugstore. How could the very land itself change overnight?

Blondie suddenly spoke up. "These creatures and all of this new terrain are clearly something from another world—just like the trees on Allen Street and the lake. There's no way to deny it. Can't you see what has happened? Parts of this world have somehow become mixed up with parts of another very different world that does have these trees and these creatures. It is the only logical explanation."

Mason considered such a possibility.

In a way, it made sense. "So, if parts of both worlds are now mixed up here, what has happened to the other parts of both worlds that we can't see any longer? Have they simply been destroyed or ceased to be?"

Blondie shrugged. "Who knows? But if both realities have become patched together, then both worlds occupy a space in reality somewhere. Perhaps in the alternate dimension—on the other side—the other world is just as mixed up now as this one. That would make more sense."

Mason pressed his skull together with his hands as if it might explode. "Mixed-up, alternate worlds and dimensions? How could such a thing happen?"

Blondie hugged his upper arms and rubbed them in the chilly air. "Perhaps it just occurred by chance, by dumb luck—a cosmic mistake. Or else someone or something made all of this happen on purpose, by some dark, insane, or diabolical design."

"Blondie, you can't even remember your own name or what boots are, how can you be sure of any of that?"

"I know what boots are; I was just tired and cold. And I may not recall my name yet, but I can still think. Just like I know my name isn't Blondie. Take a look at the evidence all around us. Do you have a better explanation for what we have seen? Or why your weapons alone seem to work, as if by magic?"

Magic? Yeah, that would explain a great deal.

Blondie clenched one shivering fist and suddenly looked very determined. "I will regain my memory. Somehow I will. And when I do, I have a very strong feeling that I'm going to be proven correct about all of this."

"Well, let's keep moving until that happens. I've got a good buddy of mine from college named David Pritchard. He lives in one the apartments close to campus near 23. After we get Howard's medicine, we'll go look him up."

"That'll be good," Howard piped up. "I need my medicine."

Another large patch of forest blocked their way right before the Portage Martin's Supermarket and the CVS drugstore there, along with a few lesser shops.

As they made their way through the trees, they picked up on the growing sounds of a commotion up ahead. They could make out many people screaming, shouting, and crying in a mix of panic, anger, and fear.

When they came out of the trees, they looked down a short slope into the parking lot. But at a glance, the Martin's was nowhere to be seen, replaced by more forest.

The CVS and a few of the other shops were there, and about a hundred or more people were just starting to break the windows and loot them.

Some had bicycles, many were on foot, and many fought over shopping carts. Gangs and small groups of thugs and looters had formed here and there among individuals. Some of the thugs didn't bother to go into the stores, but watched like vultures, and took what they wanted from people coming back out with armloads full of stuff.

Many people there had bloody noses or bruises and bleeding wounds from various altercations.

A handful of people lay knocked out or possibly even dead in the parking lot. The bodies were in danger of being trampled by the mob.

Mason led Blondie and Howard down the slope and toward the growing crowd in front of the CVS drugstore. Things looked pretty bad. Should they even go down there?

A South Bend cop in his late thirties lay moaning off to one side.

Occasionally, a punk or thug would stop and kick him.

Only some of the looters were armed with what appeared to be an assortment of baseball bats, clubs, and kitchen knives. No one seemed to be brandishing guns any longer.

"We're too late," Mason said, looking at the mob boiling in and out of the drugstore. "I don't want to risk going in there with that mob. This is a feeding frenzy; those people down there have lost it. They're acting like animals, like savages. Let's try to reach that cop and drag him out of there. Someone's going to kill him. We have to do something."

"Why?" Blondie said.

"Hell, I don't really want to, either. But it's the right thing to do."

They made their way toward the cop, chasing off some teens who stopped to taunt and hurl insults at the poor guy.

Mason brandished his cavalry saber, Blondie bent an arrow on his bowstring, and Howard menaced them with his nine iron.

"Get the hell out of here," Mason snarled at the punks.

They screamed a bunch of filth and ran off, laughing and cursing.

Mason knelt to check the policeman's injuries, and his name badge. "Officer...Reinert?"

The cop could barely sit up and nod, gasping for breath.

Mason handed him their last bottle of water after opening it.

Officer Reinert took a long drink, which seemed to help, and handed the bottle back. "Thanks. My name's Tim." He stuck out his hand.

Mason shook it quickly. "I'm Mason. My buddies are Blondie and Howard."

Tim glanced up. "Thanks, guys."

30

"These looters beat you up?" Mason asked. Reinert wasn't bleeding, but he had some nasty knots and bruises on his face and head.

"Yeah, in hindsight, coming here in uniform probably wasn't the best idea I ever had. At first, I thought somehow that they might listen to reason."

Mason shook his head, glancing around. "Not this mob. Let's get you out of here. You're beaten up, but you don't seem to have anything broken. Can you stand?"

"I think so."

Mason and Blondie helped lift Tim up to his feet.

A group of about a dozen thugs focused on them and started to circle over their way.

That was when a crowd of several dozen men in fatigues and hunting garb emerged from the trees from the opposite direction and fanned out across the entire section of parking lot.

The mob drew back in fear.

Mason noted right away how organized and coordinated this group was. Every one of them had a black band or strip of cloth tied around their right upper arm.

Then a large man emerged from their ranks out of the forest as well, astride a large, saddled horse. He held what looked to be a long, makeshift spear or lance in one hand, and an old-fashioned megaphone in the other, which he shouted through.

"Halt. Stop fighting and stand where you are. We are the local militia, and we are here to restore order. South Bend is now under martial law. We are now the authority in this city!"

The crowd resisted, bunching together closer in their numbers, shouting back taunts and curses, clutching their looted supplies.

More militia came out of the trees, and began to flank the looters on either side of the parking lot.

"I am City Councilman Mark Benton," continued the large man. "The available city leaders have formed an emergency South Bend militia to defend this area, assess the damage, and restore order. Follow our directions and you will not be harmed. We don't want fight you unless you force us to, but we will use force to restore order, if we must."

More taunts and curses from the mob. But even they began to notice that the militia unit almost matched their numbers by this time. And all of the militia were armed with bows.

Benton continued to shout the mob down. "I repeat, martial law is now in effect for this area. I say again, the authorities have declared martial law. Stand down and do as you are told. Looting and fighting will not be tolerated. Supplies will be sorted and dispensed to the public on the basis of emergency need—not taken by thieves and thugs."

A new swell of curses and taunts erupted.

Benton lifted his spear. "Militia…prepare to fire on this crowd, if they do not stand down and comply with our instructions."

About a hundred and fifty men with hunting bows and arrows bent on the string took aim at the looters from three sides.

"Comply with our orders, or be cut down!" Benton warned.

The mob pulled back, gasped, and got really quiet all of the sudden. Many of them dropped to their knees at the show of such force. Some began to cry and beg not to be shot or killed.

"Militia, lower your weapons, but stand ready," Benton ordered "Shoot anyone who tries to run. This looting ends here and now. Half of you close in and secure this site."

The mob became very docile in the face of a such a large, well-organized force.

"We have no wish to harm you," Benton said. "Cooperate and we won't have to. Form a line. Militia, screen these people and disperse them one by one from this area. Let each of them keep one or two items if they really need them. But confiscate all shopping carts, bags, and boxes of stolen goods. No exceptions.

"People, once you are searched and ordered to disperse, you must leave this area and return to your homes or to one of the nearby shelter areas being set up at local churches and schools. Further instructions will be given out by the authorities.

"Militia recruitment stations will also be established to help defend the city and this area, if you are able-bodied, and between the ages of sixteen to forty-five—both men and women—report to one of those stations."

The looters were searched and released one at a time. Each of them walked away with something. While the process continued, Mason and his friends approached the militia, trying to bring Officer Reinert before the city councilman. Finally they got through, and their basic story was presented.

Benton more or less ignored the three of them and focused on Reinert. "Officer, with your training, the South Bend militia could use your skills and knowledge of the city. We're not completely sure what we are up against or the extent of what has happened. Can we count on your assistance?"

Reinert nodded. "I'm a little beat up right now, sir, but I'd be glad to help, once I've secured my family. We live close by."

Benton nodded. "Good man. Once you have secured your family, report to St. Joseph High School—we're using it as one of our headquarters for the time being. Half of the downtown and everywhere else appears to be missing, according to all of the reports we've had thus far. We're still trying to determine what is still here, and what is gone."

The city councilman finally glanced at the three of them. "Are these three fellows with you? My people say they protected you from the looters."

Reinert nodded and put an arm about them as much as he could. "They probably saved my life after I got beat up."

"Well...bring them along with you. If those things that attacked the city late this morning return in force, the militia is going to need all the able-bodied help it can get. You fellows want to join up with the militia?"

Howard looked a bit worried and shook his head. "I can't fight. I'm too old, and I need my medicine. That's why we came here in the first place."

"They say this man has a heart condition," Reinert said. "Can we see if the drugstore can fix him up?"

Benton looked to one of his militia aides standing nearby. "Frank, go with them into the pharmacy and see if they can get that man his meds. Gentlemen, perhaps I will meet with you later at the high school. My people and I must finish securing this area and move on. Good luck to you all." The militia leader turned his horse away from them and rode off with his guards following him.

Mason turned to his comrades. "I still want to go by the university and find my friend David."

"I'll go with you," Blondie said.

Howard shook his head, looking exhausted and weak. "I just want to get my medicine, and find a safe place to lie down and rest."

Reinert took Howard by the arm. Frank was waiting nearby. "We'll check on his meds and then I'll take him home with me," Reinert said. "It's only a few blocks off Elwood." He jotted the address down on a piece of paper and handed it to Mason. "You boys do what you need to do and then meet us at my house within about four hours. Then we'll all walk over to militia HQ at the high school together. That sound okay?"

Mason nodded. "Should give us plenty of time. We'll meet up at your house like you said. Take care, guys."

They moved to part company, but the militia lines stood in their way. Frank waved them through at Reinert's insistence.

Once they were clear of the militia, Blondie grinned and spoke up. "Mace, I noticed that you made no mention of your...new abilities," he said.

Mason glanced over at him. "There didn't seem to be a good point to bring it up."

"That might have been wise on your part. Once that information does come out, I'm sure that there will be a great deal of curiosity and explaining on your part. You don't know how people are going to react to what you are capable of now. Those in authority might try force you to hang around and do their bidding."

Blondie was pretty shrewd. "Yeah, I've considered that," Mason said. "Once we figure out what the hell is going on, my main goal is still to reach Elkhart somehow and find my girlfriend, Tori. I won't rest until I make sure she's safe."

They followed the strange trees and patches of normal South Bend back past Leeper Park to 933, where they could at last cross the St. Joe River. By then, survivors were scurrying about in all directions, everyone still in shock and panic. Some were using small boats to ferry people back and forth at other points.

They walked up Angela Blvd and past the university, where Mason and Dave were both sophomores. Just like the rest of the town, half of the campus seemed to be missing also, replaced by more patches of the strange forests and dark, rolling hills.

They continued east, but the basketball arena, Eddy Street Commons, and most of the off-campus apartments up that way were all gone, replaced by more hills, trees, and strange pools of water that had collected in countless places.

Mason eventually resigned himself to the fact that wherever he was, his friend David Pritchard was gone, whether he was dead or over on the opposite side of this strange new, alternate reality.

He paused and said a little silent prayer for his good friend, and for Tori, and everyone else he knew.

What about his folks in Cleveland? His parents? His younger brother Jerry and his little sister Katey, both of them still in high school?

Were they still alive? Would he ever find them one day? Were these strange violent monsters everywhere?

So many questions just left him numb. If he thought about everything too much, he'd break down and cry and flip out.

He could only focus on the now. Dave was gone. Stay alive, and find Tori. That was enough to deal with, for now. Keep going. Keep busy.

Everywhere he looked, people just like him struggled to deal with the shock of all of the changes of this new reality. As Blondie suggested, if the mix-up was like this here, it was most likely worldwide in their dimension or reality. Mason felt crazy and just silly even pondering such things, but there it all was.

What had happened? Why had everything stopped working? Was there some evil force behind all of this?

On their way back from looking for David, Mason tried to find the Blackwoods over on Calvert Street, older friends of his and Dave's, not far from Mason's ruined duplex on Allen Street by the new lake. But there were trees in place of the Blackwoods' house as well. They were gone, too. Hopefully alive and well on "the other side," just like David.

Mason sat down and thought for a bit. Blondie was silent; he did seem to be very stoic and quiet much of the time.

"Blondie, I know we're supposed to meet Howard and the cop back at Reinert's place, but my girlfriend Tori lives in Elkhart with her parents and her sister."

"Is that where you want to go? How far away is that?"

"About twenty or twenty-five miles of more. If we found some bikes and enough connected roads we could probably reach it in a couple of days at most. Once I find Tori, I can put my mind at rest."

Blondie paled. "We don't know what's out there, Mace. Just two of us, out all alone at night, against huge bands of those monsters? You won't be able to help your girl–or anyone else, for that matter–if we get killed. And what about your people here? Won't they need your help, with what you can do now? I think they're going to need all the help they can get."

Mason sighed heavily. "You're right, Blondie. All good points."

"Besides," Blondie added. "I have absolutely no idea what a bike is."

Mason looked at him. "Bikes are those things we've seen other people on all day. The contraptions that they peddle with the two wheels."

"Ohh…"

"And just now, you said 'your people.' Aren't they your people, too?"

Blondie shrugged. "I don't know why I said that."

A cold shiver shot up Mason's spine. "What if…what if you aren't from my world, Blondie? What if you're from the other world, and you just can't remember? That would explain your strange boots."

A couple of attractive young women walked by. One of them glanced Blondie's way.

Blondie smiled back and stared after them, running his hands through his longish, golden hair. "Hmm…I suppose it's possible. Then, except for my boots, why was I wearing clothing from your world? How did I learn to speak your language?"

"I don't know."

Blondie continued. "If I was from the other dimension, then perhaps I had a way to cross over between the two. Before the...the Merge happened."

"The Merge?" Mason asked.

"Let's just call it the Merge for now. But getting back to our main line of conjecture. To obtain your clothing and learn your language and some of your ways, I must have spent a significant amount of time here on your world, prior to the cataclysm. I learned to more or less pass as one of you."

"But why?" Mason asked. "Why did you come here? What was your purpose for doing so?"

Blondie shrugged. "Perhaps I was an explorer. Or maybe my people feared or knew the Merge was going to happen, somehow. Perhaps I was sent to warn you?"

Mason swallowed hard. He couldn't help his mood darkening. "Then why didn't you warn us right away about what was coming? Why study us and learn our ways first, if such a cataclysm was coming?"

Blondie shuffled a bit. "I don't know, Mace. This is all your conjecture, not mine. We don't know it if–"

Mason just blurted it out. "What if your people were the ones who made all of this happen? What if the Merge was deliberate?"

Blondie nodded. "That is also quite possible. I guess for now, there's still just too much that we don't know. I don't even recall who I am, so don't start blaming me for this entire mess."

"No, you're right." Mason pulled out the piece of paper Reinert gave him with the address. "Let's check on Howard at Reinert's place. Then we'll go with Reinert over to the high school and check out the militia. If it feels right, maybe I'll show them a little of what I can do. We'll see if we make it through this next night before we try to reach Elkhart. Does that sound fair?"

Blondie shrugged. "We don't have anything else to do. I don't know anything, so I'm following you. Let's go. Do you think they'll give us some food and drink?"

Mason smiled as they walked, other people streaming all around them. "I think they will, if they have any to spare. We did save Reinert's life, after all. But let's be polite and let them make the offer."

"I don't understand. The man is indebted to us for saving his life. He should owe us a great deal. We shouldn't have to beg for his help. Wow, will you look at the way she's built!"

"Blondie, pay attention. When you talk like that, I start feeling like maybe you were from the other side and–just maybe–you weren't such a nice guy, after all. Hey, are you even listening to me?"

Blondie grinned, keeping a distracted eye out for more pretty women. "Perhaps. I'll follow you, for now, Mace. You can blow stuff up, so lead the way. But if we meet some pretty girls, just let me do the talking."

36

"Seriously? You have amnesia…but you're good with women."

His strange friend smiled even wider. "Mace…some things you never forget."

5

David looked around them in the twilight where they sat on the cold curb, freezing his butt through his jeans. Remnant patches of snow and old, matted-down oak and maple leaves lay fused together. The metal cable and electrical boxes nearby, blocked part of their view. The light yellow, two-story Victorian across the street stood on the corner. White wrought iron fence, high bushes, wooden fence down by the river, near the bridge.

A weird mixture of chaos and ominous silence closed in all around them. It was almost suffocating. Like the chill in the still air, in the bare, wraithlike trees all throughout the neighborhood. No sign of a full spring yet.

And yet somehow, everything around them had changed. Anyone could sense that. And they had not changed for the better.

"We're in a lot of trouble, aren't we?" David said to the strange girl from another world.

She nodded, looking as if she were in just as much in shock as he was.

"Do you know what's happened, Jerriel?"

"I natta zhure, Daeved. Batta eet iz verry natta goo-ud."

He took in a few deep breaths.

"What world are you from, Jerriel?"

"Eet is culd Tharanor. Eet is verry mush lahk yoor woorld...in some vays. Baht een uzzer vays, yoors is verry stra-hange."

He looked around again instinctively. "These monsters. They're from Tharanor—your world?"

Jerriel nodded. "Yaes. On Tharanor, theez lands are, how you zay—vild. No peeples. Jest mon-sters. Verry bad. Much danger."

He rose up and put his hand on his sword.

"We should go," he said. "Will you come with me, Jerriel?"

She thought about it. "I weel, Daeved. I amza weery. Yoo help me. I help yoo."

"Sounds good. We should go. I have friends nearby."

They walked down Northshore as the dawn rose golden in the sky. It was all so crazy.

David couldn't help noticing, again: no cars were moving. No trucks. People stayed in their homes for the time being. Dogs barked and cats screeched here and there. People screamed and shouted in the distance.

Jerriel smoothed her long black hair from her pretty face, fixing it up with her gleaming metal hair clips. She glanced at him and finally relaxed enough to smile slightly.

An incredible smile.

David wished they weren't in so much trouble. That she was just a pretty coed he met in the Subway line at the Huddle. But it just wasn't that way. Not now.

Maybe not ever again.

That realization really shook him up.

They could not cross 933 at the bridge over the St. Joseph River, curving up Northshore toward Angela.

Because the river was still there, but the bridge and a long section of the street weren't. Just more forests on both sides of the rushing St. Joe.

In the end, they had to circle way around by the Portage Road turnabout.

Both of them remained very nervous. They tried to keep talking and learn more about each other, despite the language problem. The cracked gem in Jerriel's headpiece continued to flash and spark at times.

Talking together kept them sane, even if it was with someone from another world.

Still no traffic. No street lights worked.

They'd reach his friends in a few miles as they circled around—Mason Tyler, Tori Nelson, and the Blackwoods.

Just let him and Jerriel make it there safe.

Then Jerriel pointed down along the river as the view opened on their left over the bridge. Her voice sounded both frightened and sad.

"Look, Daeved. I'm zorry."

Bodies. Corpses lined both river sides. Some of them were snagged along the banks. More in the water.

Several were human–two of them children.

Dead monsters, too. It was still a big shock to see that many bodies.

"The smaller creatures are called torgs," Jerriel said. "Dere are beeger ones like dem, called ka-torgs."

He remembered, all too well. "I saw an even bigger monster," David said. "Very tall, with long, hairy arms."

"Mor-kahls. Very strong. Then there are gozogs. They are even beegger and more powerful. They all eat everything. Even eech other. Anything they can choke down."

Great. Voracious monster killing and eating machines.

A vast shadow. Without warning, an enormous green dragon swooped down over the river, scooping up bodies in its massive claws. It wheeled deftly away and sped off low over the trees, sweeping swiftly out of sight.

Holy kah-rap. It was a hundred feet long!

David staggered back, jabbing his finger frantically at the sky where it disappeared. He couldn't breathe. He could hardly speak. "D-d-dragons?"

"We call them shallavoks," Jerriel said. As if spotting one was an every day thing. "Verry dangeruss."

Okay. He was seriously on the verge of flipping out once more.

They continued on the bike path on the left side of Northshore to Angela Street and crossed the bridge there. A chilly breeze cut across the bridge from over the river.

They crossed to the right-hand side of the bridge. An old dead locust tree lay jammed up again the bank on the right. More bodies.

His college buddy Mason Tyler lived off campus with two roommates on Allen Street. Mason's cute, redheaded girlfriend Tori was probably with him.

Mason and Tori were lucky; the two of them were obviously head over heels in love. David himself had only had two girlfriends throughout high school. He had dated a few college girls, but nothing ever developed. He just never felt a spark.

When he looked at Jerriel, it was like lightning bolts zapping him silly.

When they were halfway over the bridge, both of them stopped and stared north, but David more than Jerriel.

Strange trees dotted the riverbanks, their numbers increasing into the curving distance. Dark forested hills rose up beyond the river farther to the far north.

He went by that way often.

There had never been hills like that before. South Bend, Indiana, was notoriously flat. What in damnation was going on?

"It's...it's worse than I thoot," Jerriel said.

"What is?" David said.

"Yoo felt a breef instant of great pain earlee this moorning?"

David recalled that very well. It startled him awake, right before everything went completely nuts. "Yeah. Really awful."

"I filt eet too. I feer evereeone in both oor deemensions did. There has been a verry greet event. A cataclysm."

David looked north again. His hands shook. His knees almost buckled. What she said was completely insane, but from what he had seen, it all started to make sense.

"That's not Earth out there anymore, is it?" He pointed at the hills in the distance and the strange trees.

"No." Jerriel said. "It iz Tharanor. Parts of our deemensions have gotten meexed up, somehoo. They must be sister-worlds. This is incredibly bad, Daeved."

"You're telling me. That must be why nothing's working." He dug his cell out of his backpack and checked it again, and dropped it back in. Nothing. Everything technological had been disrupted. If even part of what Jerriel said was true, the world David knew was pretty much gone. Just like that.

Those ramifications alone were pretty grim. Even without the frickin' monsters.

"C'mon. Follow me," he managed to say. David took her by the hand. At first they walked up to Portage Road and turned left, crossing the street. When they spotted Sherman Street, David led them right and started to trot. Then they ran down Vassar. At Vassar and Allen they turned left around the corner.

Jerriel kept up with him.

They stopped abruptly.

Past the first house on the other side of Allen Street, all the houses were gone. They just weren't there anymore. And all of Allen Street beyond that.

Where Mason's house had been.

Instead, they stared at a wide swath of dark, dangerous-looking forest, leading down into a deep hollow and a brackish pool. Old growth forest all around. Ancient, massive trees. Weird trees that were like and

41

yet unlike trees that he knew. Something was off about each one. Oak, maple, hickory, pine, fir—all with strange bark or weirdly shaped leaves or needles or odd colorations. And like the trees, some of the heavy brush and brambles, thorns and weeds, also defied description.

Where did it all come from? The streets and houses on the northwest side just ended. And then the eerie forest began.

Trails led off into those grim trees. Animal trails and trails with booted feet and many strange tracks. David smelled blood, smoke, and something rank.

Monster stench—still lingering.

As they skirted the forest's edge, several of the nearby houses looked broken into. They spotted blood trails and darker gory patches where victims had been cut up and dragged off. A few houses still burned or had been reduced to smoking heaps of ruin on their foundations.

As crazy as they looked, some yards and houses on the edge of the change were half normal and half part of the other dimension's forest.

Tharanor.

"What if someone was caught on the very edge of the change?" David asked.

Jerriel grimaced. "They would be torn in half like everything else. The effects of this merging would keel them."

They started calling it the Merge. So be it.

David held his head with both hands and rocked a little. Hell, if the Merge had taken place worldwide, even at random that would mean millions of deaths from that event, alone. An intense disaster on a planet-wide scale had taken place—for both dimensions.

He feared the worst for his friends Mason and Tori. Mason's rowdy roommates were also gone for spring break. What was happening to them? And to his own family in Cleveland.

Mason and his girlfriend Tori had looked forward all month to some serious alone time together. Now they could all be dead.

"The parts of Earth that are gone," David asked. "Have they been destroyed completely?"

Jerriel held up her hands. She looked lost, too. "Perhaps yess. Perhaps noo. Weeth our dimensions touching, our sister-worlds could be jumbled up, half and half on booth sides. It is amazing that booth dimensions were not completely destroyed in the Cataclysm. We could all have been obleetorated."

He looked straight into her large violet eyes. "How do you know all of this?"

Jerriel shook her head. "I don't. I'm jest guessing. Jest like yoo."

"You're from another dimension. Another world. This Tharanor…
How can we even speak to each other? You should be speaking another
language, and yet I can understand you more and more every minute."

She sensed his panic and gently took him by both arms. "Eet's all
right, Daeved. I'm scared and confoosed, too." She touched the dark,
cracked gem on her forehead. "Thees enchanted jewel normally allows
me to speak and understand any tongue eezily. But eet has been
damaged. Eet only woorks een part, now. Eevan woorse, I can't get any
of my other magicks to woork. Not at all. No spells. Nathing." The fear
and frustration in her words were palpable.

David needed to sit down again. He felt dizzy, and plopped down
on the curb. Jerriel sat beside him while he rubbed his eyes. His brain
was on overload.

"Are yoo sokay?" she asked. She sounded worried.

How much more of this could he take? David looked over at her,
still completely flabbergasted.

"Magic?" he inquired.

6

Mason knocked on Officer Reinert's red front door.

The sound of feet came pounding toward the other side from within, along with muffled sounds of scuffling and whispering.

"No, I'll get it."

"Don't! Let me do it."

The front door was suddenly yanked open and two young boys, one nine or ten and the other about twelve, almost fell over each other trying to manage the door between them. Blue eyes, blond crew cuts, freckles.

The nine-year-old brandished a plastic sword. The twelve-year-old wielded a battered police nightstick.

A woman's voice shouted from further inside with some anger and alarm.

"Dennis Michael and Harold Thomas! We told you *not* to open that door for any reason. Oh, my gosh. Who's at the door?"

She came close enough that Mason could see her. Blondie simply stared. Mason smiled and lifted both hands to show that they were empty. "This is Blondie. I'm Mason."

The woman looked afraid, and glanced at a large kitchen knife sitting on the dining room table, on top of a bunch of other stuff—an assortment of bills, backpacks, schoolbooks, papers, two coffee cups, and an open tool box.

The kids remained oblivious, and things remained tense between the adults until Howard poked his head up from the other side of the couch, where he had apparently been sleeping. He looked at them bleary-eyed, raising the nine iron still clutched in his hands.

But recognition spread over his drowsy face. The mother of the boys, most likely Mrs. Reinert, took a hopeful cue from the old man, their new house guest. "Howard, do you know these two boys?"

"Sure do. These are the two boys who saved me and your husband. Tim and I said they'd be by later."

Mrs. Reinert relaxed and her face brightened instantly. "Come in, come in." She went behind them and quickly re-locked the front door. "Make yourselves at home. I can't thank you enough for helping Tim. I'm Helen. Denny and Tommy, go play in the family room and stay out of the way. Now, go!" The boys took off, laughing.

She turned back to her new guests. "Would you two heroes like some lemonade? The fridge stopped working, but it's still kinda cold."

Mason kept smiling. "Sure. Thank you, ma'am."

Denny and Tommy popped around a corner and shot Mason and Blondie in the back of the head with some of those foam gun bullets.

Blondie turned around, raised both of his hands like claws, and growled. "Arrrr!"

The two boys burst out laughing and ran away.

"Mace...I hate kids."

"You can't remember anything...remember? But you're a womanizer who hates kids."

"Well, I've recalled that much, at least. I do distinctly recall that children annoy the hell out of me."

Helen returned in a few minutes with four glasses of lemonade in green Libbey glasses with stripes. Mason thought his own mom had the same glasses in their cupboards back in Cleveland.

By that time, Mason and Blondie were so thirsty, they nearly inhaled the lemonade and swallowed the glasses whole.

Helen laughed. "You guys are thirsty. Let me get a pitcher of water; you can drink as much as you like. We have one of those old hand pumps out back that still works."

While she fetched the water, Mason called over to Howard. "Where's Reinert?"

Howard set his empty glass down on the coffee table as well. "Upstairs, resting. He took some medicine. His head was still hurting after that beating he took. He said to wake him in time to go over to the high school. I'm staying here. Everyone's afraid there'll be another attack tonight."

"I hope not," Mason said.

"Think about it," Blondie said. "Those creatures only had a few hours this morning, right after the Merge happened, to do all of the damage they did. How much more do you think they can do with a full night of darkness to work with?"

Helen had heard everything they said as she returned and set the pitcher of water down on the coffee table. Her face grew very worried, and she looked nervous, as if she was trying not to break down and cry.

"Do either of you boys know what's going on or why all of this is happening?"

Mason shook his head. "I'm sorry, ma'am. Nobody does."

"Has anyone figured out what happened to the moon?"

"What's a moon?" Blondie said. Helen just stared at him in confusion.

"Blondie got hit in the head somehow, ma'am. He doesn't remember anything anyway. People are saying the moon's gone?"

"I think I'd remember a moon, if there ever was such a thing," Blondie said, sounding like a loon.

"The moon is gone," Helen stated. "It's just...not up there anymore, and people are really scared about that and a lot of things. There's a lot of other strange stuff going on."

Helen questioned Mason and Blondie quietly over the next two hours while Howard and her husband slept, and her young boys played, mostly in the family room.

It gave the adults something to talk about and pass the time, but nobody seemed to know anything for certain.

Mason and Blondie told her everything that they had seen and heard.

Dinner with the Reinert family that late afternoon was tuna sandwiches, instant mashed potatoes, and unfrozen peas. Tim the cop woke up and ate with them all. They spoke about things a bit more, but they didn't want to scare the kids.

Tim got his coat and hat on to walk with Mason and Blondie over to the militia station at the high school. Nobody knew what was going on our what would happen. The militia was still being formed, and to avoid panic, the word went out for people to barricade themselves in their homes and be prepared to hunker down or evacuate, as needed.

Mason wondered how much that was going to help if the monsters returned in force.

Helen looked worried, and made Tim promise her that he would be back home well before nightfall. Tim held her in his arms while she leaned against him and shook. He softly reassured her once more that he would be certain to make it back.

She finally let them go, and started doing the dishes out in the kitchen while the boys played cards with Howard.

Along the way, Mason revealed to Tim what he could do with his pistols.

He asked Tim to approach the militia leaders and tell them about his new abilities. Mason had decided that despite his fears, he must try to help out his town.

But first, it took some convincing for Mason to get Tim to believe him.

Words couldn't do it.

One lesser shot from an empty pistol did the trick.

At the high school, Tim left them quickly, to go speak with the militia commanders. Mason and Blondie walked around, observing what was going on.

People from all over the city came together there, bringing with them whatever weapons they could find, and anything that would pass for armor.

A few people from the local MHS medieval group actually walked around demonstrating various helmets, suits of chainmail, and other types of armor. They pointed out how to take them on and off, with or without assistance, and explained how they were made.

They also instructed groups of militia on how to use medieval-style weapons. Some of them looked familiar to Mason, but David and the Blackwoods probably knew many of those folks better by name, since they were in all in the same local reenactor group.

Mason wished again that his friend David was with them. Dave was an expert at fighting up close with swords and other such weapons.

All sorts of football, baseball, and hockey protective gear was piled up on tables. It looked like an attempt had been made to sort them out by size: extra small, small, medium, large, extra large, and larger.

There were lots of football helmets, batting helmets, and catcher's masks, hockey helmets, motorcycle helmets, and military-style helmets.

Some of the cops present were lucky enough to have full suits of riot gear, complete with big clear riot shields and long riot clubs.

One entire section was devoted to assembling various types of shields out of plywood, sheet metal, even metal and plastic barrels. Another held stacks of various poles, where spears were being fashioned.

Archery bows and arrows were at a premium. Any bow hunter or person with archery skill was tested at targets outside and assigned to the ranks of the archers. Some few had crossbows—but the big fear was the shortage of ammunition for the archers.

There weren't enough arrows to go around.

Everyone looked pretty scared.

Blondie finally put it into words. "Mace, these people aren't ready for this kind of fighting," he said flatly. "Everyone's still in shock from the Merge and what happened this morning."

"You're right. They're used to fighting with guns, grenades, machine guns, tanks, and jet fighters and bombers—missiles and drones. But if this is the only way we can defend our people now, we're going to have to learn it all over again—and fast."

Tim suddenly came running up to them. "There you guys are. Come with me, Mace. The militia leaders are very anxious to test you and your abilities. Hurry."

"I'm sure that took a little convincing," Blondie said.

Tim nodded. "It sure did. They thought I was joking, at first. Then they accused me of being crazy, drunk, or both. But I finally convinced them to let Mason put on a little demonstration for them. They've set up some targets out on one of the practice fields. Let's get out there before they change their minds. Most of them still think this a big waste of time."

Mason was nervous. He wanted to help, but he didn't want to be kept from going to Elkhart to find Tori, either. But it also might be safer working with the militia than being on their own.

Tim led him out past the school into a vacant construction lot. There was nothing there but some burned-out vehicles and houses along the street, and a few archery targets.

Six militia people, three of them cops and the others in fatigues, paced around waiting, skeptical looks on their faces. All six heads turned as Tim, Mason, and Blondie came up.

The apparent leader, a younger guy in his late twenties with fatigues and a crew cut, put his hands behind his back. "I'm Lieutenant Larry Watkins of the Army Reserve."

"Mason Tyler."

"His friends call him Mace," Blondie said.

"Whatever, son. Officer Reinert here says that you have firearms that still work, after some strange fashion. I don't know what to believe from what he told us. It doesn't sound possible. So why don't you just up and show us? But let me warn you, son. We don't have all day, and this better not be some kind of joke, because none of us will be laughing, my friend. If you've got something to show us, step up to the line here and do your thing."

"Yes, sir," Mason said, striding up to the line.

First he readied a pair of his empty, single-action six shooters. Those would be good to start with.

He fired one, and then the other, and quickly blasted one of the burned out SUVs full of holes.

The six onlookers jumped as the red-orange blasts of energy ripped out of Mason's pistol barrels.

For good measure, Mason fanned one of the pistols and fired more than twenty times out of the one empty gun.

His barrage of rapid shots reduced the SUV to smoking, glowing scrap.

All six of the observers stood there pale and staring with their mouths hanging open. Lieutenant Watkins came forward and held out his hand.

"By the Lord God Almighty, that was something, son! How in the hell did you manage that? I didn't even see you reload–and you fired over eighteen times that last burst, from what I counted. Those are just six guns. How is that even possible? What kind of ammunition are you using in them things? How do you load them so fast?"

Blondie chimed in. "Sir, he did that with the pistols unloaded. It's some kind of magic, and it only works for him and his guns–no one else."

Watkins stared at him as if he was a nut. "Magic? You're shittin' me. Lemme examine one of those weapons, son. This can't be. Magic my white-hairy ass."

Blondie continued. "How else do you explain it? How can you explain any of this stuff that is happening all around us?"

Watkins examined the weapon, and then tried to fire it. Nothing. The action just clicked. He check it, and then checked it again. Then he handed it back to Mason, still skeptical. "There, now I know it's empty and you can't switch it on me. I'm watching. Go ahead. Make that empty gun fire again."

Mason took the pistol from him immediately. He held it at arm's length and didn't even aim. He kept staring Watkins in the face, meeting his eyes.

He proceeded to fire off several more blasts into the ruined SUV as fast as he could.

Mason watched as the blood drained out of Lieutenant Watkins' face.

Dozens of people came running from several directions, hearing the blasts.

"Someone has guns that work? Who is it? How come those guns work and no one else's will?"

Watkins shouted at the onlookers. "Stand back, people. We're with the militia. That's what we're trying to find out, here."

Blondie was still grinning, apparently enjoying himself immensely. He tapped Watkins on the shoulder.

"What now?" Watkins asked.

"Have Mace show you what happens when he *does* fire one of his guns fully loaded. Once you see that…you just might decide that you have need of him."

Watkins paled again. "Christ the Holy Lord from Fresno, I'm afraid to ask. All right, son. We're not in Kansas anymore, and you're the pistolero here. If you have one of your rigs loaded, fire off a test round and show us what happens."

Mason took aim, and everyone present except for Blondie took a step back.

That one shot swept a wide, cone-shaped swath of flaming destruction before Mason in the flash of an instant. It was sixty yards in length and half that wide, and it tore up and melted the asphalt of the street, obliterated the remains of the SUV, and took down most of the partially burned building beyond that.

The six militia observers and all of the onlookers fell back in amazement. They got back up and stood there, freaked out and astonished.

Watkins was the first to react. "Holy jacking Jehoshaphat! You're a walking artillery unit with those damn things. Need you? By thunder, you bet we'll need you. Load up and walk right next to me, son; you are not leaving my side. Bring your friends, too. All of the commanders will need to hear about this. And here we thought this was some kind of hoax. My greatest apologies."

On the way back, Mason did his best to try to explain his situation. "Sir, I want to help out around here, but I'm no soldier. I also need to get to Elkhart to locate my girlfriend. Her name's Tori—Tori Nelson. I love her more than anything, and I need to find out if she and her family are safe. They could be in danger."

"We are all in trouble, kid. If we make it through tonight, we will find a way. If I have to, I will personally carry you on my back all the way to Elkhart, and you can whip me bloody with a riding crop all the way there."

"I'm serious, sir. I must find her."

"I am as well. Give me your gal's name and address, Mace. We have riders and messengers trying to reach Elkhart. We'll have people check on that address. If we can locate her, we'll bring her here, safe and sound. Is that good enough for now?"

Mason nodded with appreciation. "Yes, sir. Thank you, sir."

"Well, Mason. I don't know what exactly we're up against tonight. But our Pistolero here is our new secret weapon. We've got to hurry up. There's only a couple of hours left, and we don't even have our forces organized and in place yet. It's going to get dark pretty soon."

That fact didn't really make Mason feel any better.

7

David looked back over his shoulder at the strange forest where Mason's neighborhood and house should have been. His friends were gone, replaced by weird trees and plants, and monster trails. Everything tunneled in on him.

Destroyers, monsters, and dragons on the loose. A cataclysm that changed everything in an instant. Jerriel. All of it was too much to process, but he'd seen it all firsthand.

Find a way to handle it. Don't go off the deep end.

A person from another world, another dimension, sat right beside him—however pretty she was.

And now—on top of everything else—now there was magic to deal with.

"So, you can do magic?" he asked. He had a hard time breathing; it was even hard to say.

She waved her hands again and grimaced. "I could, before the event. Now I can't seem to make eet woork."

David nodded. "Great…just like our technology," he noted. "So, magic isn't working, either?"

"Is that what yoo call yoor magic?" she said. "The magic yoor people used to live and run their woorld?"

He rubbed his aching head. "I guess you could call it that. Nothing seems to be working now, for either of us." He'd never thought of it that way

before. But to someone from another world–a very different world–
Earth technology would in fact seem like extremely powerful magic.

He wondered what Jerriel's magic was like.

The wizard girl shook her head. "A dimensional event of this
magnitoode could disrupt booth of our realities in many ways. These
changes put us booth at a very serious disadvantage…and oor peeples.
The monsters, as yoo call them, Daeved, will come back tonight een
force. And they will take great advantage of yoor people's confoosion
and vulnerability. Many moore will perish, I fear."

David rose up. "Then we need to do something. First things first.
We need to organize a defense against the monsters when they attack
again. Everything else can wait. If they kill and eat us all, nothing else is
going to matter."

Jerriel stamped her staff on the pavement. "I agree."

He pointed the way. "We're going down Portage to Cushing." Even
though that all looked blocked by trees now.

"I'll follow yoo, Daeved. I cannot read yoor language, so the signs
yoo point to tell me nothing."

"Sorry. I keep forgetting. With any luck, the Blackwoods are still
there. Dirk was a Special Forces colonel in the Army before he retired.
He'll be a big help." He still worried about Mason and Tori. But whether
his friends had been blasted to atoms or were fighting for their lives on
the mirror-side of two mixed-up dimensions, he couldn't do much to
help them at the moment.

For the time being, he and Jerriel had their own survival issues.

If what she guessed was right, the other side was going to be just as
mixed up and chaotic as their side was.

Would there ever be a way to cross over, back and forth?

More importantly, was there any way to undo the entire mess, and
return both dimensions and their worlds back to the way they'd been
before the event? The Merge?

They weren't entirely screwed, but they were pretty damn near it.

Finally they spotted the Blackwoods' house.

The home was an old white and blue worker house from the
thirties, wrought iron fence out around the front, with a pink concrete
pig statue on one of the dark brick risers of the front porch. Two pink,
plastic flamingos guarded the garden spot on the right. Skunk cabbages
and crocuses had already popped up all over the neighborhood.

A growing crowd of at least thirty people gathered in front of the
Blackwoods' house, complaining and talking about what to do. Dirk and
Belinda stood on the porch, directing the debate.

"If nothing works," Dirk said, "then we'll have to go back to using bicycles and maybe horses if we can get some. We've already sent messengers on bikes to the County City Building and the police station on Sample."

"What the hell are they going to do?" some whiner shouted. "If they've even there still. Whole chunks of town are just gone. They aren't even there anymore!"

"Where'd these weird patches of forest come from?"

"And the monsters!"

"We can't defend ourselves!" People in the crowd wept and moaned.

"You can't give in to fear and panic," Belinda said. "You have to stay focused and strong." She was a sharp, taller woman. Glasses, green eyes, long silvering hair tied back. She wore a big dagger on the belt of her long blue skirt.

Dirk and Belle were the former baron and baroness of the local MHS medieval club, longtime family friends of David's dead parents. In his forties like Belle, Dirk stood at medium height, still Stocky and strong. Straight, steel-gray hair tucked under a black French beret. Tough gray eyes and a long, gray moustache. He drew the sword he wore at his side.

"We can and we will defend ourselves, our homes, and our families," Dirk said. "But we can't just panic or hide. We need to get organized and work together. We've still got tens of thousands of people in this area, and anyone who can fight needs to arm themselves. We'll form a militia—starting right now."

"Who in the hell are you to order us around and tell the rest of us what to do?" another loudmouth said.

Dirk rested his sword on his shoulder and shook his head.

"I'm the guy who will fight these things to the last breath. My wife and I killed three of them this morning when they crashed through our picture window. I know how to use a sword, a spear, and ax, and I can shoot a bow. I can teach others how to fight. I was in the Army and I can lead people in combat. What about you, buddy? Will you arm yourself and stand with us when these things come back tonight?"

The loudmouth looked down and melted away, back through the crowd.

Others stepped forward and volunteered.

David saw his opening and pulled Jerriel along with him up to the side of the porch and stepped up.

"Hey, Dirk, Belle. Mornin'. Can you use two more volunteers?"

Their grim faces brightened in recognition.

"David!" Belle said, hugging him. "Good to see you."

"You're a sight, son," Dirk said. "We could use a hundred sword fighters like you. Folks, this is my young friend David Pritchard. One of the best swordsmen I ever helped train. He's pretty good at throwing 'hawks and archery, too. He'll probably be training some of you directly, if you want to join the militia."

Belinda went up to Jerriel. "David, you haven't told us who your pretty friend is yet. She's wearing garb, but I've never seen her at any events."

David smiled. "This is Jerriel. She's...she's new."

Dirk appointed block leaders and told them to spread the news and continue organizing each block from there on out. Everyone needed to secure their own home first. Then check house to house. See who was still around, who wasn't, and if anyone needed help. They needed to recruit fighters for the militia and have them arm and armor themselves with anything they could find. Then meet up at the Century Center at noon for organization and training.

People looked scared and nervous, and still had too many questions, but at least they had things to do now. There was some kind of purpose. Even those too old or too young to fight could help out: securing homes, boarding up windows, checking supplies, and caring for others.

Some people wandered off and vanished. But most were willing to pull together and face the crisis head on. David admired that.

He and Jerriel went inside with the Blackwoods. Their living room was always chock full of medieval camping gear and supplies from the many re-enactment events they went to year round. Plus all of their various crafts and projects. They were so much like David's parents had been that it was scary.

There was still some broken glass around, but the ruined window had a big piece of plywood over it, making the room a lot darker, even in the morning light.

Dirk and Belle were admittedly exhausted, but they threw together a hurried breakfast of sausages, eggs, fried potatoes, and toasted bread. Belle cooked on her brazier on the back porch with the screens. The Blackwoods also had a fire pit out back where they liked to cook over open flames. That would also come in handy.

Dirk pointed out the three dead torgs that he had dragged out back by the shed and the alley, with a piece of plastic pulled over them.

"We'd better eat what's going to spoil first," Belle said. "No more refrigeration, at least for a while." They slurped down milk and juice.

"Thanka yoo," Jerriel said. "Yoo are moost kind."

Dirk stared at her, picking up on her strange accent. "We've only got a few hours to gear up and rest up before we go help organize the militia," he said. "Do either of you know what in the hell's going on? We felt that really nasty spell of pain this morning, and then these things started attacking from out of the darkness. Everything stopped working."

David looked at Jerriel, took a breath, and told the Blackwoods what they had figured out so far.

Even that much was a lot to handle, and they still knew next to nothing.

The Blackwoods looked a little paler and stared at Jerriel even more. "How come we haven't met others of her people?" Belle asked.

8

Mason Tyler–the Pistolero–the living weapon.

The strange monsters did in fact return that night, and in even greater numbers. They seemed to hit South Bend from every direction at once and went on a rampage of burning and destruction.

It was widely reported that most of the untried militia units broke and ran. Many panicked defenders were cut down after they were routed, while they were in the process of running away.

Even worse, many good potential leaders and fighters perished in the chaos when they could not hold their positions or their units together.

Anyone could see that the inexperienced defenders of South Bend were in for a long, grim night of terror and bloodshed. After the initial three hours, much of the west and the north of the city was on fire. The enemy seemed intent on burning everything to the ground.

But the worst unexpected factor was thousands and tens of thousands of non-combatants–women, children, the elderly, and the infirm–turned out into the cold night to flee. They quickly became a swelling tide of panic-stricken refugees. Those who were not hacked down, killed, or captured outright fled east or south, struggling to hide or get away from the chaotic fighting and the unpredictable enemy hordes.

Mason barely had time to think, let along focus on how scared he was. He rushed to whatever location Lieutenant Watkins directed him to, unleashing a torrent of destroying fire against the packed enemy hordes, wherever they were massed together and pouring through the defensive lines.

His blazing pistols and their devastating blasts helped stem the tide somewhat. But he couldn't be everywhere at once, and the conflict flexed and buckled at several points and along several major battle lines. In the end, it seemed as if all he did was keep them from being completely swept away.

The defenders just barely survived.

In between battles, Mason struggled to keep his various pistols reloaded. To do so, he had to focus and keep his hands from shaking. Necessity forced him to get a handle on his fears.

He tried to always keep a couple of his guns loaded with what he began to call his special "devastator" rounds. Loads that, when he fired them off, cleared the widest path of destruction possible out in front of him.

Anything caught in the kill zone was obliterated. Mason had no control over that.

Then, even the slow-witted brutes started to get wise after suffering repeated losses and setbacks at his grim handwork.

The enemy started watching for him, trying to track the unit that brought him around. If they spotted him coming at them from a distance, they would break up and try to avoid him, choosing to attack other high value targets that were far away from his location. They knew that it would take him too much time to reach them.

At that exact moment, Mason was downtown, helping defend what was left of it.

Then the enemy forces pulled back and seemed to vanish.

A militia captain and some skirmishers raced up on bicycles.

"Lieutenant Watkins, General Benton orders you and all of your forces to proceed directly to the area around the university in all haste. The enemy is converging there in great numbers in an attempt to overrun our defenses."

"Yes, sir. Tell the general that we're on our way."

Watkins swung them around and marched up Colfax and then Notre Dame Avenue.

Up ahead, as they approached the campus, they could see that the enemy had already cut them off. Numerous buildings in that entire area were already up in flames.

They could hear the unmistakable sounds of heavy fighting. There was lots of smoke, and shouting and the clash of weapons filled the air. Frightened civilians scattered in all directions.

Unfortunately, it looked as if the defenders had already broken, and reeled in full retreat.

Watkins raced them up to General Benton on his horse. "We're here, sir. I've got our secret weapon with us."

Mason hated the sound of that when they said it that way—as if he were just a thing, a tool, not even human anymore.

"I prefer being called, the Pistolero," he started to insist. That was a lot better than just being referred to as "the weapon," secret or not.

Benton looked at their retreating forces and snarled. "You're too late," the general shouted. "We ran out of arrows. The area has fallen. They're sacking and burning everything, flooding into every building like cockroaches. By morning, they'll have burned this whole part of town right to the ground, and we can't stop them."

Terrified troops shrieked, "Here they come. Run!"

Oh, hell. Mason wanted to join them.

A dark mass of monsters formed a long, deep swarm like a plague of death itself, and charged at the militia. They roared and screamed like demons.

Perhaps they were.

"General," Watkins said. "We can throw them back. Turn our people around and let's fight. We have to stop them!"

Even the general shook his head. "There aren't enough of us left here, and there are too many of them. Save yourselves to fight another day...if there is another day."

The general rode off on his horse, chasing after his fleeing troops, who were already way ahead of him.

Watkins wouldn't give in. He shoved Mason in front of him. "Start blasting, son. Let's show these sons of bitches what you can do. Put on a show. Cut them all down!"

Mason hesitated only a second. If he was going to die there, so be it. At least he wasn't going to be cut down from behind. He was going to go down fighting.

His only regret was not finding Tori.

Mason drew his guns, felt his adrenaline hype up, and held nothing back.

The enemy charge stalled in the face of sheets of fire and death. But then pockets of fleeing defenders accidently strayed into the killing fields in several places.

"I can't fire with our people mixed up in there," Mason protested. "And my blasts are getting too close to the houses and buildings as we move in. We'll be killing our own people along with the monsters!"

"No, keep firing." Watkins insisted. "It can't be helped. The enemy is stuffed inside of those houses and buildings, ransacking everything and putting them to the torch. They'll burn them all any way. We have to reduce their superior numbers, at all costs!"

Their small band strode forward, Mason's weapons blazing, leaving a wide radius of total devastation in their passing. The vicious faces of the monsters vanished before him.

He fired until all his rigs were empty, breaking the back of the enemy assault in that vicinity and putting them to flight.

A cart was brought up, pulled by four troops, so that Mason could sit inside and reload his several pistols rapidly and efficiently during the lull. Another cart lugged his gear box behind them.

The surviving defenders saw what was done and rallied around them, for protection if nothing else.

"Form up, troops," Watkins called to them. "Form ranks the way we taught you. Turn and fight. Stop running. We can turn the tide if we stand together!"

"We're low on arrows, sir." That was the common complaint.

"We do what we must. Glean what we can from the battlefield. Take the black arrows off the enemy dead. They're shorter, but they'll still work in a pinch. Gather up their spears and javelins, anything to fight with. We'll take them down with whatever we have. Halt the retreat and call our fleeing forces back. Send word, send word!"

Word came that the enemy was regrouping and preparing to counterattack once more, from several directions at once.

Mason just finished reloading his last pistol, and just in time.

"Here they come again!" the warning sounded.

"We're almost doing as much damage as the enemy," Mason said.

"It can't be helped," Watkins insisted. "It's us or them. It's that simple. Keep firing, no matter what!"

The foe streamed at them like an onrushing flood.

Mason systematically fired in several directions, striving to hold back the dark tide. The militia fired all of their remaining arrows. Troops flung spears and javelins. They even hurled axes, hatchets, and knives right into the faces and bared fangs of the enemy advance, and barely managed to hold.

The sheer weight of the enemy numbers finally forced them to retreat behind the sheets of destroying flame that Mason's weapons unleashed.

His guns held the enemy at bay and kept the defenders from being routed once more.

But they could not maintain such an intense level of fighting, and eventually, all of Mason's pistols would need to be reloaded.

They were seconds away from being swallowed up.

They could only keep fighting to the last, as they became an island, trapped within an ocean of swirling foes.

Mason only had eighteen devastator rounds left. He took aim and tried to make each one of them count—cool, calm, and precise.

His roaring guns cut the horde down in droves, incinerating them in waves of raw, destructive power. He slew the foe in great swaths at a time. Burning buildings broke up and collapsed, shredded and brought to ruin during the course of the tumult that raged all around that key point.

The enemy went mad trying to get at them and sweep them away.

All of his pistols were at last empty. With no time to reload, Mason poured his lesser, direct fire into the enemy as they surged in up close.

The fear of death gripped him as the monsters closed in.

Just as it seemed that all would be lost, defenders poured in from countless directions, now surrounding a large surge of the monsters and cutting them off, hemming them in and spearing and hewing them down from behind a shield wall.

Further assault by the enemy became impossible. The enemy became trapped. The monsters turned every which way, attempting flee and fight their way out. More perished each second as the trap closed in around them.

Mason kept firing until he could no longer stand. He suddenly felt hollow.

All strength left him, and he pitched forward onto his face. Watkins and others feared he had been hit somehow. They checked him for wounds and tried to give him water.

The militia had the enemy on the run at last.

After hours of such fighting, all at once Mason felt more than exhausted, more than completely drained. Firing his weapons seemed to suck him dry of his very lifeforce. For the first time, he had finally reached his limit, and he knew it.

He could barely lift his head, and he gasped for air, soaked with sweat. He felt as if he were in the grips of a deadly fever. He couldn't lift his guns in his hands, or even stand up, even if he had wanted too.

"I'm completely spent," he said. He rolled over on his back, and struggled not to pass out. His entire body went numb.

"Pick him up," Watkins ordered. "Get him behind our lines to a safe place. Try to get him to eat and drink something. He's more than earned it this night." Mason thought he saw Blondie's face above him here and there.

The world around him and his spinning, swirling vision seemed to transform into a burning, smoking ring of fire and death.

Many of the buildings around them were roaring up in flames, consuming the bodies of friend and foe alike, trapped within where they had been fighting.

The sweet, sickening stench of burning flesh was terrible and maddening.

Mason could barely move, but he did not black out.

A portion of his strength slowly returned to him. He sat up from his stretcher and looked around.

Fires were burning nearby where they had placed him in a shelter. He did not see Blondie, but someone outside suddenly called out for Captain Watkins.

Watkins had apparently been promoted for his actions that night.

Mason staggered out to see what was going on.

Troops brought in more than about two hundred men and women, a sad-looking lot. All of them had their hands bound in front of them with cable ties. Most of their armor and gear had been stripped off of them.

None of them had weapons.

The other troops bullied and spit on them as if they were all criminals.

But if so many were criminals, what was their crime?

Watkins called out to his junior officer, Lieutenant Avery. "Bill, what's all this? Why have you brought these people here?"

"General Benton said for you to dispose of them as you see fit, Captain. These are deserters. No matter where we put them, they run and they keep running, every battle, every chance they get."

Watkins snorted. "What of it? Most of the militia ran away at some point tonight. What am I supposed to do with so many of them?"

Avery frowned. "At the very least, I think Benton wanted them beaten and driven off. He even suggested that perhaps hanging a few of them might set a proper example."

Watkins stopped. "Do you bear any direct orders to do any of that?"

"None, Captain."

"If they won't fight, then we won't waste any further time or effort upon on them, Lieutenant. Disband them in dishonor and send them on their way. Nor will we waste food or drink on them."

Some of the troops still serving volunteered. "Captain, if you please, the troops gathered in this area would happily give these cowards a drudging. Give us that pleasure."

"No!" Mason croaked, getting up. "No, do not touch them!" he shouted. "Don't you do that!"

He drew his pistols and dragged himself forward, even though his arms still flopped at his sides like noodles, and he no strength to lift them.

Time for a bluff.

"Captain Watkins, Lieutenant Avery, we can't turn on each other like this. We can't start doing this kind of thing to our own people. I saw everyone run tonight, including the general himself. By God, I swear it, if you abuse those poor people any further, I will start shooting in all directions, and I will not stop until someone cuts me down!"

"Mace," Bill Avery said in shock. "Calm down. You can't mean that."

"No, you and the captain listen good. We can't do this to our own kind. Everyone isn't cut out to be a warrior, a soldier, or a fighter. But they are still human—they are still our people, worthy of respect. There are so few of us left; we can't waste anyone. Find another way for them to serve with honor. They don't have to be able to fight and kill to contribute."

"Calm down, Mace," Watkins said. "I just want to get rid of them. They can go their way."

"That's not good enough. Instead of beating or dishonoring them, give them all a choice. Some could serve in the medical corps or with the injured. There are children who need watching and educating, elderly who need to be cared for. Some people are good teachers or trainers. Some are good with animals. Others are good at sewing or fixing things. Some are good at building stuff. There are those who are good at logistics, or planning, or counting. They could work in the damn fields, if nothing else."

Captain Watkins looked befuddled. "Mace, I'm listening to you, but you're delirious."

"Damn it, everyone's good at something. So they're not fighters. So what? Find what else they're good at and let them do that."

"All right. We will. I'll do as you ask, Mace. You have my word. Why do you care so much what happens to these cowards?"

Mason laughed weakly.

He let his Spillers fall into the dirt.

"Because...we all know what it's like to be scared out of our minds. Without my guns to hide behind, I might be right there among them."

9

While they spoke, Jerriel got up and walked around the Blackwoods' living room, systematically studying everything she came to. She looked at their gear and supplies, Belle's' plants and bird pictures on the walls.

She gasped suddenly, and zeroed in on an old globe on the dining room table.

She went straight to it, turning it over in her hands, and staring at the continents and the writing.

David turned back to his friends. "Jerriel told me that this region is part of a wild, unexplored continent on her world–the world of Tharanor. Her people are just starting to explore and colonize it, but the Wildlands, as her people call North and South America, are overrun with fierce creatures and these monster tribes that we are now fighting. We even saw a dragon by the river."

Belle and Dirk looked at each other, then back at him. "Are you sure it was a dragon?" Belle asked.

David blinked. "Pretty damn sure. It swept right over us."

"If all of that is true, and there are none of her people around here—then what was she doing here?" Dirk asked.

"She was using her magic to travel between one colony city state and the next when the Merge struck, disrupting her magic and dumping her here."

The Blackwoods gaped.

"Did you say, magic?" Dirk asked.

"Yeah, I know. It sounds crazy, but I believe her. On Tharanor, she was a wizard, in fact. Only the Merge has messed up her magic, almost just as much as it has disrupted our technology. That cracked gem she wears on her forehead is magic, but it was damaged. Now it barely lets her understand us and slowly learn to speak our language. But she's still getting better at it all the time. When we first met, I could barely understand her words."

"And that's proof of magic?" Belle said.

"Look, I know it sounds crazy, but then, all of this is crazy."

Dirk smoothed his gray hair back and put his worn beret back on. "Okay, Dave. It's just a lot to accept all at once. You said her people have colonies in this region...on her world? How far away are they from South Bend?"

"I'm not sure. I'm guessing at least a hundred miles or more to the east and west of us. She said it was a few hours travel between them, via magic. She was about halfway along her journey to what we call Toledo when the Merge struck."

"Hmmm...so let me follow this," Belle added. "If her people are as dependent on their magic as we are on our technology, then they're going to be almost just as hamstrung. We might not be able to make contact with them for weeks, perhaps months. Just like our people in Chicago, Indianapolis, Detroit, and Toledo."

David shook his head. "And we're all in danger pretty deep. Jerriel says this entire continent is overrun with warring monster tribes and other dangerous creatures—especially this region."

"That's not very good news, Dave. People out in the small towns and rural areas are going to have a tough time surviving."

David didn't want to say anything, but it wasn't looking so good for the people in the cities, either.

Belle pointed at Jerriel. "What kind of magic or spells can she normally do?"

David shrugged. "I don't know. I haven't had time to ask. She just says her powers aren't working because of the Merge."

Dirk glanced at her, then back at David. "Maybe it's just an act," he whispered. "Could she simply be a little...you know. Whacko?" He shook his hands in the air for emphasis.

David's eyes went back and forth. Jerriel smiled that smile of hers. Pretty, but not crazy.

"I considered that, but I honestly think she really is from this other dimension–this other world she calls Tharanor. That world is mixed up with ours now. Think about it; it all makes more sense than anything else. These monsters and the weird patches of forest had to come from somewhere. They aren't from Earth."

Jerriel rushed back in, clutching the globe upside down.

"This woorld. It is Tharanor. I recognize the coontinents, but the markings are all stra-hange. I cannot read them."

"Your world must be an alternate Earth, similar to ours," Belle said.

"Yes, a sister-woorld," Jerriel agreed.

They spoke for a while, about Earth and Tharanor. Belle was smart enough to whip out a notebook and write as fast as she could whenever Jerriel poured out information about her homeworld, its peoples, and their cultures.

Dirk drifted off to sleep after about thirty minutes. He started to snore on the couch.

"Let him rest," Belle said with a smile. "We've had a tough morning, fighting those scary things. Chills my blood to think about them coming back in force tonight."

Jerriel looked as if she was ready to nod off, as well. David suddenly felt the same way.

"We've all been through a lot this morning," Belle said. "And it's going to be a long day and night."

She pointed at Dirk snoring. "I'll rest down here in my comfy chair with sleeping beauty. You two drag yourselves upstairs and use the beds in our room and the guest room. Or bed...if you're so inclined." Belle winked at David.

Jerriel stretched her slender, luxurious body, shaking her mane of dark hair. The elegant curves of her lips and her nose were so exotic. David kept catching himself staring at her.

"Thanka yoo, Belli," Jerriel said. "A bed wood be verry nice. Are yoo coming, David?" She waited for him at the foot of the stairs, smiling.

David gulped, not sure what to think. "I sure am."

They got up the stairs. Jerriel took the guest room. She smiled at him again as she closed the door behind her. "Wake me when yoo need me, Daeved. Sleep weell."

"I will. You too." David shuddered. What he wouldn't give to–

He stopped himself from thinking in that direction. Otherwise, he wouldn't be able to rest.

He left the other bedroom door open, threw himself onto the Blackwood's un-made, king-size four poster and passed out in a few minutes.

#

David went downstairs after what he guessed was a nap of about two hours. Jerriel's door was still closed. Let the pretty wizard girl rest.

Outside in the back under their gigantic hickory tree, Dirk and Belle got four bikes ready from their garage, two with carriers behind them for gear. Dirk had his loaded up with armor pieces and weapons.

David sat down on the loveseat in the living room and went through his backpack. Not much help there. He took out his textbooks and smirked. He wouldn't be going back to class any time soon, he guessed. Smartphone. Still dead. His pad, also dead. Some notebooks, pens, and pencils. He might need them. Half a bottle of water, an apple, and a peanut butter granola bar.

Yep, ready to save the world.

He looked at his parents' picture, touching their faces with his fingertips. David sighed.

"Mom, Dad. Stay close to me. I'm in a blivet full of trouble." He put the picture back in and zipped up, gathered his weapons, and joined Dirk and Belle outside in the back.

"I got rides ready for you and your wizard gal," Dirk said with his usual grin. "Yours has a trailer, an old kid carrier. You still have more of your gear at your place?"

David nodded, walking around the bikes, checking them over.

"The monsters burned my apartment building down, but most of my gear is still in my car's trunk. Jerriel and I can fetch it before noon, once she wakes up. I don't know if she can ride a bike."

"I can learn," Jerriel said. She stood stretching a few feet behind him.

"You're pretty quiet," David said. Not many could sneak up on him.

She smirked. "When I have to be."

"Bring everything you can get your hands on," Dirk told them. "We're going to need it."

David showed Jerriel her bike. "Let's go have a little crash course in bike riding," he said. Bad choice of words.

"Cra-hash?" she said, putting her staff down. "That does not sound soo good, Daeved."

Within fifteen hilarious minutes she got the basics down and stopped running into cars, trees, and hitting the curb or falling over. She learned to brake, turn, and turn around.

The little bit of laughter they shared helped David relax somewhat. His muscles repeatedly knotted up with tension and worry over their situation. The threats they labored under felt like heavy weights bearing down on him.

But steadying Jerriel with his hands on her slender arms and waist took his mind off quite a bit, including the terror they faced.

Everything about this dang girl was pretty. She even smelled good. Getting close to her made it difficult to stay focused. It was hard to think.

Geez, snap out of it. He couldn't daydream about girls like some teenage idiot. In less than a few hours they'd be fighting for their lives, against what number of monsters, they still didn't know. From what Jerriel told them, it sounded as if they were surrounded by tribes of countless lethal creatures.

He clenched his fists briefly, watching Jerriel pedal away and then come back to him. Oh, man. Check that smile. If only they weren't in such deep crapola. What he wouldn't give to have things back to normal. To get to know Jerriel and spend time with her. Damn it all, straight to hell and back.

The monsters would attack again that night. They all felt pretty certain of that. They could all die.

There was still so much they didn't know. It knotted his guts up all over again.

Jerriel came to a stop. She motioned with a toss of her dark hair. "Get yoor bi-hike, Daeved. I will get better. We need yoor armor and other supplies. I will follow yoo."

Beautiful, and practical too, while he daydreamed and fumed. He needed to keep it together better.

They rode side-by-side from Cushing up to Portage to Angela, around patches of dark trees. At 933, David pointed out the ND Golf Course and many red maples, white oaks, and cotton wood trees that obscured the area, and across the street between the houses on the other side of Angela.

They had to cut through some of the back streets to get downtown and reach the Century Center. People already gathered in the parking lots and the open streets. There was safety in numbers.

More and more bikes filled the roads. More people walked, carrying bundles, pulling and pushing all kinds of carts—most of them shopping carts. Traffic passed in all directions.

David pointed to the Century Center parking lot, HQ for the city authorities now that the County City Building was gone. "This is where we need to meet Dirk and Belle in about two hours. They're going to help organize the militia to defend the town tonight."

"Where are we going again, Daeved?"

"To get some things out of my car, if it's still there."

They peddled a few miles and reached his ruined apartment building, back up near Angela and 23. The monsters had done a job on it–burning it to the ground. The wreckage still smoked and burned.

No signs of any weird glowing pools like the one he had seen earlier. And there wasn't any way not to notice several bloody "kill-spots" in the area. Those got him angry again. The monsters had to go down.

At least the calamity struck during Spring Break. Otherwise, there might have been even more victims. But with many of the students gone, that also gave them fewer able-bodied defenders in town.

He could only guess what was happening elsewhere across the globe, but if they all died here in Michiana, all of that wouldn't really matter.

At least his faithful old car still sat in the parking lot–with all the other now-useless lumps. A silver 1992 Toyota Corolla four door, rusting out on both sides, banged up by fender-benders. All caused by others, of course. David's car wasn't much to look at. Just a worn-out heap, many would say.

Yet even with more than 200,000 miles on it, it still remained the greatest car David had ever owned. Or ever would. The engine still ran perfectly and got him wherever he wanted to go.

At least, it did before the Merge. Except for a cracked rear window, it was still the same heap he knew and loved. They got off their bikes. He dug out his keys. His keys jingled and his hands trembled.

David loved that old car. His parents had bought it new and then given it to him after they got their Sienna. Because the Corolla was silver-gray, they had nicknamed it Gandalf, and the name stuck. That car never let him down.

It cut him to the bone to think that he might never climb in and drive it anywhere–ever again.

He knew it wouldn't work, but he opened the creaking rusty door, sat down in the comfy, threadbare seats, and tried to start it up.

No good. Not even a click from the starter. Nothing.

All over the planet, cars and vehicles no longer worked.

David couldn't help weeping–at everything his world and his people had lost–overnight.

10

Birds sang. The air was cool and crisp, but Mason felt warm.

He didn't have the strength to force his eyes to open just yet, no matter how hard he tried. He was either still too weak, or too deeply asleep.

But he took the sounds of the spring birds singing around him as hopeful sign.

At least he wasn't dead. Birds meant morning. Daylight. The hope of another day.

Then he tried to move.

Big mistake. Everything hurt when he tried to move.

New strategy–don't try to move.

But he was awake enough to make out voices now, out in the hallway beyond his room. He made out General Benton's voice, filled with irritation, worry, and doubt–talking with Captain Watkins and Blondie.

"I don't give a damn about anything else. None of it matters. But we need to know if he's going to be able to fight tonight. What if the threat comes back for a yet another shot at us? We barely fought the bastards off again last night–even with the Pistolero."

"Sir," Watkins tried to explain, "we won't know what his condition will be until later today. I will notify you and the other leaders as soon as we know anything. We have a doctor and a nurse nearby looking after him."

"Well, keep him safe, Watkins, and don't let anyone near him, especially civilians."

"Why is that, sir?"

"Because, unfounded rumors about last night are spreading. Many people don't exactly care for the Pistolero's handiwork. Many are saying he took out too many friendlies with some of his blasts, along with the enemy. Some are even calling him a murderer and want him to be hanged. Idiots, I know. Why, without this kid, most of us and them would be dead right now. None of us had any choice in what happened last night."

"I quite agree, sir."

"Do we know what happened to him yet, Captain? How is he able to do these things? Can it be replicated somehow with others? We've had reports of strange incidents–of people suddenly developing other weird abilities–but nothing like this."

"Not that we can tell, sir. We sent people to check out the new lake on Allen Street, but the water isn't glowing any longer. No other effects have been noted. His powers seem unique and exclusive to him alone right now. And most of us have been too busy trying to stay alive to do much of anything else."

"General," Blondie jumped in, "Mace is not a machine. He's still flesh and blood. Last night was the first night that he pushed himself and his new abilities to the absolute limit. We're lucky he didn't kill himself or burn himself out somehow. Nobody knows how any of this works. He fought until he couldn't go on, after many hours of sporadic and intense fighting and racing around. There are rational limits to everything. If you want to keep your precious Pistolero healthy and fighting, you're going to have to work within those apparent limits."

"Very well. Get him healthy–whatever it takes. Just get him back on the line...tonight. Like you said, no one knows what's going to happen. After last night, we're still having trouble assessing our losses and recruiting more troops. And we have thousands of dead and wounded casualties to deal with now as well."

"Yes, sir." Watkins said.

"So don't either of you attempt to lecture me on our limitations and the unexpected. Make it happen, Captain Watkins. Make it work. And don't let the boy slip away to Elkhart, either. He's worried about his little girlfriend, when we have thousands of people dying every day? I don't care if he has ten wives with kids or an entire harem over there in Elkhart. He's staying put, right here. That's the last thing we need is for him to wander away and disappear on us."

"Yes, sir."

Mason didn't ever recall signing up with the militia, or reciting any oath. Neither had Blondie.

Yet here they were, just as he feared. The authorities weren't about to let him go. Too much depended on him now. He was too valuable a commodity.

Only he could make the magic work. He was the only one who could do whatever it was he did.

Mason Tyler–the Pistolero–the living weapon.

There was a chill in the air and on his face. He was on a bed in a house somewhere. There wasn't any heat, but he had warm blankets over him.

He didn't like the sound of people being angry at him, either. If friendlies got caught up in his wildly destructive blasts, perhaps that was just one of the costs of war. But, on the other hand, he could understand people getting angry and upset at friendly fire losses from his guns.

It didn't sit well with him at all that he had killed others–even by accident. But he could see the militia's side of things as well. They were the only defense the city had, and they were all barely hanging on. There wasn't any exact, precise way to do any of this. And he recalled vividly that, despite his own misgivings, he had been under direct orders, several times, to keep firing in order to prevent them all from being overcome.

Screw the pain. He needed to get up and start moving around.

He needed to decide what he was going to do: stick around South Bend, or head to Elkhart on his own, if need be.

Mason winced and tried to flex his sore body. He had to loosen up, but moving hurt so bad that it brought tears to his eyes.

Blondie came in and then called out to Watkins. "He's awake and out of bed."

Captain Watkins came back in with the doctor and nurse. The medical people started checking his vitals: pulse, blood pressure, breathing. Mason put up with a little of that and then grew frustrated and waved them off.

"I'm fine. Just stiff and sore," he told them. "Let me walk around and limber up."

Watkins smiled. "You did good last night, son."

"Yeah, I guess that's why some people want to string me up."

"Oh...you heard that?"

"Yeah, and according to the general, I'm not going anywhere. Be honest with me, Captain. Did you send anyone to Elkhart to try to locate that address and find my gal, Tori Nelson?"

Watkins looked offended. "Son, I can't speak for others, but I keep my word when I give it. There are three different groups of messengers and scouts trying to make it to Elkhart at this very moment. Things are pretty wild, so I can't promise they'll make it there or come back. But if any of them do make it, they're going to try to find that address and locate your girl. A lot of people are risking their lives do so. Is that good enough for you? And like the general also noted, this isn't a game. Lots of people are dying each day. Deal with that, just like the rest of us are."

Mason looked down for a second. "I'm sorry, sir. Thank you. Of course I'm grateful for everyone's help. You'll have to forgive me. I feel like crap, and I'm young and dumb and self-centered as it is. I know that for a fact. I don't have a lot of patience, either. But I'll try to do my best. Do you really think there's going to be another battle tonight?"

"That's what we expect. And if there is, we're going to need you badly, once again. There's no avoiding that fact."

"How long do you think it will take your people to reach Elkhart and get back?"

"With as tough as things are and the roads all broken up, we gave them up to three days out, and three days back. Less if they can make it happen. They left yesterday, so with any luck, they should return by the end of the week, if not sooner."

"Well, I can't really say that I could get there any faster or at all, so I'll wait. And I'll do my best to help out here. But I don't want to be treated like a prisoner."

"You're not, Mace. Go anywhere you like, within reason, and we'll go with you. Consider us your bodyguards."

"All right. I like and respect you, but I'm putting you on notice, Captain. If no one comes back with any word on Tori, I'm going there myself. And no one is going to stop me—not you, and not the general."

"Let's cross that Rubicon when we reach it, and don't do anything rash, son. A lot of people are depending on you."

"Yeah, like the ones who want to hang me." After stretching and loosening up, he felt a lot less stiff and sore.

"You shouldn't focus on them, "Watkins told him. "They're an ignorant, vocal minority. Most people who know or learn the real facts are still very grateful that we have you on our side. We could all be dead today."

Mason nodded, grabbing his jacket and hat. He belted his pistols on and loaded up. "I want to go back to my duplex and see if there's anything else I can salvage. Ready to go for a little walk?"

Watkins smiled. "Ready whenever you are."

Once they were outside, Mason determined that they were less than a mile away from the lake. He and Blondie walked ahead of the rest.

"You remember who you are yet, Blondie?"

"Nope. But once I got to sleep, I had some very weird dreams last night. They didn't make any sense, however. I'll let you know when anything coherent comes to me. You put on quite a show last night, Mace."

"To my mind…I kinda had to."

"I know. Don't feel guilty. Don't let anyone ever blame you for anything."

"Thanks, Blondie. I'm trying not to."

Bands of militia, refugees, and civilians were out and about now that it was daylight and safe. There was much to do, and little time until the next sunset. Lots of bodies to be buried.

Teams of volunteers struggled to identify human remains and prepare them for the burial details, wrapping them up in whatever could be found—even trash bags. That was all harsh enough by itself.

The dead monsters slowly dissolved into foul-smelling vapor and slime if left in the sun, and blackened the earth where they lay. Some people tossed such remains into partially burned houses or burn piles, and immolated the bodies in order to cut down on the stink.

Bad smells abounded almost everywhere as it was.

Mason and Blondie recognized some faces among the refugees: Officer Tim Reinert, his wife Helen, and Denny, their twelve-year-old. All three of them looked wounded and beaten up. They just had the clothes on their back. They stumbled along, bandaged up and staring straight ahead.

Mason turned to Watkins, pointing out the Reinerts. "Those people are our friends. We need to help them." Watkins nodded, and called up their doctor and nurse, who had come along with them as ordered. They and the militia pulled the Reinerts out of the shuffling mob and started checking them over. From their injuries, it looked as if they had passed a very rough night on their own.

It worried Mason greatly that he didn't see Howard or the younger boy, Tommy, along with them. For the moment, he was too afraid to ask, but he knew that he'd have to work up the courage to do so.

"The Pistolero," someone whispered. "That's him right there, in the gunslinger hat and dark brown duster."

Mason turned and stared at the whisperers, who pointed at him and then nervously looked away in fear.

Other voices and interest grew and turned his way, as people passed by, in all directions. People continued to point him out, and look his way in a mixture of fear, wonder, and sometimes anger.

Various emotions played across their faces as they stared, or smiled, or scowled at him. And the hushed voices continued to whisper.

"Are you sure? Is that him?"

"He looks so young–like a college kid."

"Look! They say that's the Pistolero."

"That's him, all right."

"Don't look at him. Don't piss him off or get too close. He could blow us all away with one shot."

"They say he blew up half this section of town last night."

"So what; he killed thousands of those monsters, everyone says. We might all be dead if it wasn't for him."

"They say he saved the militia's ass last night. They all ran, and he stood his ground and kept shooting until his guns were empty, and the only thing left around him was a ring of dead monsters."

"Yeah, because he cut down everything around him–friend and foe."

"What the hell do you know? They say his guns are never empty. He fires them like magic...somehow."

"We should be thanking him."

"They should string the bastard up. He cut down a bunch of our people, too. He went crazy and started killing everything in sight."

Mason finally tried to ignore them and walked up to Tim and Helen, while their wounds were being looked after. "What happened?" he asked.

Both of them glanced up at him and broke down. They started crying. They couldn't speak.

Denny piped up, still carrying his old nightstick clutched in his hands. It looked even more battered than before. He almost sobbed when he spoke. "The monsters attacked our house and set it on fire. Mom and Dad fought their way out the back, but the monsters were waiting for us there, too. We tried to get away. They–"

The young boy's red eyes got real wide, and brimmed with tears. "They got Tommy and he was screaming. Howard tried to save him with that golf club. He whacked a couple of them before they dragged him down, too. There were just...too many monsters."

Mason put an arm around the kid and tried to comfort him. Denny was having trouble getting the rest of his words out.

"I watched them...kill my little brother Tommy and Howard. The monsters enjoyed it. They kept laughing and stabbing them with their rusty weapons, over and over. So much blood. Mom and Dad grabbed me and dragged me away. We kept running, hiding, and fighting. It seemed like that's all we did, all night long. I was never so glad to see the sun come up. But Tommy's still dead. They killed my brother."

Captain Watkins dispatched a squad of militia to look after the trio. "Get them to one of the shelters. Make sure they're safe."

But Mason looked all around them. There were too many people ambling around just like this family. An entire sea of them homeless, wounded, and in shock.

Their band regrouped, minus the squad, and kept going.

At Mason's ruined duplex, there really wasn't that much to retrieve. Most of Mason's belongings from his room had been tossed into the new lake when the Merge happened.

But he did manage to worm his way back into the collapsed house, along with Blondie, and drag out a few personal items: clothing, boots, leather saddlebags, and shoes.

When he got around to it, he'd have to ask the general for two horses for him and Blondie, and some kind of pack animal.

For the rest of that day, they returned to the house they were using nearby, and made ready for battle that night.

Mason went over, cleaned, and loaded all of his guns and tested them. Blondie focused on making crossbow bolts for his new crossbow, which had a scope and everything. He made dozens and kept making them.

Mason didn't ask where his strange new friend had acquired that crossbow—most likely on the battlefield somewhere, the night before. Blondie was normally tight-lipped about anything he did, and Mason didn't bother to prod him about much.

To Mason's great joy and relief, all of his remaining powders and shot all functioned the same way as the others. He only used half loads to save on his precious supplies, but he also experimented with mixing different components, either in the powder or mixed in with the lead shot.

The effects of those experimental loads also varied widely.

Iron filings and aluminum seemed to produce more incendiary effects over a longer, but narrower, area of effect. Whereas copper and brass increased the explosive yield of each shot, and did greater damage over a wider area closer up.

He spoke to Captain Watkins and Blondie about experimenting further with various types of other materials. He was anxious to try small quantities magnesium, if they could find one of those fire starters.

Mason thought about what had happened to the Reinerts, and what had happened to the city in general. And he still spent a lot of thought on hoping that Tori was still alive and okay, somewhere. They were both just two people in a mixed up world gone insane.

At sunset, Mason and Blondie waited with the militia for another enemy attack.

No attack came that night.

No attacks came for the next two nights after that.

But no word returned from Elkhart, either. None of the scouting parties or messengers returned.

11

So many memories of growing up with his parents and becoming a man in that car. David's car–Gandalf.

To him his reliable, faithful car had been more than a companion–it had represented his freedom, his adventure.

Now it all meant nothing. So much of David's world was now gone, lost so abruptly and completely.

Jerriel must have sensed his shock and discomfort, as he sat there helpless, almost paralyzed with loss and regret. She put her slender, white hand on his arm, but how could she know what he was going through?

She had to be just as confused, if not more so.

Jerriel had no idea what a car was.

Perhaps losing her ability to do magic was just as upsetting for her.

There was no way in hell for David to even begin to explain to her what a great car meant to someone on Earth. What it *had* meant.

In a world that once depended on safe, economical travel, David's old car had taken him everywhere–all over the U.S., Canada, and even parts of

Mexico. Just one of the many aspects of modern technology that Earth people would probably never take for granted again.

They never knew how good they had it. They might not ever get a chance to understand and appreciate that all over again.

All of that was gone now—perhaps forever.

He swallowed hard and faced many cold facts.

Even if humanity survived the Merge, they had still suffered great harm—and losses that they would be dealing with for centuries to come. Many would yearn for the golden ages of the past.

They had gone from being Earth, to being *Urth*.

And that loss would mess with humanity in many serious ways, from this time forward.

Damn the Merge.

"Daeved..." Jerriel said softly.

"I know." He'd already wasted too much time feeling sorry for himself and his dimension as it was. Time to push on, and do what needed to be done in the present.

The old Earth was already gone. What the new Urth would become remained to be seen, as did whether they would even survive and have a say in it.

David climbed out and ransacked his now useless car, filling the bike cart with his katana, wakizashi, and other spare weapons, more bolts for his crossbow, arrow-making supplies. He had several spear heads that would come in handy once they were set on poles. There was plenty of medieval garb, and a couple of shields someone could use. He preferred to fight two-handed.

And finally, his suit of armor. A fully-functional suit of fourteenth century field plate, complete with coat of plates, chainmail, tassets, gorget, and gambeson. Shoulder, arm, leg, and foot armor.

It all weighed less than forty-five pounds. From years of practice jousting and dueling at events and Ren Fairs in it, David could move around and fight in that armor for an entire day or more.

Dirk Blackwood and the other armorers from the local medieval club had helped him make it out of sixteen gauge stainless steel. He bought the helmet and the mitten-style gauntlets from another armorer, but everything else he had made, riveted, and put together with his own two hands.

If he took the time to don it, he could even ride a horse or a bike in it.

As soon as he finished loading up, they pedaled back to the rendezvous point downtown.

By then it was noon and a crowd of several thousands volunteers milled about on such a chilly, sunny day. David spotted Dirk and Belinda helping out. Dirk already had his own battered suit of medieval armor on to show off for the crowds. Like David, Dirk was used to wearing armor and could do so all day, if need be.

But they would shuck it off to save their strength, when and where possible.

Belle carried her longbow and a quiver of arrows and stood with Dirk, but she remained slightly behind him when he stepped up to speak.

Communication continued to be a problem. Big megaphones had been set up on stands for people to give directions through.

The chaos and confusion only intensified with so many nervous people coming together. If the authorities weren't careful, the attempt to raise a militia could easily turn into a riot. People weren't in any mood to be messed with or to mess around.

But *hurry up and wait* seemed to be the order of the day. Typical military.

Dirk sensed the frustration building and took charge, just as David and Jerriel joined him and Belle near one of the main stands. Belle waved to them.

"I'm provisional militia commander Dirk Blackwood. Quiet down and listen up, people. Let's get this started. There's a lot to do."

"C'mon," David said to Jerriel. "People need to see more of us ready to fight. Let's go behind the stand. Help me put my armor on." He picked out the gambeson and the coat of plates from the bike carrier.

Jerriel nodded, grabbing his gorget and the arms. "I know what to doo. I grew up among armed warrioors."

She continued to impress David. Jerriel made a great squire. Having her hands moving all over him was also thrilling.

Above them, Dirk shouted over the big megaphone in front of him. His hardened voice rang out over the mob.

"Listen up, people."

A messenger ran in and handed Dirk a note.

"This is an important general announcement for anyone listening. The search teams have encountered several strange pools of glowing water in the area. At this time, we don't know what they are, but reports state that these weird pools of liquid can at times be dangerous—even fatal. There have already been a number of unusual losses and injuries."

David thought of the incident he'd witnessed involving one of those strange, glowing pools. Did the damn things appear randomly, or was there some pattern to them? Were they permanent? What happened when the pools dried up or drained away?

It continued to frustrate him that they knew so little about all of the many threats they now faced.

Jerriel rushed up to Dirk, tapping on his arm. He turned to her in surprise.

"Dirk. I must examine these strange pools. They may be magic. I must see them." She looked back at David.

"Go ahead," David told her. "We're going to be swamped training the militia until tonight."

"I will come back, Daeved, befoore the sun goes down."

Dirk turned to Belle. "Send her out with some of the searchers. She must be kept safe. Take her with you tonight if you have to."

"Got it," Belle said, noting it in her book. "Come with me, Jerriel." The ladies left. Dirk and David turned back to the monumental task at hand.

They divided the volunteers into units of three: sword and shield, spear and shield, and archer or crossbow. Three such units led by a corporal formed a squad of ten on the line. Three squads of ten, led by a sergeant, made up a platoon of thirty-one.

Three platoons comprised a company of ninety-three troops, led by an additional field command staff of seven—normally three second lieutenants (one attached to each platoon), a first lieutenant, a captain, and two aides or messengers.

Three battlefield companies of a hundred troops made up a battalion of three hundred troops plus support personnel, led by a major. Three battalions made up a legion of a thousand, or what was also called a regiment, led by a colonel, and support staff. Three legions or regiments of a thousand each made up a division of three thousand, led by a brigadier general, and support staff.

And finally, three divisions formed an army or battle group of ten thousand troops, led by a general. Support and supply units were also formed, but organized separately from frontline fighting units.

Dirk gave David the acting rank of first lieutenant, and sent him to help get the companies forming up, getting their weapons and gear, and begin drilling and training to fight and move as a unit.

"We don't have a lot of time before nightfall," Dirk told him. "Get the basics down. Impress on everyone the need to stand and fight and not break and run. With green militia, that's going to be a big problem tonight—holding our lines together. Very few of these people have ever fought in any kind of battle, let alone one that's going to be as up close and personal as this one will."

"Got it," David said.

First they had to get everyone suited up.

Staff had pieces of makeshift armor broken down into types and sizes, as more continued to pour in from the community.

Criers had been sent out by bicycle and on foot, asking for donations of anything that could be used as armor or weapons. Workers cut pieces of metal to be tied on and used in overlapping layers to protect chests, arms, and legs. Sometimes they were merely fixed in place and glued on with caulking guns.

First thing, each militia trooper got a set of dog tags with their name, serial number, and any basic religious or medical info. The local military recruiters and ROTC people from the colleges had brought along several tag imprinters and boxes of blanks and chains.

Next came a helmet, shoulder and neck protection, torso armor, arm and leg armor, boots if they needed them, and tie-on protective plates or caps for their feet fashioned out of metal or plastic.

Next came weapons.

Everyone got a small hand weapon, usually a long hunting knife or a hatchet, to wear on their canteen belt. Every trooper received two canteens filled with drinking water, and a butt pack filled with bandages and basic first aid supplies.

Sword and shield fighters naturally received swords or machetes, and larger shields for the shield wall. Spear fighters got a six- to seven-foot spear and a smaller shield. Spears fought behind the shield wall, spearing as many foes as quickly as they could, while the shield wall held.

Archers had a bow or crossbow and were tested. They had to demonstrate some minimal skill or ability to fire it. They were issued two dozen shafts, and a hammer or hatchet with a hammer head on the reverse side.

The archers could cut and drive picket poles into the ground for position defense, and then sharpen the exposed end with their hatchets or knives. In a pinch, the pickets could even be yanked out and used as last-ditch spears. Picket lines could slow enemies down so that the spears and archers could cut the enemy down at close range.

Dirk and David knew that ammunition for their archers was going to be a running problem from the get-go. Entire teams of older and younger volunteers were organized by the emergency town council to do nothing but make arrows and crossbow bolts as fast as possible. Teams of runners were organized to distribute arrows and bolts by cart and backpack to each company on the line.

Finally, the troops received a backpack with a foam sleeping pad and wool blanket. They ran out of ponchos very quickly. Troops could use their own tents, sleeping bags, and camping gear if they had any, but non-coms made sure their people did not carry too much gear.

If the troops were too heavily encumbered, they wouldn't be able to move or fight very well. All packs had to be kept behind the lines during actual battles.

Time passed quickly.

Three hours before sunset, and the city only had one single division of three thousand green militia troops to send out, marching to take up defensive positions at key points.

Dirk Blackwood was appointed acting brigadier general.

David and the other leaders did their best to keep the units together, and attempt to train and instruct them as they marched–a very tall order.

There were three lines of defense: shield wall, spears, and then archers in direct support. Protect the flanks. Don't get cut off or surrounded. Hold the strategic access points to the city, and take the enemy down. No negotiations with these creatures. Kill the bastards dead on sight.

It grew closer and closer to nightfall as more militia units came online each minute across the city.

David rode up and down his sections that he could reach on a bicycle in the fading light, checking their lines and positions. He tried to make sure that the militia had the basic formations in place: sword and shield wall, spear, and archer. Three lines deep–archers up in higher positions to shoot down at the enemy, whenever possible.

Everyone looked pale and scared.

David's gut ached. They could all be in for a very long night.

12

Another night, with no further sign of the enemy.

"I'm leaving," Mason announced that evening for all to hear, including General Benton and Captain Watkins. "With or without your help, I'm going to Elkhart. I need to go there myself, and find out what has happened to Tori."

"You can't do that," Benton said.

"Watch me. It's been over a week, and I'm done being patient. General, there have been no further enemy attacks, and we've also had no word from Elkhart in all that time. None of the people we've sent have been able to make it back. We need to know why."

Benton looked as if he was about to lower the boom.

Mason rested a hand casually on one of his pistols.

Watkins broke the tension. "Let him go, General. Someone needs to get through, somehow. If anyone can, he can. Mason's right—he needs his answers, and we need to find out what's happening in Elkhart."

Benton sat back and hesitated still. "What if something happens to him? What if we're attacked while he's gone?"

"Then we handle it the best we can, sir. And then we summon him back. Our recruitment is up. The militia is four times its original size now that we've had a few days to fully recruit, stabilize, and organize the city's defenses. He's young; he's no good to us this hostile and distracted. Let him go—two problems solved."

Benton waved one hand. "Very well. Send him. Give him and his friend horses or bikes—whatever they need. Go to Elkhart, Mr. 'Pistolero,' as people have taken to calling you. Do whatever you need to do there and make contact with whoever is in charge. Then return back here and report, as quickly as you are able. But if you hear we're under attack, I want you back here—pronto—girl or no girl. More lives than just one depend on you. But let me still wish you good luck. You have already saved us, more than once, and we should all be grateful to you for that. I hope you find that young woman you are looking for, alive and well."

Mason didn't know what to say at first. He didn't expect this level of compassion. Watkins had really come through for him. "Thank you, sir, and everyone else."

He and Blondie stayed up two more hours, working with Watkins getting their horses, pack horse, and gear ready. Then they turned in.

"Do you mind if we get an early start, just before dawn?" Mason asked Blondie.

His new friend held his hands up in the air. "Like a guy who still doesn't know who he is has anything better to do."

Mason grinned and clapped his buddy on the shoulder. "Thanks, Blondie. Let's hit the sack."

Blondie grinned. "Mace, as much as I have come to adore your company, and your light snoring and mumbling in your sleep, I've arranged to have my own room next to yours. I hope you won't mind."

Mason looked at him. "What brought this on?"

His friend grinned even wider. "A certain young lady has made it very clear to me that she wishes to keep me company tonight. I thought I might oblige her."

Mason raised both eyebrows. "Well, okay then. Have good time, my friend."

"I fully intend to."

Good for Blondie. Mason was happy that his strange friend had found someone so quickly, but Blondie did happen to be just the kind of bad boy character that many young women probably went for.

Mason knew what it was like to really want to be with someone, but his Tori was the only woman he needed or wanted.

For the first time, things seemed to be on the way up.

85

Mason stopped being happy for Blondie and whoever his new gal was very quickly over the next three hours or more.

Not only were the walls between his and Blondie's room right next door apparently too thin, but this young lady was definitely a screamer—and quite possibly a budding opera star or something.

Despite being dead tired the night before a big mission, Mason was forced to endure the torture and annoyance of repeatedly listening to said young woman cry out in passion at the top of her lusty lungs.

And she only had two modes that she switched back and forth between. She was either incredibly agreeable to what Blondie was doing to her, or she kept calling on the Almighty Himself for either some kind of divine notice or assistance.

After three hours, he could hardly stand it any longer.

Mason seriously considered shooting a few lesser holes through the wall.

But even as Mason cocked the hammers on his Spillers and aimed high, Blondie and the young woman apparently collapsed and passed out from their exertions—at last.

If the young lady in question had lost her voice by morning, it would not come as any surprise. The entire county must have heard her cries that night.

Mason collapsed to grab what rest he could.

Whoever it was came for him in his room two hours later. They were quiet, and Mason was exhausted. But something tried to tell him he was in trouble.

They jumped him a split second before he grabbed one of his pistols. Someone cracked him on the back of the head with something hard, and the last thing he recalled was being dizzy and mostly out of it while his wrists and ankles were being bound with either duct tape or zip ties.

He never completely blacked out, but when Mason could make sense of things, it was still dark. He could determine that much, even with the dark bag or hood that had been shoved over his head. His skull still ached where his abductors had struck him.

When he tried to move, he discovered he was sitting on some kind of a metal, perhaps a kitchen chair, tied down to it by his wrists and ankles. His muscles had gone stiff and there was duct tape over his mouth, the adhesive of which tasted lousy.

He couldn't do much but breathe through his nose. Even though the room was chilly, having a bag over his head made him hot, sweaty, and uncomfortable.

It was quiet around him. He was probably alone.

His bonds held fast. The metal chair was very sturdy. Tipping over in it would just make him more uncomfortable, and risk bashing his head on something.

If it had been a wooden or folding chair that might break apart or collapse, he would have risked doing so. Things did not look good.

After a while there was nothing to do but sleep and keep his strength up. Perhaps a chance to escape or break free would come later, when they cut him free from the chair.

When Mason woke up again, it was already getting light out. The bag was dark, but not completely dark. People were moving and talking around him in hushed voices, but he could still make out what they were saying.

Mason considered his situation. Someone in the militia had to have helped these people. This had *inside job* written all over it.

"Did you try the guns?" one voice said.

"Yeah."

"All of them?"

"None of them work, just like I told you. They only work for him."

That would be a militia person who knew that.

"Then that's a damn shame, cause this bastard's going to swing. My brother and another good friend of ours were in one of those buildings fighting the monsters. This jerk blasted them and that entire building to bits with his damn guns. He killed them all and he doesn't even care. He has people thinking he's a hero—when he's just a filthy murderer. He doesn't give a damn who he cuts down. We've all heard that."

"Then let's get this over with. They're already looking for him everywhere. If you want to do this, we need to move on it and get it over quickly."

"Everyone's here now. We're all ready. Let's string him up and get to it."

Now Mason was scared. These people obviously hated him fiercely. They were going to hang and kill him—no trial, no questions, no chance to explain or defend himself.

They just wanted him dead. It was that brutally simple.

"Keep his hands tied. Cut his feet loose and bring him out to the tree. We've got the rope ready."

"I think he's awake. He's probably listening to us right now."

"Good. Then he knows he's about to die."

Mason started kicking and trying to get away as soon as his legs were free. It wasn't very easy to go on the defensive with the bag on his head and his hands still bound.

They all cursed and grunted.

His captors shoved him down and kicked him into submission.

Then they jostled him back up to walk. He was stiff and hurting, but they shoved him out what was most likely the back door of a house.

They led him down some short steps.

No, he couldn't die like this.

He couldn't even speak. Somehow that made it worse. He couldn't yell or scream at them or call for help.

Mason still didn't even know how many of them there were around him. It could be an entire mob, for all he knew. He had only been able to parse out three, maybe four different people breathing around him and then hitting and kicking him during the struggle.

Only the two men had spoken, and he didn't recognize either of their voices.

Was he really going to die this way, hanged like a criminal?

Tori. Whenever he was close to death, he could only think of her and everything they'd miss out on together. Damn it.

His captors made him step up and stand on something—something wooden that creaked—maybe a picnic table. Mason heard and felt the cold wind lashing through some kind of tree branches.

Then they cinched the rope tight around his neck. Four pairs of hands worked on him. Mason started to panic in terror, grunting and mumbling through his gag.

The angry guy whispered, taunting him further. "Getting a little excited, are you? You just suck on that and twist in the wind, scum. We're all going to stick you with knives and cut you, also, while you jerk like a fish on a hook. This is for my brother and all the other innocent people you killed, you no good mother—"

Scores of bows twanged.

Arrows zipped through the air like angry hornets.

People grunted, moaned, and dropped. Some fell very hard. Mason could hear their skulls smack into either brick or concrete.

Something or someone heavy still managed to shove him off of that table.

The rope tightened and burned around his neck like a band of sudden fire.

Mason couldn't breathe.

His legs kicked wildly, but he still could not breathe or reach the table again with his toes.

Feet pounded in toward him.

Someone grabbed him by the legs and hips and hoisted him back up, taking the tension of his weight off the rope.

A blade swept through the air with a whoosh at the same time.

The rope was cut and his dead weight slammed both him and the person holding him to the ground hard.

He was still trying to breathe.

Blondie yanked the dark bag off Mason's head and tore the tape from his mouth. His friend proceeded to cut his hands free with the same razor-sharp cavalry saber Blondie had severed the rope with.

Five people lay bleeding and dying on the ground near Mason, riddled with arrows.

Two of them were women, and all five did, in fact, have knives—either in their hands or on their belts.

Captain Watkins checked the conspirators, but with all of those arrows in them… "They're all done for," Watkins noted. "As it was, we couldn't take any chances. Search the house; they took some of Mace's guns when they abducted him. I want every one of those weapons returned immediately."

Mason studied the faces of the dead people who had wanted to kill him so badly. He barely recognized one face from the militia among them, but he didn't know any of the five conspirators by name.

Why did that shock him so much?

He didn't know any of these folks, but they had certainly been hell-bent on killing and torturing him—revenge for Mason taking the lives of people they cared about during the chaotic fighting. Now, all five of his abductors lay dead as well, because of him.

All because Mason's special talent for destruction made him too valuable to let anyone kill him.

Blondie sheathed his saber finally and grinned. "I was all set to ride for Elkhart this morning, Mace. Where the hell were you?"

Mason groaned, slipping the burning rope from his raw neck. He hissed in pain and took in a sweet breath. "Oh, just hanging around, I guess."

Blondie grunted. "Stick to your guns, Pistolero. You sure aren't any good at comedy."

Mason nodded. "They say it's all timing. We're still going to Elkhart, just as soon as I finish catching my breath."

"I know we are," Blondie said. "We're all packed up. Everything's waiting on you."

Mason hugged his friend with both arms, truly thankful and grateful. "Thanks, my brother. Thanks for finding me, and for coming to my rescue. I sure owe you one."

Blondie pulled away, catching his own breath from being bear hugged so forcefully, but looking both proud and pleased with himself. "You got it, Mace. I'm going to hold you to that some day. So what happened? I thought you were a light sleeper? No one can sneak up on the Pistolero."

Mason stared at Blondie suddenly, his eyes wide and a little annoyed as they walked away from that scene of death. "Well, it just so happened that I was dog-damn-tired from being kept up for hours by you and that shrieking banshee you had in bed with you!"

"Yeah, I'm sorry about that, Mace. She was a bit loud, but real eager, let me tell you." Blondie sighed.

"A bit loud?" Mason said. "A bit loud? They must have heard her over four states!"

Blondie chuckled. "Man, you're still pissed about it. I can tell."

"You don't wanna mess with a man who likes his sleep like a good steak, Blondie—I swear to Jehovah Himself, if that gal howled 'yes!' or 'oh, God!' once more, I was going to blast through that paper-thin wall and shoot you both right in the ass. Give you both something to goddam scream about with burning holes punched clean through the fleshy parts of your buttocks for the wind to whistle through!"

His friend laughed so hard, he couldn't speak for a moment. "Well, Mace, I'm sure glad you showed some restraint. Neither of us need any extra holes. By the Powers, maybe you do have a knack for comedy—we just have to get you good and mad."

They both laughed together, continuing to relieve some of the tension.

The rope burn that still scorched and scarred Mason's neck was bloody where the nylon noose had bit and burned into his flesh under the agony of his own weight. Those wounds needed to be tended to and dressed so that they didn't get infected.

They would also serve as a constant reminder of his hanging.

No one was going to do that to him ever again.

No one.

It still hurt and bothered Mason greatly, deep inside and personal, that those five dead strangers had wanted to murder him so badly.

He didn't want to become too paranoid, but he would have to watch his back now, and be a great deal more careful.

Yet none of any of that was going to prevent him from going to Elkhart and search for Tori.

First, see to his injuries. Next, after he ate and rested enough to recover from his ordeal, he and Blondie would hit the trail.

13

At least it didn't rain. The sky stayed partly cloudy, with patches of sun here and there around Portage and Angela on the northwest side. The wind in the bare trees swept in cool and breezy, about ten to fifteen miles an hour out of the southwest.

During those last two hours before sunset, another hasty division organized at the Century Center rushed up to reinforce the lines in the last few minutes.

That made it six thousand militia set to defend South Bend from whatever came against them that night.

Word came from General Blackwood. Because of his knowledge and skills, David quickly went from first lieutenant to become the captain of 2nd Company, 1st Division, a hundred troops anchoring the left flank on Portage Road around Angela Street just before the roundabout and the crucial bridge there and the old train trestle that was blocked off. Their position was a strategic choke point that protected the river and that entire area, not to mention the new emergency centers set up among the churches and nearby schools.

Attacks had been heavy in that area the night before. David knew that firsthand.

He wished he knew for certain that Jerriel was safe.

While it still remained light out, David instructed his people to post sentries, stay warm, and maintain their formations and positions. They moved derelict vehicles to form a defensive barrier on the far side of the road.

Troops also had boxes and crates of rocks and bricks to hurl in the face of the enemy when the monsters charged.

It seemed to grow dark around them very quickly, especially from the east.

Tension and fear tainted the air, along with a faint stench on the wind.

David knew exactly what that stink was from. Monsters.

One of his runners biked back to him from downtown; David couldn't remember the kid's name. "Where's Jerriel?" he asked. "Did she ever report back to HQ?"

Thus far, only a few people knew just how valuable and important the wizard girl was to them all.

"We haven't heard anything," the messenger told him. "Perhaps she—"

Whistles and horns sounded up and down the line, all along the near northwest side.

Major Hammond's runner came to them from up the line to the east, a terrified blond kid from one of the high school cross country teams. There were a bunch of new officers that David hadn't even met. Hardly anyone knew each other.

"Captain Pritchard. The enemy has been spotted. They're sweeping this way, pouring into town between us and the west side units. There's a big wild area of forest there that stretches all the way out to where the airport once was."

David put his hands on his weapons. "How many strong?"

The messenger shook his head. "Reports say it's difficult to estimate accurate numbers in the dark. But they're rampaging this way, across Olive Street and down Ellwood—at least several thousand strong."

The enemy obviously intended to cross the river again and go on another rampage—this time with far greater numbers.

"Good work letting us know. Return to Major Hammond and tell him we need to hold the line here at all costs. Any available units should reinforce this location."

The runner remembered to salute this time. "Thank you, sir." David returned it and the boy ran off.

David didn't feel like much of a leader, but he couldn't let that show.

He walked up and down Portage Road, spear and sword swinging easily in his hands. He tried to settle his troops down, trying to ignore the chaos of the attacking hordes growing ever closer.

The sound of breaking windows, screams, and fires erupted.

They couldn't protect every house. That was just the way it was.

He only had a few minutes before they'd engage the monsters. The first stroke of the enemy hammer was going to hit their position first.

"All right, people. Get up to the line and maintain the shield wall. Hold your ground. Prepare to fight. We back each other up. Take out the enemies around you, and then the next."

They had finished rolling up a defensive line of vehicles bumper to bumper all on one side of Portage Road.

"We're defending our homes. Our family and friends are counting on us. We can't let the enemy break through. We can't let them reach the river, or the bridge."

The militia stood poised and ready to fight.

Yet even at a glance, their lines were obviously too thin. What was going on?

David shouted. "Platoon and team leaders, get everyone up here, now. Everyone on the line!" Voices erupted all at once.

"This is it, sir," someone said.

"Sir, a bunch of people behind us just turned around and ran off."

"What do we do, sir?"

David held his breath, checking left and right.

Half his troops—were already gone.

And the monsters were mere minutes from falling upon them.

"Everyone to my right and left, within the sound of my voice, close ranks. Keep the shield wall in front. Set spears to receive a charge. Spread the word down the line on both sides. All units, close in and get ready to fight!"

David loaded his crossbow. His hands shook.

Horrific roaring filled the air. Trees and houses rattled. The cold ground rumbled at the pounding of charging monster feet. Monsters attacked throughout the northwest, smashing and burning everything in their path.

"Hurry!" David commanded. "Pass the word. Close up the line toward Angela on both sides. We'll form up and defend that intersection leading back to the bridge!"

Fighting erupted in several places along Portage, even as they continued to try to close ranks.

If the enemy caught them thin and off-balance—they were screwed.

"Archers and rock throwers, hold your fire. Remember, the enemy will drive human refugees in front of them, just as they did last night. Don't get confused and hit our own people. Let them through the lines! Tell them to get to one of the safe zones."

More screams where unlucky people hadn't left their homes for the evacuation, hoping the trouble would pass them by again.

And it didn't.

Within a few minutes, scared and wounded survivors biked and ran down the street. Even little kids, half naked in the cold. Some troops wrapped them in blankets and tried to get them to safety.

"Let them through, troops. Keep them moving—but stay on the line. You cannot go with them. Hand them off to others!"

"They're coming," people screamed. "The monsters are coming!"

"They're killing people, eating people, taking prisoners. There's hundreds of them!"

"They're everywhere!"

In the night, terror took hold easily. David sensed the uneasiness of his remaining troops.

Those troops without bows still had the boxes of rocks, stones, and pieces of concrete debris to toss at the enemy at the outset. The idea was to inflict whatever damage they could from a distance.

The last terrified stragglers ran toward the line, some of them injured.

The militia still shifted toward Angela. David spotted the main dark mass of foes, swelling and growing as it swept forward.

"Prepare to fire. On my—"

He didn't even get his whistle in his hand.

A few terrified refugees still crossed Portage. A hail of sporadic arrows and rocks tore into the advancing mass, taking down friend and foe alike.

The last refugees dispersed or crawled under cars or houses.

David started shooting, still leading his people to protect the intersection. He aimed at enemy torsos, scoring hits. The missile barrage checked the enemy advance for a few precious moments.

He dropped a torg with a bolt in the chest, less than ten feet away.

Then he slung his crossbow over his shoulder, secured the clip, and tightened the strap down behind his back. He hefted his broad bladed spear. The enemy bunched and charged across Portage. Missiles still struck among them.

He dropped a torg with a bolt in the chest, less than ten feet away.

Then he slung his crossbow over his shoulder, secured the clip, and tightened the strap down behind his back. He hefted his broad-bladed spear. The enemy bunched and charged across Portage. Missiles still struck among them.

The barrier of vehicles barely slowed them down.

Monster drums boomed in the distance. There had been no drums the night before.

Drums and weird horns blared, strange cries and screams. More fires erupted.

"Shield wall. Set for charge!" David yelled. He snapped his head left and right.

Holy shit. He had maybe fifteen people on either side of him. Everyone else broke and ran down Angela back toward the bridge.

There was no way they could hold now.

"Everyone retreat. Fall back to the bridge and the river. Keep fighting all the way!"

The Portage line quickly collapsed inwards and dissolved.

Now those who hadn't bolted would need to fight like hell just to try to save themselves.

"Fighting retreat. Stay together and fight, or we're all dead!"

David stabbed three more charging torgs with quick jabs of his spear, giving ground every second.

A ka-torg, taller and stockier, jumped on David's spear haft and cracked it. David ducked under the sweep of its broad-bladed scimitar. He whirled to the side and ran the monster through with his broken spear.

He drew his longsword and swept up, clipping another creature in the arm. Then he thrust forward suddenly and stabbed it in the throat. It gurgled and fell back.

More foes rushed in. David backpedaled around the nearest house.

The enemy didn't know the area and quickly bogged down among the confusing obstacles of houses, cars, yards, and fences.

But so did some of the militia in their attempt to retreat. Several got cut off and dragged down. David heard their screams end abruptly. He wished he could have helped them.

They were nearly overrun at Angela and Woodward, only a few hundred yards from the bridge.

Damn it. They had lost good people to cowardice and stupidity. The shame he felt at his own failure to lead them better sank in pretty deep, but there wasn't much time for any of that.

It was all he could to help support the troops near him. What remained of his company—two dozen out of a hundred—fought a feeble retreat back down Angela and across the roundabout past Brownfield Park. They retreated toward the natural barrier of the river, where Dirk Blackwood and several other companies still held the bridge.

This was now the crucial choke point for the battle.

From the screams and cries for help, many militia got cut off and surrounded along the steep riverbank. Many jumped into the cold water to get away from the monsters. The collapse and its losses made David sick, even as he and his people fought their way back toward the bridge.

But the monsters wouldn't go into the water. Apparently, they couldn't swim. That gave the humans one advantage.

14

The day was cool and partly cloudy with some gusts of wind. Mason and Blondie rode through what remained of South Bend and into Mishawaka. The raiding and fighting hadn't been as bad there. Not yet, at least.

He liked their three mounts, and had forgotten just how much he enjoyed the company of horses. His mount, Winger, was an eight-year-old bay quarter horse mare—smart, strong, and good-natured. Blondie's mount Patton was a tall brown gelding who looked to be part mustang, seven years old, fast and agile.

Patton didn't seem as clever and intelligent as Winger, but he was strong, calm, and obedient. Their pack horse, Ginger, was a smaller, tough, ten-year-old riding horse who looked docile, and also had a lot of mustang in her, from the way she was built. She faithfully carried their supplies and Mason's shooting gear.

Their old western saddles and other tack were sturdy and passable. Mason sighed and breathed in deep. Horses simply smelled good to his nose.

In the morning, they would lightly feed and groom their horses before setting out, giving their mounts about at least an hour to wake and warm up. Then, once Mason and Blondie had eaten and were ready, they'd saddle up and set out for the day. Mason and Blondie routinely checked the horses' legs, hooves, and shoes.

Mason recalled that an old cowboy once told him that it was better to feed horses many smaller meals throughout the day; it was supposedly more natural for their digestion. Feedbags made that possible, even while they traveled along. If they made short stops, they used long leads they kept with them to let the horses graze a bit on the spring grass that was up. That helped conserve their feed, but they had to be careful their horses didn't get tangled up.

Luckily, all of the horses seemed to like one another.

Once they rode through Mishawaka, they'd make their way into Osceola and on into Elkhart, which was spread out even worse than South Bend. But Mason knew exactly where they were going. Barring any trouble, they might make it there in as little as two days.

Although the fighting hadn't been as bad out this way, there had still been many intense raids and probes by the monsters to test the defenders. There were still burned houses here and there and many signs of fighting and violence.

They periodically passed large groups of refugees in bunches, all ages, most of them heading away from South Bend. Naturally, they were trying to escape from the heaviest areas of fighting.

People in the crowds pointed at the two riders and whispered. Mason did his best to ignore them.

Blondie finally spoke up. "Mace, I don't like this. We're getting a lot of weird, angry looks from time to time."

"Yep. I think I'm going to have to somehow live with that."

Blondie sounded a little nervous. "For a second I thought some of them might actually rush us, or attack us with weapons. A few people have bows or crossbows. They could shoot us in the back, right out of our saddles."

Mason looked around and rested a hand on one of his pistols. "Some of them might try."

"Careful, there, Mace. If the Pistolero blows a bunch of them away—self-defense or not—you'll just make more enemies, and more problems for us."

"Damn it, Blondie. I'm not going to shoot anybody if they don't force the issue. Don't worry, I'm not as dark as you yet. But I can't change the past, either. I'm trying to be more careful, but I tell you what: I'm not letting anyone put a rope around my neck ever again."

"I don't blame you there, Mace."

Mason sighed again. "I can rationalize it all, but part of me still feels guilty. It was never my intention to kill anyone on our side, not even indirectly or by accident."

"Well, don't lose too much sleep over it. If people only knew how many of those monsters you took down... Tell me, how many people would those monsters have killed if you hadn't wiped them all out? So what if a few eggs got cracked along the way?"

"They weren't eggs, Blondie. They were living, breathing people, and its hard for those who knew them to accept that. But I'm still not about to let anyone abuse or hang me."

Someone buzzed the other way on a bike, pointed the two of them out, and taunted and sneered at them. "Hey, that's the Pistolero...and his darling boyfriend."

The crowd of refugees seemed to boil over and erupt. Some voices shouted in praise, while others shouted in rage and anger.

Someone yelled. "The Pistolero saved the entire city of South Bend. If it hadn't been for him, the city would have been overrun by the monsters. That's a known fact!"

Another person shouted, "And he cut down lots of militia and innocent people while doing it. He killed them all, and the authorities won't bring him to justice for it. He's a goddam murderer!"

"Don't curse him. He cut down thousands of monsters with his guns. Most of us would be dead if he hadn't done so. We ought to be thanking him!"

"He killed innocent people without even a thought."

"It couldn't be helped."

"Killer. Killer. Killer!"

"No, he defended us all!"

"Hanging's too good for him!"

It looked like a fight was going to break out among the crowd of refugees. Some of them flung trash, garbage, and mud, clumps of dirt, and even rocks at Mason and Blondie.

"Aaughh!" Mason cried out, feeling the burn of a stone that struck him on the back of his right arm.

Both of them grunted and cursed, feeling the further sting of a few more missiles. Their horses jostled and neighed in fear, getting spooked. Blondie and Mason found themselves pelted with debris until others in the mob rushed forward to try to stop the throwers. It came to blows.

Mason reached his limit. He drew and fired two shots—one in the air—another over everyone's heads that vaporized a nearby tree and gouged out a big smoking portion of a muddy field.

That got their attention.

"Everyone calm down," he shouted. "Unless you really wanna see what my pistols can do. What in the hell do you fools think you're doing?"

He kept shouting at them. "Keep the peace, you idiots. Damn it to hell. Isn't it bad enough that everything's so messed up and these damn monsters are trying to wipe us all out? We can't turn on each other like this. We can't afford to be fighting each other. We don't know how many of us are left. Stop all this crap and pull together. Work together and help protect each other."

"Why should we listen to you...you bloody killer!"

"And as for that, how many of you cowards were actually there, on the lines, defending the city? Tell me that? Speak up! You don't know how it was—you were too busy running away. All you've heard is a pack of lies. I'm sorry about what happened to those people. I wish there had been another way, but there wasn't. We didn't have a choice; there wasn't time. It was kill or be killed, and those monsters were coming at us from all directions. But I'm still sorry for it!"

The mob just stared at him.

"Come on, Mace," Blondie said, clearing his throat and spitting. "Don't waste your breath on them. Let's get the hell out of here."

They put their heels to their mounts, clucked their tongues, and cantered away from the refugee mob. Until they spotted another similar mob up ahead, converging on the next intersection of roads.

Mason hissed. "We're not going through all of that crap all over again."

They ducked out into the country until they found a partially burned-out farmhouse, hid their horses out of sight, and ducked down until the next swarm of refugees passed through.

Blondie finally spoke up, still pouting. "I'm not anyone's boyfriend," he said. "Why in the hell do they even say crap like that?"

Mason burst out laughing, and soon both of them were.

"Seriously," Blondie said. "I've come to recall that I'm a born and bred womanizer. I have never met any guy who looked as good to me as women do."

"Well, as comforting as that is to hear, maybe you just haven't met one as pretty as yourself, with the right kind of lust in his heart and a twinkle in his eye...just for you."

Blondie laughed. "No thanks, Mace. I like women, hot and willing. Just send those gals my way."

Mason shook his head. "That part's up to you, my friend. I don't care either way what you or others do. I've already made my choice. I just want to get to Elkhart and find Tori."

For the first time, Blondie clapped him on the shoulder, a serious look on his face. "I hope we find her, Mason. I hope your lady's okay."

"Thanks, Blondie."

Then Mason yelped and jerked away, feeling a burning pain on his shoulder.

His duster was on fire.

Blondie's hand glowed—his fingers like orange glow sticks, lit from within.

Both of them looked just as startled as the other as the glow faded.

Mason put out the small spurt of fire on his shoulder. Blondie stared at his hand and started shaking.

"What in the hell did you do?" Mason demanded.

Blondie's mouth fell open. "I-I don't know."

"What are you? How can you do that?"

Blondie ground his teeth in frustration. "I don't know."

"This proves it. You must be from the other side."

"It proves nothing. This from the guy who can shoot magic bolts out of empty pistols? How do we know you aren't from the other side?"

Mason snorted. "I know that much, at least."

"Well, maybe the Merge is affecting me just as it affected you—or perhaps in a different way."

"Can you control it…can you make it happen again?"

Blondie tried to focus. He tried to concentrate.

They both watched his hand.

No change. Nothing.

"I've got an idea," Blondie said. "I had my hand on your shoulder. Maybe whatever it was, was reacting to the power or energy in you."

Mason nodded. "Try it again—just don't make me burst into flame."

"No promises." He rested the same hand on Mason's shoulder.

Nothing happened this time.

Both of them breathed a sigh of relief. Blondie rubbed his fingers before his eyes.

"Did your fingers get burned?" Mason asked.

Blondie shook his head. "Not a bit. No pain, no damage to my skin. But while my hand was glowing, I felt a strange tingling sensation."

"I bet you did. I feel something like that whenever I fire my pistols."

"Hmm…well, it's gone now. Unless it comes back, we won't be able to experiment with it."

"Let me know if it does."

"Don't worry. I think we'll both know." He looked out the window. "The refugees have moved on. I think we can head out now, Mace. There are very few people on the roads."

"We have a much bigger problem."

"Nighttime?" Blondie said.

"You got it. In a matter of hours. We don't know what's out there or what's going to happen. We can keep going while it's light out, but I sure don't want to be traveling at night. Not unless we have to."

"Then let's keep going as long as we can, while we can, Mace. We'll find a safe place to hide out during the night, but we'll have to make sure we keep the horses quiet. Horses can be pretty noisy, and easily give us away at night."

"I know that, Blondie. How do you?"

"I just do, I guess."

"You ride a horse pretty well, too. And you instinctively know how to care for them. I've been watching."

"So what? So do you. And what I don't remember, I've just learned from watching what you do. What, still convinced I'm an alien, huh?"

"Maybe not an alien, but possibly a person from the other side—from the other dimension. Nothing so far has convinced me otherwise."

"And what if I am? So what?"

"I just wonder what those people might be like. Why haven't we met more of them? Why are we coming up against all of these monsters, instead of people like you—like us?"

"Who knows? Perhaps on the other side, this continent is the home of the monsters, and people like us come from somewhere else?"

"Then why were you here posing as one of us?"

Blondie shrugged and smirked with his hands up in the air. "Tell me and we'll both know."

"You don't remember anything, yet?"

"Not really. The last thing I can recall, I just have a feeling that I was running from something. Or maybe I was chasing after someone. Perhaps both."

"Were you running from the monsters?"

"I don't know. But that doesn't explain why I would be dressed in clothing from your people and your world."

"No, it doesn't. Well, time to cover some more ground. Until something changes, we stick to our current plan—if we survive the night. Remember, no one else has made it to Elkhart and back yet."

"Then we'll be the first. We'll just be sneaky about it."

Mason grinned. "Blondie, you don't exactly strike me as an optimist."

"I am when it comes to us staying alive. Right now, I figure the safest place I can be is behind you when you're blazing away with your pistols."

They left the remains of the farmhouse and got back on the road with their horses.

15

David wielded his long fighting dagger in his left hand, his longsword in his right. The strange thing was, once they actually started fighting, he felt surprisingly confident in his own combat abilities.

He had been training for something like this all of his life.

In his brief experience battling these monsters, torgs and even ka-torgs proved vicious, but not especially clever or competent fighters. Their weapons were crude, and they were only capable of fighting as a pack—a horde to overwhelm.

Other than raw ferocity, they possessed little skill or discipline.

David had cut down a dozen more on his way back to the bridge. Then he lost count.

He heard Dirk's powerful voice shouting. "Shield wall! Shield wall! Three lines deep. Put the longest spears and pikes behind them. Make the enemy pay. Stand fast. Don't give an inch!

"More shields line the sides of the bridge and protect our flanks and overhead from enemy arrows. Be ready to cover up! Our archers, fire overhead into the enemy's packed ranks. They're going to do the same to us. Set up the same defenses on the opposite side of the bridge!"

Arrows already fell among the militia on the bridge. Cries of agony marked where some missiles hit. Shields went up pretty quickly after that.

All the spotters had to cry was "Arrows!" or "Incoming!"

Both sides took turns firing volleys back and forth.

Any wounded were pulled back off the bridge to be attended to by medics.

Finally, the militia had halted the enemy advance, but mostly due to the natural barrier of the river. Thank goodness it was there.

"Dirk!" David shouted. "You're packed too tightly on the bridge. Spread them out. Let me and my people pass through!"

"Suck it up and form a path down the middle," Dirk yelled. An escape path opened up. "Let our people through to the other side!"

The monsters chased more militia troops down the steep riverbanks and right into the cold waters of the river itself.

"If they can't get their armor off, they might drown," David shouted.

Dirk was already on it. "Send in the boat details. Rescue as many in the water as you can!"

Rowboats, canoes, and kayaks, armored with sheets of plywood, already sped out along the banks and out from under the cover of the bridge to help the troops struggling in the icy water. Several of the boaters carried lengths of nylon rope with floats that people floundering in the water could grab and then get pulled across to the other side.

Archers and crossbows from some of the boats and along the bridge fired at enemy archers and forces bunching up on the shore.

Once more, it was very clear that the monsters didn't like to swim or didn't know how. The militia continued to exploit that weakness. All the more reason why their foes needed to take that key bridge, in order to attack all of the areas beyond it.

On the bridge itself, David wiped his weapons off with a rag, sheathed them, and went back to using his crossbow. He methodically picked targets along the lost shoreline.

More and more arrows fell among the bridge defenders as enemy archers came on line in greater numbers. Militia troops lifted their shields turtle-style to block some of them, and dropped their guard only long enough for archers to shoot back.

Enemy troops massed in front of the bridge by the hundreds. But beyond what could be seen, it was hard to determine their exact numbers in the dark with nothing but a few torches and lanterns to fight by. The militia archers poured missiles at the massed horde with great effect. The defending shield wall and spears held against the first probing enemy charges.

Then a team of big mor-kahls charged up, flinging glowing things from afar with their great, shaggy arms. The shadow of something even larger, perhaps a gozog, loomed huge in the darkness behind them, booming out commands in a deep, harsh voice.

A barrage of enemy firebombs suddenly blasted the shield wall. They even struck some of the boats in the river. Militia troops screamed.

Some whose legs were on fire jumped over the side into the water.

The front line defenses crumbled in flames and fell back.

The firebombs came as a complete surprise. The enemy had never attacked in this manner before.

But now the flames of the enemy's own devices blocked their way. They had to wait until the flames died down, and that gave Dirk and the militia a chance to regroup.

The enemy charged onto the bridge in force, and crashed among the spears and shields of the second shield wall. Yet the remaining flames continue to work against the monsters. Many of them were taking damage, with all them packed onto the bridge.

But the monsters hurled a few more firebombs.

This time, Dirk was prepared. He had called up fire extinguishers used to help rescue people from burning buildings. Now he use them to put out only the flames that Dirk wanted put out.

He kept a line of fire burning in front of the bridge where some of the bombs had fallen short.

Militia archers fired point blank into enemy faces, especially anything taller than man-size. Monsters up front were speared and pitched over the sides. Dirk helped maintain the center, and the spears held fast. They even advanced to the edge of the fire line, three rows deep once more.

Enemy dead piled up in front of the bridge, held back by the militia and the enemy's own flames.

David braved sporadic enemy arrows. He stood upright on the bridge to survey the forces on the other side. He didn't understand their language, but it was obvious that they called out for something to be brought up to them.

He finally spotted a tall cart wheeling up, just at the far edge of the militia's missile range. Mor-kahls started handing things out of it.

Torches lit more of the enemy firebombs in the darkness.

Scores of the creatures came running at the bridge to hurl them.

A firebomb barrage that massive could incinerate Dirk and all of the spears in one blast.

"Archers up on the bridge with me. Aaughh!" An enemy arrow clipped his left ear. It stung horribly. He ignored it and pointed over at the bomb wagon. "Concentrate your fire over there—at that wagon of firebombs and anything near it!"

Dirk spotted the firebomb wagon as well and saw the danger they were all in. "Use fire arrows if you have them," He commanded. "Shoot anyone carrying one of those bombs. Hit that wagon. Take them out before they burn us all!"

David and the militia archers got off one full volley before enemy arrows cut several of them down. Some grunted, slipped off the bridge, and fell into the dark river.

But the effect was almost immediate. The cloud of militia arrows cut several foes down. Those foes dropped their bombs among the charging enemy horde.

Several flaming arrows arced into the wagon at nearly the same instant.

Then the entire wagon detonated. It cooked off and became an instant, roaring bonfire.

Dirk and David led a cheer from the militia.

That broke the enemy assault. And they remained exposed to concentrated archery volleys that continued to cut many of them down.

Against such losses, and with no hope of taking the bridge, the monster horde quickly retreated back up Portage Road, and then toward the north.

Dirk and David clapped hands and embraced, while all of the militia continued to celebrate their first victory.

But the night wasn't over. More battles were yet to come.

Word reached them by kayak messenger.

They were in danger of being cut off. From the north, another enemy horde had taken the bridges over the river on Darden Road and fought its way down 933 north of Roseland. Now all of the remaining monsters were rushing that way to pour into town from that direction.

"Listen up," Dirk shouted. "Leave five companies to guard this bridge. Hold it the same way we did. The rest of us will fight our way back up to Angela and 933 and help defend Holy Cross and St. Mary's. A lot of innocent people are holed up there. With the river, that's a major safe area. We can't let them down!"

More than a thousand more troops swelled their ranks as they marched, some of them troops that had run away at first. Dirk and David and the other commanders struggled to keep them all in good order.

Their rear guard became a skirmish line that also turned back anyone else who attempted to flee or desert.

They raced up to engage massed foes once more just past Douglas Road, 933, and Saint Mary's—right near Toll road exit 77. Dirk brought up every archer they had for direct fire support. Pikes and spears stuck out over the advancing shield wall.

If they could hold, thousands of more militia were heading that way to support them. Dirk and David guessed that they were outnumbered five to one at the outset.

"Make the enemy pay for every foot!" Dirk shouted. "If we bleed them enough, we'll break them. Watch out for those firebombs. Keep shooters up on buildings and up in high spots and in the trees. Pour arrows at any of these creatures carrying one of those bombs. Watch for them being lit or more of those firebomb wagons."

Over the next two hours, the night battle raged back and forth down 933, the carnage growing.

The enemy slowly pushed and fought the defenders back toward Douglas Road, taking horrible losses. But hundreds of militia forces also fell.

Other bands of retreating defenders joined the militia on either side, swelling their ranks.

One advantage to being bunched up tighter was safety in numbers. The defenders felt stronger and more confident when they weren't spread out so thin.

David fought beside Dirk, taking turns at the forefront. The two of them kept order and rallied more and more troops to them. Reinforcements continued to march up on both sides every moment.

If the enemy seized the schools beyond, where so many noncombatants had gone to for protection, bloodbaths would result.

The fighting grew so intense that they lost track of their militia losses in the chaos. There was nothing to do but keep fighting.

They cycled in fresh units to keep the front line troops from getting exhausted and ripped to pieces. The militia systematically kept slaying enemies wherever they fought. But more always seemed to pour in. Steadfast discipline made a huge difference for the defenders.

"Where are they getting such numbers?" David yelled.

"No telling," Dirk said. "Bring up three new companies left and right. Prevent them from flanking us! Ram steel into those freaks and take them down!"

The rotating companies did their best to drag their wounded back with them out of the meat grinder of the battlefront. Many people weren't used to such stress. Some fell over from heart attacks.

Yet on the whole, the defenders held. They had to.

"We're breaking them." Dirk shouted. "We're finally thinning them out and wearing them down!"

Another great cheer went up and down the militia lines. The roar from almost five thousand defenders was deafening.

"We need to counterattack," David suggested.

Dirk nodded.

"The last of our reserves are already on it. They're racing to flank the enemy in Roseland and smash into them from the east, while our troops push north up 933. I only wish we had enough forces to cut up all the way from Cleveland Road to Darden and encircle them. Then we'd have them completely surrounded."

Messengers came in on bicycle and on foot.

"General Blackwood, the enemy's retreating. We held off another mass attack on the Portage and Angela bridge area."

"Good work. How are they retreating?" Dirk demanded. "Which way are they heading?"

"Sir, Major Hammond reports that a large mass of the creatures are surging south, back through what's left of the downtown. Others are fleeing from Portage to Olive, receding west and southwest toward Lincolnway."

"They initially came from the deep forest where the airport used to be, sir. It looks like they're heading southwest. Dawn is still hours away."

Dirk sighed and removed his helmet, sucking in a few deep breaths and wiping his brow. "My brave friends, I think we've beaten them. At least for the moment."

16

Mason and Blondie took shelter in another old, abandoned, three-story farmhouse with a small, attic cupola off Douglas Road that night. In the middle of nowhere, the old place sat up on a low hill, and provided a good view of the surrounding area and even back toward the parts of Michiana they had just left behind.

First they saw to their horses in a sturdy part of the old barn that did not appear to be ready to collapse, as some sections were. Each evening, they would need to unsaddle their mounts and make sure the horses didn't stay wet.

Next came wisping the quarters, shoulders, and necks of the horses, and then give them a gentle rubdown. That could be relaxing for both the riders and their horses. Mason and Blondie always needed to find the safest, most secure place they could for their horses to bed down at night. They had to guard their mounts jealously.

Oddly enough, Blondie developed a crush on Ginger, their pack horse, and was always kind and extra good to her thereafter. She was a sweetie.

They didn't make any fire or light any lamps, and snacked on cold rations until they were full, drinking water from their canteens. The night was also partly cloudy and cold, and now that there was no longer any moon, the nights were also much darker.

Their plan at night was to take turns keeping watch for three hours at a time, so that the other one could get some solid sleep. Then two hours more for each of them, making it five hours apiece, ten hours total.

Young, strong guys in good health could get by on five hours of sleep each night for a long time. Long enough for this trip.

That way they could make good time during the day.

It was bad enough that when he did sleep, Mason had more nightmares about monsters chasing Tori, or himself being hanged once more.

But Mason quickly found that staying up alone at night was not much better. The human mind worked overtime either way. Watching out for horrid creatures that might want to kill and eat you got one to thinking.

Mason felt overwhelmed and troubled by a great deal. He seemed to go around in circles in his own mind. Nothing he had done or decided to do seemed exactly right.

Was he doing the right thing? Was he just being immature, stupid, and selfish? Were more innocent people like Howard and Tommy going to die in South Bend because the Pistolero wasn't back there, fighting to protect them? Could he only think about himself and Tori...about one girl weighed against the lives of so many others?

Yet he loved Tori with everything he was. He needed to find out what had happened to her. His mind would not rest until he did so.

Then again, playing devil's advocate in another direction, what did he owe Michiana or anyone else? What were they to him? If they did die...so what? Why would that be his fault? Why was he responsible for anyone else? Some of them didn't even try to understand him. Most came to their own conclusions about what he was and what he had become. What did they know? He and his powers were now something to be feared. And fear often led to hate.

Some few people wanted him dead.

He suddenly thought about what Tori would say if they could talk about it all. What were the facts? What was the main issue at hand that no one could avoid or walk away from?

Since the Merge hit, everyone in Michiana was facing a terrible threat from these monsters who wanted to kill and eat anything and anyone that was meat. That threat was bigger than any one person—even the Pistolero and his missing girlfriend.

Even with his new powers, he couldn't fight all of those monsters on his own. No way.

110

In that moment, Mason realized, that if anyone including himself or Tori, was going to survive, the remnants of what people were now calling Urth—and its humanity in that area—had to band together to save each other, or at least as much as they could save.

The threat was simply too great. None of them was going to make it on their own.

Mason still resigned himself to trying to find Tori. He and Blondie were almost halfway there.

But at some point, he would need to go back and rejoin the main fight.

And he and everyone else would be forced to become a lot less selfish and egocentric. If Urth humans were going to survive, they would need to stand and fight together. He was just as bad as anyone else.

Truth be told, he just wasn't that great of a human being.

Throughout the night there were flames in the distance that lit the sky in small patches back toward Mishawaka and especially South Bend. They didn't look widespread, but to Mason's eyes, it appeared as if the enemy was back, at least to some degree. They were most likely probing for weak spots to exploit. That seemed to be their nature.

But they weren't flooding in to be wiped out in great swaths of packed numbers by the Pistolero any longer. At least not yet.

Perhaps they finally reached a limit to the size of their forces, and needed to start being more cautious. Even the monsters apparently learned from their mistakes, and strove not to repeat them.

Mason swallowed hard while watching those flames in the distance.

He thought of the Reinerts once more and people just like them back in South Bend. Had he made the right decision to go to Elkhart, risking the lives of so many for the life of one girl?

Tori. His Tori. Not just any girl.

What would the enemy do when they figured out that the Pistolero and his blazing guns weren't in South Bend anymore? How long would it take? Could he get back there in time to help if he tried?

Even worse, what if Tori wasn't there in Elkhart? What if she was on the other side, with David and the Blackwoods? What if she was already—

No. Mason couldn't go there. That was exactly why he needed to find out for himself—one way or the other. He had to know or it would drive him insane.

"Doesn't look so bad," Blondie said, getting up for his shift and looking out at the same patches of fire. At least Blondie seemed to have a pretty good internal clock. Mason checked his wind-up, travel pocket clock and saw that almost exactly three hours had passed.

Mason was ready for his next rest, and a break from his worries and racing thoughts.

"Any traffic?" Blondie asked.

Mason shrugged. "A few runners and refugees on the road, on foot or bike. Just stragglers, too scared to stay put or too dumb to avoid traveling at night. No monsters yet." He handed Blondie their binoculars.

"Let's keep it that way," Blondie said.

Mason already snuggled down on the old musty bed mattress and yawned. He pulled the sleeping bag over himself and dozed off, while his friend kept watch in the night from the farmhouse cupola windows that looked out in all four directions.

17

Another messenger arrived and exclaimed, "General Blackwood, commanders along Edison report the enemy massing again down Eddy Street in large numbers. Many smaller groups of monsters have filtered back in quietly without attacking, moving fast in the darkness, bunching together in the center."

Even in the dark, David saw Dirk's eyes widen.

"The clever bastards," Dirk yelled. "We've beaten them back in two key places. But they're forming a horde in our center while the other hordes keep us busy on the outskirts."

"Sir, heavy enemy attacks are already pushing down Jefferson Avenue from downtown," the messenger added.

Dirk rubbed his face and thought for a moment. He snapped his head up and looked at his runners. "That's just what I'd do if I was them. Send two messengers, call back our people from Roseland, and break off the pursuit. Get them back here!" He turned to David and the others.

"The enemy isn't retreating at all. They've finally found a weak point, and they're going to keep us all spread out while they exploit it. They'll concentrate their remaining forces to push through that weak point into our center and break us all up. They will spend the rest of the night doing as much damage as they can to whatever we're trying to defend. My guess is the key to their attack plans is Jefferson Avenue."

"Makes sense," David said. "From there they can get at us down Ironwood, Edison, Twyckenham–any direction they want. Lots of civilians in those areas to feed off of, too. But this begs another question, Dirk. Who's really leading these creatures? None of them seem to have the brains to orchestrate a tactical plan this complex."

Another messenger ran in. "General Blackwood. The bulk of the enemy forces are funneling toward Jefferson Avenue. They're deliberately bypassing many of our other defenses and flooding across Main and Michigan streets where they've broken through. They're trying to penetrate as far east as they can go. They're not even stopping to attack civilians or set fires yet."

"Just like I thought," Dirk said. "They're trying to crush us at our core. It's a race, people. Get as many of us on bikes and ride like hell up Ironwood, Edison, Greenlawn, and Twyckenham."

The militia double-timed it back to Angela to where the bikes were amassed on both sides off the sidewalks. More commanders rushed up, bunching around Dirk and David.

Dirk issued orders all along the way. "We cut them off, flank them, and break them up on both sides in force along Jefferson Avenue. Take your orders and go. Get to your new positions. Send word to the other commanders. Keep enough troops at the key points to protect them, and companies staggered along the way to fend off enemy skirmishers from the roads. We need to move, and move fast!"

Dirk pulled David aside for a moment. "If we get there fast enough, we can still cut them to pieces. But I want you to reach the area around the Haywards' house. Take as many stout fighters as you can find and secure that entire area. Hold it for all you're worth, Dave. Belle and the ladies and a lot of other people we know and care about are holed up there with their kids. They're depending on us to keep them safe. Jerriel should be there with them!"

Dirk sent sixty troops with him, on top of the forty that still followed him from his original 2nd company. David picked up another spear on the way.

As soon as they could, troops grabbed bikes from nearby and rode as fast as they could pedal. Dave took a bike and joined the front of the second wave with his forces, spear at the ready.

He tried not to think about it, but the enemy push drove right toward the Haywards' house in that exact area. That was going to be ground zero.

If Jerriel wasn't at HQ, Dirk was most likely right. She must be there with Belle and Rosalyn Hayward, and many other friends' wives and kids.

David ignored his fatigue, all of his cuts and bruises. His company joined the squads going up Ironwood. They rode for all they were worth. It only took minutes, but the time dilated into what felt like an eternity.

People cried out from time to time or crashed and flipped over. Enemy skirmishers tried to slow them down and delay them with arrows, rocks, even a few fire bombs. David and the militia went around the fallen and kept riding. Troops guarding the roads chased down any skirmishers they could find, but reacted only after an ambush revealed itself.

There was too much open territory and too much chaos. The roads couldn't be kept completely safe against clever and determined foes.

Then, at Ironwood and Jefferson, David spotted a large group of enemies already holding that key intersection. Dead defenders littered the street, and a huge gozog in armor, ten feet tall, commanded the center with a guard of several huge mor-kahls, dozens of ka-torgs, and about a hundred torgs, half of them archers.

"Take that intersection!" David shouted. "Archers, pour it at them! Let up when we charge in. Spears and lances to the front. Rip through them! Swords and hand weapons follow on and cut them down. Everyone focus on those big bastards. Fill their guts full of steel!"

The militia shouted.

David helped lead the first massed bicycle attack in human history. They used the speed of the bikes to add to the ferocity of their attack. David and the spears went in first, even while the other archers peppered the intersection with one last volley of missile fire.

But the enemy lifted their shields and held tough, even though some of them went down.

They all knew how important that intersection was. The monster sortie made a determined stand there.

The spears broke through the front line and blasted through the torgs and ka-torgs in their way. They rammed into the mor-kahls like hitting a brick wall. Fierce hand-to-hand fighting with the big armored monsters erupted.

Three of the huge creatures went down, but the others struck havoc among the militia, snapping off spears, flinging bikes and riders forty feet away to either side.

The intersection choked with mangled dead and wounded.

"Fling your bikes to either side and charge in!" David said. That's what he did, his spear already lost in a mor-kahl chest. He rushed in from the left, switching his longsword into his left hand and drawing a tomahawk from his belt.

It whizzed through the air from his hand and smacked another one of the seven-foot-plus mor-kahls square in the face. The thing roared in agony and fell back, its broad face split open.

He switched his sword back, drew his second tomahawk in his left hand, and charged with the other heavily armored militia fighters who rushed in on either side of him.

They fought together in a chaotic mass of shifting friends and foes.

David cut down three torgs, and bashed a charging ka-torg in the face with his tomahawk.

David swung his sword in fierce, whirling arcs, chopping and bashing with his 'hawk. He and the other fighters buzzed through the horde of lesser monsters hurled against them.

Black blood exploded and gushed in torrents. Severed parts of monsters flew in several directions. David used every ounce of skill he possessed, and slew the foe by instinct, cutting through them two and three at a time with each stroke. He killed in his very own Zen-like flow of battle without thought—without hesitation or mercy.

A sharp pain suddenly stabbed him in the back of his right leg. He whirled, and saw no foes. But he reached back and yanked out a human target arrow from the outer flesh of his calf.

"Sorry, man!" an embarrassed militia archer shouted.

Great. Some unstoppable hero he was—shot by his own people from behind. The wound was annoying, but not serious.

The big armored gozog up ahead wielded a massive tree club and a big sledgehammer. Nobody could get near him. The enemy rallied around him and surged forward. He smashed humans to mush left and right and flung their mashed bodies aside.

"Take them down!" David yelled. The militia around him roared into battle. Fresh troops charged up from behind.

By then archers pincushioned the gozog with arrows and crossbow bolts. But the creature was so big and well armored that none of the missiles struck a vital spot.

The missiles only served to piss him off.

Once more, the fat, giant pincushion swatted militia troops every which way, roaring and screaming.

A half-dozen troops, men and women with swords and axes, dragged down one of the mor-kahls and cut it to pieces, even while it raged and struck at them. David saw his opening and leaped forward. He sprang on top of another mor-kahl's broad, thorny back as it reared up. Many weapons pierced the creature, finally killing it.

David used the force of the thrashing monster's fall to propel himself forward. It fell back and flung him through the air right at the gozog. He rammed his longsword up to the hilt under the stinking thing's boiled leather armor and full into its chest.

Boy, did that thing smell.

The gozog ducked and tried to brush him off with its massive club, even as it dropped back. David twisted his blade in the monster's chest and rode the huge creature down. It smashed into the ground and dropped its hammer. With his tomahawk and his long fighting dagger David chopped and stabbed repeatedly at the monster's face, neck, and throat.

That big bastard was going down, no matter what.

A spurt of black blood gushed from the gozog's throat like a geyser, coating David. The creature roared and shuddered. Humans boiled over it, stabbing and cutting it with their weapons.

With a final heave, it rolled to one side and swatted David into the darkness with a massive hand. A blow like a brick wall slammed into him. He soared through the darkness and crashed into the branches of a tree.

He toppled to the ground with a cold splash, momentarily stunned and winded. He rolled onto his back and lay gasping and alone in a small, frigid pool of glowing water in the tall grass.

Then the water flashed blue-violet, glowing even more intensely all around him.

Oh crap. Not one of those damn pools.

David felt his spirit wrenched free from his body. He tried to gasp, but he couldn't breathe. Completely weightless, he floated above his stricken body, still lying in the pool below.

What the hell happened? Was he dead?

18

Mason and Blondie ate a quick, cold breakfast and made ready to travel within the second hour after dawn. They intentionally brought a lot of rations with them so that they would not need to bother cooking.

Once or twice each day, they would also canter their horses in the fields on good terrain and even make them run for a spell. They didn't just walk and mosey down the trail. Good horses such as theirs needed exercise, and were glad to get it.

If they got into trouble, which Mason guessed was only a matter of time, having their mounts in good shape might mean the difference between life and death for them all.

But there always seemed to be more refugees on the road. They came in waves of human misery, drifting in one direction or another. There was no avoiding them.

At least, in a grim way, it was better to see living refugees rather than dead bodies all over the place.

Mason put on a baseball cap instead of his outlaw hat. "If I don't wear the Pistolero hat and keep my guns out of sight, maybe we won't get hassled so much."

Blondie grinned, putting aside his cavalry hat and tucking his long hair under a red bandana. "I don't know, Mace. Our outlaw look also keeps people from messing with us. Our horses and saddles are suddenly going to be worth a lot these days. Some folks might just decide to try to take them from us, if they think we're just a couple of regular guys."

Mason grinned. "Then they will quickly learn the error of their ways. We still have your saber at your side and your crossbow on your back to discourage petty thugs and horse thieves. I have a short sword...somewhere that I can sling on my saddle. That's enough of a display. I just don't want to get stoned again or have people throwing garbage at us."

"It's up to you, Mace. I'll follow your lead."

"Let's try this for now." He concealed his Pistolero hat away with his gear on the pack horse. "This way, we can travel incognito and gather some news from the refugees."

Another good thing that made horses better than bikes was that they could go cross country a lot easier at any time, when the roads were cut off by the weird new patches of forest.

They learned right away that rumors quickly multiplied and exploded on the open road. They heard everything possible, from South Bend wasn't attacked at all to the city was completely destroyed, all of the survivors were fleeing, and the monsters had taken control of everything.

Mason and Blondie guessed that the actual truth was probably somewhere in between those two extremes. And as they got more than a day or two away, who knew what else they would hear?

But it did appear that the refugees continued to steadily move away from South Bend, and into Mishawaka, Osceola, and toward Elkhart. They had yet to meet any refugees coming from Elkhart, but they didn't know yet if that was a good or a bad sign. Yet it was strange.

At least wearing the baseball hat worked, more or less. No one called them out. Although some people still gave them dirty looks. Blondie kept wearing his bandana, and then a straw hat he traded for, to avoid sunburn. Mason introduced him to sunblock.

Blondie was right about one thing. Their horses did attract a lot of attention. They had numerous offers to buy them—even with gold coins—but they wisely refused. Whenever anyone dangerous started to follow them, that was when they decided to exercise their horses and go off on their own for a while.

Most people were too scared to leave the relative safety of the roads and the crowds.

It was just after they had ridden off into the woods that the refugees behind them were waylaid by a large team of bandits who swooped in.

The banditos were about fifty or sixty in number from what could be seen through binoculars. They rode horses and bicycles, and had even acquired what looked to be a couple of Amish-style buggies and wagons, some with obvious bloodstains still smeared on them. Many of the horses looked badly cared for, even from a distance.

The bandits stolen them, but weren't used to caring for horses. Not everyone was.

Suddenly Mason felt guilty for being more angry about the way these goons treated their horses than what they were about to do to the refugees.

Mason spotted lots of bows and crossbows, swords, spears, axes, and knives. These bandits were well-armed and making a definite show of force to intimidate the refugees. The leaders even seemed to have crossbow pistols. They encircled the batch of refugees from all directions and hemmed them in. A couple of hundred refugees in all.

The bandit leaders shouted over megaphones they must have made out of what looked like bright orange traffic cones with the bases sliced off.

"Don't resist or we'll kill you," one of the leaders warned the civilians. "Now, listen up and listen good. We are going to take whatever the hell we want. Anyone who protests is going to take a beating. Anyone who hurts one of us is going to die. Don't provoke us, and we'll be on our way soon enough."

The bandit archers and crossbowmen formed a gauntlet for the people to pass through, keeping their weapons trained on everyone.

Other bandits lined the gauntlet with sacks and plastic tubs. They quickly searched and stripped the refugees of any weapons or food or drink that they had on them—anything the bandits wanted to take.

Not only that—they separated three teen-to college age-girls—all of them very attractive. They tied their hands, and blindfolded, and gagged them, despite the women crying and screaming. There were a few females among the bandits, but most of them looked to be male, and eyed the three women with obvious bad intent.

The few people who tried to protest the women being taken were quickly beaten down, kicked, and clubbed into submission, as promised. The bandits left them bleeding in the road.

A few people tried to break loose and flee during the commotion, but archers cut most of them down and left them dead or screaming. Only one person, a young terrified girl, managed to get away out of range, fleeing into the trees. Some of the bandits retrieved their arrows, even from those hit by them. And they weren't gentle about doing so.

Mason retrieved his Pistolero hat, but kept it hidden for the moment. "We gotta put a stop to this," he said.

"Think about this," Blondie told him. "There's nearly threescore of them and they're too spread out. That's too many, even for you. A couple of lucky arrows hits on their part and we're both dead."

"Both of us know what they're going to do to those three young women. That's enough reason by itself."

"Is it worth dying for, Mace? Are you prepared to kill every one of them?"

A thought occurred to him. Any one of those girls could have been Tori.

Mason nodded. "If need be. I'm making this my fight. Trust me. They're a bunch of newly minted thugs, robbers, and killers, preying on the weak and the helpless. Only a few of them have any guts. The rest are followers and gutless cowards."

"You're hoping that's the case. They could be hardened criminals already, for all we know. None of this makes them cowards or weaklings, and there are still nearly sixty of them."

"Either way, let's see if we can throw a scare into them. If we do this right, we can run them off. We might not need to fight them at all."

"Yes, I'm sure all will be well, despite the fact that we could slip away right now or just wait for them to finish up their business and leave. What are any of these people to us? I thought you wanted to get to Elkhart so badly and find Tori?"

"I do, but if I can put a stop to this, I feel obligated to try. That's who I am now, my friend. Mount up if you're with me, or stay behind and watch."

Blondie scowled, climbing up on Patton and readying his weapons. "All right, Mace. I'm with you, damn it."

"Good. Thanks. Follow my lead. We'll try to fool them first with an offer to trade—just to get in close."

Mason was getting much better at managing his fear. Being angry helped a lot. Pissed off was even better. The trick seemed to be to make the energy of your emotions work for you, not against you.

Together, the two of them got back on the road and started cantering straight toward the bandit leaders at the head of the line.

Mason called out boldly. "Who's your leader? Get him up here. Wahoo! Boy, have we got some deals for you!"

A pocket of goons pulled closer and shuffled nervously toward the incoming riders. But from what the bandits could see, it was only two riders. One had baseball cap on, and the other a straw hat. The bandits appeared a bit startled at first, but none too worried, overall.

Two of the thugs stepped out a bit further in front of the lead wagons. They appeared to be the biggest and the baddest thugs of the bunch.

Mason guessed, from the looks on their faces, that their curiosity had gotten the better of them.

Several bandit archers still turned and waited with arrows on the string, while their friends behind them kept processing the refugees without stopping.

Mason and Blondie both smiled, grinning and waving. "We've come to trade. We've got treasures to barter with. Something you folks can't live without these days."

The tallest of the two was in his late thirties, with black whiskers and eyes, and a broken nose. He smelled like booze, even in the morning. "And what would that be?" he snarled. "This better not be a trick, you punks. What could you possibly have that we couldn't live without?"

The second man was shorter, but broader, almost forty, with slightly graying hair. He finally spoke up. Neither of them smiled. "I see three more horses and gear we could sure use."

Mason kept grinning and nodding as he dismounted and waved them both back toward the pack horse, continuing to distract them. "Just wait until we show you what we've got."

He could tell by their faces that they had taken the bait, and focused eagerly on the gear on the pack horse.

"Excuse me while I put my trading hat on," Mason said. He hung his ball cap on one of the pack carriers, and then pulled his Pistolero hat out and popped it on.

"What is this?" Tallboy said.

"What are you selling?" Stocky added.

Quick as vipers, Mason's hands flashed full of steel.

He jammed his pistols right into their faces before they could catch their breath and held the bandit leaders off.

His hammers were cocked.

"Life insurance," Mason said. "I'm selling life insurance—against death. Order your goons off, clear out right now, and no one has to die—especially you two right off."

Both men swallowed hard.

"Both of you are dead," Tallboy muttered. He had a wild look in his eyes.

Stocky looked cold. "You're bluffing. Everyone knows guns don't work."

Mason smiled and shoved the barrels in their faces. "Is that a fact? Well, mine still do. In fact, they work better than ever. Perhaps you've heard tell of me? Maybe you recognize my faithful compadre, Blondie. Wave to the not-nice men, Blondie."

They glanced over with their eyes.

Blondie had his straw hat on his back. He took his bandanna off and shook his long blond hair loose like a shampoo model. "Hey."

Tallboy still didn't believe. "You're full of–"

Mason looked him in the eyes and snapped off a quick shot, mowing down a swath of the dark trees in a wide blast of exploding flames without even looking.

That got everyone's instant attention. Everybody flinched.

Quick as winking, Mason recocked and brought his hot, smoking pistol barrel back in front of Tallboy's face.

Both bandits turned even paler and their eyes got very wide. They continued to swallow hard as if their throats were dry.

"Just think of what they'll do to your heads if my trigger fingers slip–everything from your chest up will just vanish in a flash. Gone. Just like that. What's left of you will flop and twitch in the mud like a bloody fish."

"It's the Pistolero!" Stocky shouted for all to hear, including the other bandits. "Nobody try anything!"

Blondie sat on his horse and yawned. No one else dared to move.

"That's right. I'm the Pistolero," Mason yelled. "Nobody get crazy, or you can all start dying, real fast. I'll cut you all down–I don't give a damn. You've heard and seen what my guns can do. You don't want to experience them firsthand."

Tallboy was sweating bullets by then, but he still looked a bit crazy, and he had a mouth on him, too, as it turned out. "What? You really think you can take us all down?"

"Shut up, Chuck," Stocky tried to warn him. "We've heard about this guy. He looks young, but he's stone-cold killer. He kills everyone, and doesn't give a shit about it, either."

"That's right, Chuck," Mason said. "You'd better listen to your friend. I've faced down worse odds than this, and won. But I'm feeling sweet today. I don't have to kill you; all of you don't have be dead. And keep in mind, if anything does start up, you two are the very first ones to go–whatever happens. Now, do we do this my way, or the easy way–that doesn't involve me blasting you two nimrods straight to the fires of perdition."

"W-we can go easy," Stocky told him.

123

Mason kept talking loud enough for everyone to hear. "Good. Now, give the orders. You goons kindly stop robbing these poor folks. They have it bad enough. Give back whatever you took from them. Let those pretty young ladies go, too. I see 'em over there. Then all of you clear out. It's that simple. Everyone stays alive."

"Do as he says!" Chuck stammered.

"Do it now!" Stocky added.

The bandits threw down what they had taken in frustrated disgust and pulled away, as quickly as they had swooped in to attack.

Chuck and Stocky looked around. Some of the refugees scattered for safety. Others held back to regain their lost goods, or the three young women—actually, it was four women by that time. The bandits were apparently a very lonely and greedy bunch.

"All right, we did as you said," Chuck noted.

"Now let us go," Stocky said, as if he were going to die, anyway.

Mason grinned. "Never let it be said that I don't keep my word."

He uncocked, twirled, and holstered both rigs, blindingly fast. Being a good showman was all part of building the mystique.

Chuck and Stocky relaxed a bit and started to breathe easier, but Mason stepped up to both of the men, really close, and gave them the eye. His voice went very soft and low.

"But know this. If I come across you robbers again, I'm just going to start shooting. No parlay, no questions asked. And if I ever hear tell of you or your kind terrorizing refugees or survivors like this, I will come after you and I will find you. I will make it my sole purpose in life to hunt you down and kill your rat-bastard asses. And I will not stop until I kill each and every one of you. I will kill you while you sleep, while you eat, while you take a leak or a dump. You have my word on that, as well. Comprende?"

Both thugs nodded. Then they turned and ran toward their gang.

Mason shouted after them. "And find someone to teach you morons how to take care of your goddam, sorry-ass-looking horses, before you fools kill them all!"

The gang cleared out fast, without looking back.

With the bandits gone, more of the refugees came forward to reclaim their stuff.

Several families and individuals walked up, and although they kept their distance, they all quietly thanked Mason and Blondie.

"Thank you, sir."

"Thanks for saving us from those cutthroats, Mr. Pistolero."

"Why, he's just a young boy," a woman said. "My son in the militia isn't any older."

"Thanks, guys. God bless you!"

A mother with her younger kids came to them with one of the pretty girls who had been taken, all of them crying, but now looking much relieved. The girl was about seventeen and couldn't speak, and still looked a bit afraid of him and Blondie. But the mother came forward, and before Mason could stop her, she kissed his left hand and wept on it.

Mason pulled back, embarrassed and not a little ashamed.

Then she looked up at him. Mason had never seen anyone look so grateful. "Some say you're a killer. But I don't think that's right. You don't even know us. You could have just ridden away, but you and your friend risked your lives against those criminals. You saved my oldest girl, Shawna. Those bastards were going to rape and kill her and dump her in a ditch somewhere–I just know it. But you saved her from all that. Thank you. We can never thank you enough."

Mason choked up and nodded. He thought of his own family in Cleveland. Were they still alive? Did they have anyone there to protect them?

He tipped his hat to the woman and the people watching. "I was happy to oblige, folks. Try to be more careful. Defend yourselves better, if you can. I can't say there won't be more bandits like them out there."

The crowd continued to disperse and move on in several directions.

One of the released girls still wept on the far side, kneeling over the body of an old man who looked as if he had been beaten and stomped to death by the bandits. The girl was about Tori's age, and had shoulder-length dark hair, almost black. She looked up at Mason and Blondie on their horses with pleading brown eyes that were still suffused with grief and shock. She rubbed her red face. "He was my grandpa. He tried to stop them when they grabbed me. They beat him so bad. They murdered him."

Mason bowed his head. If this was Tori, what would he have done? Then he got angry and looked at the receding bandits. Maybe he should still go after them. "I'm sorry, miss. Sorry I couldn't have run them off sooner than I did. I'm sorry for you and your grandpa."

Mason looked around and called out. "How many are dead? How many people did the bandits kill?"

Blondie rose up in his stirrups and glanced around. "Looks like five that aren't moving. Several more that are wounded."

Mason clenched his fists. "I should have taken all of those bastards out."

Blondie looked around.

"No, son, you did the right thing," an older man in his fifties said, coming forward. "If you had started shooting, a lot more of us would have died in the crossfire. Thank you for not using violence as the first resort. You handled the situation as best as you could."

The dark-haired girl panicked suddenly and began shuddering and freaking out. "With grandpa gone, I'm all alone now. What's going to happen to me? What am I going to do? I don't have anyone else. Where will I go?"

Mason paled.

What if this helpless young girl was his sister? His mother? His grandmother? Tori?

But he couldn't help and save everyone. There was too much tragedy and misery out there as it was. He and Blondie still had to reach Elkhart and find Tori. They couldn't get saddled by a string of orphans and strays all along the way. They'd never get anywhere.

And, just maybe, Tori was also lost and alone just like this girl, without anyone to help her. Maybe she was hurt somewhere, with no one to care for her. The worst possibilities always came to his troubled mind.

The third girl who had been set free came forward and rested a hand on the dark-haired girl's shoulder. They were about the same age. "Get your stuff. You can come to Elkhart with me and my family; we have relatives there. My mom says it's okay."

"Thank you, but I can't. I can't leave grandpa like this. What do I do?"

Mason shouted out to the crowd again. "Can anyone stick around and help bury the dead and see to the wounded? Blondie and I will stay here to protect you, if you do."

Thirty-nine people stayed back, including the family and friends of the dead, and the family who said they'd take in the one orphan girl. Three people had shovels. Another one of the older men stepped forward to Mason. "Son, I'm a retired church deacon. If no one has any objections, I can say some words over the dead."

Mason nodded. "Thank you, sir—but you don't have to bother asking me for any permission. Does that sound all right with everyone?" No one objected.

The five victims total were three men and two women of various ages, either beaten or shot down by arrows. It was a great deal of work digging five graves off the road where it wasn't too muddy. They only made each grave about four feet deep, but all of the adults—including Mason—took turns digging and were exhausted by the effort. Blondie snorted and said he didn't dig.

They covered the bodies up in sheets or blankets, and lowered them down with ropes. Once the ropes were pulled up, the retired deacon spoke his peace for the departed.

Then the graves were filled in. People put rocks on them and made crosses out of sticks tied together. That was about all that could be done. The day grew longer, and a new pod of refugees came down the road. The thirty-nine people left the dead behind and passed on with the living.

Just five more deaths during a war where thousands had already perished. Who knew what had happened nationwide, or even across the world, after the cataclysm of the Merge?

Some of the people came to Mason and asked him questions, as if he knew something. "Why is all of this happening? Where did the moon go? Why are all of these horrible creatures attacking us? What do they want? What does it all mean? Are we being punished?"

Mason frowned and shook his head. "I don't know anything more than anyone else. I wish to hell I did. It appears that we've all been dealt a mighty rugged hand, folks. I guess we just have to play it out as best we can."

One of the other cute gals finally got brave enough to give Blondie a quick look and smiled at him. He winked back and tipped his hat. He did have a way of making gals look. Who knows, maybe it cheered her up.

Their world needed some cheering up.

In a reality gone mad and turned upside down, there wasn't yet time to comprehend and deal with everything that was going on in the wake of the chaos.

All Mason wanted was to find the woman he loved and make sure that she was safe. After that he'd be able to think straight. Then he could decide what was the right thing for him to do next.

19

David stared down at his body while the fighting raged nearby. The light of the glowing pool slowly faded.

He drifted down closer. If he was dead, why was his body still breathing there on the ground? What was going on?

He looked out into the darkness in confusion, struggling to see into it. His spirit swept forward suddenly, insubstantial. He passed swiftly through buildings and trees and then over them up into the lower part of the sky.

It was both exhilarating and terrifying.

On a high, southwestern hill with a vantage point overlooking much of South Bend, deep in the wild new forest nearby, David noted more glowing pools of light of various colors and hues dotting the land.

He swept toward the area with barely a thought. His force of will seemed to propel him wherever he wished to go.

He noticed something else as he closed in. Bonfires, torches, and lanterns—a large camp. People moved around tables in dark robes and masks. Monsters were there too. High ranking gozogs and mor-kahls, and other weird creatures he hadn't even seen before stood at hand.

The strange, robed figures pointed at maps, directing troop movements.

Mirrors sat up behind them. Images of people and more odd creatures flashed in and out, passing information back and forth to the dark-robed people.

David recognized the area on those maps as he circled in closer from above. The enemy concentrated all of their remaining forces on the same key points that Dirk and the militia tried to defend.

He who appeared to be the leader stood tall—well over six feet—but human, at least from what David could see. He wore an expensive-looking cloak that seemed to be made of darkness itself, adorned with a mantle of black gems. So black were those jewels, of some kind of weird stone, that each glowed like a dark hole in reality itself.

A long, deadly looking black saber hung at the leader's side. His cloak was pulled back over one shoulder. David spotted the sword and other weapons and pouches on the leader's ornate leather belt and baldric.

This was someone important. All eyes and ears fixed on him.

And even more bizarre: in his spirit-form, David clearly understood everything these people said, somehow.

"You fools should have crushed these pitiful weaklings by now!" the leader told. "They are soft, weak, and confused. Divided. Leaderless. We've taken their magic from them. How is it that we cannot destroy them?"

"We will," the gozog leader insisted. "But Master, there are many more of them than we thought. Even so, it's only a matter of time."

"They are not leaderless," a hissing, evil voice from one of the mirrors said. That inhuman voice made David's skin crawl—even though he could not feel or sense anything physical. He couldn't even feel the wind.

"My lord, these Urthers have proven much more troublesome than we originally expected," another of the robed men admitted.

The master flipped the heavy map table over with a wave of one gloved hand. "Idiots. Incompetents! We have wasted enough precious time here. Raze this insignificant hamlet. My masters and I sent you more than enough forces to do so. You will be punished severely if you fail. More importantly, I shall be punished severely! Urgent matters on other more important fronts call myself and the mages away. We must depart now, with all speed."

He shook the same fist at them. They backed away as that fist glowed with dark power. "Throw everything you have at these insects. Destroy them! Search the dead and the captives for the missing traitor and any other Tharanorians helping them. They should still be powerless."

One of the robed men suddenly started, and pointed up into the darkness near David.

"Ware. Ware! I sense an astral form nearby, my lord!"

"A spy?" someone exclaimed, in disbelief.

"Impossible!" the leader said, whirling about. "The Urthers have no such abilities. Nevertheless, I will negate this entire area!"

He motioned with his hands. Weird, glowing symbols expanded into waves of shadow that lashed and rippled out from him.

When those waves of darkness struck David's spirit, they flung him back in pain. He shot back through the air in agony, speeding through the night.

Light. He saw light and halted abruptly.

Little flowers like violets, but glowing white, came in and out of focus. His blurred vision tried to fix on them. David heard harsh voices, sounds of battle once more. He looked up from the long grass beneath the trees, aching in several places.

Cold and soaking wet.

He could feel again.

He actually felt the grass around him. His spirit had made it back into his body somehow. Now, back to the battle.

More foes. Dozens of them wheeled and scattered through the nearby yards. Some of the monsters headed his way.

David couldn't get up. He tried shouting a warning. He was still too weak and gasping. His longsword was still far away, stuck in the dead gozog leader. His tomahawks were both gone.

A few arrows zipped into the advancing foes. At least someone on the militia side had spotted them.

David drew his katana and wakizashi to make his stand. He finally managed to get to his feet and put his back against a nearby red maple.

Alone, he had no chance. If he could run, he might make it back toward the intersection. But he could barely stand.

He caught his breath before the foremost foes tore into him, and struggled to lift his weapons and set his stance.

The first three torgs and two ka-torgs clearly spotted him in the shadows and rushed in for the kill.

No, he wasn't going to go down that easy.

He took one torg out with a short sword thrust to the belly, another with a side cut of his katana.

David staggered around the bole of the tree. He spin-blocked and cut the torg coming around from the left in the throat. The ka-torg raced around the right and sprang at his right arm to wrestle the katana from him.

David staggered and fell back, allowing the ka-torg to impale himself on the sword. It thrashed and convulsed and bit at him.

David rolled to his hands and knees and lifted both blades, fully expecting more foes to overrun him.

20

Both Mason and Blondie thought it very odd that they had not heard of or seen any sign of the monsters in their area for more than two days. And by all reports, even the monster raids and probes on South Bend remained scattered and lackluster. They were barely a threat now.

What had happened to all of those thousands of monsters? Where had they gone in such numbers? Did they simply hide out in a certain place, or did they actually leave, and go somewhere else? Where did that many of them conceal themselves during the day?

It was perhaps impossible to understand the motivations or behaviors of such brutes.

Heavy thunderstorms rolled in after dark. That night, Mason and Blondie slept in a trailer park in Osceola, with their horses locked up in an old garage next door to them.

They briefly used candlelight and lamplight. They took turns sleeping again just as they had before.

Mason risked a little more light under the cover of the storm and the drenching spring rains. He used a good part of his time awake to go over his shooting gear. He cleaned and reloaded as needed, all except for the two pistols he kept empty for general shooting. His Spillers were pistols that routinely fired accurate blasts of the strange energy at will, even though he almost never loaded them—outside of war.

As long as they continued to function that way, he wasn't going to risk doing anything that might make them stop. When the magic worked, it was wise not to tamper with it.

Yet Mason also continued to experiment with reforming and melting both round balls and bullets with his lead dipper and various bullet molds over candles. He laced each round with additional components or reagents that seemed to react with the magical energies at work. Then, each following day when possible, he would check how the test rounds performed, and kept careful track of what the differences were. He maintained very careful notes in his logbooks.

He could make six to a dozen new rounds each night, depending on how much sleep he wanted to lose.

Another factor was continuing experiments with adding new components into the black powder of the loads themselves.

Both practices seemed to produce wildly different results to different degrees, depending on what components, amounts, and combinations were used.

Since some kind of strange magic was in fact at work, this resulted in a new kind of alchemy, specific to him and his firearms.

If he didn't figure out the secrets to it all, eventually he would run out of both powder and shot, and then be reduced to firing weapons that only worked on the lesser level—when he fired them dry.

If he could only figure out the phenomena, he might be able to prolong and replicate it its effects, and perhaps even make it work for someone besides himself.

Where did the energy come from? How did the magic in that glowing lake infuse itself into him, and his weapons and components? It appeared that they all needed to be saturated with it at the same time.

Mason shook his head and yawned. He never imagined that he would be experimenting with magic. He was a mage—a pistol mage. Thus far, he could shoot small accurate blasts of energy from his dry weapons, and sweeping, destructive waves of devastating fire from his various loads and ammunition types, somewhere within the range of either fire or explosion.

Was it possible to produce effects that were somewhere in between, or entirely different? He even began to experiment with small quantities of stone, wood, crystal, and even gemstones that the militia had obtained for him.

The rain let up by the next day. Having the last watch, Mason let his friend sleep in, ate quickly, and saw to the horses first thing.

After that, he and Ginger took his guns out early to a remote location in a valley to have a bit of target practice and record the results of his reloading experiments.

Mason patted Ginger and realized that none of their horses were gun shy, which was also a very good thing. They had most likely grown up around hunters, or shooters at the very least. Firearms didn't spook them, not even the Pistolero's.

Thing's might not work out so well if their horses spooked every time he needed to shoot.

Mason set up his targets and got out his notes and notebooks to record the results of his experiments.

Small, precisely measured quantities of rose quartz, and especially diamond helped produce incredibly devastating explosions, which nearly engulfed him in the blast radius itself. The trade off was that the range of the shots was greatly and dangerously reduced. He could use those on enemies who managed to get right on top of him.

Very intriguing.

But his range of effects remained more or least constant—flame, explosion, or a combination of both. Not that he was complaining.

As he expected, various types of woods and metals, especially iron oxide, aluminum, and magnesium, continued to produce various incendiary effects.

He had also finally acquired one of those camping fire starters, thanks to his militia contacts. Magnesium turned out to be quite spectacular—just as he expected—and produced not only a tight, terrible explosion, but an instant blast of high intensity flame that ignited anything that might burn.

Blondie was still sleeping back in the trailer park, if the nearby blasts didn't periodically jar him awake. But he seemed to like to sleep a lot, given the chance to grab some extra shut eye.

Mason collected his gear and led Ginger back to their camp. He tethered the pack horse, and double-checked the other horses, getting them ready to travel for the day.

Then he pounded on the side of the trailer.

"I'm up," Blondie yelled from within. "Just getting dressed. I'll be out shortly."

What, Blondie just didn't sleep in his duds like Mason did?

Maybe he was just changing his clothes.

Then Mason heard the baying of strange dogs in the distance, very distinctively. Definitely hounds of some kind, but unlike any baying he had ever heard before. It chilled his blood.

These sounds came from far off in another direction at first, southeast and well away from the nearby vale he'd been conducting his morning firearm experiments in. These sounds were far away at first, but seemed to be approaching rapidly from that direction. They grew louder.

What in the hell kind of dogs sounded like that? And from their strange baying, they were obviously chasing something and growing closer to their quarry.

Then one dog suddenly yelped in pain, actually more like a high-pitched shriek. After that it went silent.

Also not a good sign.

Mason mounted up on Winger. "Something's happening in the distance to the southeast," Mason shouted to Blondie. "I'm going ahead to investigate. Follow along and bring Ginger."

"Give me a few minutes, Mace, and I'll just go with you."

"No, I've got a feeling we need to check this out. There's something strange about it. Follow along when you can."

"All right. I'll catch up and find you."

"I won't be moving that fast, I hope."

It was daylight, after all. It couldn't be the monsters. They didn't come out until night time.

Mason rode Winger cross country, avoiding patches of heavy mud from the rains. He tried to stay out of sight and under cover. He picked his way carefully through the fields, brush, and forest, drawing ever closer to the sound of those strange dogs in the distance.

Then he noted rapid movement in the brush and trees near a hillside, above the edge of a muddy field. He spotted the amazing sight of a lone figure running very quickly for one so large.

A female warrior; she was an absolute Amazon, seven feet tall if she was a foot. Dressed all in armor somewhere between Viking shield maiden and something out of *Conan the Barbarian*. This gal was tall, but perfectly formed and rippling with muscle, a warrior goddess if he had ever seen one.

Just looking at her running in the morning sunlight took his breath away. Even his good buddy David would have been impressed.

She simply bristled with all sorts of swords, axes, and daggers. She carried a round, bossed shield on her left arm and a throwing ax in her gauntleted right hand.

If this vision wasn't amazing enough, suddenly the dogs in question shot out from the edge of the brush and loped over the open field, snarling and leaning forward as they gained on their quarry. They growled as they hit a patch of mud and it slowed them down.

These weren't your average hounds.

These were monster dogs—four feet at the shoulder, lean but with powerful hind legs and short, bobbed tails. They had enormous, wide-splayed front paws. Their block-like heads sported short ears and wide, vicious maws filled with gleaming, bone-crushing teeth.

The damn things were bigger than ponies, and much stouter and powerful, built for running prey down over long distances at the lope. They made the biggest, nastiest pit bulls look like mere puppies. They had weird furry hides that were short, mottled bluish-red coats mixed with purple and black.

Wicked, iron-spiked war collars bristled around their thick necks.

The warrior goddess realized they were closing on her.

The lead dog was almost on her.

Even as she kept running, she halted slightly. Her throwing ax whirred through the air. Mason could hear it from where he was, many yards away.

Smack! The ax sunk into the thick skull of the lead monster dog and not only dropped and slew the beast, but flung it backwards with the force of the impact.

The great hound rolled end over end and lay dead.

The other three encircled their prey and closed in: heads bent, ears back, and eyes narrowed.

The warrior goddess kept her shield on her left arm and drew a broad-bladed, short stabbing sword and switched it to her left hand, point down.

She slipped one of the double-bladed battle axes from the carrier on her back and hefted it deftly in her right hand.

She voiced a war cry that seemed to split the very air and turned at bay. Not waiting for the onset of the monster hounds, she charged them, wheeled and swept her weapons around in what looked like an elaborate, violent dance.

The armored boot of her foot crunched into the face of the next hound while she scythed him open with her battle ax the next instant. The great stroke laid open the beast's chest and ribs. The woman warrior kept moving past the severely wounded creature.

The second dog sprang at her to drag her down with its weight.

She smashed it to one side with her shield and stabbed it in the guts with her sword, tearing intestines free.

With the third monster, she ducked low and smashed right into it head-on, rolling, cutting, and slicing at the wailing beast as they tumbled together.

She sprang back up to her feet and stomped on its thick head, mashing the skull into bloody pulp as the legs kicked and went still.

The second hound was horribly injured and dying, but tried to drag itself and its entrails away from the warrior woman in whining terror.

The Amazon stabbed it through the heart without thought or hesitation. The creature stiffened and went limp.

The first tough beast still had some fight in him and sprang at her throat. She yelled another war cry and whirled completely around, splitting its vicious face wide open—like chopping through a length of wood.

She fell back into her long, loping run, now that she was free of pursuit. She skirted some trees that led up the hill to help conceal herself. Mason would have done the same exact thing.

She no more went out of sight when two score strange men in plain helms and studded armor or light field plate raced onto the scene to encircle the hill and close in to trap the warrior woman. They still had a few of the monster dogs like the others on chains with them, held back in check.

To Mason, this did not at all appear to have the makings of a fair fight.

He skirted the nearby road and went down into the dry, leafy sloughs that crisscrossed the roads and the various farm fields.

If he kept low and then used the heavy brush and thick trees, he might reach the next hill's crown before the menacing riders overtook the Amazon.

Boy, could that girl scramble. Incredible. And she did it with all of her armor and gear, as well. Here he was, traveling pretty light and riding flat out—on a horse.

Mason wasn't any slouch at running, either. He had completed a marathon six months before and placed seventeenth against good competition. Not bad for an amateur runner, winding up in the top twenty.

At the moment, he was worried that he and Winger might not even catch her at this rate. The warrior goddess was that fleet of foot.

He saw her glance at the wide-open terrain extending out in front of her.

She instantly turned away and chose to make her stand around the large oak tree at the top of that forested hill, and among the rocks, lesser trees, and brush crowning it.

Mason saw it, too.

Even with her speed, she wasn't going to get much farther. If she remained exposed, out in the open, the riders would run her down with ease.

More than half of those two score riders carried various spears, lances, and shields. Most of them also had horse bows.

Mason's primary question was, who was in the right, here? And did these riders want to kill, or capture this woman? That would remain to be seen.

He charged Winger up the backside of the hill, and the horse labored to get up quickly, making its way toward her.

The Amazon wasted no time preparing her defenses.

Some small dead trees lay up to slope to one side, possibly taken down by a wind storm and then moved up there with a tractor at some point.

The Amazon grabbed them and dragged them over in front of the big oak, forming a hasty, V-shaped picket in front with the large tree at her back.

Mason grinned.

So, not just fast and powerful, she was smart, too.

That way, the riders couldn't simply charge in at her in waves from several directions and sweep over her.

But she was still up against forty to one odds. Pretty stiff, even for a warrior goddess. He wondered how she was going to even those odds.

Mason fully intended to see if he could do something about that, as well, if he could get close enough to her without the Amazon splitting his head or body cavity open, just as she had done to those monster dogs.

21

The wind turned sharp and cold in the later hours of the morning. Another dark mass of enemies swept David's way and toward the hotly contested intersection.

Yeah, the main body of the enemy would catch sight of him any second.

Then the line of bushes and trees behind David sprang to life.

An entire flight of camouflaged militia archers rose up. They must have crept forward, concealed from view.

More than a hundred compound hunting bows thrummed in unison. Razor steel broadheads ripped through the enemy like a sheet of whispering death.

The enemy advance withered and collapsed under deadly, point-blank, concentrated fire.

A second rapid volley nearly eradicated them, before they could even react.

Still gasping, David staggered to his feet. The archers marched in, ready to shoot again.

Fred and young Steven Hayward, more longtime MHS friends, stepped out and took him by the arms.

"Dave, we thought that was you."

David swallowed hard. "Thanks, Fred. I was about to die again. You guys just saved my ass."

"Die...again?" Steven asked.

"Finish catching your breath," Fred told him. "The intersection's ours. We have to push on toward the house! Get your people together. There's heavy fighting all through out this area."

"There's worse coming our way," David warned. "They're going to throw everything they have at us, here. We might very well get overrun."

"You mean they haven't done so yet?" Fred sounded worried. "How do you know all this?"

"Trust me." No time to explain about the pool or everything he had seen. He still didn't understand all of it himself. "Have you guys seen Jerriel?"

Fred leaned on his personal longbow and shook his head. "She's been in and out with Belle and Rose, Dave. She went searching for some kind of glowing pools everyone's been worried about. I got kinda mad at them, and told them to stay put near the house. But you know them women—they don't always listen so good. Not to anyone."

Young Steven looked worried. "Dad, I wanna go protect Mom. She could be in real trouble."

"We will. Trust me, son. But we have to get more people to go with us."

"I'm with you," David said. "Dirk sent me here to do just that." He thought of Jerriel's pretty face once again. "Fred. Put your archers on our left flank and behind us. I'll send two squads to guard our rear."

David called to his remaining forces. They and many others rushed toward him.

More militia troops poured in, thankfully.

Dirk rode up, an arrow through one arm and another sticking out of his armored thigh. "Let's go, guys."

David warned him about the impending enemy counterattack—even more massive than what they expected. "The enemy is going to throw everything they have at us right here."

Fred immediately looked to Dirk's wounds, and then glanced at David's leg again. "Dave, you're bleeding, too—from the back of your leg."

"It's just a flesh wound. I'll be all right."

"Steven, bandage that up for him like I showed you. Dirk, hold still, dammit."

"We don't have time for this, Fred. Leave me be. Aaughh!"

Fred pulled the arrow out of his leg and pulled the armor aside for a moment. "That one barely nicked your thigh through the armor. I'll plug it up with some superglue and a bandage."

"Damn, that hurts, Fred. Leave it the hell alone!"

"Belle will kill me if I let you bleed to death, you ornery bastard. Quit your complaining. You're no good to us bled out. Now hold still, you idiot!"

David winced as young Steven finished bandaging up his leg tight where the militia field arrow had struck him.

Fred used a Multi-Tool to cut off both ends of the arrow in Dirk's arm. "If I pull out the rest of the shaft, any punctured arteries and veins might bleed free. We can leave it in to plug you up for now. It'll hurt, but you should be able to still fight for a long while."

Dirk gritted his teeth. "Oh, I can fight all right. Just wrap it up good and tight and let's go."

David retrieved more bikes for them.

"Fred, you and your archers protect that northern flank and catch up to us when you can!"

David and Dirk rode back up toward the front.

"General Blackwood, Captain Pritchard!" their troops called out. David still wasn't used to having rank. He didn't know if he deserved it.

"We heard you were both badly wounded," someone said.

"We're okay. Just banged up a bit."

"Great to hear it."

"Glad to have you two back with us!"

"We can't stop now, people," Dirk said. "We've got a bunch of the enemy trapped. But there's a massive counterattack on the way. Now we have to finish this batch off before their friends bust them out. And they're going to fight like hell to break out any way they can."

"They're not going anywhere but straight to hell," David said. "But they'll still throw all their reserves at us. That's what I'd do—all in and go for broke."

A bunch of troops moved an enemy cart up along side, ten men pulling it.

"Commander Blackwood. Look at this! We captured a cart of their firebombs. It's almost full!"

Dirk's pained face brightened. "Great job, people. Outstanding! Bring up some of those lawn torches and keep them handy! We can use their own firebombs against them. Let's go. Wahoo!"

A cheer went up from the defenders. "Hey," David said. "Keep a few of those bombs aside so that Kevin or someone at the college can

141

study them afterwards. You know, to see what they're made of and how to make them."

"All right, sir. Will do."

Very heavy fighting exploded in the next block over, very close to the Haywards' house. Dirk and David advanced on the front and the right flank with pikes and spears massed together.

They struck the enemy hard and drove a wedge of fighters deep into the enemy ranks. David wheeled the right wing of his forces to shatter the enemy's exposed right flank. The central mass of militia spears and pikes retreated behind an advancing shield wall, and kept hammering the enemy from behind it, attacking repeatedly. David found another shield and joined the wall, his katana in his right hand.

Sporadic firebombs landed among the humans. It looked as if the enemy had started to run low on the devices, and were using them sparingly.

Word came from Fred.

"You're overextended," the messenger warned. "Pull back a little!"

"Like hell," Dirk said. "Bring up more troops and follow us in. Let's end this and kill these fuckers!"

Flames roared up behind them. A massive firebomb assault cut them off from the rear.

"Damn it! Now we're surrounded," Dirk said. "Everyone circle around and prepare for an enemy push. They think they can wipe us out now. Well, we have enough people for one good charge. Let's ram everything we have right down their throats! The rest of our people will follow in behind. They won't let us down once they see what we're doing. Bring up that stuff we captured!"

The enemy struck everywhere around them, in vast numbers. It was hard to tell in the dark just how many there were.

Dirk and David and the other leaders led the charge with their best fighters out in front and protecting their flanks.

Two of the firebombs got passed to each trooper in the center with free hands. They sheathed their swords to light their bombs on the lawn torches and fling them into the faces of their foes as the monsters flooded at them.

Blasts of flame caught the enemy off guard and confused their packed ranks.

Then the Urth humans tore into them.

The militia charge only lasted a few moments, but it broke the entire right side of the enemy ranks. Dirk and David shouted and screamed like berserkers, fighting wildly. Battered and exhausted, they and their forces dropped back among the neighborhood houses to recover and defend themselves.

But the enemy wheeled on them with a vengeance and poured everything they had at the defenders in an attempt to crush them.

"Hey, look where we are," Dirk said.

Behind them, only a block away, sporadic fighting had erupted around the Hayward's house.

"Let's head there," David said. "If we're going to make a stand, let's make one there."

They cut down any foes between them and the house and arranged their forces in the neighborhood in good order. They held their last firebombs at the ready.

Belinda and Rosalyn stood out in the backyard helping the remaining guards beside them. Both women had their bows out and arrows on the string, swords and knives at their sides. They had ladders set up nearby, incase they had to fight from the rooftops.

Three dozen dead foes littered the area, and about fifteen dead humans. Dirk yelled at his wife, "Belle, get back inside, woman!"

"Like hell. We've been out here fighting for over an hour. You need everyone you can get!"

David went to Fred's wife, Rosalyn. "Rose, where's Jerriel?"

"I don't know, Dave."

"You don't know?"

"We tried to keep her inside with us. But things got dicey and we went out to shoot. She must have slipped away again."

"She's gone? You let her go?"

"We were too busy to watch her constantly," Belle said. "She can handle herself, David. Don't worry about her. We're the ones in trouble here!"

More messengers poured in. Their situation worsened.

"Rose is right," Dirk said. "This is the hot spot. The enemy knows they're partially trapped now and that this area is the weakest point. They're going to try to break out here and get away, where they know we're already tired. But we can't let that happen."

David looked around. They had maybe three hundred people or so left who could still stand and fight. The enemy had maybe ten times that number or more.

Dirk pointed with his sword. "We'll make a stand down Jefferson and on either side of Greenlawn. A gauntlet of death that they'll have to pass through, with us plugging up the end."

"They're going to butcher us as they pass through us like crap through a goose!" David said. "But we're still the goose; they're still the crap."

"We'll be butchering them at the same time," Dirk said. "We just have to spread them out and hem them in long enough for our friends to get here and fall upon them from every angle."

"Dirk, we don't have enough people to hold these positions. It's a good plan. But we need five hundred more troops to make it all work."

"Damn it, Dave! We don't got no five hundred more people. We've got us! And that's going to have to be enough. So everyone suck it up, tighten your belts, and get ready for the main event. Get our archers up on the rooftops with every shaft they have. We're stuck here, and we're going to give these bastards the fight of their lives!"

And that fight that wasn't long in coming straight for them.

The first enemy wave hit them just before the intersection of Jefferson and Ironwood again, and slowly punched west.

David fought side by side with Dirk in the main shield wall, ten rows deep. Alternating rows of shields and swords and spears and pikes, bleeding the foe every step, every inch they fought.

The militia was slowly forced to give ground.

On the flanks blocked by a hasty wall of derelict cars, trucks, and SUVs lining the street, more human fighters hemmed the enemy in and fed them down Jefferson, forming the entire street into a corridor of death. Archers, crossbows, teens throwing bricks and stones, anything with weight that could be tossed: appliances, boom boxes, potted plants.

All types of debris rained down upon the enemy and smashed into them.

Anywhere the monsters turned or tried to break out, a wave of flanking defenders dogged their steps and met them with steel and threw them back.

The enemy had no choice but to fight their way forward down that corridor of death.

David laughed a grim bitter laugh. They became a meat grinder, with them as the blades.

And the enemy became the meat fed into them.

They cycled their troops in a flow pattern of lines, fighting for a few fierce minutes and then back out to retreat and rest for their next turn to come. He spotted their friend Pete Steiner nearby, from Mace's Civil War reenactor's unit. Pete was tall, strong, and wearing an old Army helmet, makeshift armor, and his tall horse boots. He sliced deftly at the enemy with his long cavalry saber up close, a big bowie knife in his other hand.

He chopped, sliced and, stabbed at rushing torgs and ka-torgs.

There wasn't time for Dave to do anything but give his buddy a quick nod and a salute with his katana.

If the militia didn't spell each other, all of them would have been worn out and simply beaten down, little by little.

As it was, even short bursts of intense fighting were incredibly exhausting.

David lost track of the blows he struck and the foes he cut down when his turns in the rotation came.

He tried to use every trick—spins, parries, thrusts, snap cuts, push cuts, draw cuts, back cuts. He went after openings and weaknesses one after another in blinding fury, efficient without thought. Just keep blocking, ducking, thrusting, and cutting.

The street ran black and red, slippery with the blood of both sides running down the gutters.

Many defenders fell or were struck down, falling beneath the trampling feet of the horde or pulled back by the militia if they could be grabbed.

The mass of fierce creatures seemed virtually endless in the dark.

"Hold on. Hold on!" Dirk cried. "At Greenlawn, the last of our reserves will hit them hard. We're almost there. We're almost—"

An armored mor-kahl suddenly powered its way to the fore. It raked Dirk across the legs with its hand claws, and flattened him to the ground with one massive blow of its war club.

General Dirk Blackwood went down, and the enemy horde rushed forward to sweep over him.

22

Who were these warriors and where did they come from? Mason merely guessed that they had to be from the other side. They certainly weren't from Urth.

The mounted troops broke into several groups with trained precision, and brought out weighted nets. They unfurled them, expertly deploying each of them between two riders.

So, they meant to capture the warrior woman. They didn't just want to kill her. That would help their cause out a lot.

Mason was now close enough to the forested crown of the hill, already in the trees. He dismounted, and quickly secured and hid Winger as best he could in a brake of small fir trees. He covered the horse's eyes to keep her calmer and quieter.

Then he bounded up the slope.

The riders with the nets surged up the hill at several strategic points, looking as if they had done this all before.

"I'm a friend," Mason called out to the Amazon with his empty hand extended. "I've come to help you!"

The woman whirled his way, a throwing dagger poised in one hand. Mason prepared to duck or dodge.

He held up his open palms again. "I'm not one of them. I want to help you. My name is Mason Tyler."

She cocked her head at him as if he were nuts. "I am called Thulkara, little man. You want to help? Then get ready to fight."

Thulkara had an odd accent, but at least they could understand each other. That was amazing in itself.

She lifted her shield at that moment, and several blunted crossbow bolts, meant to stun her, pattered against her shield and deflected off with smacking sounds.

Mason turned and drew his Spillers. He snapped off accurate shots that blasted the nets out of the foremost riders' wringing hands, and then the scarlet-feathered plumes off the tops of their helmets.

Monsters were one thing; killing other humans was another, even if they were from the other world or dimension.

He didn't know anything about any of these people, or the causes for their apparent quarrel. He would kill if he had to, in self-defense, but he hoped that he could scare them off, or at least get them to break off their attack and talk.

Perhaps these humans from the other side could become their allies against the monsters. Simply mowing them all down wasn't going to be the answer.

The lesser blasts from his guns certainly gave the mounted men some pause. They immediately broke off their attack to what they apparently thought was a safe distance.

Did they have some knowledge of his guns and their effectiveness? How could that be?

They also broke out all of their horse bows and arrows.

A leader or officer rode forward slightly and rose up in the saddle to address them.

"Surrender, wizard. You and the barbarian woman are trapped. There is no escape. You are surrounded. Come down and give yourselves up. You will not be harmed. You have the word of Captain Areglio Lokadoglio of the Scarlet Vipers, Swordmaster of the Crimson Swords of Morrad."

Thulkara came a bit closer and laughed under her breath. "Well done, wizard. Your mighty spells have given them pause and caused them to banter with us instead of attack."

Mason held up his pistols to show them to her. "I'm not a wizard. I'm a shootist. They call me the—"

147

She clapped a heavy hand on his shoulder with what felt like the strength of a gorilla. "Oh, so you are a sorcerer, then. Your words are strange. No matter. I'm not judging you. At least you're not a filthy necromancer. Keep those funny metal wands of yours handy. We could have great need of your powers very shortly."

"Uh...okay."

Thulkara looked around her and took in a deep breath, gripping her weapons. "Ahhh...the sun is up, the cold wind is sharp, and a hawk soars high in the sky. All good omens. It is indeed a good day to die!"

"I'd really prefer to leave out the dying part," Mason said. "Say, for–sixty or seventy odd years?"

Thulkara laughed again and shouted at the warriors below. "You filthy sellswords can sit upon you bloody blades and spin on them. My sorcerer and I will take you at all hazards. Come against us then, and let us show you the paths to hell itself. We dare you to try!"

"That is ill-advised, Thul," Captain Areglio said. "From this distance, we can easily feather every inch of that hilltop with arrows, and both of you right along with it. We wish only to question you. Who are you? Where did you come from? Who sent you into the Wildlands and why?"

Mason opened his mouth to speak again, but Thulkara beat him to it once more. So, if these troops were mercs, who was paying them and why were they here?

"We don't answer to bloody mercenaries in the wild, scum. You have no authority over us. Our business is our own. Go you way and stop pursuing us. Or come ahead and taste steel and magic."

"Very well, Thul. Cohort, fire a volley. Ring the ground right before them. Show them how easily they can both die."

Almost every one of the mercs fired their bows, including the captain.

A cloud of arrows soared up into the sky and came down, with deadly precision, in wide arc not a yard from where the two defenders stood.

Areglio wasn't bluffing.

But again, what was so important about capturing or silencing two travelers? What were these mercs doing out here, if these were the Wildlands for them also, as they said?

Captain Areglio and his horse archers prepared to fire another volley.

"Hold it," Mason called out.

"You are the sorcerer?" Areglio asked. "You and the Thul should prepare to meet your makers, if you have them."

In answer, Mason drew two different pistols and blasted the terrain to either side of the mercs with full devastator loads.

The blast on the left gouged a wide fan of dirt up, stripping back everything in its path. The blast on the right did about the same, mowing down a few saplings dotting the hillside.

Either blast would have taken out most of the mercenaries with one shot.

Captain Areglio quickly pulled his forces back once more.

"We're just travelers passing through," Mason said. "There's no reason for any of us to die today. Let us be on our way, and you be on yours."

"Very generous, sorcerer. Your destructive powers are indeed very impressive. I did not catch thy name?"

"I did not give it. Do you know either me or my companion?"

"Not in the least. We are under orders for this entire region. Our patrols stop and question all who travel this way. But we have seen none such as you two, thus far."

Thulkara roared back. "Whose orders do you follow, Captain? Under whose authority do you do these things? There is no law in the wilds."

"There is now. Our law. And you and all are subject to it."

The big Thul raised both her weapons. "Then I say lay on and be damned! Come ahead then and see what happens when you attempt to enforce thy will."

Areglio paused, and remained where he was. "Let us not be too reckless and hasty," he said. "We are paid troops, and paid very well, mind you. You two travelers obviously have valuable skills that would earn high pay as well. Would you by chance consider joining us?"

Mason shook his head. "Not without further knowledge of who you are working for—and who would hire us unseen."

"A pity, then. I am not at liberty to provide any information. We shall meet again, mage and Thul. And soon, I would say. You can only travel so far in one day. Until our next meeting, then."

With that, the mercenaries wheeled about and rode off quickly, just in case they were attacked again.

Thulkara laughed and clapped Mason on the back so hard that he pitched forward on his face, the air slapped out of him.

The Amazon merely lifted him up bodily like one might pick up a small dog or cat, and jammed him back up on his feet.

Thulkara bowed to him. "I'm sorry, my little man. Did I hurt you? I can never judge my own strength enough. My deepest apologies, great sorcerer. Your amazing powers surely saved our lives and drove those scum away by the fear of thy great might!"

For the first time, he got a good look at her up close. Thulkara was athletic, even very attractive with her high, noble face and fierce blue-gray eyes. Her long dark hair was braided and pleated with precious metals and gems. Her gigantic shape was still perfectly proportional, all woman, and all solid muscle.

Everything about Thulkara was huge, like that of a giantess fashioned for the express purpose of doing battle and making war. The armor and many weapons that she wore only added to her stunning overall look and effect.

Thulkara held out her huge right hand in its steel gauntlet and armored forearm. "Well met, Mason Tyler."

"My friends call me Mace."

She bowed to him once more. "Thulkara Rajan, at your service, Mace. I am glad to know you and count you among my boon friends and valiant companions."

He shook her hand and arm as best he could, but his hand wouldn't even fit around hers. She pretty much shook and jostled all of him until his teeth rattled.

He rubbed his arm and shoulder when she released him. At least she hadn't yanked it out its socket.

"Thulkara, what are you doing out here in the middle of nowhere? If these are the indeed wilds—"

"They most certainly are."

"Then why are you here?"

"I'm looking for someone—a good friend of my people. He is one of my kind, who came this way to scout the area and investigate what was going on in these parts."

"Why would either of you do that? And for that matter, who are you, where did you come from? If there are more of your people, then where are they?"

"I could ask you the same questions, sorcerer. I never expected to find one of your kind wandering out here, but I guess I shouldn't be too surprised. Last fall, a very large host of mercenaries disembarked their troop ships on the eastern coast of the New World. Then they formed up their companies and marched into the interior of the wilderness, and toward the wilds. No one heard anything from them again until now. My people, the Thulls, including myself and my missing countryman, have been trying to pick up their trail ever since."

Mason had to sit down and catch his breath. He finally had someone from the other side, with their memory intact, to talk to directly—a person from this other world. The mercenaries were from the other world, too, but they were apparently working for someone—perhaps the people or beings responsible for the terrible cataclysm that was now being called the Merge.

Where to begin? "Thulkara. You said this was the New World. You wouldn't have a map of it, would you? Does it include this region of the wilds?"

"Certainly. It is one of the latest colonial maps from less than two years ago. I've added some notes of my own, but these areas are still mostly uncharted and unexplored." She produced what looked to be a bamboo tube with cork caps and canvas straps. Thulkara opened it and took out a roll of parchment that instantly smelled of some kind of waterproofing.

"Do you know how long the New World has been under colonization?"

"Within a lifetime. Barely threescore years since mariners discovered it. But word of it has existed in legends since the dawn of time. The Old World knew something had to be out here, but our ships were not strong enough to cross the wide seas to reach it. Once they were and we finally found these new lands, we flocked here."

"And there were no humans living here in the New World?"

"None. The colonists have just barely been able to survive and push inland against the monster hordes."

"But I take it that the Old World is quite civilized and run by humans?"

"Of course. That's why everyone there wants to come here to get away from it, and to exploit the new lands and riches in this place."

As soon as Thulkara spread the map out, Mason understood that he was looking at a world parallel in most respects to Urth—a sister world from an alternate dimension, most likely, with a different history, peoples, and creatures.

As rough and crude as Thulkara's map was, it was still, very clearly a representation of the eastern half of what Mason knew to be North America and the U.S., yet with different terrain, cities, and towns. All marked in the runic language of the alternate world.

And apparently: wizards, sorcerers, and necromancers existed in this alternate world as well—all of whom could make use of magic in some form. Very interesting.

The mercs had been startled by the power and range of his blasts from his guns, but they still accepted them and reacted to them as fact. To them, his pistols were some kind of strange metal wands. These people had experience with mages and their powers, perhaps in warfare, as well.

After he demonstrated his powers, they and Thulkara naturally assumed that he was a mage of some kind, a magic user, and they had referred to him as a mage and a sorcerer from that point on.

151

So much to take in. He examined Thulkara's map once more. Most of the cities were naturally on the coast, if the New World here was a recent discovery. But he did see a small number of fledgling cities located in expected points along the east coast, leading west along the water ways of their version of the Great Lakes.

He wished that he could read the writing on the map.

The furthest west the colonial cities went appeared to be what he knew as Chicago, and St. Louis to the south, and then New Orleans. This new world had its own version of the Mississippi River, which seemed broader and more or less a wide, inland sea that split the entire lower part of the continent in half. Or perhaps it simply had been charted badly. It was hard to know with hand-drawn maps. Yet they seemed accurate to a degree–enough to travel and navigate by.

Just like the north, the south had a few points of cities founded along the eastern coast, and a handful within the interior. But it appeared that the interior of the New World, including the Appalachians, were all still part of the Wildlands, and ruled mostly by violent hordes, tribes, and bands of these various monsters.

The closest cities nearest to the Michiana area seemed to be what he would call Detroit and Toledo. There was no equivalent city for Indianapolis, but further east, there was a city in the place of Cleveland. Imagine that.

His family could be interacting with these other humans at that very moment. Mason hoped they got along peacefully and worked together.

Mason studied that map intently for a long while.

"What language is this written in?" he absently asked.

Thulkara grunted and smiled. "Thuldoran, of course. The language of my people, the Thulls. I thought all mages could parse and speak the languages of the six lands and the six peoples of Tharanor?"

"I guess I never got around to learning them all."

Thulkara suddenly nodded down the hill. "A rider with golden hair comes this way, drawing a packhorse behind him. He carries a crossbow and a saber at his side. He searches for something or perhaps someone. Do you know this fellow?"

Mason nodded. "He's a friend and companion of mine. Do him no harm. I will get my own horse and call him up to us. Wait here, and keep your map out."

"I will."

Mason retrieved Winger and called to Blondie. "Up here. Come up here. I've made a new friend–she's from the other world."

Blondie came around the lowest side to make his way up to them. Mason secured his horse and kept talking to Thulkara while he got his notebook out and a pen. "What do you call the world–the entire planet?"

Thulkara blinked at him and shrugged. "Tharanor, of course."

"And the six lands and peoples of the Old World?"

"Thuldor, the Thull Nation. Sylurria, the nation of mages. Khairun, the land of sellswords. Jattar, a nation of wizards and horse riders. Darshia, a nation of mages and great swordmasters. And finally Marrandor, a land of knights, great archers, and enchanters."

Mason pointed on the map to what he would call Detroit. "What city is this and who rules there?"

"Why, that is Tornhold, the westernmost colony of the Thulls."

He pointed to Toledo. "And this one?"

"Kellendra, the furthest, western city state of the Marandorians. How is it that you do not know these things? Have you just recently come here from the Old World? How did you get so far into the interior without a map or any knowledge of the colonies?"

"Let me ask a question," Mason said. "What happened to the moon?"

"Moon?" Thulkara said. "What the hell is that?"

"I figured as much. This Tharanor probably never had one, for some reason."

The Amazon suddenly gave him a hard look. "Who are you? Where do you come from?"

He pointed at Cleveland. In a way, it wasn't lying.

"You're from Dorundia? Funny. You don't look like a Darshian—their eyes are slanted. Or perhaps you merely came over on one of their ships." Thulkara began eyeing him suspiciously and pulled her map back, rolling it up.

Perhaps from being out in the wilds, Thulkara did not fully understand what had happened with the Merge.

Blondie rode up just then. He looked a little stunned to see Thulkara, and started rubbing his head as if it suddenly pained him. "Oh, ghods—a Thull!" he exclaimed.

Thulkara looked him up and down, and said to Mason. "You're traveling with a Sylurrian?"

"How do you know he is a Sylurrian?"

She pointed. "His boots are. None of the other peoples would wear boots such as those, or their hair that way."

"Thulkara, Blondie. Blondie, Thulkara. I knew it. I just knew it, Blondie. Get this. She says you're a Sylurrian."

Blondie folded his arms in front of himself. "And just what the hell is a Sylurrian?" he asked.

Thulkara pointed at him. "You are. Now I can tell so by your voice as well."

Mason turned to Thulkara. "He must have hit his head at some point. Blondie doesn't know who he is, or where he came from. Nothing."

He turned back to Blondie. "You're probably from Vaejan—what I would call Chicago."

Blondie shook his head. "That means nothing to me, either. You two are giving me a headache."

Perhaps that was a good thing. Confronting him with a bunch of Tharanorian stuff could jog his broken memory.

"Why would you call Vaejan that?" Thulkara said.

Mason ignored her for a moment and turned back to Blondie. "She doesn't seem to know about the Merge."

"What is this Merge you speak of?" Thulkara asked.

"Where has she been for the last week or so?" Blondie asked. "Hiding in a cave?"

"No…traveling through the barren wilds, Sylurrian. But now that you say something of it, after I woke up one day, things around me started to look very weird. I began to see many strange things along the way. Things that should not be. I've kept to myself, and remained out of sight—especially after I rediscovered several mercenary armies out this way. Then one of their patrols spotted me briefly, and their gulluk hounds picked up my scent."

She laughed. "The rest Mace knows. He chased them off with his sorcerous powers. I have never seen powers so strong or used in such a manner." She let her glance rest on him with a certain gleam in her eyes that made Mason slightly nervous.

It was as if she admired him, and perhaps something beyond that.

She caught herself and quickly looked at Blondie, and actually sniffed at him. "You stink like a mage, but all Sylurrians seem to smell of magic. What sort of mage are you?"

"I…I don't know," Blondie said. "I still don't recall very much since the Merge."

She looked perplexed. "You two keep babbling about this Merge? What do you mean by that?"

Both of them tried to explain the current situation.

Blondie went directly into his theory on the matter, but that just seemed to confuse and worry Thulkara. She even looked a bit frightened, if it was even possible for a Thul to comprehend what others would call fear.

Mason chose a more subtle approach. "Thulkara, you said that you've seen many strange things in this area recently. Haven't you noticed the strange houses and buildings and structures? Odd people wearing strange clothes, speaking in strange languages?"

She nodded. "I have seen many strange things, but the languages would not be a problem, if they spoke some other tongue," she said flatly.

Now Mason and Blondie were at a loss. "Why not?" Mason asked.

She pulled an ornate silver medallion on a strong silver chain up from around her neck, set with many runes and symbols.

She acted as if they should know what the artifact was, but the two of them simply stared back at her and the necklace.

"These medallions and other similar devices are quite commonplace on Tharanor–throughout my world. Ages ago, the mages of our world devised a way to create many such devices with heavy enchantments on them. This type of magic allows the wearer and many within range of them to converse freely with one another, no matter what tongue each of them actually speaks."

"Prove it," Mason said. "Take it off and try to talk to me."

Thulkara shook her head. "It would still work. I would have to take the enchanted medallion far away from us, nearly out of sight, and then return."

Mason remained skeptical. "How do I know such magic works?" he said.

Thulkara reached over with a long finger and hooked it under the neckline of Blondie's T-shirt. She pulled out a chain and a very similar golden medallion with different markings from another language on it.

"Because your Sylurrian friend is also wearing one, made by his people."

Blondie stared at it and studied it as if it were a king cobra. Then he quickly stuffed it back down his shirt, out of sight.

23

"No, save Dirk!" David shouted. He leaped directly in front of the seven-and-a-half-foot-tall monster that towered over him like a tree. Four other fighters joined him to help keep the huge mor-kahl busy.

More defenders swept forward on either side.

They stabbed and cut down the torgs and ka-torgs trying to drag Dirk away.

Pete Steiner rushed in with them and booted a ka-torg in the face, and then ran the creature through with his saber. Pete helped the troops fight off the enemy and pull Dirk, battered and bloody, toward the rear to safety.

If Dirk was even still alive.

David grappled with his enormous foe, and rammed his wakizashi into the mor-kahl's chest—up to the tsuba.

Then he thrust his katana deep into the thing's maw as it snapped its sharp teeth down at his torso.

He pushed and leveraged all his weight. With the help of his comrades, they toppled the stricken monster to one side. David lunged forward, shoving the sword all the way back through the thick skull.

He rolled free, yanked his swords out, and came up slicing, battling beside the foremost twenty militia fighters.

Then the southern militia line collapsed to their right.

Countless more foes poured in from the south and west to aid their comrades.

These were the last of the enemy reserves—the final heavy counterattack.

They collapsed the thin militia lines, lines that had already been in confusion and disarray.

Only seconds, minutes at most before they all went down.

They were going to be completely routed and swept away.

The only logical choice was to withdraw.

"Pull back!" David shouted. "Wheel north to Greenlawn. Direct them down Greenlawn. Shields! All shields up front. To me. To me!" He gathered every remaining defender not struck down and formed first a skirmish line, and then a hasty shield wall.

They retreated, fighting among the yards and houses around the Haywards' place once more.

Dozens of human archers on the rooftops poured murderous fire down into the enemy horde, heedless of any return fire—which was sporadic.

But the larger monsters flung smaller torgs up onto the roofs by the dozens to attack the archers.

The human archers cut down the torgs and took their arrows.

But all of that took time away from both sides.

The enemy charge faltered and stalled before it could completely sweep David and the others away.

All the while, the militia archers kept up their lethal fire.

The militia defenders in that spot dwindled down to a few hundred against many hundreds of monsters, perhaps thousands more behind them.

The enemy piled up at Jefferson, but already spilled over and raced down Greenlawn. There wasn't any help for it. They'd most likely break out and do as much damage as they could in the area until close to dawn. Then they'd rampage back through the downtown and into the safety of the strange dark forests and hills to the west.

Only to attack again the next night.

David and his people could contain them only for a few more moments—fully expecting to go down fighting.

He backed up hard against a tree in the Haywards' backyard. Two of his best fighters went down on his right.

"They're coming!" someone cried. It sounded like young Steven Hayward up on the roof, protecting his mother. "Help's coming. Hold on. They're only a block away!"

A city block might as well have been a country mile. The relief would not arrive in time for them. He fought on, and thought first of Jerriel's smile, and then his parents.

David and the militia killed foes each second, calmly and efficiently.

But it was Captain Pritchard who led them and held the line each precious second by force of will and his skill with swords. Even his own troops protected his flanks, but gave him room to fight.

No one wanted to be cut by those flashing blades.

David slashed throats and severed hands, arms, and legs—spinning, slicing, and cutting like a cyclone of steel.

His swords were steel razors, two and three feet long, wielded with a surgeon's skill.

If the monsters could be called living things—nothing living came near him that was not cut deeply more than once or sliced completely in two. Any foes who got in close to try to hit the captain were quickly impaled on a forward rush of spears and pikes or cut down.

The enemy advance stumbled and climbed over piles of their own dead and dying.

But exhaustion could eventually bring down anyone.

David and his people had been fighting all night. They were at their limit, and began to falter.

He dropped to one knee, cursing his own weakness. Damn it, he was failing everyone.

Their foes smelled blood and came at them fresh and fell for the kill.

A small, blazing comet smashed into the ground twenty feet into the horde and detonated. A blinding hot wave of white-orange energy incinerated the first few ranks of foes and flattened the rest onto their backs, fifty or sixty yards beyond that and into the street.

The blast wave leveled everyone who was up close.

Asphalt buckled and melted.

The enemy shrieked in terror and tried to pull back from the destruction.

As dust and smoke and debris cleared, David gasped in wonder and fell back on his elbows. Troops tried to help him back up.

What in the hell had happened?

Jerriel rose up out of that smoldering crater like a glowing star and twirled her glittering staff above her head. Lines of force and runes glowed all along its length.

She chanted singsong in her tongue faster than David could follow. The air around her crackled with energy, and her long hair and her garments rippled around her as if in a strong gale.

She looked like a young goddess enraged. His heart leapt in his breast to somehow be able to reach her side. But everyone stood back before her revealed might, friend or foe.

She cried out spell words and unleashed the gathered force around her as the enemy surged forward once more.

A wave of blue-violet lightning blasted out before her in an ever-expanding arc. It crackled and jolted into the enemy, slaying and sweeping them in several directions. Scores fell, lying smoking and convulsing on the ground.

The glowing might of her staff wavered.

Jerriel hurriedly pulled out a pouch from her belt and sprinkled something glowing and powdery all along the staff's length.

The enemy noted this, too, and rushed forward again to overtake her.

"Jerriel!" David cried, and charged in beside her at last.

"No!" a voice screamed. Steven Hayward jumped down from the roof and flung his longbow and empty quiver aside. He drew two short fighting swords, one in each hand, and came to their side on Jerriel's left. Ten other militia fighters joined them, forming a protective arc around her, ready to do battle. Two troops were instantly struck and wounded by enemy arrows.

Shields, they needed shields.

Yet all they had were their weapons and their bodies.

"Daeved!" she shouted happily, her eyes bright and wide when they met his. Then she continued to focus on recharging her staff and preparing her next spell.

Three armored gozogs rushed to the front of the enemy lines, trampling lesser creatures underfoot, and driving a final charge forward to crush all of the humans.

David recognized the leader. He had seen it talking to the enemy wizards in the dark, hooded, black robes on those hilltops in his strange, out-of-body vision.

David and his fighters formed a wedge in front of Jerriel to meet the enemy charge head-on.

Jerriel rose up into the air behind them and unleashed another spell barrage at the last moment.

Blasts of magic green ice shards scythed into the enemy from above the heads of the defenders. The shards swept through the enemy's packed ranks. Ice blades pierced many monsters and shredded them.

159

The terrifying spell caught the monsters in a hurricane of magic, glass-like blades of ice wherever Jerriel directed her staff.

David stabbed one of the huge gozogs directly in front of them deep in the groin. Then, spinning to his left, he dodged a heavy blow and slashed behind the gozog's left knee with a deep backcut. Finally, he thrust both of his swords up into the monster's vast, stinking gut from behind and to the side. It roared and toppled back and to the right. He nearly lost his grip on both of his blades.

Cheering erupted. Fresh waves of militia finally poured through the yards and around the houses from all directions, falling upon the last of the enemy push. The late arrivals shattered and broke up the enemy, who had first been staggered by Jerriel's amazing spells.

The enemy panicked and became tangled up with each other.

David tried to follow after them as they receded, but he could barely stagger forward.

The lead gozog rose up like a mountain of flesh, and lifted a gigantic battle ax to strike down Jerriel from behind

With his last strength, David dove under its guard, avoiding the sweep of a massive armored forearm. He drove both swords deep into the gozog's armored chest, up under the ribs.

Then he released his blades, dropped back, and collapsed onto his hands and knees.

Steven Hayward sprang up onto the gozog's ax arm like a monkey. He barely deflected the stroke with his weight.

The huge ax slammed deep into the ground just behind Jerriel, barely missing her.

Steven rapidly scissored his short swords into the leader's face and throat. Even as it died, the leader swatted the young boy away like a bug. Steven landed and rolled to his feet, black blades ready once more.

Militia troops swarmed over the gozogs like army ants.

None of them ever got back up.

"Daeved!"

He turned, still gasping for breath on his knees. Jerriel melted into his arms.

Filthy and bloodstained, his armor dented and in tatters, David wrapped his arms around her. He dropped to the ground, struggled and gasped for breath, trying to hold her closer.

"We beat them, Daeved!" Jerriel cried. "We've woon!"

24

Mason knew now that he was right, even if Blondie couldn't remember his past. His new friend was, undoubtedly, from the other side—just like Thulkara.

But if all of that was true, then countless questions still remained. In fact, they only proliferated.

Just these magic language translation medallions by themselves were an enigma.

What was magic? What forms did it take on Tharanor…on Urth? How did any of it work? How was all of that affected by the Merge?

"If these enchanted medallion things work to translate language," Mason asked, "then how come I can't read those symbols on either of the medallions, or on your map?"

"The enchantment affects the roots of language as it is centered in the mind," Thulkara said. "What we say, think, and hear. They have no power over the written word; that is a very different thing. Such skills must be learned on their own. I myself can understand all of the other tongues with such a device—but I still cannot read or write them."

Even with that caveat, Mason remained impressed. The best Urth computers had only been able to translate complex languages, subtleties, and nuances in a limited, unnatural way. Tharanorians used their magic in the same ways that Urth people had used their own advanced technology—and apparently in many other similar facets of their lives.

To Tharanorians, Urth magic in the form of technology would most likely have seemed just as strange, frightening, and impossible.

Yet it still begged more questions: Why had virtually all of the vital Urth technologies that could be used in defense been nullified by the cataclysmic effects of the Merge?

Mason still suspected that somehow the Merge had happened on purpose.

Perhaps it had been some strange plot to weaken Urth and leave its people vulnerable to subjugation. In that case, who was behind it all?

Someone or some power had planned it all very neatly, and well ahead of time, in order to cripple Urth and leave its people nearly helpless.

And just what had Blondie's role in all of that plot been, if any?

It still took them the better part of an hour to explain the Merge to Thulkara and convince her that Mason and his people and their culture were part of another separate world and reality entirely—a world the Tharanorians referred to now as Urth.

"Well, I guess that would explain all of the strangeness, at least," the Amazon finally admitted.

"And neither of you know what has happened to the moon? The satellite that revolves around the Urth?" Mason said.

"Tharanor has never had any such satellite," Blondie said. "Everyone knows that."

Mason grinned. "Everyone from Tharanor, you mean? If you were from the other world you refer to as Urth, you would remember that it does have such a moon. And you didn't recall that fact, either; not until Thulkara said so."

Blondie threw up his hands. "I don't even care anymore. Can we talk about something else or give it all a rest? My head is splitting. Are both of you happy, now?"

"No," they both said in unison.

By then it was closing in on noon. Mason quickly explained his mission to reach Elkhart and locate his girlfriend Tori.

Why did it sound so silly and simplistically petty when he put it into words? In the larger, cosmic scheme of vast worlds and dimensions, it did sound goofy. But it was still Mason's driving factor.

"You're welcome to come with us, Thulkara," Mason told her. "You could be a big help to us. You've already been through parts of that area and made it all the way this far."

"Almost. If the mercenaries had not spotted and come after me. You want to go back there into all of that, just to locate a girl?" She also seemed slightly disappointed that Mason apparently had a lover already.

He hated to tell Thulkara, but it would never have worked between the two of them any way.

Mason didn't date giant girls, even ones as pretty as Thulkara.

In fact, just the thought of it made his blood run cold. Gosh, what would something like *that* be like? Scary. She'd probably grind his bones to meal.

Luckily, she seemed to accept the fact that the Pistolero was already taken.

He sure felt grateful for that. Once again, not that Thulkara was unattractive at all. Quite the opposite, in her own, buff, bulging muscles, Amazon sort of way.

But he still couldn't shake the frightening image of making love to someone as huge and powerful as the barbarian goddess.

She'd pulverize him as if he were made of dried sticks.

Thulkara folded her arms before her and set her feet a little wider apart. "I am not going back that way, and neither are you. The mercenaries have encircled this entire area with their armies. They capture and take away anyone they can find. They already have several slave camps set up all around this city you refer to as—the heart of the elk."

"That explains that much," Mason said. "That's why nobody has been able to get into Elkhart and get back to spread the word yet. These mercenaries have everything out this way completely locked down and under their control. Any refugees from Michiana who go that way are captured and enslaved. I wonder why the monsters plaguing South Bend aren't attacking these mercenaries or their slave camps?"

"They might, eventually," Blondie said, "once they finish dealing with South Bend and Mishawaka."

Thulkara spoke up. "The monster hordes fear nothing but raw power. They will attack anything that is meat for them to devour—even each other. Even the great number of these mercenaries would not dissuade them. The monsters would see them as a challenge to their territories.

"Before the Merge, there were no lesser, human cities or even colonies or settlements here in this region of the New World. Not yet. Little else could survive in this region. The monster hordes must see the

163

appearance of so many strange humans, mysteriously appearing among them and their lands, as a terrible insult and a threat to their territory. They will do everything in their power to destroy such threats, regardless of where the humans came from–this Urth as you call it–or Tharanor. They guard these lands fanatically, and fight over them even amongst one another. The presence of this many humans must be driving them insane with hatred and bloodlust."

"I want to see one of these merc slave camps," Mason said.

He had a sudden stabbing fear in his heart.

What if Tori had been captured and was in one of these camps? His heart sank. She was so young and pretty. What if the bandits found her? What would these mercs do with fair young Urth girls like her under their power? The answer was pretty obvious.

His fears always raced in the worst possible directions.

"Are you certain?" Thulkara asked him. "There is one such camp less than a half a day away from here. But it is guarded by one of their armies. Each of the camps is."

Mason didn't like the sound of that. "Sheesh, how many mercenaries are there?"

Thulkara looked as if she were doing the numbers in her head for a moment, looking up. "I would guess there are thirty or forty thousand of the sellswords here. Perhaps more. It's difficult to say."

Mason gaped. "Thirty or forty...that many? What are they doing here? Who are they working for?"

Thulkara shrugged. "I've been trying to learn that, as well."

"We still have half a day left," Mason said, slapping his leather gloves in his right hand on his leg with purpose. "We can still reach that slave camp by nightfall."

"Armies?" Blondie asked fearfully, still trying to catch up. "Mace, you want the three of us to go up against armies? Thulkara, refresh my memory. Just how many of these sellswords did you say are there out here, just waiting to capture us?"

Thulkara sighed. "Enough to surround this Elkhart of yours, the slave camps, and more. Tens of thousands. And what's more, many of their numbers seemed to be repositioning themselves in this direction, perhaps in fear of the monster hordes."

"I've still made up my mind. Can you show us where that slave camp is?" Mason asked. "I don't even like the sound of that–my free people being made slaves."

"Oh," Blondie chipped in, "and the thought of vicious monsters killing and devouring them is somehow better?"

"I must ask something before I join you," Thulkara said. "Has there been any sign in this region of a great warrior–a Thul such as myself–but male. He has golden hair like the Sylurrian, yet a bit darker. But this Thul has no equal in battle. Such a fighter would be hard to miss. He was the one I came looking for."

Both of them shook their heads. "Thulkara," Mason said, "it would be well known if someone like that–like you–turned up out of the blue. No. No one like you has been met with or spotted. Not that I know of. And rumors do seem to travel quickly."

She suddenly looked very concerned. "What could have happened to him, then? You are correct. Wherever he is, we should have heard of him or his great deeds by now. That much would be very plain."

"What if he is on the other side of the Merge?" Blondie suggested. "That might explain why you haven't heard of him or been able to find him. There are many people we haven't been able to locate on our side here. As the Merge theory goes, if half of everything is mixed up, half of Urth would be on the other side with the other mixed-up half of Tharanor. That includes half of the people, too."

She nodded slowly. "Indeed. It is a fearful thought. Then we must seek out a way to cross over to this other side–this alternate dimension, as you call it."

"There is no way to do so that we have heard of yet," Mason said. "Although, the time that has passed has been both brief and chaotic."

Thulkara clapped her hands on her thighs. "Then I shall go with you two, and continue to search for a way. Until that time, I shall aid you as best I can, and we shall see what we shall see."

She checked the sky and the birds nearby. "A dark, broken sky and squabbling blue jays–troubling omens. We need to be careful."

Blondie snorted. "Yeah, like we need superstition to tell us that."

A short while later that afternoon, Blondie switched saddles on thickheaded Patton for a time and rode Ginger. She sure seemed to get a kick out of that. Dumbo Patton didn't care either way, whether he was a pack horse or not.

Mason smiled, knowing full well that his new lady Winger would have been severely insulted by such a grave indignity.

25

Not a single monster escaped that final battle. The militia surrounded as many of the creatures as they could, just as Dirk had originally intended.

The few monsters that they took captive and tried to question proved worthless. The brutes were far too dangerous to keep alive.

David ordered them dispatched.

He and others realized quickly that these creatures were a lot like soldier insects. They seemed to have been bred to fight and kill, and were almost mindless in other respects. Their sole purpose for existing seemed to be to fight, kill, enslave, and eat all other living things.

Thunderstorms and heavy rain kicked in before dawn the next day. People tried to clean up in the aftermath of the big battle. But they quickly gave up in the face of a deluge of relentless, frigid, pouring rain.

Stubborn militia troops on duty still managed to drag heaps of stinking enemy dead off through the mud, and piled them up out of the way for later burning.

They identified human casualties when possible, and took them to morgues and mortuaries in preparation for quick funerals. More bikers and scouts went out to map and explore the area around Michiana and to reach out to other towns and communities.

Niles, Michigan, for example, had almost been completely wiped out by the heavy enemy advance that swept down from the north.

Searchers also reported powerless plane and jet crash sites amongst all of the other growing bad news. More casualties from the cataclysm.

Thousands of refugees and injured people still poured into the Michiana area from all directions. Anyone who could travel and get there in any way, shape, or form, did so. They became the Urth human rally point in that region. Getting there meant life.

The wilds were simply too dangerous.

General Dirk Blackwood returned to his house with Belle, badly battered and bruised, but still tough. He finally got that chunk of arrow taken out and his arm patched up. The Blackwood house ended up damaged, but not burned down.

The drenching rain actually did some good—quenching most of the monster-set fires in the area.

David and Jerriel took over a house on Churchill whose owners, a retired couple, had unfortunately been slain the night before.

It was a smaller, older red brick ranch home close to the Haywards' and Twyckenham and Ironwood. It was not that far from downtown. It still had working fireplaces and propane heat—even an old fuel oil furnace and stove that could be used again, with some work.

The well provided good water through an old-fashioned hand pump out in the garden, next to the garage.

Despite his exhaustion and intense soreness, David couldn't tolerate the stench of filth and death that covered him.

The first thing he did was find some towels and soap, go out to the open garage, and strip down to his boxers.

He stepped outside into the cold, pouring rain to suds up and rinse off a few times.

Ugh, get rid of that blood, grime, and dirt. The rain was chilling, but no more than mountain waterfalls he'd bathed in while backpacking.

When he went back inside, Jerriel had some oil lamps lit. While he toweled off, shivering, she cleaned up with simple magic.

Hair, body, and clothing—she wiped her accumulated grime off on some paper towels and tossed it all away.

Well, if it was that easy-peasy for her…

She glanced at him in the entryway. Jerriel blinked, stared, and gasped. It was about that time that David noted just how heavily bruised and lacerated his entire body was. The damage was spread over several places and many lesser wounds.

But right then, he didn't give a crap how badly he was banged up. He just wanted to get warm and sleep. He would feel better thereafter.

Jerriel murmured a spell and drew the excess water from his body and his clothes. In an instant, he was completely dry—even his hair.

Wow. That was a pretty convenient spell.

Jerriel carried the small orb of floating, muddy water through the air into the kitchen and dropped it in the sink.

She came out and pointed back to the kitchen where Rosayln Hayward had briefly showed them around. Rose was the one who knew about the house and the former tenants.

"Daeved. Are yoo hungry?" Jerriel asked.

He smiled at her, his eyes heavy and drowsy. "No. Not hungry."

"Sokay."

He folded his hands and leaned his head against them. "I'm very tired, Jerriel. I don't know about you, but I just need to sleep."

"Yes. I am tic-hard also. Wee shall sleep then. Like at yoor friends' hoome."

"Sounds good." He could have dropped right there and slept on the floor. Only the thought of a nice warm bed kept him from doing so.

He pointed to an open bedroom with light blue walls and a queen-sized bed. "You take that room. That is now Jerriel's room."

She followed him.

He stumbled in through the next door. "And this is now David's room." All he saw was a full-sized bed, green covers. He fell into it.

His head, heavy as a rock, found the heaven of a cool linen pillowcase.

#

The sky was still dark and raining later that day. Thunder rumbled. David opened his eyes. Jerriel? Probably sleeping in her room. Time? 1:23 in the afternoon, according to the wind-up clock on the night stand.

Most mechanical stuff still functioned, just nothing electronic. Guns still worked mechanically, but somehow the Merge messed up the chemical reaction of gunpowder and explosives and most highly refined fossil fuels.

He groaned in agony when he moved. Oh, hell.

Very sore. Incredibly sore. Even jousting all weekend never left him that beaten up. He felt painfully stiff—as if his body were made of dry sticks. Sticks of pain that ground, popped, and splintered with every move. He lay there, moaning and grunting.

Damn it all.

So much change. So much uncertainty.

So much death.

The world he knew was now gone—in an instant—probably forever.

Part of him wanted to remain alone with his grief, frustration, and pain. Part of him wanted Jerriel holding him again. He wanted to scream.

He stuffed the pillow into his mouth and shuddered, sobbed, and yelled.

As usual, there was nothing to do but keep going forward. Figure things out, and do the best that they could do. At least Jerriel could use her magic again. That was really something. She could cast her spells—very powerful spells, as it turned out. Good thing she was on their side.

But those other wizards, sorcerers, or whatever he'd seen that distant, enemy camp. All of that, after he stepped into that weird glowing pool and his spirit left his body. He had seen and heard them all plotting against Michiana as plain as day. Those mages and those other weird creatures were behind all of this. They were directing the monsters, organizing the attacks. They were clearly on a mission, but who did they work for?

They didn't seem to have any trouble using their magic. They talked about the Merge as if they knew exactly what it would do to both worlds, both dimensions.

Had they planned it? Did they help cause it?

That possibility enraged him. The militia needed to take some of those bastards alive and force them to talk.

But the night before, during the battle, most of those wizards had been about to depart in a great hurry. Their leader said they were badly needed somewhere else. Where had they gone? Yet they could still return and use their magic against David and his friends in the future. Even Jerriel couldn't stand up against a dozen other wizards who had powers similar to her own.

He had to get up, despite the pain. He needed to speak to Jerriel and learn more about her and her world—Tharanor. Half of that reality was now merged with half of Urth on both sides of their two mixed-up dimensions.

Knowledge was going to be the key to freedom or slavery—life or death.

They now existed and struggled to stay alive on a mixed-up, double-sided jigsaw puzzle. Only on a 3D, worldwide scale.

Their survival, perhaps the survival of both worlds, depended on understanding exactly what had happened. And next, what was going to happen.

David had a great deal to figure out, and he guessed that there was not enough time to do so. He staggered to the door and sniffed the aroma in the air.

But first, before he saved the world, he had to find out what smelled so great. His head was still fuzzy. Thoughts came and went.

He rubbed his empty gut; he was starving.

Downstairs in the kitchen, he could see at a glance that Jerriel didn't know how to use the stove. The gas was cut off anyway. Instead, she heated a pan with a reddish, glowing heat spell emanating from one hand, while she hummed and stirred the contents with a wooden spoon from one of the drawers.

He peeked inside the pan from behind her. Creamy stuff bubbled and boiled. To one side on the counter, he saw the mess of spices, cans, and bottles Jerriel had amassed from a concerted search of the pantry and cupboards.

Her face lit up when she saw him.

"Daeved!" She left off heating the stew, put her spoon down, and flung her arms around him. He stopped smelling the stew.

Suffused in Jerriel's embrace, suffused in her own luscious scent, and the wafting fragrance of her long dark hair was a new form of paradise. All he could think of was holding her close to him, breathing in the scent of her skin, her hair. She took his breath away and didn't give it back easily. After two days of terror, they were still alive, and she was in his arms.

Jerriel and all of the wonderful ways he felt around her. Just having her near him.

She pulled away, leaving him so wobbly that he clung to the doorjamb. He smiled, noting every line of her pale, happy oval face. He couldn't get enough of her big violet eyes, dark brows, and long lashes. Her pretty nose and mouth—the way she concentrated and bit her dark pink lower lip. She had not painted her lips today, but they were just as alluring in their natural state.

She went back to stirring her stew or whatever the concoction was. A nice sweetened white sauce, what looked like canned chicken. Peas. Carrots. Maybe some cubed potatoes. Did he smell rosemary?

"Did yoo sleep good, Daeved?"

He nodded, still staring at her.

She laughed. "Hungry now?"

"Famished."

"Sokay. Me too. Let's eat."

David set the table and discovered where to find the plates and silverware. Most Urth houses were set up pretty much the same way. Everything in them had to be somewhere.

He did feel a sudden twinge of guilt about taking over the dead couple's house. He felt sorry for them. Rose said they had been good people. They didn't deserve what happened to them. No one who perished in the attacks did.

Somewhere their kids had lost their parents, just like David had. He knew what that was like. But things were tough. Lots of people were already gone, and he and Jerriel needed a place to stay. Theirs wasn't the only empty home in town. And the living needed to survive. He did his best not to feel guilty about that.

Frankly, at the moment, David simply enjoyed sitting with Jerriel, enjoying their little pot of magic stew, served up in stoneware bowls. Very tasty.

He didn't know if he could have done as well with the same ingredients. And he considered himself a pretty fair cook. Both of them ate two bowls and split the rest of what remained between them. They washed it down with warm apple juice.

The milk in the non-working fridge had already gone sour.

Jerriel licked her spoon clean deftly with a slender pink tongue and her pretty lips. David looked into her eyes and smiled, his belly nice and full.

He felt so much better.

She put her hand on his and looked back into his eyes.

"We need to talk with more of yoor people, Daeved. There is much to doo." She pointed at a bookshelf full of books. "I want to learn to read yoor language. Perhaps yoo and some of yoor peeple should learn to read and speak mine. It is only a matter of time before you meet oother Tharanorians. I'm guessing our many nations, peoples, and languages are as different as yoors."

"I agree," he said. "There's so much we need to know about each other. So much we have to talk about. But we need to stay alive first. We have to make sure the monsters don't come back tonight."

Her eyes widened. "We defeated and destroyed so many of them," Jerriel said. "I doubt they will be able to attack yoor city in such noombers again. Not for a loong while."

"We have to be ready all the same. Let's go check in at headquarters and go from there."

They left the house, with its broken windows boarded up. David gave her one of the sets of keys he found on the key rack.

He showed her how to lock and unlock the doors front and back.

They rode their bikes to the courthouse and the County City Building in the rain, wearing the plastic ponchos David found for them

At HQ, the militia scrambled to train more recruits. There was no new word on how Dirk was recovering. David got his orders for that night, and was asked if he was fit for duty.

He told them that he would report to his unit at nightfall.

171

But there were several urgent messages waiting for them both from the new town council. The council was swamped, but doing its best to gather facts and information about the Merge.

Dirk and Belle had informed the remaining city leaders about Jerriel, and the council was extremely interested in having various local linguists, historians, and experts speak with her as soon as she was available.

Before they left HQ, David located an empty meeting room that wasn't being used. This one had a bunch of donated school and office supplies sitting around in boxes. He gathered a few notebooks, drawing pads, pencils, and pens. He put them in a decent, almost new black backpack for Jerriel.

They'd both need to take a lot of notes in the weeks ahead.

Jerriel especially liked the colored markers he found for her. She delighted in them. To her, they were a kind of magic.

On a whim, David went to the white board and taught her his Urth alphabet.

Jerriel wrote the characters down quickly. Then they went through the sounds of each letter with him correcting her.

She took the marker from him and they switched places. Jerriel drew corresponding symbols or runes that matched some of the same sounds in her language. Tharanorian had a runish alphabet all its own. David made notes on those. He had always enjoyed studying other languages, but had never taken the time, thus far, to master another besides his own. This was a starting point for both of them and their peoples.

"We could do this for hours," he told her. "But people are waiting to talk to us, and the day's almost over. I'll have to report for duty tonight."

Jerriel slung her backpack on the same way he did.

"I'm going with yoo, Daeved. Wherever yoo go, I go."

At least it had stopped raining. They got back on their bikes, and reported to the town council think tank, conveniently set up at the main branch of the public library downtown.

Half of the town was gone. Half of everything and everyone was gone. Everything that remained suddenly became very important, fortresses for protection and centers of knowledge, training, and learning.

Crews of workers labored to fortify buildings and brick up exposed, lower level glass windows and doors.

From the public library, aides and advisors to the acting town council made many busy appointments for both David and Jerriel the next day. Then they took them to a section where local linguists were setting up an office.

They located the office and went inside, but the linguists had already gone home for dinner that day, and to prepare for nightfall.

Two grad students, Danielle Callahan and Theo Miller, were ecstatic to meet Jerriel. They fell all over each other trying to talk with her, made quick notes, and begged her repeatedly to come back early the next day.

They ignored David almost completely, but that was to be expected. Until he showed them Jerriel's alphabet. Then they almost fainted. They were soon drooling as they copied down the symbols in their own notebooks. David wouldn't give his up.

Jerriel's partially working language translation crystal that she wore on her forehead fascinated them all to no end. The sudden prospect of magic, mindstones, and alien languages boggled Urth minds.

But in no time at all, the sky darkened once more. Time to go.

Another night approached.

No one knew if another enemy horde would attack again or not.

"We're going to hole up in one of the storm shelters," Danielle told them.

"You should, too," Theo suggested to Jerriel. "We can't afford to have anything happen to you."

"I will be sokay," Jerriel said, smiling at David.

They biked home to their new house.

David quickly patched up and repaired his battered armor as best as he could. Jerriel helped him put it back on. He readied his weapons.

Fortunately, his troops had retrieved his longsword and tomahawks. His crossbow was in his bike basket. His katana and wakizashi were already at his side. His troops also brought him another quiver of bolts.

And, of course, the rain started falling again.

A nice cold, drenching April rain. Poncho time for everyone.

Jerriel went with him. He didn't try to stop her. With her spells working, she could definitely handle herself against any kind trouble.

The air smelled full of wood smoke, propane smoke, and charcoal grill smoke from everybody cooking. Some people even found a way to burn coal they had gathered. Only the rain kept everyone from choking.

An hour passed.

Then another.

The militia waited—in the dark. In the drenching rain.

"There's no attack coming tonight," David finally said, both relieved and disgusted at the time they had wasted. "Any attack would have already started. Send word to Dirk and the other militia commanders. Stand down most of the troops and let them rest. Keep large patrols at all of the intersections and near the borders. Rotate them in shifts."

Finally they caught a break. Either they had defeated most of the enemies in the area, or their foes didn't appreciate the rain. Or both.

Then word reached them.

"Captain Pritchard," another commander said. "Our scouts have discovered an enemy base in the deep forest, in a hidden vale in the hills, three or four miles west from here. The remnants of the enemy have a large group of captives there that they've been…feeding off of. It appears that they were preparing to bug out, but got stuck in the rain."

"Hmm… We definitely need to free those people, and fast," David said. "I guess there will be some action tonight after all, folks. I hate to think about what's been happening to those poor people. We'll surround that area, take out those bastards, and free the captives."

Jerriel twirled her staff. "Then let's go get thoose bast-hards."

He chuckled slightly at her eager bravado. "We'll need to be careful and quiet. They'll kill or injure as many of the captives as they can if they get wind we're coming. We have to take them by surprise. At least the rain will help dampen our scent and the noise of our approach."

They waited for a response from HQ. The rain let up a short while later. Great. Just great.

Now that they wanted rain, it stopped. "How many enemies?" David asked the scouts, as they continued to relay information. "We need to know."

"The scouts say around four to five hundred, sir," his current runner said. "Including several of those big gozog creatures."

"Hmm…we'll probably need about a two thousand fighters, just to be sure." He sent out another runner, asking for that many troops.

"General Blackwood must want to be real sure," Lieutenant Craft said, upon his return, with the reinforcements. "He sent us three thousand, and as many archers as he can spare. He insisted on you leading the assault, Captain Pritchard, and Captain Hayward leading the archers."

David laughed. "All right, then. We'd better hop on our bikes and join up with them all at the head of the strike force. I'm glad Dirk's up and around."

Jerriel put a hand on his arm. "I have a few spells that might help."

He smiled back at her. "Sounds good. It's going to be a wet, dark walk in the woods. And then a battle. Hopefully a quick one."

26

With Thulkara's help, they reached the nearest mercenary-controlled slave camp shortly after dark. They circled the area and studied the camp from all directions. They watched and learned everything they could about the enemy organization, patrols, and troop movements.

The entire area already reeked of human waste and despair. Even in the dark, the camp seemed to hold over ten thousand souls, and was guarded and patrolled by more than a thousand troops. The camp was built like a spiral, and when patrols brought more people in, the sloppy, sprawling camp of tents and flimsy huts expanded and continued to spiral out in size, and misery.

They watched how the new arrivals were processed. Much like the bandits, the mercs took anything from the refugees they wanted, and beat down anyone who protested or tried to escape.

They were slightly more civilized. They didn't exactly force females to become comfort women. But they made a point of separating attractive women at first, and announced loudly for all of them to hear.

The mercs made it very clear to the slaves that any who signed a contract to become comfort women would get special treatment that the regular slaves would not.

Comfort women and their children would be housed separately in cleaner, much nicer facilities, and have access to good food and medical care.

The standard contract to become a whore for the mercenaries was for a year and a day. The terms were briefly explained at certain locations in the camp on the hour, for the benefit of all.

Mason guessed that after the pressure of being in that terrible slave camp for a few days, some might break and sign up out of fear for themselves or their helpless families. Especially if someone they cared about became ill and needed medical help. Camps such as these with bad water, food, and sanitation were perfect breeding grounds for sickness and disease.

There were no good choices for slaves. It sickened Mason to see slavery returned to his a nation and his people—brought back by outsiders. It made him incredibly angry to see his people treated in such ways.

"Stay your wrath," Thulkara said. "We cannot free them. What is it that you have come to do here, Mace?"

"At least they're not being outright killed and eaten," Blondie said.

Mason snorted. "This isn't that much better, but you are correct. At least they still live."

"There is no chance or rescue from death," Blondie added.

"I want to get into the camp and speak with some of them."

"You are mad," Thulkara told him. "What more do you think they can tell you? Most of their stories will be the same: they fled and were taken prisoner by the mercs. And you will risk being killed, or captured, and made a slave yourself—just to be told that?"

"She's right," Blondie said. "What more do you hope to learn?"

"Wait. Something's happening," Mason said.

The mercs opened up a gate at the back end of the camp, leading southeast. Four wagons left the camp, each of them piled with dead bodies. Mostly the elderly, plus anyone else who died of wounds, infection, or illness.

In a camp of tens of thousands, there would be casualties each day.

Behind them came five slave cage wagons with about a hundred able-bodied men total, guarded by a platoon of thirty mercs on very poor horses, but horses nonetheless.

Mason thought he spotted two militia men from South Bend. Perhaps that was a break. He told Blondie and Thulkara, "Let's follow these wagons at a distance and see where they go. We might have to free those men, but I'm curious about where our foes are taking the dead bodies."

Three miles south, the two groups split off. The slave cages went east, and the dead bodies west.

"We can catch up to those slave cages later," Mason said. "I still want to see what they do with the corpses."

Less than two miles later, they had their answer.

A patrol of a hundred mercs guarded the next intersection. They seemed ready for battle and tense, as if they were waiting for something or someone they didn't trust. Possibly even an attack.

Then a tall man in tall boots and long black robes rode up, guarded by a score of warriors all dressed in black, much like himself. But the leader wore what looked to be an iron mask, and the eyes of the mask glowed bloodred. His guards simply wore strips of black cloth masking their faces, all except their eyes.

Behind them came five empty wagons, each pulled by a pair of the larger monsters they had seen. And an assortment of monsters followed behind them.

Mason couldn't make out the words they spoke up close, but it was clear what was happening.

The man in black with the mask had control of the monsters, somehow. The two groups were trading the empty wagons for the full ones.

They were allies, giving the dead bodies to the monsters to be used as food. It also got rid of the dead and the greater chance of disease.

Yet this did not seemed to be a perfect alliance.

Someone among the mercs said something wrong, and one of the monsters lunged forward and tried to gut the merc leader with a jagged sword.

The dark man in black with the iron mask gestured with one hand.

A beam of darkness shot out from the masked one's hand and struck the monster in the back. Mason had never heard any living thing shriek in such agony. The monster stood up on its toes, transfixed by the beam, as its flesh steamed, boiled, and melted off its bones into nothing but goo.

Then the bones clattered to the ground.

"Bloody necromancer," Thulkara muttered under her breath.

The mage grew angry, stepped forward, and backhanded the merc leader, before waving him and his entire platoon off.

"The larger monsters are pulling the wagons away," Blondie said. "Why are the mercs bringing the horses back?"

Thulkara snorted. "So that the monsters don't eat them as well."

The mercs quickly hooked the horses up to the empty wagons.

"It must be mages like that necromancer who are in charge of both the monsters and the mercenaries," Mason noted.

"That would not be so unusual," Thulkara said. "Except for the fact that they are controlling so many of them. They must have a new spell or enchantment that allows them to do so."

"You said the monsters obey only raw power," Blondie noted. "We just witnessed a demonstration of such might. Even those dumb brutes would fear power such as that—one that can destroy in such a terrible fashion, at a whim."

"Very intriguing," Mason said. "Now let's catch up to the slow-moving slave wagons and effect a rescue."

"There are thirty mercenaries and three of us," Blondie said. "That's ten to one."

Thulkara shrugged and grinned, thumbing the edge of one of her battleaxes. "I like those odds. And, we have a sorcerer with us. I think we have a fine chance. But we must surprise them."

"Just follow my lead," Mason said. "No way around it. This is going to require killing, but I also want to capture as many prisoners to take back and interrogate as we can. Thulkara, once I begin the fireworks, do you think you can charge in and knock out the merc leader?"

At first she almost looked offended. Then she whacked her huge fist into her open palm. "Consider it done."

"Blondie, shoot down anyone who tries to run. Anyone I miss."

"Will do." His friend nodded.

"Now, we just have to find the right place to jump them."

About an hour later, Mason jumped out of a tree and onto the top of the third wagon. With guns drawn, he used lesser fire to blast the majority of the thirty guards off their horses. Most of the mercs were down before they even realized they were under attack.

Thulkara knocked the leader completely off his horse with her shield and laid him out cold.

Then she proceeded to drag down the drivers from the front two wagons, one after another. She knocked them out as well.

Mason shot the two drivers behind him, and smashed the third right below him in the face with the butt of his pistol, and then kicked him off the wagon.

Blondie shot three riders with his crossbow who were trying to get away. Mason and Thulkara went around and counted, finishing off any screamers or those mercs who were already too badly wounded.

That left fourteen new prisoners, including the merc leader.

Mason searched the man and found one of the enchanted necklaces. He quickly took it and put it around his own neck. They found three other such medallions around the necks of other mercs. Those would come in handy as well.

Blondie tried to keep the freed slaves quiet as they clamored to be set free.

Mason found the keys to the cages while searching the leader. Another backup set was located in the lead wagon, under the driver's seat.

He turned to the slaves and tried to explain their situation. But most of them simply clamored to be set free.

"Shut up and listen to me," he told them. "How many of you are from the South Bend or Mishawaka militias?"

About three dozen of the hundred raised their hands.

Mason handed a set of the keys to Blondie. "Get those militia people out first and have them hide the dead bodies nearby. Listen up, people. I can't just let you all go running off in every direction. We have to make it back out of enemy territory and into friendly hands in Mishawaka. That means that we have to put on a show that everything is cool and normal. The cages will remain open, but held shut by just a piece of string. Most of you can just enjoy the ride, and keep acting like prisoners in a cage. The militia people will don the mercenary uniforms and pretend to be mercs, drive the wagons, and ride their horses. We'll spread what weapons we have around. If we run into trouble, everyone boils out of the cages and we fight for our lives. Got it? Keep it simple. Play it cool if we encounter any patrols, and keep your mouths shut."

"What about the enemy prisoners?" one man said, with murder in his eyes. "These bastards took some of us from our families to go work in the farm fields south of here. To be slaves!"

"They took my wife to be a whore for them."

"They took my daughter, too. I want to gut them all!"

"Men, if it was up me, I'd hold them down and let you cut their throats right here and now. But we're at war. These mercs need to be questioned. They might have valuable information. Our leaders need to know whatever these men know about what's going on. That knowledge could save countless lives. They are worth far more to our cause as prisoners than they are dead. The militia will keep them bound hand and foot and gagged, and they won't let any harm come to them, either. So keep your distance and don't try anything stupid. Keep cool and we'll all get out of this alive."

"You're just a kid. Who are you to order us around?"

One of the militia people stepped up. "You damn fools. He's the Pistolero, and unless you forgot, he and his friends just saved all of us. So shut the hell up and do what he says. Hurry up switching into their clothes and let's go. We're wasting precious time!"

They turned the wagons around and headed back toward Mishawaka, taking lesser known roads and skirting fields and patches of forest. A handful of the men knew that area pretty well, and advised them which ways to go.

Yet by morning, they were still moving through Osceola, and Mishawaka remained hours away.

When they thought it best, they sent some of their people riding up ahead on a few of their better horses. They already had outriders on their flanks and their rear, half a mile out.

Mason and Blondie had grabbed a couple of hours' sleep in the wagons. Thulkara just laughed and said she'd be fine until they made it to their destination safely. She easily strode next to the wagons, keeping up with them and trying to stay out of sight, as much as a giant Amazon could.

After Mason woke up, he spoke with the militia people as they went along. "It is imperative that we get back to the militias and warn them about this army of mercenaries surrounding Elkhart, and working with the monsters. They have to stop refugees from heading out this way, and then we have to try to liberate those filthy slave camps. Perhaps the fighters in Elkhart can help us."

"I'm militia lieutenant Chet Monosso," a midsized, Stocky man in his late twenties said. "I was in the National Guard. Captain Watkins sent me and my platoon to reach Elkhart. We got in, and spoke to some of the leaders there. They are very well organized and prepared to defend their city and their people, but they're hampered by being so spread out. That's a disadvantage for both them and the enemy mercenaries, who've been watching the city but not assailing it directly, thus far.

"At first some of the monsters infiltrated Elkhart and began attacking and burning homes in many places. Then the monster attacks stopped, and the authorities in Elkhart realized that the mercenaries had surrounded them, allowing no one in or out, and refusing to negotiate or answer any questions. Overall, the mercs seem more bent on seizing much of the rich farmland in the area and trying to organize enough slaves to plant it than anything else. But now they are on the move again."

Mason snarled. "I think their strategy is one of containment. After the monsters finish off South Bend and Mishawaka, I'm sure they'll attack Elkhart next–with the help of these mercs who are currently containing the latter and keeping it from sending any help to the rest of Michiana. They're keeping us all divided so that they can defeat one, and then the next. Classic divide and conquer."

"What do the monsters have to do with all of this?" Chet asked. "All we've seen are the mercs."

Mason explained what they had witnessed.

It was hard for many to believe. "And you say they're all being led by these dark wizards?" Chet asked. "It sounds like a kid's fantasy story."

"Necromancers," Thulkara corrected. "And where there is one, there will be many."

"I know it sounds crazy," Mason told them, "but the people from the other side use magic the same way we used technology. And their magic can be just as powerful and destructive—like my guns. But our tech doesn't work anymore."

"Mr. Pistolero, why is that? Why doesn't our stuff work any longer? How did all of that happen? Why are we so damn helpless?"

Mason shook his head. "Lieutenant, we don't know all of the reasons for that yet. Perhaps some of these prisoners can tell us, but I think we'll need to capture one of their leaders, who all seem to be mages. I'm guessing that they know. But we can still resist and fight. We are fighting back. We're not helpless."

"Sir," Chet added, "for your personal information, Captain Watkins sent us to an address in Elkhart, looking for a young woman named Tori Nelson, with red hair and brown eyes."

Mason snapped his head up. "Did you locate her? What did you find?"

"Sir, we located the address and the house and searched it. The monsters had attacked in that block, I'm sorry to say. We found many old, bloody signs of fighting and death nearby. Neighbors still in that area said that no one has lived in that house since the attack. They said that agents from the militia came through directly thereafter and made records and descriptions of everyone wounded or killed, before the casualties were taken away for medical treatment...or burial."

"And?" Mason asked. "What did those records say? What happened to Tori and her family?"

Chet shook his head. "Our findings were inconclusive at best. There wasn't time to track down the actual records of the casualties that were made that next day. And many people had left that area entirely and became refugees. But many other locals also remembered seeing the body of dismembered, red-haired young woman near that house."

"Her eyes. What color were the dead girl's eyes?" Mason demanded.

"Sir, we just don't know. Once all of this is over, it might be possible to track down those actual records that were made. They could probably tell us for certain. But I'm sorry—we just don't know any more than that."

Mason gasped and bit his right hand.

So damn frustrating. Without a positive identification, that dead girl might have been Tori, or her sister Tanya, or someone else entirely. No word of Tori's parents either way.

She could still be out there. She could be in one of the slave camps. Tori could even be on the same side with David and the Blackwoods. There was hope that she still might be alive, and he was going to cling to that hope, until he learned otherwise.

But for now, they had to reach Mishawaka, and expose what they had learned about their foes, and bring the captured mercs in for questioning.

Three hours later, their outriders rode back in a panic.

Four to five hundred mercenaries were moving to intercept them on the road, and the chase was on.

They bounced those wagons down the road and across fields until everyone in them was sore and the horses were pooped.

But about a hundred enemy cavalry on faster horses and no wagons raced ahead to cut them off before Capital Avenue. The mercs waited there, watching, while their troops on foot struggled to catch up.

Then word came.

The horse messengers Mason sent forth had gotten through. Several hundred militia from Mishawaka were also hustling that way, even now, to engage the mercs. The escapees simply had to avoid being recaptured or killed.

Mason did his best to evade.

The enemy rode straight at them to intercept.

The mercs spread out to encircle the slave wagons in a wide arc, to limit the effectiveness of Mason's mass attacks. Even if he fired every round he had loaded up, he would only take out a few of them with each blast.

Arrows began to whistle in from the enemy horse bows, fired from extreme range while the riders closed in.

"Take the wagons into the trees," Mason said.

"We'll have better cover in the forest," Thulkara noted. But their situation looked bad.

Worse yet, enemy infantry came in from two directions in the distance.

Mason and his group prepared to make their stand.

"Don't dismount," Mason warned them. "Fight around the cages and wagons, using them for cover. We still might have to break out and make a run for it. Fight on horseback and the wagons for as long as we can. Steady your mounts!"

Several of the horses were terrified and ready to bolt as it was, if they had not been so tired. Others were not used to the roaring blasts of Mason's guns, but he couldn't do anything about that, either.

Mason did his best to pick off cavalry as they raced in, but he mostly held his fire. In a minute or so, the cavalry would be forced to bunch in more up close, in order to press their attack, and then he could use his loaded weapons on them.

The defenders only had a few arrows and bows. They waited and stayed under the cover of the trees, holding their fire.

The cavalry came in to encircle, and then stopped, dismounted, and advanced in good order on foot, behind light shields.

The defenders spent what arrows they had, taking several mercs down. The mercs closed in for hand-to-hand combat.

Mason cut loose with his guns, sweeping batches of them away in waves of flame. Blondie fired his crossbow quickly and coldly. Thulkara tossed two throwing axes and two daggers. Each weapon found a target.

An enemy mage, wearing one of those black, hooded cloaks and a cloth mask like a ninja, stood up on Mason's right from out of nowhere.

He raked their right flank directly with scarlet lightning, ending by focusing the attack directly at the Pistolero.

Mason was caught switching guns and could not respond fast enough. The enemy mage had apparently watched and timed his attack just for such a moment. He might have even counted Mason's shots.

Thulkara lifted her round shield in front of Mason to protect him at the last instant.

The ground beneath their feet also seemed to explode and burst upwards. Thulkara saved Mason, but both of them were blasted backwards. Even Mason's horse Winger was knocked screaming off her feet and toppled over, nearly crushing her rider.

The enemy mercs knew enough to hold back for an instant and let their mage do his thing. They didn't want to be caught up in an attack such as that.

Mason sat up and shook his head, trying to still the dizzy ringing in his ears. He watched, partially stunned and helpless, as the next few seconds of the battle unfolded.

The secondary effects of the magical blast had knocked Blondie off Patton. His crossbow fell out of reach.

This close, the red lightning had blasted the nearest slave wagon behind Mason, exploding it and killing several people and one of the wagon's horses outright.

Blondie tried to rise and draw his saber, but several enemy archers rushed in and had him dead to rights with their horse bows, in the confusion after the spell.

Their packhorse, Ginger, smashed into those archers on the run, knocking down some even as they all fired. The brave little horse put herself right in front of Blondie to save him.

She took an arrow in the neck, arrows all along her pack saddle and gear, and in her top hindquarters. She screamed and fell back at Blondie's feet.

Blondie lifted both of his glowing hands and strode forward, enraged. Torrents of burning black fire incinerated the faces and heads right off of the archers and enveloped the enemy mage.

The sudden, withering attack stemmed the enemy rush, and disrupted the enemy mage's next spell.

The mage fell back, trying to shield himself from Blondie's sorcerous fire.

The enemy mage looked Blondie right in the eyes and screamed, "Shaeddor!"

Blondie got in close enough to punch the mage in the gut and wind him. When the mage doubled over, Blondie booted him hard in the face, knocking him out.

Two militia troops had the good sense to drag the stunned enemy mage under a wagon.

Blondie tried to cast more magic, and the enemy mercs gasped and drew back, trying to cover up.

But his hands weren't glowing any longer, and Blondie's fickle powers no longer obeyed his will.

He was forced to draw his saber.

By then, Mason was back up. He and Thulkara jumped back in beside their friend, and none too soon.

The battle reverted once more into a free-for-all, up close and personal. Mason relied on his Spillers and their lesser fire. He fought back-to-back with Thulkara and Blondie.

He shot mercs at point-blank range. He blasted them right in the face and torso up close.

But in the end, it was Thulkara who saved them all. She met the brunt of the enemy wave attack with an absolute mastery of toe-to-toe combat. She anchored their position and never wavered. Her weapons flashed and slew and maimed with each stroke, with each thrust.

The defenders formed up behind her and protected her back, following her lead as she tore through the enemy ranks like a locomotive covered with steel blades.

For the moment, they were holding their line and even winning. Yet with each second, the enemy infantry reinforcements charged in closer.

A crossbow bolt just missed Mason's head and grazed his jaw with burning pain.

"Mace!" Thulkara shouted. "Get up in a tree. Focus on reducing that oncoming infantry!"

Mason nodded and struggled to climb. A militia man gave him a boost up, but the fellow took an enemy arrow to the shoulder while doing so.

Once actually in the tree, Mason scrambled up about eighteen feet more to an excellent vantage point.

More arrows zipped through the leaves and sank into the big tree branch in front of him.

He blasted the archers up close first thing.

Then Mason switched guns and launched devastator blasts into the charging ranks of the infantry, focusing on the foremost enemy troops first.

It still looked as if they were all going to be overtaken any second.

Then clouds of arrows rained down and slew the mercs from both flanks.

The militia from Mishawaka raced in from three sides and the enemy saw their own serious disadvantage.

The mercs promptly and wisely withdrew. The few remaining merc cavalry also melted away. Within another minute, the mercs voided the field entirely, leaving behind their dead and wounded.

Blondie begged Thulkara to help him tend Ginger's wounds, removing the weight of her saddle pack. The Amazon helped him remove the arrows. Both of the packhorse's wounds looked painful, but not particularly fatal.

They'd have her up and around again in no time. In a way, that little horse had saved them all, and brought out Blondie's powers for a few precious instants in ways that even he couldn't manage.

That proved it. Blondie was a sorcerer, similar to what Mason himself was. Yet the question remained.

Whose side had he been on to begin with?

And what had that enemy mage been trying to say to Blondie?

Mason had some trouble climbing back down out of the tree, now that the adrenaline rush of battle ebbed. After days of almost constant running and fighting, he definitely needed both food and rest. He was exhausted.

But he steeled himself, knowing that he could not rest until he made a full report to the militias and their leaders. The humans of Urth and Michiana were up against more than just monsters. And that fact worried him greatly.

He had a definite feeling now that larger wheels were turning and moving against them. They might not have that much time.

It was vital that the defenders learned what was going on around Elkhart. Whatever the enemy prisoners revealed, he and Thulkara could help fill in many of the gaps in their overall knowledge.

Their next task would be to try to help interrogate the enemy mage that they had captured, with Blondie's surprising assistance. This individual was one of the enemy leaders. Perhaps now, they could get some real answers.

They would also continue searching for a way to contact the other side of the Merge–if there was one.

A sobering thought awoke. What if their foes already knew how to go back and forth between the two sides? The enemy did have powerful magic, after all. That much was very clear.

They seemed to possess great knowledge. Why wouldn't they know of such ways?

Ginger was back up, nuzzling Blondie with her nose. He spoke to her quietly, trying to sooth her. His face looked very troubled and pale.

"What's wrong, Blondie? You look like you're going to be sick. Hey, before you knocked him into next week–what the hell was that mage try to tell you, anyway? Was he trying to cast a spell?"

Blondie frowned and tried to look away. He seemed very uncomfortable suddenly, and rubbed his temples as if they ached. "That mage is in fact a wizard, Mace. And as such, a wizard must speak words to cast spells. But he was not casting any spell–at least, not in the way that he intended."

Mason took in a breath, since his friend would not. "Then, what did that word mean, Blondie? What was he trying to tell you?"

Blondie held Mason's eye. "He told me my name, Mace. I saw it in his face when he said it. He knows me. He recognized me. I must...I must speak with him."

Mason tried to remember the name and how the enemy mage spoke it. "So, your name is–"

His friend lifted his head. "I am Shaeddor–the Black Prince of the Royal House of Holleth, Lord Sorcerer of the mage nation of Sylurria. And at this moment, my brother, I cannot safely tell you, whether we are meant to be friend...or foe in all of these matters."

Thulkara came to them, laughing, and clapped both Mason and Blondie eagerly on the back once more. "Victory, my friends!" she shouted. She drove them both to the ground with the force of her elation, flat on their faces.

She yanked them back up like puppets, with many profuse apologies.

Thul warrior goddesses...and Sylurrian princes. What the hell next?

27

Within two hours, Captain David Pritchard's strike force encircled the western monster camp beyond the abandoned ruins of the South Bend airport and Mayflower Road. They surrounded the camp with three thousand troops and tightened the noose.

The cold spring rains came in once more, complete with thunder and lightning.

"More reports from the scouts, sir," Lieutenant Craft said softly. "Several troops have been injured and three killed by enemy traps set in the woods. Such traps take the form of stake pits, deadfalls, and trip lines."

"Damn it," David muttered. The battle hadn't even started and they were already losing good people.

"What is wrong?" Jerriel asked. David told her about the traps. Everyone had to be more careful.

They came upon one located nearby–a stake pit set with spikes.

Jerriel nodded. "Torgs use many traps to guard their camps and villages. Bring some of your scouts to me, Daeved." She shook her staff.

He summoned the nearest scouting team. Four men and one woman in heavy camouflage, all with bows or crossbows and binoculars.

First Jerriel cast a spell all about her, even on David. A band of dark energy covered his eyes. He blinked and found that he could see much more effectively in the darkness. The light around him took on a gray-green hue, similar to night vision.

It was at least as good as seeing in dark twilight. He looked around. The spell affected about forty people within Jerriel's range, including herself. Now they all had the same band of magical energy over their eyes, giving them the "darksight," as Jerriel called it.

Then she spoke some more magical words and cast another special spell, just on the four scouts. They gasped slightly. Their bodies turned into what looked to be dark mist. They flowed effortlessly through the woods like silent phantoms.

"A mistshadow spell," she told David. "Tell one of them to shoot a tree."

David turned to scouts. "One of you shoot that big oak to our left."

The mist arrow turned substantial again after it left the range of the spell. It quietly thunked into the tree.

David gaped and turned to Jerriel. "You, are amazing."

She bowed. "Thanka you. The spell will only last foor one hour."

He turned to the mistshadow scouts. "That's all we'll need. I want you guys to slip in and take out as many of their sentries as you can find. This spell should make that a lot easier. Then help protect the captives once we begin our main assault."

They nodded. "Will do, sir." They nodded their thanks to Jerriel.

"Let's move in folks," David said. "Everyone keep an eye out for more traps"

Then in a sheltered glade, they stumbled upon a glowing pool of shining, white-green liquid.

Jerriel gasped in glee. She rushed forward while David and the others held back in fear.

After his last experience with one of those strange pools, David wasn't in a big hurry to take a dip in another.

"Jerriel, what are these pools?"

"Magic. Wild Magic. Concentrated magic. There are many kinds from what I have seen. Sometimes yoo can tell what kind from the aura."

She twirled the end of her staff above the pool and spoke some words in her language. The staff drew tendrils of the glowing magic up into it, sucking up the energy. But the water remained and ceased to glow.

"I have learned how to absoorb the magic foor later use," she whispered.

"Captain Pritchard," one of the troops said in a low voice. "There's more over here."

They slid over that way. Sure enough, another small glowing pool lay there. This one had a pink aura.

Jerriel went to suck up the energy, but one of the troops touching the water exclaimed, "It healed my hand. I had a nasty bruise and several bad cuts and scrapes from the fighting last night. Now they're gone!"

David blinked and held Jerriel back this time. He produced a plastic military canteen of water and emptied it. Then he filled it with the pink glowing liquid. Others did the same until they drained the tiny pool completely.

"Jerriel, do you think this magic water is safe to drink?"

She held her hands up and shrugged. "Maybe. I can't be sure, and we doon't have time to study it. If it is Wild Magic, who knows?"

"Well, pass the word. We'll experiment with this stuff later. Nobody drink any, for right now."

The message came back from the scouts. They'd taken out all of the sentries they could find. No alarms had sounded, so they must have done a good job of things.

"Move up," David said. "Our priorities and objective remain the same. Locate the captives and secure them first. Then we'll put down the enemy. Pass the word."

Moving in close became pretty grim. The enemy hordes fed off anything that was meat. Nasty bone piles and dung piles seemed to be everywhere, along with old fire pits. The monsters ate people and left the bony hands, feet, and heads.

David saw the remains of a dead little blonde girl, about four or five years old and wished he hadn't. Her hair was still in doggie ears.

The look of terror and pain on her poor, dead little face, staring up in the rain, shocked and tormented him.

The image of that little kid, eaten down to the bone, burned into his mind like a dark curse. He never wanted to see anything like that again. But he and the militia saw plenty of victims, just like that all the way in.

First it shocked and sickened them—then those feelings turned to rage. They couldn't take the enemy down hard enough, or fast enough.

David gripped his crossbow hard and sighed quietly, trying to control his fury. Even Jerriel sensed his distress and clutched his arm briefly. He shook his head in disgust.

He probably didn't need to, but he passed the word anyway. The troops looked as grim and angry as he was.

189

"No quarter once we attack. Kill every damn one of these bastards! I want them all cut down."

Every trooper around him looked just as pissed off and filled with wrath as he was. Many wept openly; some had quietly vomited.

The monster camp looked even worse up close–if that could be imagined. It stank like shit and death, even in the rain.

That included several hundred wet, shivering Urth people, penned up and picketed out in the open, with dozens of monster guards armed with spears, bows, and makeshift weapons surrounding them. The humans huddled together in the cold rain, trying to protect the children.

There were a lot of children. The enemy seemed to prefer them.

It made sense in, sick way. As prey, children would be weaker and less able to resist or escape than adults.

And from a monster standpoint, their meat would also be more tender.

David saw all that he needed to see. Half-eaten, half-stripped bodies of all ages hung roasting over several sheltered fire pits.

Some of them were still partially alive.

Slow cooking humans. The smell was awful, like burning hair, blood, and roasting hog mixed with urine and dung. No one would ever forget that night.

Just before David signaled the attack, their wave of silent, enchanted scouts swept over the guards and captured a big section of the pens. Then the shouting began.

"Attack!" David yelled. "Kill every monster. Save the captives!"

Militia shot the enemy in their sleep.

They drilled arrows and bolts through them as the foe started to rise.

They shot them down when they scattered and ran.

After three devastating volleys, the remaining foes tried to regroup and push toward the rear to break out.

That was not going to happen.

David already had his crossbow secured behind him. His longsword and tomahawk came out. He was out for blood, and charged into the camp with his forces shouting on either side.

An enormous, armored gozog, ten feet tall, emerged out of an earthen cave in the hillside. He wielded a gigantic warhammer in one hand and munched on a baby still in diapers. The little white feet slipped down his gullet. His eyes gleamed red with hate.

He smiled a broad, toothy grin and flatted several troopers with a sweep of his massive hammer.

Jerriel rose up in the air. Her staff glowed red, the symbols along its length pulsing and shifting. She swung her staff forward with both hands and unleashed a blast of red flame with a cry of strange words.

A whirlwind of fire engulfed the big gozog and his mor-kahl guards. Then the whirlwind exploded in a vortex of blasting flame.

Even David pulled back and shielded his face from the heat.

But as the tempest of flame cleared, a big stone half the size of a person shot out, grazed Jerriel's head, and knocked her out of the air.

She toppled back into the darkness behind them.

"Jerriel!" David cried.

28

The first bounty hunters tracked Mason down in Mishawaka after the initial militia debriefing there. That only took five hours.

Transcripts of the data would be rushed to South Bend.

The enemy mage was still bedridden. He'd cracked his head when he dropped and had a concussion—as well as some nasty burns. It could be days before he might be up for questioning.

Mason was in the process of walking across a street find a place for him and his friends to eat, two blocks over from a militia base set up at the Post Office. That was no easy task. Food was scarce, and as it turned out, Thulls apparently ate quite a bit—a lot, as it turned out.

Several places had been contracted to provide feeding stations for the militia. Mason carried a writ from a Mishawaka general allowing them to get food and drink anywhere in town. But the nearest food stations all made and kept their own hours. And the debriefing had gone on for hours.

Thulkara and Blondie were busy getting feed for the horses.

They had even found and accepted the gift of a huge, hulking draft horse for Thulkara to ride, from the captured enemy horses, and located the biggest saddle they could find for her to use. It was a saddle that had been custom made for a big football player a long time ago, and it wouldn't fit any other normal human being that Mason had ever heard of.

The giant draft horse was an enormous, ill-tempered brute named Goliath, and made all of their horses look like petting zoo ponies by comparison. But at least now, Thulkara could ride with them.

Of course, she immediately fell in love with the great beast. But she really didn't care either way if she rode or not, and openly boasted that she could outrun most horses over the course of a day.

Mason and Blondie took her at her word.

Mason was quite surprised by bounty hunters suddenly appearing on the streets of the Princess City of Mishawaka.

Eight thugs with loaded crossbows suddenly stepped out of the shadows and doorways and surrounded Mason on the street. They had him from every direction on the compass and then some.

"You there, Pistolero," the gruff leader of the band said, two loaded crossbow pistols aimed right at Mason's gut. "Don't move."

Mason cocked his head. "Yeah?"

"We have business with you, mister."

Mason cleared his throat and spat on the ground to his left, sizing them up. Half of them were scared. Two of them eager, including the leader. And the other two looked a little nuts. "And what would that be?" he asked calmly.

The leader sighed and shifted his weight. "A citizen's committee in South Bend sent us after your murdering ass. You're wanted back there to face a tribunal. They appointed us to bring you in. You're coming with us, one way or another, to face justice for the people you've killed."

That made nine crossbow bolts to dodge, what with the two pistols.

Quite a feat to pull off. Not good, the way they had him at close range.

"You're vigilantes. You're not the law. Jump straight to hell and burn there."

But most people with crossbows didn't shoot from the hip.

They took time to lift their crossbows and take aim.

That might give him enough time. Maybe...

"There is no law," the leader said. "We've been paid to bring you in—alive if we can. Throw your hardware on the ground and we'll tie you up."

Take out the eager and crazy, first.

Then maybe the scared ones might run, freeze, or slip up.

"Like hell you will," Mason told them. "So, you've been paid. That makes you dicks bounty hunters. But no one's putting a rope around my neck ever again. So you and your precious citizen's committee that paid you can suck ass."

"I'm giving you to the count of three, Pistolero. Then we kill you right here where you stand. One–"

"Three!" Mason yelled.

At the same time he drew, spinning and turning.

He shot the leader right through his gaping mouth and out the back of his head.

He shot the other eager in the throat, almost taking off his head, and continued to whip around.

The two crazies–he shot the one on the left through the right eye, and the one on the right through the left eye.

He wheeled again. Crossbow bolts flew thick through the air by then.

Three stuck in his duster but did not hit flesh.

Mason put his back to the dead even as they dropped, and faced down the other four.

Two panicked and ran, tossing their crossbows away; one of them hadn't even fired. The other two struggled to reload.

"Just stop it," Mason said. He shot one of the crossbows and shattered it. The other guy still lifted.

Mason shot him in the right arm, nearly taking it off. "Dumbass, get the hell away from me and live. Get out of my sight. Stay, and I will kill you, sure as Death Himself."

All of them were running after that. Mason shouted after them, "Tell those cowards not to send any more bounty hunters my way. I have no desire to waste my time killing fools. What, we don't have enough enemies surrounding us?"

They had his blood up by then. Mason remained tired and hungry, and now he was royally pissed off, by asinine dillholes trying to murder him.

Thulkara and Blondie came running down the street.

"It's all over," he told them. "Get this. Now I hear someone has a price on my head."

Blondie nodded. "In a barter system? What, you're worth a pen full of chickens...or maybe a pig...or perhaps, a cow?"

Mason snorted. "Yeah, laugh it up, Blondie."

"*Mooo*...Hey, hold still, Mace. I can add those crossbow bolts stuck in your coat to my lot."

He went around to pluck them out.

Mason sighed. "Help yourself, Blondie. Sheesh."

They left the dead bounty hunters where they lay. The local militia could take care of them, when they got around to it.

A crow cawed somewhere nearby. Thulkara laughed once more and studied the sky. "I think our dark uncles follow hard upon our road. The skies are troubled, my friends. Mark my words—there shall be more blood this night."

Blondie groaned, muttering something about more useless, superstitious crap.

Yet, the next enemy attack did come later that night, when they had almost ridden out of Mishawaka, and returned to South Bend.

The troubled sky spat rain.

Things did not begin well, and turned worse from there.

First, a large host of monsters attacked, sweeping over the unsuspecting Mishawaka defensive lines. Most of the Mishawaka defenders had yet to be hit that hard, and they weren't up to the test. Not yet, at least. It took a while to get used to.

Mason and his friends were close by and rode up to help seal the breach. Lightning flashed and thunder rumbled in the distance.

For more than an hour, they fought a pitched battle as it rained harder and harder.

Mason acted as the artillery, blazing away into the monster ranks as they surged forward just as they always did.

No. That wasn't right. Something was wrong. Even the monsters in South Bend didn't fight this way anymore.

They weren't that dumb.

Something was wrong; this was far too easy.

Then they heard a whooshing sound in the air from a distance.

"Incoming!" Mason yelled." He dragged himself and Blondie under a nearby picnic table.

"Archery barrage!" Thulkara yelled to the troops. "Shields and mantlets up. Pass the word. Turtle up and take cover!"

It had to be the merc archers, openly working in conjunction with the monsters for the first time.

Arrows covered the exact area where Mason and his friends had stood. The shields of the militia troops and the picnic table were all riddled with them.

Many of the remaining monsters up front were also cut down. They were obviously expendable.

The enemy was trying very hard to take down the Pistolero, and perhaps Blondie and the Thul as well.

"Shift forty yards to the right!" Thulkara shouted. "Hurry. Run for it. Put out those damn torches and lanterns!"

Less than an instant after they finished moving, two fireballs, a red lightning bolt, and some kind of magic blast hammered the area they had just occupied, leaving the ground blackened and reduced to smoking craters and ash.

"They've brought at least four mages with them," Thulkara warned. The wind picked up and the rain increased as the thunderstorms rolled in.

"Did you see where they fired that magic from?" Mason asked. He knelt down and struggled to reload in the gloom during the lull.

"You can spot a mage in the dark, by the magefire or glow on his hands before he unleashes his attack," Thulkara warned. "Watch for any strange lights and report them. Sometimes the military uses black canvas screens on poles at night. They move the screens around and shoot magic from behind them. Then they shift again, just like we did, and attack once more. Everyone keep watch in the darkness for any strange lights."

"I hate to say it," Blondie said, "but we aren't going to spot them until after they've already attacked us once more."

"We've been in one place too long, again," Thulkara warned. "Everyone, pull back forty yards from this position."

They were only halfway there when they heard the whooshing sound in the air once more.

"More arrows. Take cover."

"The monsters are bunching up to charge our lines again," someone shouted.

Spells came at them in the sky from two separate directions.

"I see spell lights," Thulkara shouted, looking over her shoulder, still on the run.

Other troops chimed in. "So did I."

"Me, too."

"Where?" Mason demanded.

Their people screamed and grunted as the last portion of their lines took casualties from the sheets of incoming arrows feathering the position they still attempted to flee from.

A trooper jumped in front of Mason, motioning with his hands and arms. "Dead ahead—make that twelve o'clock. I saw lights at the ten and one o'clock positions."

He grunted, taking a stray arrow through his left leg, and dropped down. "I'm hit!"

"Mace," Thulkara shouted. "I don't know what that fellow meant, but cast your magic on either side of the positions he noted. Most likely, the enemy is in motion after each attack, just as we are. They will go left or right, forward or back, and they can only move about as far as we can."

Mason gauged the ranges and fired rapidly to either side of the noted positions. His blasts struck several spots. They heard screaming from one area.

"Shift again, troops," Thulkara ordered. "Forty yards left and forward."

They were already moving.

More spells pulverized the area around them.

Several troops were engulfed in an exploding, magical fireball and reduced to charred skeletons, with their screaming skulls frozen open in death.

"Only three spells that time," Thulkara said. "We must have taken one of their mages down. Good work!"

"Three and eleven o'clock," spotters shouted.

Mason cut loose on those areas.

To make things even worse, the heavy thunderstorms continued to rage right over the battle.

Mason did his best to blast the areas the enemy spells came from, as they played their game of cat and mouse.

The enemy wizards seemed very close now.

"The enemy's charging in on us!" Thulkara shouted.

The next two enemy spells came from only twenty feet away.

But now the foe seemed down to only two mages.

The earth both exploded and rolled up on their left, flinging a score of militia back and injuring them.

Black bolts of energy pierced several troops in front of them, and those people shrieked as their bodies began to boil and dissolve.

Mason had seen that spell at work before—from a necromancer.

He dove to one side, blazing away all in front of him to the right, now that the path was clear.

One of those enemy black bolts hit Thulkara's shield, but her shield either absorbed or negated it. She yelled a Thul war cry and swung her battle-ax down at a big merc.

Mason had never seen a person split cleanly in two like a chunk of firewood.

But the two enemy mages charged in with forces swarming all around them.

Blondie rose up from reloading his crossbow and shot the mage on the left in the right lung, cutting him down. A dying monster collapsed on top of Blondie, knocking him over.

Mason and the necromancer on the right unleashed hell at each other right at the exact same time.

The guy was fast—just as fast as Mason.

A burning dark cloud of writhing black and red vapors shot out toward Mason, enveloped by an exploding, diamond-laced round from his pistol.

The resulting blast canceled out both effects in an instant. They imploded and vanished, harming no one. Both combatants staggered back.

Mason realized at that moment that it was possible for him to directly shoot down enemy spells and magical attacks. If he could spot them quickly enough after they went off, before they struck.

The necromancer in the iron mask lifted his black-gloved hands, both of which became encased in dark flame.

Mason shot off the left and the right side of the necromancer's skull mask, leaving the rest looking like a bloody, chewed-off apple core.

The corpse dropped back and flopped on the ground, spraying blood.

Then the dead body consumed itself and imploded as they watched.

Another third enemy mage rose up on their right and nailed both Thulkara and Mason in the back with some kind of red lightning that transfixed them and quickly drained their strength.

Mason was helpless. Thulkara moved at half-speed, resisting the effects.

The mercs rushed forward to either kill or seize them both.

The white-blue lightning from the sky suddenly thundered down like a net, roasting several foes where they stood.

Blondie rose up, both hands glowing with white fire.

He called the lightning down to himself and fashioned it into first a veil, and then a wall.

He walked that wall back into the enemy under his direct command.

Everything living that the lightning wall touched exploded in blasts of light, fury, and death. The enemy mage tried to counter it, and screamed. He vanished in a bloody detonation.

With their mages taken out and the rest of them facing such horrific destruction, the enemy ranks broke and fled in terror.

Blondie pitched forward onto his hands and knees, spent and catching his breath.

The enemy had failed to take down the Pistolero and his friends, thanks once again to Blondie...or was he back to being his old self Shaeddor by now?

No one knew that. Not even Mason. He wonder if Blondie knew.

Thulkara spat on the necromancer's shriveling remains. "Those bastards never go to hell easy," she said.

It was all they could do to keep Thulkara from finishing off the enemy sorcerer with the lung shot. She wanted his head very badly.

Mason and Blondie wanted the guy alive—another enemy mage for questioning—once they could get him healed up enough.

Thulkara saluted Blondie once more with her gory ax, looking at him with new respect and even a little worry.

So did Mason.

"Good work, Sylurrian," Thulkara told him. "You continue to regain more of your powers. That is well. You are a mighty ally."

Blondie stared at his hands, looking both pleased and still slightly confused. He shrugged and rubbed one temple. "Indeed, I keep recalling more and more of myself and my past...all the while."

29

"Someone check on her and keep Jerriel safe," David yelled. "The rest, in with me!"

The big gozog shielded the remnants of his guard within a shimmering half globe of blue-green energy. Its light faded as the flames went down.

The leader wore gold and lapis gauntlets. They glowed with runes just as Jerriel's staff had done.

The enemy also wielded magic. It had somehow shielded them from Jerriel's attack. It also deflected arrows and crossbow bolts.

David's militia troops fell upon the enemy bodyguards hand-to-hand.

He squared off with the big leader—the one that had injured Jerriel. "You're mine, jerkweed!"

The big gozog swung his great hammer swiftly and with skill. This creature knew how to fight, and use magic.

David ducked under a hammer stroke and sprang to one side. The hammer slammed into the ground where he had stood not an instant before.

He slashed his longsword deep into the gozog's massive forearm above the gauntlets. The leader roared in pain and booted him aside with the sweep of one iron-shod foot, as big as David's chest.

David flew back as if hit by a charging rhino, and landed among his troops. They caught him. An arrowhead nicked his right arm through his armor.

Nothing felt broken. He just had the wind knocked out of him.

The leader flattened and swept troops away to the left side, killing many with that huge hammer. Behind their unstoppable leader, it looked as if the monsters might break out toward the northwest.

David staggered forward with his troops and caught his breath. Then he rushed the leader again.

He avoided the swooshing hammer and slipped behind the leader. With a diving, two-handed stroke, he cut through the back of the leader's right leg. Black blood sprayed everywhere.

The leader staggered and went down on his injured leg, spinning around, killing more troops with that accursed hammer. David charged into the opening and rammed his longsword into the big gozog's neck. A sweep from a massive backfist clipped his helmet.

David chopped at the huge arm with his tomahawk, sinking it into the bicep like hitting a tree trunk. The weapon jerked from his hand.

He pulled out his other tomahawk and cast it into the face of the leader, burying it in the left eye. Then he drew his katana and wakizashi.

The leader turned at bay, his vision damaged, smashing anything nearby. David cut, sliced, stabbed, and dodged.

The gozog suddenly fell forward toward David, attempting to flatten him, like a hill of stinking flesh.

David sprang back and thrust his swords into to the leader's right eye up to the hilts and out the back of the head.

The big gozog finally convulsed and sagged forward, dropping its deadly hammer out of its twitching hands.

David yanked his swords free and sprang back.

He surveyed the battle. Pockets of fighting remained, but his troops had the area secured. Very few of the captives had been injured or killed. Good.

But from the looks of them, many would prove too weak from terror and exposure to walk back to safety under their own power. They would need to be carried or trucked out.

Other militia officers could order carts in and see to that. At that moment, David could only think of Jerriel.

He asked the troops around him. "Where is she? How's she doing? Where did they take her?"

"Who?"

"Who in the hell are you talking about, man?"

"Jerriel. The wizard girl."

"Oh, man. I heard she got flattened by a ginormous rock from one of those giant things. I think she's a goner."

It couldn't be.

He couldn't lose her that quickly. It felt as if someone had sucked David's heart out of his chest through his mouth. He staggered back, dropped his weapons, and sat down.

Another trooper shoved the first guy out of the way. "Shut up, you loser. You don't know anything, dude. Don't say shit like that unless you're sure. She's not dead, sir. The wizard girl. She just got knocked out."

David rose to his feet, wiped off his bloody swords and sheathed them. He still had hope.

"Where is she?"

"Man, I don't know, what with the battle and all. I think they dragged the wounded back over there by that stand of evergreen trees. Where those tents are going up."

"It's true," someone else said. "There's a field hospital set up over that way. Get all the injured and wounded over there for processing, if they need help."

"Thanks," David said. He quickly headed in that direction.

"Hey, isn't that Captain Pritchard?" the last trooper said.

"Dunno, man. What's the captain look like?"

"Like that guy, you goof!"

The field hospital. Organized chaos in the dark and in the pouring rain. Dozens of injured and wounded people lying under blankets, tarps, and ponchos. Medics propped them up against rocks and trees. Another cave had been found. Lanterns were set up within and there were makeshift tables and raised cots to operate on. Any available medical personnel–doctors, nurses, Army medics, EMTs and such–scurried around doing yeoman's service for the militia and the captives.

A battlefield triage situation evolved, where they stabilized the most severely injured, if possible. Or, in the worst cases, they simply made the injured comfortable until they slipped away. The main attention was focused on sorting out those who could still be saved.

If this small battle produced this much chaos, David could only imagine what the main battle the night before had caused all over town. He suddenly had a newly enriched respect for their medical teams.

He caught the attention of a medic who just finished sewing up a leg wound and bandaged it.

"I'm Captain David Pritchard. Jerriel. The wizard girl. Where is she and how is she doing?"

The medic swallowed hard. "She got hit in the head pretty bad, sir. Concussion. They stabilized her as best they could. I think she's under a blanket in one of the tarp shelters back that way." He angled his head. David took off in that direction. The sounds of the final fighting died down.

Like the medic said, he found her under one of the tarp shelters, pale and unconscious in the cold. Her pale face looked slightly scratched and bruised.

A young woman sat with her. Jerriel's staff lay at her side, barely pulsing with a faint glow. David knelt down and put his hands to her face. She felt so cold. The young trooper woman, about their age, sat back in the damp weeds and hugged her knees to her chest. She wore a blue-striped lacrosse helmet with a dented face mask. Brown hair peeked out above a black wool coat and ski gloves. A medical bag hung on her shoulder. An aluminum baseball bat lay next to her. A hatchet and a hunting knife were on her canteen belt.

"They put her here about ten minutes ago and assigned me to watch over her. I'm Stacy, Stacy Keller. I was in my third year of nursing training before all of this happened."

"I'm David Pritchard. How is she?" He felt Jerriel's pulse at the neck. That was weak, too.

"You're the captain. The one she works with?"

"Uh-huh. What are her injuries?"

"Concussion, mostly. They're not sure how bad. She drifted in and out for a while, in a lot of pain. They said she kept trying to get up and was calling for you. We tried to keep her awake, but she passed out. I'm sorry to tell you this, but that's not a very good sign."

David bowed his head.

"If only I could speak with her," he said. She could die now and he would never get to say another word to her. Every thought like that ripped into his guts.

"Tell me the truth, Stacy. Do you think she'll make it?"

"I don't think anyone knows. If there's an edema and her brain swells too much, that could kill her. They'll get her over to one of the hospitals, once the carts get here. But all of those places are still stuffed with wounded people from last night." Stacy wiped her nose.

Stacy tried to change the subject. "At least we rescued the captives. I sure wouldn't have wanted to go through what all those poor people did." Stacy shuddered. "Ugh, never knowing who would be tormented and eaten next? It gives me the creeps just thinking about it."

"Yeah, I guess that's something good." Inside he felt like a total jerk. The darkest part of his soul would have given up all of those hundreds of lives at that moment, just to have Jerriel back with him, whole and healthy again.

He thought about that once more. No, he couldn't have done that.

He could not have sacrificed the lives of so many innocent people–not even to save the girl he loved.

He stroked her white, pretty face with his cold, shaking hands again. "I love you, Jerriel. Please, hang in there. You can make it."

"What is that horrible smell?" Stacy suddenly said. "At first I thought it was the monsters, but I swear, it's getting worse."

"Who can tell, around here with all these stinking things?" David said. But Stacy was right. The entire area smelled even worse now after the battle. Their enemies quickly festered and rotted–could that be causing the stench?

David took a deep breath and almost choked. "You're right. It is far worse all of the sudden. Like rotten eggs, sulfur, and dead skunks." People all around them choked and rubbed their eyes, the air stung so bad.

The bushes and smaller trees parted. Something dark and massive pushed through like a big truck pulling right up to them. Stacy screamed and jumped to her feet, forgetting about her bat.

David drew his swords and placed himself directly between Jerriel and whatever it was.

"Stay back!" David shouted. "Come no closer!"

Deep rumbling laughter erupted from the thing and shook the entire area.

Intense heat wafted out from it as if a blast furnace had opened up right before him.

Two large eyes, glowing with green energy like huge searchlights, winked open from narrow slits.

An equally intense voice boomed into his mind, almost causing his head to split and his ears to bleed.

So brave, little warrior. How very amusing. And what action do you presume to take if I do come closer?

The head of an enormous green dragon stared directly at David, its long, thick neck rippling with muscle and sinew beneath the thick scales. A wreath of massive horns and spikes, steaming hot, protected that head. A huge, glowing maw sliced open between the cavernous jaws, armed with razor-sharp teeth as long as David's arm. That maw was the source of the furnace-like heat. The green dragon's head alone looked as big as a semitruck.

He glared at the great beast, gripping his swords in defiance.

Jerriel lay helpless behind him.

David stood his ground and would not budge.

30

Mason was dreaming again, but this time it was a pretty great dream.

Tori came into the room where he was sleeping and started taking off her clothes as she slowly approached his bed.

Gosh, she was pretty.

Mason loved her. Wanted to marry her. Have babies with her. Grow old together after about a hundred years of loving her, and die in her arms. That was the life he really wanted.

Then the dream shifted. Damn it.

It wasn't Tori at all. It was some other young woman, and she was definitely taking off her clothes as she approached his bed.

But she wasn't Tori, and thus, she was nothing to him. He almost cried out in heartbroken pain. His heart and his initial desire went cold and felt as if it sank through him like a block of ice.

Mason rubbed his tired eyes and looked over at Blondie, snoozing peacefully under the starlight coming in through the windows.

Was he dreaming all of this?

Yet, as the naked young woman drew closer, a strange light grew in her eyes—almost a weird glow.

Mason lifted both hands. "Miss, I don't know who sent you, but I'm not—"

Before his eyes, the beautiful young woman transformed into one of those big, hideous monsters.

Oh, hell—screw that.

Mason reached for his guns.

The monster backhanded him with a long, hairy, hulking arm and claw. It swatted him clear out of the bed and knocked him across the room. He smashed into the buckling wall.

Mason found himself dazed, in pain, and far from his weapons. He struggled to his feet.

The monster rushed forward, flipping the empty bed out of the way and knocking a very startled Blondie and his bed over and smashing him against the other wall.

It ripped a huge rent in the wall where Mason had stood.

He tried to slip between the big monster's legs, but it caught him by the lower legs and slammed him up into the ceiling, cracking the drywall and winding Mason.

The monster clutched and grappled at him with its other clawed hand. Mason struggled to fight back or escape, gasping for breath. It finally held him upright in one hand and looked as if it was about to rip off his head with the other.

With the last of his strength, Mason reared up and booted the monster in the face.

That just pissed it off. Now it really wanted to tear him apart.

Then the creature squealed in pain.

Red lines of energy crisscrossed through its entire body, transfixing it in agony.

Monster blood sprayed everywhere.

The thing just fell apart, tumbling into a heap of foul-smelling chunks of stinking meat.

Blondie stood across the room, his hands glowing bright red this time, but quickly fading.

Both he and Mason caught their breath.

"Someone is seriously trying to make you dead," Blondie told him.

Mason grunted and stood up. "Looks like a line is forming to me. Thanks again, my friend."

Blondie rubbed his hands. "Maybe I'll keep remembering things faster if everyone keeps trying to kill you, Mace."

"To hell with that. But some of your powers do seem to be returning quite nicely. I don't see you casting spells, so you must be a sorcerer–and a pretty good one, I'd say."

Blondie nodded, flexing his fingers. "Must be."

"Anything else come back to you, besides your name and some of your abilities?" Mason asked.

"Nope."

"What if you wake up one day, and remember that you both were and still are on their side?" Mason asked.

Blondie sighed with a frown. "I'm kinda worried about that, too."

"Now that you know your real name...do you want us to call you by it?"

His friend thought for a moment, and then shook his head. "Not for now. Mace, to tell you the truth, I like being Blondie. I still don't know who this Shaeddor fellow was. But I'm starting to get the feeling that he might not have been a very nice guy. No one says I have to go back to that."

Mason clapped him on the back. "They sure don't. Come on then, Blondie. Let's fetch the guards. I'm not sleeping in this stinking room now. Sheesh, look at the mess you made."

His friend looked around at everything with a wicked grin. "Yep."

The next morning they went with a full company of troops back to South Bend.

Then, along the way, Mason and his friends dodged arrows and crossbow bolts that came at them out from of the trees. Three militia troops were wounded in the crossfire.

Mason sent two pistol blasts sweeping into the trees.

As it turned out, it wasn't the enemy mercs or mages this time.

More dumbass bounty hunters, attempting a quick kill. Good thing they were such lousy shots. Damn amateurs.

Their militia captain–Captain Avery–ordered the surviving bounty hunters that they had captured immediately hanged, under the authority of martial law and summary justice.

"This madness has to stop," Avery told them. "The generals have posted articles in the old-style papers, and they are going to post notices throughout Michiana, explaining that you are–and always have been–operating under the direct authority of the militia. Just as you have always done. They want these insane attempts on your life to cease. The Pistolero is vital to the Michiana defense effort. These bounties are illegal and will be dealt with in the harshest manner. Mace, we need you desperately, back at the front. Many lives depend on it."

Mason rubbed his neck absently. "Captain, I'm not so sure I want to go back now. Maybe I'll decide to stay over in Mishawaka for a while and help out here. A lot of my own people seem to have the wrong idea about me–like I'm some kind of mad killer or rabid animal. These people are serious, and they want me dead–war or no war. Why in the hell would I want to go back to all of that?"

He remembered the way it had been when he left.

A lot of people still hated him and cursed his name.

They stopped right there, on the border between Mishawaka and South Bend. Mason had a great deal to think about and consider. And he was pretty angry.

He could also become very stubborn and unreasonable when he was angry.

Militia officers came before him and begged him to return to the front lines. "The monsters are regrouping in great hordes. By all reports, these bloody mercenaries are also maneuvering in large numbers and even bringing siege weapons against us. We don't know how many of those mages they have to throw against us or what their powers are. The main battles are going to be in South Bend, where the defenses are weakest–not in Mishawaka. A lot of people are going to die if the Pistolero doesn't help us make our stand there."

Mason shot back at them, "I'm fed up, I tell you! Everywhere I go, people try to kill me. Not just the enemy, damn it–my own people want me dead!"

"We're trying to put a stop to that."

Mason was tired of all of this crap. "Well then, let me know when you do."

Finally the powers that be sent officer Tim Reinert, his wife, Helen, and their surviving son, Denny, and a group of other civilians to talk to him and attempt to change his mind, later that same day.

"Hey, Mason. Blondie," Tim said.

Everyone present blinked and were amazed to meet Thulkara for the first time. She made a big impression on everyone wherever she went.

Too bad they didn't have a thousand more like her.

"Hey, Tim," Mason finally said. He nodded to Helen and Denny. "You guys doing okay?"

Helen forced a smile. "We're getting by. We have a place now. Tim's wounds are nearly healed. He'll be going back to the front, soon." Helen looked down when she said the last part.

"Mason," Tim said, "I know you've had it rough, and things haven't been fair to you. But all of us have come to beg you to put all that behind you. We need you in the fight to come. We can't hold South Bend. There aren't enough of us left. Too many have fled. Too many have died or been hurt. We could barely hold the monsters off as it was. And now these mercenaries and wizards are on the move to come against us."

Mason didn't say a word.

Tim took a breath. He was nervous and shaking. "Our skirmishers came up against some of those mercs and fared badly. They're all professional soldiers, experts at fighting and killing. We're not. We're just people trying to defend our homes. We can't get up to speed fast enough."

"The authorities have formed everyone else into a second line of defense," Helen said. "That includes me, and Denny, too. Anyone forty-six to sixty, the remaining younger women, and kids ten to seventeen. When the militia goes down—*we* become the front line with whatever weapons we can scrounge. Denny and I will be facing those monsters and those trained killers with all of the old men, the rest of the women, and the kids. By then, Tim and most of the younger men and women will already have been killed off."

Denny came forward and looked back at Mason fiercely, with the burning hatred of a child. "I wanna kill some of them. I don't care what they do to me. I wanna kill just a couple of them—for what they did to Tommy and Mr. Howard."

Helen gasped and pulled her young son back, and burst into tears. "Be quiet, Denny. You don't know what you're talking about."

Three hundred people got down on their knees, pleading and begging for the Pistolero to come help them. To fight for them. To fight beside them.

Mason looked down and didn't know what to say.

He just wasn't that great of a human being.

He raised one hand and looked up at them all.

They waited, silent and pleading, to hear what he might say.

"I'll be there," Mason quietly said. "I'll come and do all that I can."

Tim and Helen rose up and hugged him.

Within the hour, they were marching again, together.

Blondie rode up next to him, skimming one of the new papers from the antique printing presses the towns were using. "Mace, check this out. We're not the only game in town anymore."

"What do you mean?"

"The militia came across two young women with strange powers all their own. They don't have guns like yours, but their story is similar in many ways. When the Merge hit, both of them got dumped into a magic lake of glowing water, similar to the one you—"

Mason's ear perked up at that. "What can they do?" he asked. "How do their powers work?"

"Well, I'll tell you, if you stop interrupting me. One of them can energize a small quantity of matter, like a stone or an arrowhead. But she can't control it, and usually it explodes or burns up in an instant. Not much use on its own. But the other girl can control and direct that energy, once it is formed, long enough for her shoot it at something–and with a variety of effects."

Mason rubbed his lips. "That sounds pretty amazing. Both of them were exposed to the energy at the same time, and now their abilities work with each other, sort of in tandem."

Blondie nodded. "When the militia found them, they were defending themselves by throwing energized rocks or shooting them at the enemy with a slingshot they found. Since then, the militia has taught them archery, and the two of them are using arrows to deliver their powers. They can blow things up, set them on fire, create a cloud of smoke that makes people choke, zap an area with lightning, or even freeze everything solid within a fifteen-foot radius. Sounds impressive to me."

Mason blinked. "Me, too. I'm glad they're on our side. How do you think it all works?" He waited for Blondie's answer. At times Blondie seemed to know more than he should. He seemed extremely knowledgeable about magic and stuff like that. Stuff just came to him out of the blue when he rambled on.

Blondie paused and thought about something for a moment. "The one girl could be a sorceress, but I'm guessing she's a conjurer. She can summon magical energy in various forms, but she hasn't learned the ability to direct or do much with it. The other girl is no doubt an enchantress, who has the power to control, manipulate, and direct any kind of magical energy once it is made available. The first girl summons the energy, and the second girl makes better practical use of it–a magical symbiotic relationship."

Again, Blondie seemed to know too much about such things.

Mason began to worry more and more about what was going to happen when his friend remembered what side he had been on, before the power of the Merge robbed him of his memories.

What if Blondie's old loyalties returned?

"I hope we get to meet them," Mason said.

Blondie nodded. "I would like to study their abilities as well."

Thulkara suddenly snorted indignantly next to them. "You mages can sure be a pain in the ass sometimes. But I have to admit, it's good to have you there in a fight–especially against other mages."

"What about me?" Mason asked. "Have you observed and studied my abilities, Blondie? What's the ruling there?"

Blondie smiled, and something about that smile always made Mason a little uncomfortable. "I've watched your powers quite extensively, in fact, Mace. From my observations, you're incredibly formidable, really. An extremely unique case."

"What am I, then?"

"Clearly you are a sorcerer, gifted with a very deep source of Wild Magic that is part of you now, whatever your were before. And you have an extremely unique focus for all of that power—your guns. As I said, quite a fascinating case, really. And you keep changing the game with all of your experiments and alchemical, magical tinkering. I even saw you negate the magic of another mage—a feat I did not even think possible. Who knows what you'll be able to do with it all?"

"Yes, who knows?" Mason muttered.

Captain Avery joined up with them. He appeared frustrated. "We've questioned dozens of the captured mercenaries. Most of them will only give us their damn numbers and say only that they fight under contract for pay. The few who do talk, won't shut up unless we gag them after they spew out nothing but tall tales and lies. All useless."

They rode quietly for a long while. Everyone kept to their thoughts.

Avery broke the silence.

"The militia and I are thinking about giving you and yours a command, Mace."

"Not this again. Bill, please don't," Mason said.

"Why not? You deserve it. I'll have you made a captain, equal with me. Blondie and Thulkara will make fine lieutenants."

Mason shook his head again. "I refuse, and so do they. None of us do all of this for rank or selfish gain."

"Then what the hell do you do it all for, Mace?"

"Because we must, Bill. Because we have to. Do you think I want to be doing this? Hell no. I'd rather be searching for Tori. But I can't do that. None of us can do much of anything until this stupid war ends and these idiots are all defeated!"

"Then why not take a command?"

Mason looked him in the eye. "Bill, I am a lot of things, but I am not a leader. I'm not even a soldier, not even much of a follower. I'm a killer. I'm a weapon. Tell me where to go and I'll go there. Tell me what to do, and I'll do it—just barely."

"You're too hard on yourself, Mace. You're better than that."

"No. I'm not. I don't want power over others. I don't deserve it. I know very well what it would turn me into, and it wouldn't take very much, or very long for it to happen. You command us all, Bill. You've got a good heart, despite being a mean-spirited bastard. Tell us where to go and what to do. You're a great soldier."

Mason sucked in a deep breath. "Just leave the shooting to me."

31

David squared off with the dragon and readied his blades. The enormous beast smelled horrible. The stench was quite choking—overpowering. "You will not harm her. You will not touch her."

The deep laughter rumbled again. Its huge green eyes glowed with amusement.

The powerful voice ripped into his mind once more. *Humans stink, too, my lad—and there are many more of your kind than of my mine.*

"Get out of my head!" he shouted. But instead of malice, he sensed great curiosity on the part of the dragon. And continual hunger.

You are not disciplined enough to keep me out of your mind, are you? This is the only way that I can converse with you, little warrior. Dragons speak the pure language of thought. Thus we speak the language of all sentient beings in the limitless dimensions and all the innumerable worlds.

"Your thoughts are too powerful," David said, gritting his teeth. "They hurt. Your thoughts hurt my mind, my brain." The pressure was intense, like someone squeezing his head in a vice.

Ah, and here I thought I was being gentle. Apologies. I suppose the flesh can only endure so much. You and this world Urth of yours seem very ignorant and unskilled. The dragon sighed.

Picture an invisible barrier around your mind, your head, and then concentrate on focusing the barrier between our thoughts. Then it will be easier for us to converse.

David struggled to do so. It wasn't easy.

Pitiful. You have plenty of will, but no experience focusing it to your purpose. I do not have all night.

Ugh. David clenched his fists.

A barrier—like one of clear steel.

The force of the dragon's mind slacked off. The pain lessened greatly. David gasped in sudden relief.

"Thanks." At least he no longer felt immersed in an invisible wall of liquid force, threatening to crush him like an egg.

The dragon yawned. *Better?*

"Yes. Much. Thank you once again."

You are most welcome. You will find that courtesy can go a long way with dragonkind. Of course, it will not prevent them from devouring you, if they are so inclined, but it will make the interaction, however brief, that much more enjoyable. I would also advise you that dragons do not at all take kindly to commands or threats.

"Does anyone?"

I suppose not.

So dragons got off on courtesy and manners. Who knew?

But I should warn you—if several of your fellows assail me, from the way they are creeping up and planning to do—I will be forced to lay waste to this entire area. And that will most likely include you and your pretty little mate.

David spotted Pete Steiner with the troops and hurried to shout out. "Pete, all of you. This is a direct order from Captain David Pritchard. Do not attack this dragon. I repeat. Do not attack this dragon. Dragons are telepathic. I am negotiating with him and he won't harm us if we don't attack him. We do not want him to attack us."

Well...I didn't exactly say that, did I? That I wouldn't attack you? But I suppose it's all good enough. They've pulled back and lowered their weapons. Thank you, most kindly.

"You're most kindly welcome."

You were, however, very correct on one very important point.

"And what was that?"

You don't want me to attack you. Which still doesn't mean that I won't.

"You've made all of that very clear. You'll have to forgive me. Fighting monsters, dealing with wizards and dragons, and creatures that use magic—I'm just not very used to it all."

And yet, overall you seem to be doing quite well. No, really quite splendidly, I would say. Except for issuing commands to a dragon...but my appearance did startle you at first, I'm sure. So for now we'll just try to overlook that failing. Don't you agree?

"Certainly. That's awfully generous and gracious of you."

Not at all. Not at all. So kind of you to notice. And so forward with your true name and all: Captain David Pritchard. Not always a wise thing you know, to give away your true name. To know a thing's true name gives some power over it, if one knows how to use such power.

"I have read and heard that before in stories. Yet I do have a middle name that I never tell anyone."

Ahh...clever, most clever. A secret name? Good, very good. Dragons do the same thing.

"You seem to have me at a disadvantage here," David said. "What may we call you, good dragon?"

The creature actually drew itself up to a dizzying height and cleared its massive throat with a few booming thumps from its vast clawed front paw.

You may call me Shavalkathar the Cataclysmic, Bane of Worlds, Slayer of Armies, Great Disaster, Source of Despair–Ruinous Beyond Measure.

"Hmm, you'll have to forgive me. I'm but a simple soldier and that's probably too much for my feeble mind to remember. But I think we could remember Shavalkathar."

Oh, very well. I suppose with your limited intellect that that will have to do.

A crowd gathered around the dragon from a distance, staring at him in wonder. Stacy finally found the courage to move and pulled away slowly. Then she reached forward and retrieved her bat. She still looked ready to bolt any second.

David remained a little at a loss himself, but the initial shock of meeting an actual dragon face-to-face was over. "So, Great Shavalkathar, to what honor do we owe this visitation?"

I have grown greatly curious over the past several days. There has been a major shifting of realities. Vast cosmic energies have been disrupted and re-shaped. Parts of this world are still Tharanor–the world I was originally on. And now parts of them have changed to something else. There are many, many changes–too numerous to note. And so I am greatly curious as to how and why these changes have occurred.

David finally lowered his blades. "It's only been a few days, and most of that time we've been fighting for our lives against these monsters. But my people and I do have a few questions concerning all of this as well."

The dragon's deep laughter rumbled again. *I imagine you do. Your world was very different. I can sense that in all of your minds. These changes come as a great shock to you all.*

Definitely an understatement.

"Our world—Urth—relied on technology and science. We did not use magic very much, or at least not the way that you and Jerriel do."

Shavalkathar snorted indignantly, and a blast of sulfurous smoke engulfed the area, causing everyone, including David, to choke.

The dragon's voice grew deadly serious. *Dragons are unique, David Pritchard. Let me inform you that it is vastly insulting to us to spread such ignorance. Dragons do not "use magic" as you put it. Dragons Are Magic. They were created from the One Source of All Power. They are wild and free and unchecked, a force of nature throughout all the universes. They do not use anything. They are as they are. They are what they are.*

David bowed. "I beg your forgiveness. As I said, my people and I are almost completely ignorant concerning both magic and dragons."

Yes, I see that now. I smelled the presence of a powerful Tharanorian wizard among you, and thought that she might be able to answer some of my questions. Too bad she is dying.

David nearly panicked. "Dying?"

Yes, I'm afraid her internal injuries are too severe. She might linger for a few more hours before she succumbs. A pity. I really wished to speak with her. There are no other mages about for many leagues, currently. There's a demon nearby, but you can never count on any real help or even a straight answer from one of those foul deceivers.

David knelt down and stroked Jerriel's face, ignoring most of what the dragon rambled on about. His hands trembled

Jerriel. Dying. And he was helpless.

"Shavalkathar, I ask you plainly: Is there any way that you know of that I can save her?"

The dragon deftly stroked his chin with a great claw. *Hmmm...that depends. Perhaps the medical skill of your people can help her—perhaps not.*

David suddenly noticed that the rain stopped once more.

There is one thing you might try, but it would be desperate. Who knows if it would even work?

David lifted his head. "Tell me. I am desperate. I will try anything that might save her life."

The dragon shook his massive head. *I see. Even if destroys you both?*

"She is dying, great dragon. What choice do I have? What would you do if it was your mate?"

Their eyes locked for a moment. The dragon nodded.

I would do all that was within my power. Very well, Captain David Pritchard. Have you seen any of the glowing pools of magical energy, or the glowing flowers?

"Yes, but we weren't sure—"

Some of them are Wild Magic. Most of them are some weird concentrated, random enchanted essence. Even I don't know what that is, but this new combined world seems to be swimming in it. They are highly charged, especially after thunderstorms.

"We found some of them. Jerriel used them to recharge her staff. We kept more to study later." He called to his troops. "Hey, get some of that pink magic liquid stuff up here."

He realized that he still had some himself, in one of his canteens.

Don't bother, David Pritchard. I can smell that stuff on you. It does possess some lesser healing properties. The Wild Magic in general was yet another very curious thing that I wished to speak with the wizard about.

"What do you mean, don't bother? Can it heal her or not? Do I pour it on her or make her drink it?"

Neither. It has no major healing properties for anything beyond that of treating topical cuts, scrapes, and bruises, I'm afraid. Now, a competent healer might be able to find a way, in a few years, to concentrate that essence to perhaps—

David closed his eyes and clenched his fists at his side. He let out a deep breath. "I do not have a healer, or a few years to figure out anything like that. If you want your long conversation with the wizard, perhaps you can tell me what would save her?"

Hmmm…I suppose that would serve my purposes as well as yours. If she survived I mean. I seem to recall drinking from a magical pool a day or two ago that did have many amazing healing properties. Was it pink? Or was it blue? Yes…it only glowed at night, and it was twilight, after all, but I'm sure now that it was bright blue.

"Great. Now if you can just recall where this pool was?"

Oh, yes, of course. I recall exactly where it was. But of course—I drank it all.

David stamped his feet. "And so how does that help us?"

Shavalkathar yawned. *I suppose not every much. But if you find another blue one like that, you could pour some of it into her or immerse her in such a pool briefly. I mean, I wouldn't drown her in it. I suppose that much intense magical energy might do something beneficial. Or perhaps not. She's a wizard, and it might affect her differently. Or, you know how fickle Wild Magic is—it might simply destroy you both…or do nothing at all.*

The dragon reared up again and spread its immense wings. Even the night grew darker. *Well, I must be going. If the wizard survives, feel free to seek me out a few days west of here for our little chat. My lair is in the mountain of bones, but you might want to beware of my neighbors in that area. They're not nearly as sociable as I am. Farewell, little warrior. We may yet meet again.*

Shavalkathar took to the air, launching himself in a tempest of wind, heat, and dragon stench.

"Thank you," was all David could muster, trying to keep his thoughts clear of any bitterness or resentment. In its way, the dragon had helped him...at least somewhat.

He turned to his troops. "Send for the mappers. In the meantime, I want every available trooper combing the area looking for glowing pools of water—especially pools that glow blue. Locate them, but don't touch them. I say again. We are especially looking for any pool that glows blue. Bring Jerriel along on a stretcher. Put her in a padded wagon if you have to."

They searched the area and fanned out west, south, and north into the forest. Messengers brought word from the mappers. They sent him the location and description of every known mysterious pool that had been reported and recorded in the area. Several of those were said to be blue.

"Another glowing pool close by, sir," one of the scouts reported "Very small. According to the reports, this one glows greenish-white, just like the other five we've come across."

David shook his head. "According to the dragon, that's not what we need. Keep looking. Mark the others on the map and keep searching."

"We've found a whole meadow full of those glowing flowers, sir. Will they do anything?"

"It's worth a try and it's on the way. Let's find out. Guys, let's take her there."

They went to the field nearby. The entire area lay blanketed in a swath of the small, glittering white flowers that illuminated the area in the darkness. They smelled fragrant and sweet.

David held Jerriel's hand as they placed her down among the glimmering flowers. Her staff next to her glowed a little brighter, but that was it.

Her life still faded. He was losing her. She looked beautiful, but she was dying inside. They ran out of time with each passing second.

Dawn would come up in about three hours.

"Sir, someone stepped in a pool of blue-violet water by accident. It flashed and sucked all the moisture out of them. They crumbled into dust. No one could help them."

David had seen that effect before. "That won't help Jerriel either. Keep looking. Watch out for these pools. Many of them are quite dangerous. We really don't know what effects they'll have."

He looked at Jerriel. "Stay with her," he told Stacy Keller. "I'm going to help the searchers."

He drew his sword and rushed through the woods with the map, cutting brush out of his way. Nothing. Everywhere he turned. Nothing. They just weren't close enough to the pools marked.

Finally he fell down in the wet grass and dropped his blades. He covered his face with hands.

He was failing her. There was just so much he didn't know. But the result was the same.

He was letting Jerriel die.

Mom, Dad, God–anyone. Please, help us–help me save her.

Stacy Keller ran up, calling out for him. "David! Captain Pritchard? Where is he?"

"I'm here. What's up?"

Other voices shouted out in the darkness. "Bring the wizard. Runners and riders have brought water samples from the blue pools. They do have healing properties, just like the dragon said. They've saved others who were dying!"

He was an idiot. Why didn't he think of that? Bring samples of all the waters to her. What a moron he was.

"Bring the stretcher. Hurry!"

Stacy helped link them up with the runners. She handed him an old, two-liter pop bottle filled with the glowing blue water. It was like a lantern.

"Here, Captain Pritchard. This is the most potent sample we know of. Give her some of this!"

David took Jerriel in his arms and held her up. Stacy undid the cap.

Slowly he poured a little of the glowing water into Jerriel's mouth, and tipped it down her throat.

After a moment Jerriel stirred a little, as if in sleep.

Was he harming her? Was it working?

David gave her more. She choked and spluttered.

Her eyes flickered open.

"What...? I feel so weak. What happened? Why am I chooking?"

David gasped quietly in joy, swallowed hard, and nearly wept. "You...were badly injured. Please, drink more of this water."

She focused on it. "But...why is it glooming blue?"

"I know. Trust me. It will heal you more."

She drank deeply.

Within minutes she could stand up and walk.

David capped the two liter and shook it. "Get as much of this stuff to field hospital and the doctors as we can!" he shouted. "Make sure they use it sparingly, on the casualties who are closest to dying, first."

"Where are the rest of the troops?" Jerriel asked.

Stacy stepped forward, her lacrosse helmet off and in her hands. She wept openly out of gladness. She could clearly tell what Jerriel meant to David. Her long brown hair flowed free in the cold morning wind. "They're still helping the captives get back to town, sir."

"We'd better join them," David said. "There's going to be a lot to do."
He left the two young women together for a short time and sent out orders to
bring everyone back in. Jerriel was safe. He felt so thankful he could have
danced a jig.

When he returned, Jerriel smiled at him and even took his arm on the
way back to town.

"I think I missed something impoortant, Daeved. Stacy tells me you
faced doown a dragon for me." Her radiant eyes twinkled, her smile beaming.
"Did you think he was gooing to eat me?

He chuckled slightly. Something similar had crossed his mind once or
twice. He couldn't blame the dragon for similar temptations.

"I did at first," David said. "But in the end, he actually told me how to
save you, in his own way."

He told her the story on their way back to town. He had a great deal to
tell her, and Dirk, and the town council. But with all of the fighting, and Dirk
getting wounded, there hadn't been enough time, yet. He was still trying to
figure out how to put it all into words and explain it himself.

Dragons, demons, his little out-of-body adventure, the dark mages
plotting against them in the shadows, magic pools. Let alone the battle this
evening to free the captives. And he still felt tired, sore, and hungry on his
own. There hadn't been time to catch up on and go over anything.

But David took comfort in one very good thing—Jerriel still lived.

32

Blondie and Mason checked on the two enemy mage prisoners. No luck. The medical people told them to go away, and check back in two days.

Meanwhile, the authorities in Mishawaka and South Bend continued to have many questions for Mason and especially his friends, and kept a small team of scribes and intellectuals following hard upon their heels, taking copious notes.

Each of the scribes—or recorders, as they called themselves—had a backpack full of numbered notebooks and pens and markers. Their job was to write down anything that might be important, and then make reports and recommendations to the city leaders based upon what they discovered.

These intellectuals had been selected from the various schools, colleges, and universities in the area. Many of them were teachers, graduate students, or younger professors

They gathered valuable knowledge and intelligence on the Merge, strange new phenomena, and events as they unfolded.

From the start, they obviously spent hours asking Thulkara about the alternate world of Tharanor, and all of its peoples, cultures, and creatures. The military was specifically interested in both the monsters and the mercenaries, how they operated and made war, and what their strengths and weaknesses were.

Any vital general knowledge was printed in the daily newspapers that the authorities used to spread information throughout the Michiana area. A handful of various manual, mechanical, antique printing presses made that possible.

Thulkara endured the incessant pestering until she couldn't take it anymore and had to get away from the recorders before she started punching people.

At times, Mason and Blondie had to shoo the recorders away from the big Amazon. They hovered around her like a cloud of gnats.

Being the only Tharanorian allied with the humans became quite a burden. Blondie didn't count yet, because he still couldn't remember much of anything.

After Mason and Blondie saw how the recorders hounded Thulkara, Mason had the impression that Blondie was actually somewhat thankful for his amnesia in that regard.

Over the next three days, as tensions concerning the coming war mounted, information exploded about the Merge and the other world of Tharanor.

Mason and his people were kept near the front lines.

For the first time, experts in physics, cosmology, philosophy, and other disciplines weighed in how they thought the Merge had taken place and what the overall effects were.

The general conclusion was that the Merge had occurred worldwide and most likely affected everything in both dimensions. All of humanity was most likely dealing with all of the problems and effects on a planetary scale. And in many cities, Urth people were now thrown together with Tharanorians from different lands and nations.

On their side of the dimensional reality—their half of what was now being called Urth—the planet was mixed up with what was guessed to be an equal half of the alternate, sister world of Tharanor.

Even more intriguing, it was surmised that the half of Urth that was now missing, was most likely another parallel dimension to theirs, equally mixed up with the missing half of Tharanor.

The authorities pleaded with people to report any strange experiences or phenomena, to help determine if there were any temporary or permanent junctures or crossover points from one side to the other. Many felt that there might be, or even should be, such ways to do so. Such portals or gateways theoretically existed, or might one day even be created, and simply had to be either located or their secrets discovered and explored.

People were fascinated by the world of Tharanor and its cultures and creatures. Humans learned the Tharanorian names for the various monsters, and many other strange creatures that they had yet to encounter, firsthand.

Mason and everyone learned about torgs, ka-torgs, mor-kahls, and gozogs.

Dragons, for instance, were called shallavoks. Thulkara spoke freely of the existence of dragons and what a scourge they could be.

Yet, thus far, no dragons had been sighted. Apparently, there were none in the current area, but that could change. Thulkara told people to count themselves as being fortunate for that fact. Thulls did not like dragons one bit.

Next, Urth humans were fascinated by the Tharanorian use of magic, and wanted to understand it. Many wanted to learn magic.

Could more Urth people learn how to use such magic?

Then, people wanted to know all about the mercenaries of Khairun. Finally, they desired to know all they could about the New World on Tharanor, and the various colony city states that had been established in the wilds. Such city states were footholds for forces from the six nations of the Old World, as opposed to the New World of what had been North and South America.

There was renewed hope that Michiana could eventually link up with these other nearby city states someday, and form alliances with the humans and Tharanorians in those places. Together, they might be able to better defend one another against the monsters and threats of the vast wilds surrounding them.

But for now, the distances and threats between those distant enclaves remained far too great, and the threats close to home too real and dire.

They couldn't even get through to Elkhart—let alone reach Detroit or Toledo.

But Thulkara and Mason warned them that they feared now that the Sylurrian mages of Vaejan/Chicago were somehow controlling both the mercs and the monsters, and were most likely using the event of the Merge to make a power grab. Michiana was caught in an attempt to subjugate all that these mages could seize under their power.

As the masters of magic on Tharanor, they might have even had a hand in causing the Merge itself, somehow. Nothing was certain.

Those possibilities alone made the people of Urth very, very angry.

As plans and preparations for the coming war continued, Mason, Blondie, and Thulkara did get a chance to meet the other two Urth human girls with magical powers—the Shooting Stars.

Captain Bill introduced them all to one another, one sunny day.

"Just as you have become known as the Pistolero, Mace," "We call these two brave young ladies our Shooting Stars," Bill said. "The name has stuck and continues to give our people hope."

Dozens of other strange cases and phenomena had been reported to the authorities and were being looked into, but thus far, Mason and these two girls were apparently the only Urth humans who had magical powers that could be directly made use of.

They looked so young. Just teens.

Minnie Patterson was a short, blond elf of a girl with sapphire blue eyes—a fierce, tiny thing, barely five feet tall, who had just turned nineteen. But all the stories claimed that she and her friend had survived many harrowing ordeals and encounters with the monsters. Only their new combined, magical abilities had saved them.

Mason listened eagerly to their story because it was so similar to his experience.

At first, they discovered their powers when they came out of the strange lake after the Merge. Minnie discovered quickly that when she felt threatened, she could somehow energize a rock or something small she held in her hands. When she or her friend threw it, the rock or small object exploded and did quite a bit of damage.

She and her best friend wiped out a group of monsters at the edge of the lake with exploding rocks. But her friend could somehow control the power in the energized stones and cast them much farther.

Minnie's rocks were unstable and burst within two or three seconds, at most.

Her friend's stones exploded on contact, and could be lobbed high into the air over greater distances.

Hannah Masters was also nineteen, and only slightly taller than Minnie, with curly brown hair and brown eyes. Equally slender and pretty, they were otherwise just regular girls.

Mason realized suddenly that they were both the same age as his beloved Tori.

And now they were caught up in fighting a brutal war for survival.

The Merge had caught them staying over at a friend's house. They were then tossed into a glowing lake just as Mason had been that same morning, but when they emerged, their friend's house was mostly gone. Probably on the other side, now. As they traveled, looking for safety, Minnie and Hannah made it home to their neighborhoods. But both of their homes and families were missing, as well.

They came across some slingshots and started using them to shoot their energized rocks more effectively. They found that they could also manipulate the energies of the magic to cause different effects.

Their abilities eventually brought them to the attention of the militia, who taught them archery and switched them over to using arrows. But the two young women insisted on keeping their slingshots and a pouch of collected marbles, ball bearings, and rocks with them at all times—as a backup.

By then, Minnie and Hannah had heard all about the infamous Pistolero, and later Blondie and Thulkara, as well.

Once the introductions were made, they all went out to the target grounds to compare notes and put on a little demonstration for the public.

The two girls demonstrated how they could manipulate their magic and cause different effects. But strangely enough, to Mason at least, their combined abilities did not seem to be affected at all by the composition of their missiles. They manipulated the magical energy itself to cause their effects.

Mason explained how his various shot and powder compositions could create his various effects. But unlike the girls, he had found no way to produce lightning blasts or cold blasts the way they could. He could produce clouds of regular smoke, but not the choking smoke—a noxious gas, really—that the girls could produce. He could affect his blasts by manipulating the components involved, but he could not directly change or shape the innate magic in him that ignited those components. That factor seemed constant in his case.

Blondie piped up and said that was because Mace was sorcerer with a very specific focus for his powers, and that he used Wild Magic instead of normal magic. Although Mason questioned how normal any magic could be.

The militia leaders had heard that Mason could cancel out other magic with his blasts. They asked for a demonstration.

"Minnie, Hannah, would you fire one of your freeze arrows at the second target from the right?"

"Sure," Minnie said.

They did so.

Mason drew and fired a blast of his own at their glowing blue arrowhead speeding toward the target.

The power of the arrow erupted. It should have frozen everything near the target into solid ice.

Instead, the two effects cancelled each other out in a spray of inert gray dust.

The authorities determined that Minnie and Hannah would fight against the monsters, while Mason would fight against the mercenaries and their various mages. His magic negation blasts could be used to effectively counter them. The Shooting Stars had no way to do that.

"But consider this," Mason warned. "It works both ways. Their magic can cancel out mine, also. And, there'll be more of them than me."

"But you can fire your pistols faster than each one of them can cast their magic," Captain Avery said.

Mason nodded. "Timing will also be important," he admitted. "If either side is too slow, the magic will still go off. And after a while, I will still have to reload."

"We've considered those factors," Avery noted. "What if we provided you with a small team to reload your weapons for you, using your components? They would still work, wouldn't they?"

"I think so." Mason felt like an idiot. He hadn't thought of that. "Let's find out."

Captain Avery nodded. "Good. We've actually had four teams of four people each, practicing with weapons and components similar to yours: black powder pistols, powder, shot, and percussion caps. But, of course, ours are now all inert; they won't function. But at least our reloading teams have become very proficient at performing the mechanical reloading function itself."

Avery motioned with his hands. "They can stay with you, close by, protected by heavy archery mantlets. Just hand one of your guards your empty pistols, and they'll give them to the reloaders. The guards will slip the loaded pistols back into your holsters if they can reach them without getting in your way, or stand by to hand them to you directly when you are ready for them. Our spotters will be on hand to help direct your fire where we think it will be the most effective."

Mason tipped his hat to them. "Sounds great. But let me try something. I want to load my components into one of those other guns and fire them with my hands. Lets see if they will work.

Mason loaded one chamber and fired it at a target.

No dice, again, the weapon just clicked.

"It appears," he said, "that my guns and my components only work for me. All three factors must be present. Whatever happened to me and them in that glowing lake water, it affected all three factors."

"Perhaps with the right mage or enchanter," Blondie suggested, "you might be able to duplicate these effects someday."

Mason shook his head. "Well, we haven't found a way yet. But we can keep trying. I guess I'll have to settle for being an artillery battery on the front lines."

Hannah chimed in. "I guess that's more or less what Minnie and I are."

"Good luck to you all during the battles to come," Minnie said.

Mason and his friends exchanged similar sentiments, and offered their hands in friendship and camaraderie.

The two young girls hugged them all instead—even giant Thulkara. The Amazon lifted the two up like they were dolls in her big muscled arms. She towered two feet over them both.

Mason marveled at those two brave girls, going off to fight for their people and their homes without question.

"If they can fight so readily," he said, "how much more can we?"

"I salute them and their valor," Thulkara said.

"They're both so young and pretty," Blondie said, with a gleam in his eyes. "It would be such a shame and a waste if something happened to them. I hope they don't get themselves killed."

Mason clapped Blondie on the back. "Hope that for us at the same time, you strawheaded horndog."

Then word reached them at the front.

The two captured enemy mages were now well enough to be questioned.

33

With the sun warming the cold morning air and a light wind in the high forties, David and Jerriel left the strange, dark woods of Tharanor behind them. They made their way back through the damaged houses and neighborhoods of the west side, and then northwest back toward what was left of the downtown, and finally back home on Churchill for some well-deserved rest.

In South Bend and nearby, human beings struggled to go back to being at least part of what they had once been.

With the monster threat eliminated, at least for the time being, people began to melt down, break down, and freak out. Now they had the time and the opportunity to do so.

Fights and looting became a problem once more. Several internal, political, and social problems and disagreements simmered up to the forefront also, rearing their ugly heads.

Who was in charge of what?

Where did that authority come from? What type of emergency government did they need to form and how should it evolve? How long would martial law be in effect? What were its limits?

How would people handle the reality of the merge? Would looting roar out of control? Would suicides and killings continue to spike? Dozens of people hung themselves or jumped into the icy waters of the river, unable to deal with all of the changes—with the new realities.

After a quick rest and a meal, David and Jerriel were summoned to a mandatory meeting at the public library, the new think tank of the town council. That entire area was now guarded by several entrenched legions of the South Bend militia.

Dirk and Belinda were there with the other new town leaders, trying to deal with the crowds of people demanding further answers. Mobs could demand just about anything—rational or irrational.

The town council had a large map of Indiana up on a board. Sections that had been highlighted in bright yellow marker were new.

One of the planners from the search and surveying teams attempted to speak over the din of the crowd, pointing to the map board with a telescoping pointer.

"As far fetched as it seems..." the man said with hesitation. He looked nervous, about mid-forties, and in a disheveled brown suit. He wore big glasses and had a receding gray hairline. "We have experienced a very serious dimensional event—a shift in reality."

"Then, damn it, shift it back. Do something!"

"Yeah. We want things back the way they were before all of this crap. We want our world back the way it was!"

"Get the cars and trucks working again—the jets and airplanes."

"What about trains and cargo ships?"

"There's no phones, no electricity!"

"No TV or cable. No radio!"

"No Internet or Wi-Fi!"

"Nothing works!"

"We're going to run out of food!"

"How do we heat our homes when winter comes?"

The speaker tried to calm the crowd. But understandably, everyone was still simply too upset.

Dirk motioned to the band people to play a quick fanfare. The noise crashed out over the crowd. He stepped up to the big megaphone.

"Listen up, folks. Just stop and listen. I'm General Dirk Blackwood of the militia."

People had heard of him from the papers. He was a hero, at least for now. Most people cheered.

"Thank you. I appreciate that. But please listen. We are doing our best to tell you what we currently know and what we don't know. Give us a chance. We're all in this together. If you panic and freak out and just start yelling at everyone, that's not going to solve anything. Try to stay calm and listen to what we have to say. Then we can all try to go forward from that point, together. Please, bear with us."

A general murmur rippled through the crowd. Most of the people nodded and quieted down. A few loudmouths, drunks, and crazies had to be ushered away by militia troops.

There always seemed to be a handful of nuts trying to disrupt everything.

"There. That's better," Dirk said. "I understand. We're all on edge. These drastic changes have been very difficult to deal with, for everyone. We must accept and deal with that new reality, the same way that we pulled together and dealt with the monster threat. Now, let one of our local professors, Doctor Dietrich Barnard, talk and tell you what we currently know."

Some mild cheering and applause followed that announcement.

The professor stepped up, distinguished in his gray suit and dark classes, medium length silver hair all combed back. "Thank you, General Blackwood. We appreciate your noble service and the grave injuries you suffered on our behalf, in defense of our homes and our people."

Dirk waved and limped back to his seat again. Another cheer went up from the militia and some of the crowd who understood exactly what the defenders had saved them all from.

"We believe the change that people are calling the Merge has resulted from a mixing of two realities–two alternate worlds," Barnard told them. "It is said that this other world is known as Tharanor to those who are native to it. Except for the monsters and strange denizens that have attacked us, there is much about this other world that we do not know yet. But we are trying, every day, to learn as much as we can. Tharanor is like Urth in many respects physically–similar continents and oceans for example, but with a different history–in fact, a completely different history than our own.

"In theory, we believe this change–this Merge–has resulted in fifty percent of our world being swapped out for fifty percent of Tharanor. Parts of both worlds have thus Merged, or become mixed up together like a random, patchwork quilt. Try to picture that in your minds."

"Are the other parts gone? Forever?" someone blurted out.

"Did all those other people die?"

"We're not sure. We think that the flip side of the dimensional coin has the other halves of both worlds patched together there, just like ours are here, but on the opposite side of the two dimensions. Our counterparts are most likely dealing with the same problems, threats, and issues that we are. For the moment, we cannot reach or communicate with anyone on the other side."

"How long are things going to be this way?"

"Honestly, we don't know. It has only been a few days. We're still trying to figure out how all of this happened. We might not ever have all of those answers. But one important fact needs to be expressed: some of you have seen things that cannot normally be explained. In theory, once again, we believe that, on this other world of Tharanor, physics, and natural and chemical laws work somewhat differently. In essence, what can only be called 'magic' can indeed function on Tharanor, and now magic can also function in parts of our world, also—what we now call Urth."

A brief uproar from the crowd. Cries of ridicule and disbelief.

The professor raised his hands. "Please. Please listen. I know how crazy and impossible all of this sounds. I am a man of science and reason. This is difficult for all of us. But these things are real. We have seen them. There is no other explanation. But it seems that the magic of Tharanor was disrupted as well, just as our technology on Urth has malfunctioned. It's likely that since the Merge occurred, both worlds— both dimensions or realities—have been thrown into chaos, as well as the natural laws that function there.

"We do not know how the Merge occurred. Perhaps some cosmic accident. Perhaps some deliberate effort on the part of unknown parties, or forces that we have not met. We're still trying to find out. Keep in mind that it has only been a short time since the Merge took place. There has been very little time to gather information, and we are doing the best that we can under the current threats and the limitations to our transportation methods."

"What about trains?" some said. "We hear that old-fashioned, mechanical steam engines still work."

"They do, and we're struggling to get ahold of any antiques and get them running. But again, please keep in mind, the land all around us is not the same anymore. Remember: it's now a broken patchwork of pieces of Urth, and pieces of Tharanor, both mixed together. Even if we send a locomotive out, say, toward Chicago, we will be forced to fix and lay many hundreds of miles of new track through dense forests, hills, and strange mountains. That will be time consuming in itself. And who knows what further threats we shall meet along the way?"

Dirk rose up and stepped forward again.

"We're sending out long range and shorter range scouting teams, mapping teams, and defense teams to the outlying areas each day. It is extremely dangerous out there in the wilds. Some teams have already been completely wiped out and killed. Others simply vanished without a trace. We've sent out larger, more heavily armed groups, but it takes time for them to go out and come back. We need to be patient. I know that is hard. But we need to keep our heads on straight and deal with all of this as best we can. There are still many of our people out there in the wilds who need help. We have to reach them as quickly as we can and draw them into the protective fold."

"To hell with them! We still have monsters hiding out in our basements," someone shouted.

Dirk did his best to respond. "Defense teams from the militia are going door to door. Report any incidents and they'll be dealt with. We need everyone we can get on our side, folks. There's safety in numbers. We don't know when the next monster attack will occur. We have to get organized and stay organized. Every hand is going to be needed this spring, summer, and fall for food production, if nothing else. We don't want to starve this next winter, along with all of our other technical problems."

"But...but..."

"No buts, people. This is the way things are. They may be this way from now on. Face the facts at hand. We may never be able to find a way to go back to the past we once had. We just don't know right now. So suck it up and stop whining like a bunch of spoiled brats, and let's get to work, and keep working together. That's our best way to survive. There are only so many of us left, and we must all work together!"

Lukewarm cheering went up. Professor Barnard stepped in again.

"News announcements will be made every morning and evening. An old-style, print newspaper has being put together and will continue to be posted and issued to the public. Stay informed. If you discover something important, let the authorities know about it. Our scientists are trying to study various phenomena and figure out a way to get electricity and other basic services working again."

"That's all well and good," a banker-looking type, in a dirty suit said. "But a lot of us don't have jobs anymore. What do we do for money? How do we pay for stuff?"

Dirk shook his head. "Get it through your heads, people. Nothing is going back to the way it was. We are fighting to survive, surrounded by enemies. Everyone's new job from this point on is the survival of humanity."

Dirk yanked one of the smaller megaphones off its stand and paced across the stage with it in his hands. He was in his battered armor again, for show. All eyes and ears focused on him. "Look at Niles, Michigan. That entire town was almost completely wiped out by the monster hordes. Practically every man, woman, and child there was slaughtered and eaten.

232

"Does it matter to any of them today what their bank statements were or what job they had? Hell no. Now they're all dead! We're in a crisis situation, folks. Money doesn't matter anymore and its use has been suspended by the emergency town council until the crisis is over. Money can't save us; only all of us can do that, together. It doesn't matter right now, who has more money. That cannot be the focus or the goal of our efforts."

The banker-looking guy still gaped. David felt for him.

Money not matter anymore? How was that even possible?

Dirk gave them all the hard facts. "There's no paying bills, no hoarding, no buying or selling. Things people need will be rationed out as best as possible from what there is. Barter and trade are fine. No disorder, no looting. No turning on each other. Looters will be killed on the spot at the discretion of the militia on the ground. Any serious crimes will be dealt with harshly and swiftly by the militia. Criminals will be hanged or otherwise executed as needed, via summary military justice. Right now, in all of the chaos, there's no other way to maintain order.

"A new system of investigations and military trials will be organized by the remaining law enforcement, legal, and court personnel. They will be up and running shortly. If we hear of a black market, or dangerous illegal stuff anywhere, we'll shut it down.

"But there is plenty of work for everyone to do. Thousands have died and need to be identified and buried to avoid epidemics of sickness and disease. Even more people have been wounded or displaced from their homes. The hospitals and medical centers have been overwhelmed with wounded from the fighting. They need volunteers and blood donors; please help them, if you can. Blood stores are being given priority in the few remaining icehouses in the area.

"Thousands of homes have been damaged and can be repaired for new residents who need shelter. A new homesteading law is being formed. Pets and animals need to be rescued and controlled. Abandoned homes and businesses need to be checked for supplies and equipment that can be gathered, sorted out, and distributed to those who need them most.

"In the very near future–in a matter of weeks and months–we will face grave needs for food and clean water. Schools have to be kept open. The young must be protected and educated. Knowledge must be passed on, especially the knowledge of what still works, and what can be made to work again. Whatever our experts determine that is."

The crowd continued to moan and groan. "It's as if we've been sent back to the eighteenth century overnight!" someone complained.

Dirk nodded. "If that's the hand we've been dealt, those are the cards we must play. Get used to it. As a species, we've done all of that before. We can use that knowledge again before it is lost, and we're reduced to living in caves and grunting around fires. We can't let that happen. We can't become savages like these monsters we fear."

"How many people are left? How many of us are left in Michiana?"

"We think somewhere around forty-five to fifty percent of the local area population, around ninety-thousand in South Bend and Mishawaka. But more refugees arrive from the outlying areas every minute."

"What about on the other side?"

"What about it? We don't know how to get there. We just don't know that much about it."

"Well, hey, man, this might work for while, but some of us people might have something to say about how all of this is organized and who gets what. If you think black people are going to stand by again and let white people decide everything for them, you got another thing—"

Immediately, frustrated people started shouting complaints and racial insults.

David gaped. Where was all of this ignorance and hate coming from? Was it born out of fear?

"And the Hispanics won't, either," someone else added.

"Go back to Mexico, Juan!"

"Who said that?"

Dirk shouted into the megaphone. "Shut up! All of you. We are not going to do this. We aren't going back to the stupid mistakes of the past. We can't afford that. I thought we were already beyond all of that crap. We cannot afford to do this! Where were all of you loudmouths when we stood shoulder to shoulder and fought those thousands of monsters to the death? We stood together—and bled and died together—not as blacks, or whites, or Hispanics, or whatever, but as human beings.

"When we fought side by side in the darkness, not knowing if any of us were going to wake up the next day—we didn't care what color we were or where our parents came from!

"Listen up. Two nights ago a gay guy took a sword in the guts for me when I went down. He fought beside me for hours and died trying to protect me. I never even knew his name. His dying thoughts were about his partner, the person he loved.

"The past is the past. If you haven't noticed, we're all on the same side now, and we don't even know the full extent what we're up against yet. And the monsters sure don't care what we are; to them, we're just meat. Think about it. When the militia came into your neighborhoods to help, to protect you, did you care what color they were or what language they spoke? Hell no!

You were just happy that it wasn't the monsters knocking down your doors and crashing through your windows to gnaw your arms and legs off, while you and your kids screamed and died.

"We stand together or we fall together. For all we know at the moment, we are all that is left of humanity. Keep that in mind. The day we turn on each other is the day the monsters start to win. Then we become the monsters, and far worse than any of the kind we're fighting right now. Everybody better think hard on that. Now, everyone get out of here. Let us do our jobs and all of you go find something useful to do as well. Help each other. Protect one another."

Dirk's words silenced the idiots in the crowd.

At least for the time being.

34

Blondie managed to get his sorry ass into trouble at a local watering hole.

As it turned out, Blondie hooked up with some young, drunken gal who just happened to be somewhat married.

And as expected, her big, drunken, burly husband—they never seemed to be small and scrawny—did not take very kindly to finding the two of them together and half-undressed in an upstairs room.

Militia troops from the bar came and got Mason and Thulkara where they were eating in a nearby mess tent as soon as the trouble began. The two of them came running.

When they reached the room in question, the woman was jumping up on the bed in her underwear, cursing at everyone present.

Her big husband finally had Blondie where he wanted him, held between two of the guy's buddies on either side.

"I swear," Blondie said. "She didn't tell me she was married. How was I supposed to—"

"You rotten bastard!" the big, drunken oaf snarled, and punched Blondie right in the face. Then another fist to the gut. Blondie choked and doubled over.

"All right, that's enough," Mason said.

The drunken oaf ignored him and drew a big bowie knife out of his boot. "Pretty boy...prepare to get neutered!"

"Thulkara," Mason said, "don't make me kill this idiot."

The barbarian giantess nodded and stepped around Mason. She flung the husband through a wall with one hand, stripping him of his knife with the other in the process.

The man's two buddies holding Blondie froze where they stood. Their mouths dropped open and they stared up at her as she shoved their heads back through the drywall with a grin on her face.

Mason slipped in and caught Blondie before he sagged to the floor, his nose and mouth bleeding.

"Okay, let's get you out of here. You really need to stay away from the married ones, Blondie."

"She...didn't tell me she was...married. I swear."

"Sheesh, did you even ask?"

"Well...no...there wasn't time."

"Look for a ring, damn it. On the left hand, second finger from the last."

"She wasn't wearing any rings."

The drunken wife started cursing them, since they were the only ones still standing.

Thulkara shoved the woman down in the bed. "Shut up, you dumb slut. You're half the problem here."

"You can't talk to my wife that way," the husband said, trying to crawl back into the room."

Thulkara rolled her eyes. "Mace, get us out of here. These people are so stupid, I might accidently step on their heads or something."

"Don't do that–trust me–it's not worth the trouble it will cause you. Follow me and let's get out of this hole."

They reported the incident to the militia night watch. The drunken couple wanted to file charges, of all things, and have Blondie and Thulkara arrested for assault and battery–and, attempted rape, of all things.

Major Avery found a blunt but diplomatic way to tell them both to drag their sorry, lying asses straight to hell and remain there for the duration. Then he ordered that dive shut down. It had been a source of many problems.

Blondie cleaned up all right. As usual, he was tougher than he looked. He was more worried about his nose and his looks than anything else, and kept checking his pretty face in mirrors.

"Mace," Blondie asked, "why didn't you just shoot that big bastard in the leg or something?"

"I might have slipped up and cut both of his legs off. And he was her husband, after all."

"So what? We didn't even do anything."

"For what, a lack of time?"

"Well, yeah. So…were you going to just let him kill me, or castrate me right there?"

"Nope, the man had a right to punch you, and he did so. He didn't have a right to cut you, neuter you, or kill you. That's why I sent Thulkara in. She took care of things quite nicely, I'd say. I sure wouldn't want her thumping on me."

"I still wish you would have shot him."

"The situation did not require killing. My guns spit death, Blondie. They aren't very good at just wounding things, if you haven't noticed. While it was true that those people were dumb buttholes, but they didn't deserve to die, or even get maimed. It was as much your fault as well for getting tangled up with them. You have plenty of stupid women who *aren't* married chasing your dumb ass. For what reasons, I do not know, nor care to know. That is between you and them. But I would strongly advise you to–"

"All right, point taken. From now on, I promise–no married gals."

"Thank you, Blondie. That will make all of our lives a lot easier, and perhaps a bit quieter from now on."

"My head hurts, Mace, I really need a drink."

"You can't, you sot. We're on duty soon."

"Damn it to hell. This entire night has been a bust!"

Later that evening, the enemy mercenaries hit South Bend from the south, at the same time the monsters hit the city from the west.

The militia held their positions for three hours. Then they began to give ground.

The field of battle was simply too wide, too spread out. And the enemy still possessed a great advantage in numbers–what seemed to be endless numbers.

That fact alone was staggering, frightening, and very demoralizing.

Where were the enemy getting such numbers? It didn't seem possible. Not only were the defenders still facing the formidable monster hordes, but now they were also facing down trained, disciplined armies of skilled soldiers for hire.

Mason and his unit of defenders pulled back to another area of high ground at the next fallback position, the secondary line of defense along the patchy remnants of Mayflower Road.

Fortunately, due to the monster attacks, most civilians had already evacuated the far southern and western areas of town—or else they had been wiped out to begin with. The militia was using those areas now as killing fields—a no man's land—to attack and reduce any enemy numbers who exposed themselves out in the open.

But no one was sure how well that strategy was working.

The enemy also began fighting smart. They weren't simply surging in, out in the open, just to be cut down in vast numbers.

In fact, even with the help of the Shooting Stars, the militia continued to give ground. The mercenaries fought and moved relentlessly. They proved themselves to be expert, disciplined soldiers—professional soldiers. They were hard to beat in a straight up confrontation.

The main problem, once again, was the fact that the battle lines were so extensive. The Pistolero and the Shooting Stars could help defend only a very small tactical area. Even their amazing efforts could be rendered statistically irrelevant in the course of a massive campaign across vast battle lines.

Realistically, the defenders needed someone like them posted with the militia at about every half mile of the front lines. Mason and the two girls were, in fact, just like artillery. But it was like an army that only had two cannons to defend an entire city.

They couldn't be everywhere at once.

The defenders waited to be attacked. The defense was static. The enemy could choose when and where and how to strike, coordinating their attacks.

They played the game all night long. The militia fought stubbornly, but continued to give ground. It was a delaying tactic, nothing more. Survive to fight another day.

They bled the enemy, and the enemy bled them.

By the time the enemy broke off their assault at dawn, the defenders were close to surrendering the third defensive line at Ireland Road to the south, and Bendix Avenue to the west.

Everyone waited to see what the mercenaries would do. Unlike the monsters, they could keep fighting during the daytime.

But would they? By all reports, they had the numbers to do so.

Two hours passed. Other than holding the lines after the monsters melted away before dawn, the mercs halted their advance and saw to their dead and wounded.

The defenders did what they could for their casualties that they could reach.

Yet it was learned that the mercs took prisoners, at least, even though they enslaved them and used them for hard labor and whatever else they saw fit. In their own opportunistic way, they weren't wholly without honor.

That was still better than the monsters, who used anything that was meat for food. At least the defenders might be able to free those slaves, someday.

The dead could never be brought back.

Mason went to Captain Avery and asked him point blank, "If we keep on like this, how long can we hold them off? How long before they drive us back behind all of our defensive lines?"

Avery met his eye. "The current estimates are three weeks, a month at most, if things go our way. Then they'll have taken all of South Bend and begin to hit the lines at Mishawaka."

Mason nodded sadly, looking down at the ground. "So, it's a campaign of attrition."

Avery let out a deep sigh. "Affirmative. Either we wear them down, or they wear us down. And we can't expect any help from Elkhart. Even Mishawaka can't send us much. They're too afraid of leaving their positions vulnerable. The enemy has the advantage in numbers and can strike wherever they want to, but it's pretty clear that they plan to roll us up first–in order from west to east, and up from the south."

Mason hammered his fist against an old telephone pole. "Yeah, it doesn't exactly take a military genius to figure it out. South Bend first. Then Mishawaka. Then they'll push on and do the same thing to Elkhart. Brilliant on their part."

"It's a solid strategy–for them. If our roles were reversed, we might do the very same thing. We must somehow be in their way," Avery noted. "In their world, there was nothing here but wilds. Now we're here, messing up their plans–whatever they are. If I were Napoleons, like they appear to be, and I had all of these mercs and could control these monsters, I'd sweep east and lay siege to Detroit and Toledo. I'd take it all. Our foes have conquest on their mind."

Mason grunted. "You said Detroit and Toledo–you mean Tornhold and Kellendra."

"Yeah, whatever the Tharanorians call them. I just wish we could get some help from those city states."

"Captain, I agree with you. I think all of this is part of some big, master plan that we don't fit into. But I'm guessing that those other city states are just as up to their necks in their own troubles as we are."

"You're probably right, Mace. I'd bet they are. You'd better join your people and get some rest, my friend. I foresee another long night ahead of us."

Mason went back to his tent.

He noted that Thulkara had her own tent. He could hear her snoring loudly inside of it.

Blondie also had his own tent by now, but Mason swore he heard the distinct sound of feminine giggling within as he walked by. Blondie attracted women the same way Mason attracted trouble.

At least this new gal wasn't screaming…or hitched, hopefully.

Mason was too tired to care or investigate. Blondie was a big boy, and was going to spend his off time whatever way he pleased, with whomever he pleased.

In a way, Mason was happy for his friend. At least Blondie always seemed to have someone to be with and comfort him. Even it was a different someone every few days or so. They were now at war. Any of them could catch an arrow in the neck and die gargling on their own blood, or get blasted to dust by enemy magic, or devoured alive by rabid monsters.

Mason went to sleep in a dark mood, missing Tori and feeling very sorry for himself, although he knew all of that was pretty selfish.

He just wasn't that great of a person, and war often made people very petty and selfish. Whatever you had in you that was the worst, war brought it out and magnified it for everyone else to gawk at.

35

David and Jerriel went into a nearby meeting room at the public library to talk to another bunch of experts. The latter wanted to know as much as they could about Jerriel, Tharanor, magic, and anything else she could tell them.

A team of linguists and historians were assigned to learn about Jerriel's language and culture as quickly as possible, with Danielle and Theo heading up part of the language team. These were the same two grad students they had met before.

Jerriel outlined and detailed the grammar of the two languages that she knew best: Sylurrian and Marandorian. She filled up the white board over and over again with sample sentences, verb tenses, word lists, and basic language knowledge, such as numbers, greetings, etc. She taught them a few Tharanorian children's songs, and they sang them together and wrote down the lyrics.

Then she wrote down the incantation for a simple light spell, about a half page of words. Then she and the linguists, and sometimes David also, translated that spell into English.

Then Jerriel cast the light spell–in English–and made it work.

A small, blue-white orb of light bobbed in the air until she dispelled it.

All of them tried to cast the spell, but none of them could make it work, in any language.

"Yoo are not wizards," Jerriel flatly told them. "Only thoose trained to recognize the magic within them can foocus that energy throough themselves and make the spell words woork.

David followed along with the researchers, jotting down notes in his notebooks and making lists of words. The hours went by very quickly.

Later that day David and Jerriel rode their bikes home, just before dusk.

Both of them staggered into their house and locked the door behind them. Jerriel lit a lamp.

They ate some peanut butter and jelly sandwiches and powdered lemonade. The easiest thing they could think to make.

The days still grew dark quickly. They were so tired that they stumbled into their rooms and collapsed, still wearing their boots.

Hell, David was still in his same clothing and armor from the day before. He reeked of dirt and sweat. But he felt too exhausted to care or feel the need to do anything about any of that.

David spent the better part of three days visiting the families of his fallen troops or writing letters to them.

As their commander, he knew this was very necessary, but also found it very mind-numbing, heart-robbing, and exhausting work.

In two days of intense action, out of hundreds of troops under his direct command, his units suffered one hundred and three killed, and eighty-nine others injured. Half of those injuries had been serious or crippling.

Now he commanded five hundred troops. He had been given a service staff of fifty officers, and mostly supply, transport, and messenger troops. Plus three units of one hundred and fifty frontline troops, each unit rotating duty patrolling and guarding the city and its perimeter every eight hours.

That gave each trooper eight hours of assigned duty somewhere in town each day. Then they had eight hours of rest, and eight hours of training. Troops were given every third weekend off to visit their families and friends in rotation. Each trooper was given a place to stay, food, drink, gear, weapons, clothing, and all the training they could handle. Their families would be taken care of if something happened to them.

David felt incredibly guilty about all of the letters and back paperwork. A lottery that the militia commanders established required that ten percent of the surviving families should receive a direct notification at home. David attempted to explain the difficulties of his situation to Jerriel and some of his staff.

"The militia got cobbled together so fast, I didn't even know many of these people before we all went out to fight and they were hurt or killed. I barely met them or even saw their faces. What can I say to their loved ones? To their families? What am I supposed to say?"

"Say yoor sorry for their loss," Jerriel said. She patted his arm. "That is always a good place to start. Yoo are a good man, Daeved. They will know that yoo mean well."

Sean Pennel, thirty-two, with a wife and four kids in a house on the south side. Before the Merge, Sean Pennel had worked for a delivery service. He got cut down the night they attacked the enemy camp and freed the captives. Sean was helping hold the line, according to the reports. He took a mor-kahl sword thrust to the neck. The troops with him said he stood tall while they knew him and that he went down during a standup fight with packed forces of the enemy.

David knocked on the door of the Pennel home. A militia sergeant and a chaplain volunteer from one of the local churches stood behind him.

A woman in her late twenties answered. She had short reddish hair, and freckles. She looked like she'd been crying. No big surprise there.

"Yes."

"I'm Captain Pritchard, from the militia, ma'am. This is Sergeant Barnett. Chaplain Weiman. We're sorry for your loss." Then David hesitated and asked, "You are Carly Pennel, right?"

She nodded. "Yes. Please. Come in."

"Thank you."

She led them into the living room. Four shocked, subdued kids played quietly in the adjoining family room. A girl about eight or nine, two boys maybe six and three, a one-year-old baby.

David and his companions sat down with the mother on worn but comfortable furniture in the living room.

Carly Pennel didn't offer them anything. They didn't ask.

"How did he die?" Carly asked directly. "Did he suffer?"

"No," David said. "By all accounts, your husband fought bravely, Mrs. Pennel. Everyone who served with him said so. He was wounded in the neck during the battle. He passed out and lost too much blood before he reached the aid station. They couldn't revive him. Again, I can only say how sorry I am."

She bowed her head and nodded.

"My unit alone lost thirty-four troops that night," David said. "Almost twice that in wounded. But we took out several hundred enemies and rescued over eight hundred captives, over half of them children–from a fate worse than death. Little helpless kids like yours, Mrs. Pennel. For every trooper who fell, we saved eight people–most of them kids, like I said. Your husband was a brave man, and he was part of all that."

"What's going to happen to me and our kids now?" she asked. Her voice shook. She looked at David directly.

"You'll still need to work somewhere and do something useful, but you'll have help when you need it. You'll get food stipends and medical care from the militia. You can get help watching your kids, education for yourself and them. The militia units assigned to this area will help protect you. The work crews will also help you get your home upgraded for the summer, and especially for the coming winter. If you need something, we'll try to help."

She nodded again. "I appreciate all that. But it won't bring Sean back. It's not going to bring back their father."

"I'm sorry, ma'am. Nothing can do that. But the militia fought hard and many gave their lives so that you and your kids could stay alive and free. That's better than the alternative. I saw that firsthand and so did your husband. That's why we all fought so hard. I'm sorry he didn't make it back."

"I know. I know why he joined the militia to fight. I know why he had to go. I just wish he..." She sobbed. "I wish he..."

They left several minutes later. The sergeant and the chaplain had orders to make the survivor services check on her regularly and help her and the kids.

But nothing anyone could do or say would ever make up for the loss of even one husband, one father, or one brother. The death of a son or daughter–of any one person–affected so many other people.

And this was just one casualty.

In the sobering days that followed, David matured rapidly, took on his duties as a leader and a commander much more seriously and with a growing sense of pride and purpose.

Michiana found itself cut off from the rest of the world, surrounded by monsters. Perhaps they were doomed to fail and be swept away. But they also rose up to meet the challenge. The sense of urgency and loss crushed down on David like heavy weights. It was his and everyone's duty to learn what they could to survive and give humanity its best, fighting chance to keep living. To at least stay part of what they still were, and what they once had been.

Although a stranger among them, Jerriel busied herself working with the linguists and a crowd of curious experts, studying the magic pools and new plants people discovered, testing Urth people for magical abilities, and tinkering with her own enchantments.

As soon as she had her wizard labs set up at the university and at home, she went to David first thing.

"I want to enchant yoor weapons and armor, Daeved. I can make them moore powerful—stroonger."

"Sure, that sounds great to me."

"Sokay."

Although they were both kept busy to the point of exhaustion each day, their friendship and respect for each other continued to grow and deepen.

David often caught himself looking at Jerriel for long moments at a time. And when she noticed him doing so, she always looked back at him and smiled. But there was always so much else that needed to be done. So many dire needs and problems to face. Real life-and-death issues and so many unknowns literally surrounded them each day.

If he wasn't doing something constructive, he felt guilty. But one glance at Jerriel's pretty oval face, and her alluring form. Even just the way she moved, the way she walked, drove him crazy with desire.

At night, David dreamed of kissing Jerriel and making love to her.

Neither of them ever said anything or directly raised the subject of romance, but both of them seemed to sense that the crisis they were in really wasn't the right time for either of them to pursue anything more.

Especially in the area of romance.

So they both let it ride. They did their best to ignore the growing attraction between them and buried themselves in their various labors. They lived under the same roof as friends, roommates, and coworkers. Many difficult decisions remained right in front of them and the town each day.

And all of that really sucked, because David couldn't help falling hard for his pretty wizard girl.

36

Mason and Blondie sat across from the two enemy mages in the jail's interrogation room. It was just the four of them.

They ignored Mason entirely and stared intently at Blondie, who betrayed no emotion and simply stared back at them.

Both of the enemy mages were Blondie's age or not more than a year or two older—somewhere in their early twenties, no more than twenty-five.

The first one they had captured still had his head bandaged and several burns dressed. He was as tall as Blondie, but with a slightly skinnier build, and dark brown hair and eyes.

The second mage was shorter, but stockier, and had thick, hairy forearms. He wheezed a little and had his chest wrapped from his lung shot. He had longer black hair, similar to Blondie's in style, and gray eyes. That same hairstyle must be a trend among their people, the Sylurrians.

The prisoner's feet were shackled, their hands secured behind them with handcuffs. Since no one knew how their magic worked exactly, they had been kept gagged and with dark hoods over their head until now.

The two mages said nothing. They only continued to blink and stare at Blondie, intense looks on their faces, and sweat dripping down from their foreheads.

Mason tried to talk to them.

No response.

Blondie tried to talk to them.

No response.

Mason and Blondie left the room for a time.

"What do you think?" Mason asked.

"Let me go in with them alone," Blondie said. "If they do know me, maybe they'll talk to me. But I keep hearing this buzzing sound in my head when I'm in there. I wish I knew what that was."

"Go ahead," Mason said. "I'll be listening from out here."

So were Captain Avery and several guards and recorders.

Blondie went back in.

At first they kept staring at him.

Then he got up and went to each of them and whispered something to them. No one could hear what it was.

When Blondie sat back down in front of them, they stopped staring at him so hard.

Then one of them glanced up at the lantern.

Blondie reached up and turned the lamp way down. The room darkened. It was difficult to see.

The two mages leaned forward to whisper, and Blondie leaned in to listen.

Soon all three of them were whispering back and forth very rapidly, but no one outside the room could understand what was being said.

After about twenty minutes of such whispering, Captain Avery grew suspicious, and sent Mason back into the room.

As soon as the door opened, the two mages leaned back in their chairs and stopped whispering.

So did Blondie, as Mason turned up the lamp again.

The mages were just as impassive and as indifferent as before.

On a whim, Mason drew one of his pistols and motioned to Blondie as he spoke. "Outside."

Blondie smirked and got up, going out in front of Mason, who kept his Spiller at his hip, aimed at the small of Blondie's back.

Once they were out of the room and the door was closed, Blondie leaned against the wall and softly laughed.

"This is going to be fun," he finally said. "Nice touch, taking me out at gunpoint, Mace. I couldn't have asked you to do anything better. Sheer genius."

Mason pursed his lips tight. "I'm not laughing, Blondie, and I'm not sure I was pretending. How about we have a little chat with Captain Avery and the militia intel folks?"

"Of course," Blondie said. "I know what you all must be thinking by now."

Mason holstered his pistol. "Seriously, Blondie. What are we supposed to think? You could be saying anything to them, and they to you. They could be your best buds from back in the day for all we know."

They went into another room at the police station and Blondie received a good grilling.

"Look," Blondie said. "Let me explain. They weren't going to talk with the lights on where someone might be able to read their lips. Mages are super intelligent. I had to do things their way or they wouldn't have said anything to me."

Avery posed it flat out: "How do we know you weren't just linking up with your allies and plotting our downfall?"

Blondie slyly grinned back at him. "That's just it. You don't."

"How do we know this whole amnesia act of yours just isn't some ploy to infiltrate us and—"

Mason grunted. "I wouldn't go that far."

"Don't you even want to hear what they told me?" Blondie asked.

"Most certainly," Avery told him. "And we want to hear what you told them. Start again, from the beginning."

"Very well. I asked them if either of them knew me. They looked at me strangely and cautiously said that they did. I asked them to tell me my name. Both of them confirmed my original identity. Shaeddor Holleth, sorcerer prince of Sylurria."

"What happened next?" Mason asked.

"They grew suspicious and I think they were about to clam up on me again. Then I told them that I had suffered a major head injury during the Merge, and that I had lost my memory. Until Gellonar had told me my name, I told them that I didn't know who I had been before, and that I still hadn't been able to remember very much. I warned them that I might not ever fully recover all of my memories of the past."

"How did they react to that?" Avery asked.

"They seemed somewhat relieved. They couldn't understand why I hadn't returned to the Dark Khabal if I survived, and even worse—why I would be working with and helping the Urthers, as they call all of you from the other side."

"Is that why they were staring at you so intently at first?" Mason said.

"No. Not at all. Sylurria is a nation of mages. Almost everyone uses magic to some degree. But some mages are much more powerful than others. Telepathy is also quite common among Sylurrians. They were trying to mindspeak with me."

Avery folded his arms. "And are you able to do so with them?" he asked.

Blondie frowned. "As a matter of fact, no. One of the things we discovered is that my brain injury that caused my amnesia also cut off my telepathic abilities. The two of them could not read my thoughts at all, even when I tried to open my mind completely to them. Nor could I read their strongest attempts to mindspeak with me. All I heard were a few jumbled words and a confusing buzzing in my skull."

Mason pointed at him with one finger. "You complained about something like that at the start."

"Right. That was them trying to contact me. This is another boon to us. Since they can't read my thoughts and emotions, they can't tell if I'm lying to them."

Avery kept frowning. "And neither can we."

"Must we go through all of this again?" Blondie asked wearily. "Yes, yes…I'm in the role of the classic double–even triple–agent. The possibility for a double or triple cross is always a possibility. Live with the uncertainty and let's move on."

"Who are they?" Mason asked.

"I knew them, but just barely. Of course they knew who I was. But they're low-level battle mages attached to the mercenaries for combat, Mace. Powerful and formidable in their own right, but still just underlings. I'm afraid they're not going to know very much. The first mage we captured is named Gellonar, and he's a wizard. The second one is a sorcerer, similar to us, and his name is Zanjan."

"Now I'm interested in what you told them about yourself and us," Avery said.

Blondie nodded. "I was getting to that. They accepted my explanation regarding my amnesia. But they still reminded me that my primary duty was to the Dark Khabal, and that I had better recall that and the initial oath of obedience that I had sworn to my master, as his apprentice. They warned me that if I continued to work with and help the enemy, that very quickly I would be treated as one of the Urthers and destroyed, right along with them."

"What did you say to that?" Mason asked.

"I hedged. I grew angry and said that I didn't remember any of that, not my past, nor any such Khabal, and that until my memories returned, I didn't owe them or their so-called masters a handful of shit."

Mason chuckled. "How did they react?"

"Gellonar started to tell me things in order to attempt to stimulate my memory. Zanjan was of the mind that I couldn't be trusted any longer. Not until I had my head on straight and clearly swore my allegiance to the Dark Khabal and their masters."

"What did they want to know about us?" Captain Avery demanded.

"Surprisingly enough, they didn't seem that interested. They asked a few things. They wanted to know what kind of people Urthers were in general, and how I was being treated while living among you. I told them that the Urthers I worked with understood my situation, and tried to accept me, but that me talking with them was going to definitely raise some suspicions concerning my loyalties."

"And then?"

"They didn't care much about that. Next, they started demanding that I help them plot their escape and go back with them, memory or no memory. They insisted that it was my duty. I tried to say that I didn't see a way that I could free them. I myself was constantly being watched. They accepted that fact, and said that they were actually surprised I wasn't locked up and being tortured somewhere."

"Since that is what they would do?" Mason said.

Blondie nodded. "I suppose so. I tried to hedge again, and say that maybe I could spy on you Urthers from within and find a way to transmit valuable intelligence to the Khabal. First they said that wasn't possible—or even necessary. According to them, most mage telepathy only extends about twenty or thirty feet. Then, listen to this: they said that spying on the Urthers wasn't important...because all of you were going to be either dead or enslaved within about a month at most anyway, by their reckoning."

Avery raised both eyebrows for a second. "So, that's their master plan for us all, is it?"

Blondie nodded again. "It appears so. And neither of them seemed to have a very high opinion of Urthers, overall. They see you as fat, lazy, and stupid without your kind of magic to defend yourselves with. Both of them seemed supremely overconfident about the Khabal's inevitable victory. The enemy expects to roll over all of your kind."

"Nice," Avery said. "Anything else?"

"They were real curious about Mace, the enemy sorcerer with the strange looking, but devastating metal wands to focus his powers through. We just started to talk about that when Mace himself came back in. Oh, and they aren't going to talk to any of you, so you can just forget it. That's standard practice among captured mages. Even torture won't get them to say much, and none of it will be useful."

"I still think we need to try to interrogate them," Avery said.

Blondie held up his hands. "You can waste your time, but it's not going to do any good. Oh, and don't tell them anything I told you."

"What?" Avery objected.

"Of course not. Then they'll know I told you what they said, and they'll stop talking to me. Right now, I am the only one they will talk to, and you want to keep them talking. We want them to hope that they can bring me back around to their side and help them. That's the angle we need to play."

Avery sighed. "I will consider and advise that, but everything isn't up to me. So, what am I supposed to do, put you in with them as a fellow prisoner?"

"No, but don't send me back in with them for a few days. Let them sweat it out a little. Then they'll be eager to talk, and I can tell them I'm doing the double agent thing, and just telling you guys crap."

Mason chuckled. "How do we know you're not just telling us crap anyway?"

Blondie gave him the same grin, with a twinkle in his eye. "Like I said, you don't. That's what makes all of this so fun for everyone."

That night, the enemy tried out a new strategy. They backed up the monster hordes with flights of mercenary archers.

It worked this way. First the merc archers would soften up the defensive lines with volleys of arrows.

Then the monsters would charge in quickly to try to break the lines.

This obviously reduced the numbers of mercenary casualties. Mason wondered if the monsters were smart enough to realize that they were being used as shock troops. Effectively, they were nothing more than cannon fodder.

But they appeared not to care. The monsters wanted only to attack and kill, and always seemed bloodthirsty and eager to charge forward and fight. The enemy was probably bribing the creatures with all the meat they could ever want. That was a pretty big incentive for a bunch of dumb, gluttonous monsters. From the monster standpoint, they probably saw the war as a godsend. They had never had it so good, and they could stop fighting and eating each other. And, from Mason's experience, humans had to taste much better.

But overall, the enemy tactics seemed to work only part of the time. They were too transparent. The defenders quickly learned to predict when the merc archers would fire their volleys, and buttoned up under protective, portable mantlets. The defenders even had teams to gather up and recycle all of the enemy arrows that could be reused.

The monsters always pulled back first. Then they charged forward again after the arrows struck.

For the first half of that night, the battle lines stagnated.

For an entire hour, the attacks halted, and the enemy appeared to be regrouping or reorganizing their lines.

Then they returned to their original strategy from before—relentless, grinding attrition.

The mercs renewed their coordinated assaults from the south. The monsters took up their relentless attacks along the west. Apparently, from what the scouts and observers reported, the two sides hadn't worked well enough together. They were too different and hostile to each other.

So the enemy leaders did a reverse. Their little experiment that night had failed in its application. They returned to what had been effective for them all along—pressing the defenders, and slowly but surely wearing them down, and pushing them back.

At dawn, the battles halted at the fourth defensive line of South Bend along Olive Street. Once more, the mercs chose not to attack during the daytime.

Mason staggered back to his tent to sleep again, and witnessed a heated, open argument between Blondie and one of his latest conquests. But the half naked young woman held her own and screamed at Blondie, raving something about some promise he had made to her to get her taken off the front lines and assigned to his personal bodyguards. But apparently, those posts had already been filled by other eager young gals.

She called Blondie on his broken promise and slapped him hard.

He slapped her back and told her to go away and stay the hell away from him.

The young woman left crying, slipping the rest of her clothes back on.

Mason was drifting off when he heard another gal slip into Blondie's tent mere minutes later. The giggling and whispering started up once more.

Now that their unit kept a regular camp, Blondie continued to be quite popular and entertained female guests on a regular basis. He could apparently afford to be choosy.

But if Blondie was betraying them to the enemy, he was sure taking his own sweet time about doing so, and had a funny way of going at it.

Mostly, Blondie just enjoyed being Blondie. But it was just that egotistical selfishness and hedonism that Mason truly worried about in his friend, and not just a little.

For the present, all Mason wanted was the sweet release of sleep. At least when he slept, he could get away from everything, and shut most of his fears out.

37

Kevin Policinski, high school science teacher, and several scientist friends at a local medical lab downtown called Dirk, David, and Jerriel over to be part of the group that they made their findings report to, including the analysis of enemy anatomy and the composition of the enemy firebombs.

First, life-sized diagrams detailed vulnerable points on torgs, ka-torgs, mor-kahls, and gozogs.

"The militia will find this information invaluable," David said. "Thank you. I know it could not have been pleasant work."

They moved on to a discussion of the enemy firebombs.

"So, what are they made of, and can we duplicate them?" Dirk asked.

"I think so," Kevin said. "We'll have to substitute some of the ingredients, but it's only a matter of time before we improve on the mix."

"What are the ingredients?" David asked.

"A combination of wood alcohol, pine tar pitch from a new species of black pine, the highly flammable resin and oil from another new plant, and the soap like sap or juice from yet another. Plus, a touch of sulfur for good measure. Quite an effective napalm, really. Historically, it would have given Greek Fire a run for its money. The delivery vessel? Simple but effective. More or less a Molotov cocktail in design. Any brittle clay or glass jar or bottle will do."

"Good work, Kevin," Dirk told him. "You and your people get us the right mix, and we'll put them into production for various weapons. We can even make a hydraulic pump sprayer that will act as a flame thrower."

Kevin nodded. "That shouldn't be hard at all to work up."

"Any luck on getting anything electric or with gunpowder to work?" David asked.

Kevin grimaced and shook his head. "Sadly, no. We're still baffled. Stymied at every turn. It's as if the laws of the universe suddenly decided that they would never work again as they once did. It is maddening. Completely irrational."

"Well, keep trying," Dirk said. "Let us know if you have any breakthroughs. Be sure to say hi to your wife, Laura, for me and Belle."

"Will do, Dirk."

They said goodbye to the scientists and headed back to their other duties.

"Here, Dave," Dirk said, handing him and Jerriel older-style watches. "They're self-winding. Mechanical, not electric. You both need something that keeps time. Use them well. The faces glow slightly at night."

"Thanks, Dirk. You think of everything. This is great."

"Yes, yoo and Belle are always soo kind."

"You and Jerriel have both been a big help to us," he said. "We just wanted to find some small, useful way to say thank you. If either of you need something, let me know."

"We will." Dave slipped his watch on.

Somehow they made it through the rest of that week and into the next, exhausting themselves every day. David briefly told Jerriel about his out-of-body experience one night, just before they both drifted off on the couch. He never got to mention what the enemy wizards said about the demon.

No further monster horde attacks gave them all some breathing space, but reports of monster raids on the outskirts and in the wilds remained constant. More foes seemed to surround them in all directions, limiting travel, mapping, an exploration. Let alone hampering any attempts to reach out to other distant communities.

With no enemy to fight, internal tensions continued to mount between various racial and political factions within Michiana itself. The militia had its hands full discouraging looting, petty crimes, revenge violence, suicides, and several troubling disappearances.

Suicides continued to be a major problem, and very upsetting to everyone.

An older woman in her forties climbed up on the Angela Street Bridge near the Portage turnabout one day. David and some of his troops were guarding it on duty. "Another one!" David shouted, and rushed toward her. "Grab her!"

His right hand just brushed the flapping hem of her floral print dress. Her feet were in walking shoes.

She calmly dropped down from the bridge into the churning dark water of the St. Joe River at flood stage in the spring.

She sank without a word.

She didn't come back up.

The militia river patrol in boats, canoes, and kayaks wouldn't find her body until a few days later, downriver.

Even the dullest duty could suddenly become a tough one, like that day.

But David grew to look forward to his training sessions with his troops. Swordsmanship, fighting, and small unit tactics and strategy were all skills he both enjoyed and excelled at.

With it came the camaraderie and respect that quickly grew between people risking their lives together. David finally got to know his people relatively quickly. Together they culled out the undesirable and recruited the elite.

Not everyone was suited for the life of a warrior. And if that was the case, then other meaningful work could be found for them. But everyone had something to contribute to the cause of keeping Michiana free and alive.

Many of his troops naturally took and emulated David's aggressive style of fighting, and tried to obtain or make weapons and armor similar to his. Longsword and tomahawks, sword-hilted fighting dagger. Katana and wakizashi as backup weapons. Bow or crossbow for missile fire. Small shield or buckler, if needed.

David started calling his unit the Blackhawks, an homage to the Chicago hockey team, and the name stuck. Their valor on the battlefield had earned them no small amount of respect, even though most of them joined the unit after the first two days.

"Many of the guard duty sessions can be pretty tedious," he told Jerriel. Sometimes she went with him when he was stationed at various locations throughout town to maintain peace and order.

Sometimes she stayed home, tinkering with her spells, magic, and enchantments for hours at a time.

There were long hours of patrolling areas block by block, checkpoint to checkpoint. Where, often, nothing happened. But that was the strategy. They kept up peace and order through a constant show of armed force on the streets and at key bridges, intersections, and strategic buildings.

But one night a frantic young mother in her night gown came running to their guard post, telling them her five-year-old daughter was missing from her bedroom.

Other people, including three children and a young teenage girl, had gone missing in that same neighborhood as well. All within a space of the weeks since the Merge.

David and a full platoon of three dozen troops searched around the house with lanterns and torches, and throughout the blocks nearby.

The window had been pried open with something like a screwdriver and forced open. No footprints.

They started questioning the neighbors about anything weird going on.

David feared that perhaps a few stray monsters, torgs or perhaps ka-torgs, were still holed up somewhere nearby, maybe in an abandoned house. Those fears were the worst kind, because they usually meant that the missing people had been horribly killed and eaten by hungry monsters.

One neighbor, an older man in his fifties, had a big dead dog in his backyard. It stank to high heaven. The other neighbors complained about it too, and the clouds of flies it attracted.

The man in that house politely told them he hadn't seen anything that night or any other night. He claimed he had a bad back and would they mind burying the dead dog for him? It had been an old wounded St. Bernard that wandered in from somewhere and expired.

"Our main concern right now is the missing girl," David told him. "Tell the militia if you see or hear of anything. I'll send a burial detail to take care of the dead dog tomorrow, if it doesn't rain again."

"Thank you, sir," the man said. "Good night."

"Good night."

They walked around the house, heading for the next. David spotted the dead dog stinking up the neighborhood in the backyard. That was weird. He didn't want to get too close, but the dog hadn't been injured or wounded in any way. There wasn't any blood on it. In fact, from the bluish-white and black chemical stains on the dog's jowls, and the dried pool of bluish vomit, it looked as if the big dog had been poisoned.

Sergeant Eugene Blaylock, a short, beefy guy with black curly hair, shook his head. "Dave, there's something not right about this house. Look how tight it's buttoned up."

David looked it over. Windows and all but one door were nailed shut with boards and plywood—to the point of obsession.

"That's a lot of physical labor for a guy with a bad back," David said.

Even the upper windows of the two story colonial had been barricaded, inside and out, apparently. White aluminum siding, dark blue trim. It had been well fortified. Perhaps the owner had a lot of help from neighbors who didn't have bad backs.

"And he's only been here since the Merge," Blaylock said. "Three of the neighbors say so. A divorced woman and her three kids lived here before. This guy told everyone that the monsters took them all. His house in town was burned down, so he started staying here for protection. He had nowhere else to go."

"Well, he didn't tell me any of that," Dave said. "I'll go have another talk with him. Keep a few troops watching the house. Ask around the neighbors for more about this new guy. Let's make sure we have some reason to be suspicious before we accuse him of anything. His story could check out."

"I'm on it," Blaylock told him.

David went back to the front door and knocked again.

It took a while for the guy to come back to the door. David knocked several times. Maybe he was on the toilet or something.

"What is it now?" the man said. This time, he sounded irritated. Not so polite as before. "I told you I don't know anything. It's late and I'm tired. Go away; I'm busy."

Something smelled wrong. An odor emanated from within the house, and not from the dead dog in the backyard. It smelled like a backed-up toilet and something else.

Like death.

"I just had a few more questions," Dave said. "I'm sorry, sir. It will only take a minute. May I come in? We can sit down for a moment, if you like."

The man hesitated. "Oh, all right. But make it snappy. I want to turn in."

A few locks clicked and the door opened.

The smell wafted out again, even stronger. No mistake about it.

He let David in.

David turned as the man closed the door but did not lock it in any way.

"Would you like something to drink?" the older man said. "I have a bottle of wine open."

"No, thank you," David said. "On duty tonight."

"Oh...sorry."

David wasn't about to drink anything this guy might hand him.

"So," the man said. "You had some other questions?"

"Oh, right." They sat down in the living room, across from each other in soft chairs. "Have you seen any of the monsters around this area, especially late at night? They would move around cautiously, trying to avoid being seen. There might be only one or two of the smaller ones, and you might mistake them for a person in the dark, or from a distance."

"Like I told you. I haven't seen anything."

Something crashed to the floor upstairs. Then it thrashed and bumped around. "What the hell is that? What's up there?" Instinctively, David rushed to the stairs.

The older man snarled like an animal and tackled him from behind.

38

The following night, Mason noted that the fighting at the front had definitely returned to the same pattern as before.

Then within the hour, it changed again–this time for the worse.

The enemy mages finally joined the battle both in numbers and in earnest.

They hit the front defensive lines, apparently at random, along much of its length. They struck from both the south and the west.

A dizzying array of destructive spells and magical effects played havoc with the defenders: mostly flame, ice, and explosions. Then there were various kinds of lightning, clouds of poison gas, and bursts of acidic vapors that also burned skin, eyes, mouths, throats, and lungs. And there was magical ice that froze everything in an area solid–including troops.

Mason saw showers of magic needles, spikes, missiles, or slicing blades like shards of glass. The ground burst open violently. Great waves or rushes of water swept in out of nowhere to sweep troops away. Or areas suddenly turned into scalding pockets of super-heated steam that threatened to cook troops where they stood within such zones.

Strange rays of light zapped people and dissolved flesh or caused bones or internal organs to explode violently from within, or boils that erupted and exploded.

Terrifying illusions emerged that put entire units to flight—horrors of the mind that defied rational description. One group swore that a wave of large, flesh-eating insects had instantly swept over them. They ran in panic, although no one else around them could see any bugs at all.

Another platoon said that they were suddenly surrounded by thousands of enormous, poisonous snakes biting and snapping at them. The illusions were always horrifying bugs and other nasty creatures, some that ate their way into or even out of the body.

The defenders reeled in shock, surprise, and fright at all such magical onslaughts, backed up by the regular, conventional enemy assaults.

From what the spotters and observers could tell, there was no pattern to the attacks from the enemy mages. They could occur anywhere along the front lines at any moment.

Various lights and the illusions of lights also flickered and flashed all along the enemy lines. No one could tell if they were the flashes of spell glow from mages, or some of the enemy briefly flaring various colored, hooded lanterns in order to decoy, confuse, and throw off militia attempts at detection or attack.

The enemy clearly proved themselves to be the absolute masters in fighting in these fashions with magical support. According to Thulkara, Sylurria and other nations had used combined magic as part of their military strategy for more than a thousands years.

The foe used every trick and advantage that they could think of against the Urthers.

Mason and the Shooting Stars blasted at the enemy front lines, trying to hit the enemy mages, but their efforts were mostly in vain. They raced back and forth this way and that, trying to isolate the positions of the enemy mages and engage them—to no avail.

First the fourth line of defense collapsed.

The enemy troops and monsters backing up the mages surged forward in a great rush.

The foe redoubled their efforts, and hit the retreating defenders with everything they could muster—arrows, magic, and massive frontal assaults. They had the militia on the run now, and strove to keep things going that way and roll them up.

The fifth defense lines buckled within minutes of the retreating troops passing within, before they could even catch their breath and turn about to help reinforce it.

The South Bend militia was reeling and in great trouble now. Panic and terror took hold of the troops and the retreat was rapidly in danger of becoming a complete rout as they fled once more.

Militia began to fling their shields and weapons aside and simply run headlong away from the line of destruction. Many were cut down from behind.

Hundreds of small children were being protected at nearby grade school. The intense fighting drove them out into the open, with only a few adults to lead them.

Their militia guards did their best to hold off the enemy advance and give the children time to get away.

But the enemy was moving too fast from what Mason could see.

It didn't look as if those kids were going to make it.

Major Avery called out to Mason. "Let's sweep in among those houses and taller buildings over there and cut off the enemy before they intercept those fleeing kids!"

Bill was right. They couldn't let the monster hordes reach those helpless children.

The main unit cut off the street.

Mason, Thulkara, and Blondie ran into a wide alley between two brick buildings. Some of the kids were still streaming down that alley, the littlest ones, only four or five years old, screaming in abject terror, and in real danger of being left behind by the older kids and the few adults.

Thulkara wove her way among the kids, hewing down any monsters trying to leap among them. Blondie fired his crossbow as fast as he could.

Mason drew out his Howdah shotgun pistol and unloaded both barrels high, loads of tungsten and iron oxide, into the face of the charging horde.

The twin blasts shredded the forefront of the enemy wave and splattered the monsters behind them with the burning pieces.

Every second they fought, more of the children got past them and could keep running.

Thulkara on his left, and Blondie on his right.

The Pistolero stood his ground and poured burning death at their enemies. His friends cut down any stragglers he missed.

But the horde was insane with bloodlust and numbered in the thousands.

Thousands against three.

Mason's guns were almost empty. They pulled back. They had to. They needed to retreat and locate one of the reloading teams.

The horde rushed down that wide alley, filling it with their numbers once again.

Arrows zipped in, just missing the three.

Merc and horde archers were getting up onto the taller buildings on either side.

"Let's get the hell out of here!" Thulkara cried, just as a charging gozog smashed into her, and they rolled back, fighting hard.

Mason fired his last round.

A child's cry alerted them. A little blond girl, about three, crouched in the shadow, whimpering and crying. She was either too scared or too exhausted to run.

"Blondie!" Mason cried, drawing his Spillers. "Grab that kid and run. I'll hold them off!"

Blondie slung his crossbow over his back, crouched down, and held both of his hands out to the small child. She retreated more at first. "No, no...come to me, little one. Let's both get away from this place."

As soon as she stepped out, a black arrow pierced her through the side. She fell, her mouth open and her big eyes blinking wide.

"No, no!" Blondie screamed.

He rose up, snarling like a beast gone mad.

His hands and arms glowed and pulsed with bright red power up to his shoulders.

Scarlet lightning shot from his hands like gigantic, electrical claws. First he used the claws like extensions of his rage and swept the archers off the rooftops.

Then he ripped through the top two levels of the brick buildings to either side down the length of the alley. He collapsed and toppled them inward onto the rampaging horde, in avalanche waves of masonry by the ton.

That part of the enemy advance was now broken and crushed.

Blondie came back to Thulkara and Mason, studying the child's grim wound. She went into shock.

They broke off the barbed arrowhead, but they didn't dare remove the shaft.

"How is she, Mace?"

"It's pretty bad," Thulkara said. "And she is so young."

"Her only chance is to get her to an aid station, Blondie," Mace told him.

"There's one close by. I'll take her. You two keep fighting."

Blondie took the child in his arms without another word and ran for it.

Mason had never seen his friend run like that. Even the Thul couldn't have kept up with him.

Mason and Thulkara fought their way back to the bulk of their unit.

Along the sixth defensive lines extending along Martin Luther King Drive to the west, and Ewing Avenue to the south, all available militia reserves were brought up to hold those positions at all costs. Every attempt was being made to halt the heavy enemy advance and throw them back.

Troops focused on stopping the retreat, and forcing the fleeing defenders to re-arm and turn about to face the enemy once more.

The greater numbers of the concentrated defenders helped them all feel slightly more secure than they had at the outset.

But the charging hosts of the enemy slammed into the sixth line just as hard.

Enemy magic blasts continued to strike at key points along the line, disrupting the defenders.

Mason and his company spearheaded one part of a desperate effort to break the enemy advance.

From east to west along the southern line, and north to south along the western front, in each place, two thousand hand-picked militia troops roared out in a fierce counterattack, flanking the enemy and driving into them hard.

The Shooting Stars led the flanking attack from the east, and the Pistolero and his people led the one from the north.

They moved as rapidly as they could, and blasted and cut down anything in their path in a skirmish line forty yards in length, cutting across the battle front.

An infantry phalanx with spear and shield marched directly behind them, screened by archers and a full company of fast-moving light lancers acting as protective cavalry on their left and right.

Mason managed to get reloaded, and blazed away with his pistols, handing them off to the loaders being pulled along in armored wagons directly behind him. Runners carried the guns back and forth, but he always kept his Spillers at his side, in holsters and on lanyards. They were his fallback guns, with their standard pattern of fire, if the reloading teams momentarily fell behind.

If a runner got cut down or wounded, two stood by to take their place. When the enemy arrow barrages came in, horn call warnings from the spotters allowed most to duck behind portable archery mantlets for protection

Once the flanking sortie passed through, then the massed defenders charged into the broken, forward ranks of the dismayed enemy, pushing them halfway back to the fallen fifth defensive line.

Mason engaged and gunned down at least five enemy combat mages who tried to come against him along the way. One on one, they could not match his devastating rate of fire. At one point, he fanned one of his Spillers, not only disrupting a necromancer's death ray spell, but disintegrating the enemy mage where he stood.

Then the bulk of the enemy mages seemed to retreat from the front lines, not wanting to be swept away. The defenders saw no more of them for a long while after that.

The enemy mages did not enjoy becoming casualties. When the going got tough, they almost always broke and ran. They only liked to attack when they had all of the advantages in their favor.

The defenders had succeeded at last in pulling their own surprise off on the attackers.

But once played, such attacks grew difficult to make them work a second time. Surprise was fickle on the battlefield. Just as the militia would, the enemy would also regroup, recalculate, and respond—ever striving to come up with some way to counter such tactics, and make them far less effective, if they were tried again.

By the time both sorties had traveled and fought the length of three miles, well over an hour had passed. If they kept driving forward, they could meet up with each other, but by then there was no need. They had broken the enemy advance, but they were also all fought out and utterly exhausted.

They had to retreat back behind the sixth defensive line, while the rest of the militia and reserves fought back and forth the rest of the night, just to hold what they had partially regained.

But the enemy mages voided the field completely for the rest of that night. They most likely regrouped to rethink their own strategy from behind their lines. It became very clear that the enemy mages did not like being eliminated so easily, and sought to protect themselves during the conflict in every way possible.

Militia spotters and observers could not be certain of their estimates, but they calculated—from the spacing and positioning of dead mages found near the battlefront—that the enemy might have as many as two hundred mages supporting their troops. At the very least, no fewer than a hundred and twenty, divided up evenly between the two lines of attack, from the south and west.

What the actual numbers of mages the enemy had in total was not known, or what their reserves might be. Thulkara told them that the entire nation of Sylurria were practically all mages. Every man, woman, and child.

Very few of that race were non-magical. That did not sound very promising or encouraging.

According to recent history, entire boatloads of mages had crossed the ocean of Tharanor from the Old World to the nationalistic colonies of the New World. Entire fleets had come from Sylurria, bearing them and their mercenary armies to bloat their city states on the southern coast and found the city state of Vaejan far to the north, up through the inner seas. They also controlled the southern city states of Kavendo/St. Louis, and Jashakal/New Orleans.

The Sylurrians had fought legendary battles all along the inner seas of the Mississippi to found and hold their new colonial territories, and some of the mages and their mercenary armies were apparently making a huge power grab after the cataclysm.

Mason shuddered and wondered what was it like now, after the Merge, to have city states like Vaejan mixed up with the vast Urth population of Chicago, not to mention all of the monster hordes of the wilds surrounding those regions. It boggled the mind.

And how many of the enemy had been sent this way to wipe out the pesky Urth humans isolated in Michiana? How many more were there that could be sent?

They were already outnumbered as it was. If only the defenders had some way to expose the enemy mages to direct fire, and concentrate attacks on their positions at the front. A war of attrition could go both ways. If the defenders could degrade the numerical advantage of the enemy mages, that would be an enormous help.

If they could kill enough of the enemy mages, perhaps the foe would reconsider their military strategy and withdraw.

The defenders had a large number of wounded to deal with after the battle. More wounded than ever before. Everyone was enlisted to help retrieve and process them. That included Mason and his unit.

It was definitely not a time to be selfish.

The medical corps set up triage stations all along the front. At first, the dead were left on the field. Only those still living were brought in, as quickly as possible.

Triage was brutal and efficient.

Anyone who could be saved was transferred further behind the lines to the aid stations. Troops or people who were expected to die anyway were put in a comfortable place, given painkillers if possible, and left with someone to comfort them until they passed. This could be both random and somewhat arbitrary.

Mason got paired up with a badly wounded guy in his early forties, pale, his torso awash in blood. The medic slipped him off the stretcher and spoke quickly, propping up the trooper's head and shoulders with the man's own bedroll.

"Multiple stab wounds to the gut; he's a goner. I gave him a pill that should take away most of his pain. Stay with him until he slips away. I've already black-tagged his boot."

Black tags wired around a boot meant KIA, to be collected after the wounded.

The medic got up to move on as the triage team kept the stretcher waves sweeping across the battlefield.

The poor guy had been staring up at both of them the whole time.

Mason glanced at the older guy, and then shouted at the medic, his voice trembling. "What do I do?"

The medic was obviously overtaxed as it was. She shouted back while checking another casualty. "Hold his hand, dumbass. Talk to him."

"I'm Mike...Mike O'Connor," the dying trooper said.

Mason took his hand and held it tight. "Mason Tyler." Mike squeezed back at about half-strength.

"The Pistolero?"

"I guess so. Call me Mace."

Mike grinned. "You know, I was in a lot of pain until she gave me that pill. Now it's like I'm going numb. I wanna get up and walk, but I can't get my legs to do it."

Mason didn't know what to say.

"You know, I don't feel like I'm dying. It's funny."

"Is there anyone you want to send word to?" Mason asked.

"The bastards killed my wife, my Jane. I'm glad I took a few of them down before they got me. Our twin kids, a girl and a boy, were away at Ball State when the Merge happened—Mark and Elizabeth. I thought I'd never see them again. I guess...I don't have anyone left in town to send any kind of word to."

"I'm sorry about that, mister."

Mike sighed heavily. "I guess it's all right. Mr. Pistolero, it was a real pleasure seeing you fight for us. I saw you jump up on that wagon and unload on those creeps. You mowed them down with those guns of yours. It was a thing of beauty to watch. I wish we could kill all of these bastards for what they've done to us. You must be the bravest of us all."

"I'm not as brave as guys like you, Mike. Tell you the truth, I'm mighty scared the whole time, every time we go in on the line. I just try to do what I have to do and keep going."

"Aww...you're just saying that to make me feel better. All of your amazing powers? You sure don't look afraid to me."

"Mike, it takes a lot more courage for guys like you–without any powers–to stand up there on that bloody line and fight toe-to-toe with our enemies. Since I can do something special, I'd better get off of my ass and do whatever it is that I can. It's an obligation, the way I see it. But that doesn't make me any braver than guys like you or anyone else."

"You got a girl, Mace?"

Mason bowed his head. "Yeah."

"Young guy like you…famous. I bet you have all you want."

Mason licked his lips. "I only want the one."

"Yeah, that's the way I was with my Janey. Twenty-one years together and we still made love three to five times a week. God, I couldn't get enough of her. It was even better after the twins went to college–like we were back in our twenties again. You like loving that girl of yours, Mace?"

"Can't think of anything much better than that."

"Good man. Love her all you can. Life is short." Mike paused. "Those rotten sons of bitches killed my Janey. I joined the militia the next day. I wish I could have taken more of them down before they got me. From now on, Mr. Pistolero, every time you put fire on those assholes, you just blast the living shit right out of them for me and my Janey, and all the other innocent people they've cut down–for nothing!"

"I'll do that, Mike. Any else?"

"No…I guess that's it. I am feeling kinda tired now, Mace. I think I might…close my eyes and rest for a spell."

"That's fine, Mike. I'll stay here with you for a while."

"I've already asked the Almighty to forgive me for anything I've done wrong, and to forgive others who have wronged me. To watch over my kids, if they're still alive somewhere. I've made my peace."

"That's good, Mike."

"Mace, it's okay for you to slip away…if I don't wake up."

"Sure. Don't worry about any of that, Mike. Rest if you want to. Keep talking to me, if you like."

"Do you think I'll find my Janey waiting for me somewhere?"

"I sure hope you do, Mike."

"I do, too. Boy, I'm kind of looking forward to that, now."

He had a smile on his face.

Militia trooper Mike O'Connor's hand slipped out of Mason's a few minutes after that, his eyes already closed.

Mason found his friend Blondie about a half hour later, way out behind one of the aid stations set up behind the lines, sitting in front of a tree in the dark with his head in his hands.

Quite plainly, his friend was sitting there bawling his eyes out.

Mason had never before seen Blondie cry. Not once—not even when Ginger got hurt that time. He left his friend to it for a while.

When it appeared that Blondie's grief was letting up, Mason stepped forward and made his presence known.

"It's just me, Blondie. Don't worry about a damn thing. I've had a rough night of it, too." Mason hesitated. "The little girl?"

Blondie nodded and hung his head once more. "She didn't make it."

Things got real quiet for a long while. Neither of them said anything.

"Why, Mace? All the power you and I have, and it don't mean shit!"

"Blondie, we only have the power to destroy, and thank goodness there are powers far greater than that."

"I...I didn't even know that little girl's name. I ran as fast as I could, but by the time I reached the aid station, she smiled up at me and then her eyes just glazed over. She went limp my arms and that was it. She was gone. I couldn't save her...and she was so beautiful, and so little. I'm not worth a shit, Macc. I would have given my life for hers, right then and there...if only I could have."

Blondie sobbed again for a while.

"They put a black tag on her tiny foot and took her from me. I lost it and fell to pieces. I've been here ever since."

"Come on, Blondie. I'm your friend, your brother. Think about all those hundreds of kids we did save tonight. People are dying every day. We can't save them all. Let's go back to the unit." He held out his hand. Blondie took it and stood back up, wiping his eyes.

They made their way back to their camp. Both of them had their hands in their pockets.

"I told you, I hate kids, Mace. Hate 'em. Don't you remember me saying that?"

39

The crazy old guy wrestled with a great deal of power. He was surprisingly stronger than David and almost as quick.

Almost.

David flipped over and grappled with him. The man tried to whack him in the face with a small ball-peen hammer. He must have had it hidden in one of his pockets.

The blow bounced off David's helmet as he turned, like a bell being struck.

He kicked the older man under the chin and flung him back down into the entryway. Then, instead of pursuing the assailant, David raced up the stairs

He did not slow down, and crashed through the locked bedroom door where he thought the noises had come from.

A small, frightened girl matching the description of the missing five year old flopped on the floor, thrashing around. She had beaded cornrows similar to the picture her mom had showed, and lay tied up and gagged, wrists and ankles taped and bound with nylon rope. She wept and moaned, her eyes big and streaming with tears.

The small child was frantic.

Lengths of the same rope had her tied to the bedposts. Somehow she slipped free and bumped around, striking her bleeding head against the floor, the bed, and the upended nightstand and lamp.

Something else was very weird.

David suddenly noticed it.

The walls and ceiling of that entire bedroom were covered with various mismatched mirrors, both framed and unframed.

The perp came roaring up the stairs like a wild man, a fireplace poker in one hand and the small hammer in the other. David still had the advantage of his armor and superior weapons.

"You get out of here!" the crazed lunatic screamed. "This is my house now. You have no right to be in here. This is my business. I'll fix you!"

David drew one of his tomahawks and rapped the insane bastard across the face with the flat of it and then back again.

He blocked a jab from the poker with an armored forearm. Then he clipped the guy up under the chin again with the flat, and tapped him on the top of the head. The man dropped and rolled back down the stairs, just as Sergeant Blaylock and some of the troops rushed in.

"The girl's upstairs," David said. "She's alive. Get her mother here, quick. Search this place and hog-tie that no good son of a bitch. Watch out— he's stronger than he looks." David cut the little girl free of her bonds and tried to dress her minor wounds. But the child was terrified. In a state of panic, she stamped her small feet, screaming and crying for her mother.

"Mama, Mama. I want my mama. Please, don't let the bad thing in the mirrors get me. Don't let it get me. Please, keep it away from me!"

David wrapped her up in a blanket and quickly carried her downstairs and out of that freaky house.

Their medic had finished checking the girl over when the mother arrived and quickly wrapped her hysterical daughter up in another blanket and took her home, guarded by several militia troops.

David went back inside and helped finish searching the upstairs. Not much else out of the ordinary except for the strange room with the mirrors all over the walls. Crazy. That room spooked everyone.

Then he heard shouts and cries of dismay and rage from his troops downstairs.

Three veteran troops ran up from the basement. Two of them vomited right there in the hallway.

The reek. The stench of death that wafted up from the basement.

Nothing could match or describe it.

The rotting dead dog smell outside paled in comparison to what rose up from that fearful basement.

Up from those dark, bloodstained steps.

David guessed that the guy had poisoned and killed the dog to decoy everyone else from the smell emanating from his own basement.

"Don't go down their, sir," one man warned.

"You don't want to see it," another man said, still dry heaving.

David steeled himself.

It had to be pretty bad.

"No one has to go with me if they don't want to," David said.

Only two troopers went with him, all of them holding lanterns.

In the basement, they found their missing people from that area.

Including all of the children.

Including the divorced mother and her three kids that the man claimed the monsters had killed and taken away.

All dead, hanging upside down from the wooden rafters. Some of them on hooks, some with their feet nailed right into the wood. Each of the bodies had been savagely mutilated. Now they were just long strips of shredded skin, flesh, or entrails hanging down over bones. Some of the bones had been torn out, split, and splintered.

From the looks on their tortured faces, many of the victims had still been alive while they had been ravaged.

Blood, shit, and death—wall to wall. It was inhuman.

More mirrors downstairs, ringed along the basement walls.

Mirrors splattered with gore. What was up with this crazy, fricking bastard and all of the damn mirrors?

But the corpses and the reek had to be the worst.

Dead faces and staring eyes, frozen in agony and terror. No human being should die like that.

Even the monsters didn't kill people like that.

The stench alone was horrifying—beyond imagining.

"We're going back up," David said, struggling not to breathe.

The two troopers with him did not argue one bit, and came up quickly behind him on the run to get away from that horrible scene.

David went to the killer, who was now sitting on the couch with his hands tied behind him and his legs hobbled with rope.

The serial murderer looked up at David and laughed. He just babbled like a freak.

"Do I get my nice trial now? I wanna be famous. I'll get my trial and I'll go on and on in detail about everything I did to each one of them. And it'll be a matter of public record forever and ever! I'll be immortal. A celebrity! Too bad there's no more TV. No more Internet or movies. I'd have my own website! They'd surely make a movie about me. But they can still write a book about me. I'll tell them everything so that the whole world can read about what I did, forever and ever!"

"Gag him and shut him up," David said, completely sickened. He felt nothing but disgust and loathing for this wretched creep. This was much worse than finding outside monsters responsible for the deaths of these poor people. If it hadn't been for this dickhead, all of those innocent people would have survived the attacks–they would still be alive.

My God, David thought, those poor kids. The agony and horror frozen on their little dead faces. He wished he had never seen it.

The internal monsters like this sick putz were even worse than the vicious denizens of Tharanor.

Once they had the perp shut up, David looked the bastard in the eye, remembering a few conversations he had with Dirk.

Short shrift and summary justice for any truly heinous crimes.

Crimes exactly like these.

"No one will ever know your name, you demented loser. You wanted to become famous…for this? Well take this with you straight to hell. No one– *nobody*–but God and the Devil–will ever know your name or what you did. You will be dismembered and buried face down in a nameless grave. And there you will rot like a forgotten piece of shit and turn to dust, as if you had never existed. Under martial law, I pass summary judgment on you. You will never torment or harm anyone ever again!"

David sank his tomahawk deep in the killer's forehead.

And then ran him through the chest with his longsword.

David twisted and jerked his weapons free, and stepped back from the spurting wounds as the body collapsed. He wiped the blades off on one of the curtains at hand.

The troops flung the killer's body down into his own blood. Some of them spat on the wretch.

"Bury him just like I said," David told them. "Stab out his eyes, and cut off his head, hands, and feet. That's a direct order."

They left the house of death. David looked around, still wanting to puke.

"No other houses near enough to worry about, Sergeant Blaylock?"

"No, sir."

"Then burn this hovel to the ground. No one needs to see or find out what happened to those poor people, here. That's exactly what that sicko wanted–exposure and notoriety. He's not getting any of that."

David nearly sobbed just thinking about it all. It was hard to get it out of his head.

"Especially those poor little kids," he muttered. He gasped and wiped his eyes.

Blaylock nodded. "Don't worry, we'll burn it to ashes, sir."

"The bodies can be collected afterwards from the wreckage and given proper burials. I'll file a brief report to Dirk."

"Yes, sir. Will do."

David shook his head and shuddered, still trying to shake off what he'd witnessed. His thoughts were very dark. Even war on the front lines with people dying everywhere wasn't like this sort of insanity.

"Sergeant, I've had enough duty for one night. I'm going home. Any of the troops who saw any of this can go home, too. If they need help dealing with any of this, get them some. Please carry out the rest of our duty shift."

"Will do, sir. Have a good night, if you can. I hope you and the others feel better."

"Thank you, Eugene. I will not have a good night, but I will try to feel better, after this darkness passes."

At least they had saved the one little girl, and put a stop to this guy. He obviously would have kept on killing.

The defiled house went up in flames by the time David and a small group of troops marched away–away from that stinking house of death.

They made their way home, to be troubled by their own private nightmares.

40

Mason grabbed what sleep he could and rose up early the next day, which was finally sunny and slightly warmer. Guards informed him that Blondie was already speaking with the two mage prisoners once more in a nearby tent. Major Avery had sent for him.

The prisoners had been brought up in one of the captured enemy slave wagons.

Blondie was definitely getting an early start. Mason suited up and went to collect Thulkara, who usually rose on her own and went to help train the militia fighters.

"Good morning, Mace!"

"Thulkara, can you break it off and join me?" he shouted.

"Sure thing," Thulkara said, still wrestling with an entire militia platoon by herself. She rolled around laughing, and nearly crushing them all with her weight alone. She abruptly sprang to her feet and ran to catch up with him.

"See you, guys!" The platoon she had been pummeling lifted their hands if they could and groaned.

"The sky is bright, all the robins are merry. This shall be a good day and night to feast…and sing!"

Oh, God, Mason said to himself, as Thulkara broke out into some kind of booming, Thul ballad.

Something about a hero who slew a thousand foes, single-handed, upon a mountaintop of skulls…during a blizzard.

Thul songs and merriment were just chock-full of skull-splitting, gut-ripping, and spine-hacking frivolity such as all that.

So very jolly.

Soon every dog in the county was barking and howling before she broke off.

By the time Mason and the Amazon reached the intel tent, Major Avery and Blondie were already walking away from it.

Mason and Thulkara quickened their pace and jogged up to them.

Major Avery motioned for them to remain silent until they were all further away. Perhaps the prisoners were still somewhere nearby.

Avery led them about a quarter of a mile away and into a tall house that was being used as a spotting station and a command post. There was a table in the dining room where they could speak freely.

"Hey, Blondie," Mason said. "Anything new?"

"Not too much. Our guests are really pressuring me to help them escape. I've put them off, telling them that I still don't see that as being very possible. They have no concern for whether I get killed or not. But they still remain confident that the war will be over soon."

"They've been asking him a lot about the Pistolero again," Major Avery said. "Blondie hasn't told them any more than what the enemy could figure out on their own."

"I've convinced them that I'm feeding the Urthers misinformation in order to get the chance to talk to them. That, at least, makes them see me as some sort of spy or double agent on their side. I've asked them to tell me what they knew about me, in an attempt to bring back my memories. But there isn't much. None of us were ever friends. I was a prince, one of the nobility. Neither of them ever directly worked with me, or knew me personally. I barely knew their names.

"On top of that, they had heard that I was continually going off on some kind of secret missions for the high masters of the Khabal—for years. I was often gone for months at a time. I showed up a few days before the Merge, reported to my master, and then vanished once more."

"Who is this master that you served?"

Blondie grinned. "That's where it does get interesting. As it turns out, I was an apprentice to Gorrial Lankorro, the Supreme Leader of the

Sylurrian Mage Council and regent of the Sylurrian New World Colonies."

"We still don't understand the Sylurrian society and its many, confusing hierarchies," Major Avery said.

"That's for sure," Mason said.

Thulkara had already grown bored and sat down in a corner, leaning against the wall and snoring, with a line of drool running out of her open mouth. Politics and intrigue put her to sleep like a lullaby.

As long as she stopped singing.

"Where does the Dark Khabal fit in with all of this?" Avery asked.

"My master Gorrial also happens to be the High Magus and the head necromancer of the secret Dark Khabal. He is its ranking mortal leader, and is in contact with the Dark Ghods, receiving directives from them."

Mason gaped. "Mortal leader? Dark Ghods? Come on, Blondie. This is starting to sound like a fairy tale."

"Tharanor is a world of magic and the supernatural," Blondie told them. "Joke about it at your peril. The Dark Ghods do in fact exist...or, at least, powerful, dangerous beings from yet another dimension, who call themselves and consider themselves as such. As it turns out, I have recently recalled that my alter-ego Shaeddor was a staunch atheist, strangely enough."

Mason blinked. "An atheist? Then how can you believe in these Dark Ghods?"

"You really must improve your listening skills, Mace. Just because I stated the fact that they do indeed exist, does not mean that I accept or worship them as such. I do not believe them to be actual ghods."

"Huh? But you just—"

Blondie held up a hand and rolled his eyes. "These creatures, these beings exist, the same as do you or I. There is no denying that. Our universe is filled with many entities and beings and things that we can scarcely imagine, Mace. So they are powerful, indeed, and extremely dangerous, verily. In the best of worlds, we should probably avoid any interaction with them at all costs, but does that mean that we should bow and scrape before any such beings of darkness or light and become their slaves? I say no. We should not. And I will not."

Major Avery still had all the color sucked out of his face. "Let me get this straight. First we have to deal with monsters, and mercenaries, and wizards. And now we have to fight beings with godlike powers? When does this begin?"

"No, no," Blondie told him. "Thankfully, the Old Dark Ones are far removed from us, tucked away in their own dimension. They wouldn't bother coming here to our little squalid, insignificant mudballs."

Avery let out a breath. Mason felt about ready to do the same. It was all a lot to take in.

Then Blondie went on. "Not when they can get their cults like the Dark Khabal to do all of their dirty work for them."

Major Avery gaped. "And this Shaeddor, this guy you were before, you were part of this cult?"

Blondie sighed and sat down. "I can see this is going to take a while, so let me explain. The Dark Khabal is a secret society—forbidden, actually. Back in the Old World on Tharanor, the practice of necromancy and membership in the Khabal are illegal, punishable by death. Most of Sylurrian society would be appalled and frightened by them, and demand that they be killed, once they were exposed. The Dark Ghods and their fanatical followers are consummate destroyers of everything they touch."

Mason and Avery simply stared back at him.

"Look at it this way. Mace has told me stuff about your world's various religions, in passing. They sound just as whacko and as crazy as ours, quite frankly. Why do you think I'm an atheist? Think of the Dark Khabal and the necromancers as the equivalent of your satanic and devil worshippers, but with real magic and actual supernatural powers to back up their madness."

Major Avery snorted. "Hell, is that all? Now that you put it like that, I feel so much better."

Mason asked his friend, "When you were this Shaeddor guy…you were a part of all of this?"

"Some of my knowledge and memories have actually returned," Blondie said. "I don't think I was actually a full-fledged initiate into the cult itself. At the highest levels of the Dark Khabal, to enter the inner circle, a dark mage must perform a certain ritual involving the human sacrifice of a family member or a close friend. He or she must kill someone he or she loves, drink the blood from their heart while they still live, and offer the victim's blood and soul to the Dark Ghods. Then he or she must swear eternal loyalty to the Dark Ones. This is called the Dark Oath or the Great Oath by some. I think, somehow, that I would have remembered all that…if I had done such a thing."

Mason let out a deep breath. "I feel a little bit better, knowing that."

"Back then, I didn't even know for certain that my master, Gorrial, was a member of the cult, let alone their leader. But I had my suspicions, and I guess it does all make sense now.

"However, my past self was quite the opportunistic scoundrel on his own, who sought out power only for himself. My master was also a powerful man in accepted society—the supreme leader of all the Sylurrian mages. A perfect example of duplicity and deception. And even as his apprentice, even without being a member of the Dark Khabal, I would have been sworn to obey him and do his bidding. What's more, I think that I did so willingly, in order to enrich myself and gain strength and power on my own."

Major Avery struck the table with his fist. "Did the Khabal and these Dark Mages cause the Merge? Are they they ones behind all of this insanity and death?"

Blondie nodded slowly. "They are indeed, and their masters, the Dark Ghods, gave them the knowledge and power to bring about the Cataclysm of the Merge."

"But why?" Mason asked. "Why do such a terrible thing?"

Blondie shrugged. "Because they can. That is what they are and what they do. They see a chance to cripple and enslave not one, but two worlds. And they still fully intend to do so. This is all just the beginning. They have plans far beyond this region—plans to conquer everything and everyone on both Urth and Tharanor. And they mean to crush and subjugate all who oppose them."

Avery glared at Blondie with venom in his eyes. "And once more, we still ask—what role did you play in all of this?"

Blondie shrugged. "I believe that I was a spy, of course. They sent me back and forth between the two worlds for the last three or four years. I learned your languages; I learned your secrets. I gathered information about Urth and gave it all back to my Master—I was one of about twoscore people. All spies. And it was surprisingly easy. Your libraries and your…Internet gave us all of the information my master could ever want, quite openly and mostly free."

"So," Mason said. "You did work for them; you were one of their advance scouts—their spies. You and the other spies helped the Khabal and the Dark Ghods cripple our two worlds, and murder tens—maybe hundreds of millions of innocent people in the process of achieving that."

Blondie looked down slightly. "Yes," he said softly.

Avery muttered, under his breath. "You don't sound very busted up about all of that."

Mason held up one hand. "Shh…"

The three of them sat there for a quiet moment. Then Mason asked, "What does that make you now, Blondie?"

Blondie stared back at him. "I have only just begun to remember it all. Yet all of this has made me your friend, Mace. You are like the brother I never had. And quite frankly, that is the only thing right now, that is keeping me from going back to my own people, especially when they are winning."

Major Avery's head snapped up suddenly. "I've just figured it out. Our enemies must have a way to go back and forth between both sides, and it must be somewhere nearby."

Blondie grinned. "And here they say Urthers are stupid. That is correct, sir. They have a handful of ways to go back and forth, most of them very costly to employ. But the most reliable method existed before the Merge, and still exists today. It has not been disrupted. Within a week to ten day's journey to the northwest, in the mountains near the inner seas, there is a little-known cave. One end opens here, and the other end...on the other side."

"I knew it," Avery said. "That's how they keep getting such heavy reinforcements. They can send them back and forth at will from anywhere or, for that matter...from either side."

"How do they control the monsters?" Mason asked. "I keep wondering about that."

"Quite simple, really. Such weak-willed darkspawn already worship and obey the Dark Ghods who made them, and they can be forced to obey those who serve the dark powers. On top of that, they can also be easily bribed and tempted by the base prospects of violence and food. And they are easily cowed by any power greater than themselves."

"I suppose," Mason said.

"You are well aware that you must still keep all of this knowledge a secret," Blondie told them. "If word gets back to the two captives that you know about that secret place, they will know for certain then that it was I who told it to you. They'll stop talking to me."

"We don't want that," Avery said. "We want you to keep them gabbing. But we also have to be very careful about how you continue to play them."

Mason studied Blondie and still wondered who was playing who.

He called his reloading teams together, and got with the militia leaders. Mason thought about what he could not control, and what he could. The enemy had stepped up their game.

It was high time for the Pistolero to do the same thing.

He made a list for every type of metal, crystal, gem, wood, stone, and chemical he could think of to experiment with, and notes on how he wanted all of the re-agents prepared, stored, and brought to him, organized and labeled.

If he was a sorcerer now, he needed to start thinking like one. A sorcerer needed a sorcerer's laboratory.

Mason went without eating until well after noon.

They took stock of his reloading supplies. He was definitely burning through them very rapidly. At this rate, he'd be out of powder and shot within ten or twelve days–long before the war would end.

Of course, he could still fire his pistols empty, but at a much reduced rate of destructive effectiveness.

What would the mighty Pistolero do then?

If his reloading supplies had been saturated with Wild Magic somehow, he needed to locate some more of that magic, and have more powder and shot ready to absorb it.

It all sounded much more feasible that it actually was. Magical energy just wasn't readily available.

The authorities had multiple reports of glowing pools of water, especially after thunderstorms. But whatever strange, magical energies the pools contained, they apparently did not last very long. Often, by the time teams reached them to investigate, the pools of water had dried up, drained off, or stopped glowing and had become completely inert.

Then there were the reports of glowing plants, flowers–even glowing trees at times. But even if they did have magic within them, how could he tap into it and transfer that power to his inert reloading supplies, in order to empower them?

Magic and the use of magic was still too new to them. The Urth humans didn't know enough about how it worked and how to manage and produce it. Whereas the Sylurrians and the other peoples of Tharanor had been using magic as the basis for their society, technology, and culture–for centuries.

Crows in the trees around them called to each other, cawing.

Thulkara laughed. "Our black-winged uncles sing of coming battles."

She was always full of warnings, signs, and superstitious omens based on birds, beasts, the sky, and weather. Everything seemed to have some deeper purpose for her.

Blondie spat in the dirt. "Crows are crows, and like carrion and garbage," he noted. "Like rats and roaches, they thrive wherever there are men. I do not need ignorant, meaningless birds and the weather to tell me that more fighting and corpses are coming." He licked his lips and lay down to take a nap.

Mason turned to Thulkara, who was checking her armor and weapons, and sharpening and oiling what needed it. "I've seen your shield either absorb or deflect a mage's spell in combat. How does that work?"

Thulkara shrugged. "Thulls are naturally resistant to magic on their own, by their very nature. But my shield was enchanted by a mage to negate magic and spells. I don't know exactly how it works; I'm not a mage. Very few of my people are, and that is rare. We are primarily a warrior people. Yet neither are we fools. We hire wizards and pay them to work with us, and for us, to enchant our weapons and armor to help protect us from magic. Magic is too great a power in war to ignore its proper use."

Mason grimaced and nodded. "I hear that. I wish we could get more of it to work for us. The enemy has more mages than we do, and that's just one of the deciding factors stacked against us. They're using magic to whip our asses on a regular basis."

Blondie suddenly mumbled something, half-asleep on his cot, hiding out in secret where his gals couldn't find him.

In truth, they were starting to run him ragged, the debauched goof. He couldn't go back to his tent because he couldn't get any sleep there. Half the time, Blondie's bedmates fought over their shifts with him.

Mason kicked his friend's boots slightly. "Speak up, Blondie. What did you say?"

"Don't kick me, damn it. I said you can detect magic and mages with equal parts sulfur and ground silver–it makes mages and anything magical glow for several minutes before the effect wears off."

Mason stared at him. "Why in the hell didn't you tell us all that before?" he said.

Blondie blinked at them. "Tell you what? What the hell are you talking about?"

Mason repeated what Blondie just told them.

"I said that? Then I must have only just remembered it. Things keep coming back to me, in strange ways, at strange times. They just pop in and out of my head...even when I'm half asleep."

Mason got with Captain Avery and sent word to the militia and the city leaders.

Then he made up some special loads laced with plenty of silver and sulfur for his double-barreled howdah pistol and his carbine. They had to try something. The enemy mages were just too much for them. The defenders were getting murdered each night by an enemy superiority and strategic advantage in both magic and mages that the Urth humans simply couldn't compete with.

Now the militia had a few more tricks up their sleeve to try out as well.

Night came, and the attacks started up, just as they normally did.

Backed up by the enemy mages, the mercs and monsters pressed the militia defensive lines harder. The defenders were forced to start falling back, working their inevitable fighting retreat.

A surge of enemy magic tried to rout the defenders once more. Even the heavy, protective archery mantlets couldn't hold up long under magical barrages.

Just as it seemed that the defense would collapse, the militia activated its traps and devices.

Catapults and ballista casters flung up clouds of sparkling dust over the forward half of the enemy front lines.

In the darkness, the enemy mages suddenly blazed to life like big lanterns, glowing yellow, orange, and green. The enemy struggled in various attempts to conceal their mages with blankets and screens, but they were simply too bright.

Mason immediately targeted several enemy mages that were within range of his most powerful blasts and guessed that the Shooting Stars did the same thing around their positions.

So did the militia archers and siege weapons.

The result was that once more, the enemy mages and the combat advantages they provided were driven from the field. Many of the shining mages ducked into buildings in order to conceal themselves and escape. Or, at the very least, until the magic detecting effects wore off.

After two precious hours, the enemy responded. They brought up their own catapults, trebuchets, and ballistae and used them to open up on the defender positions.

After the third hour, they began using flaming missiles and missiles that were enchanted to explode with great destructive force on contact with other matter.

Mason and his unit rode up and down the line, trying to take out any enemy artillery pieces within range of his guns. Yet the enemy had gauged and measured his powers quite effectively by then as well, and kept most of their siege weapons just outside of such range.

In order to take out a single device, the Pistolero and the militia had to make a sudden push, driving toward the device and fighting their way through the enemy lines to get close enough to those targets to engage them. Such operations often proved very costly in lives. And the instant they destroyed the device, they would be forced to retreat to avoid being cut off and swallowed up by the superior enemy numbers.

The seventh defensive line was barely holding when the sun finally rose, and the defenders could get a break and see to their dead and wounded.

As usual, Mason was exhausted by that time, after a full night of heavy fighting and maneuvering.

Then the scouts picked up signs and sounded the warning.

The siege engines renewed their barrage, pummeling the militia lines once again, but this time the missiles unleashed an enveloping smoke that obscured the battlefield.

The enemy artillery fire only increased. Spotters reported even more siege engines and their crews and ammunition being raced forward by the enemy, and fresh mercenary units charging up to the line behind them—even from the west, where the monsters usually fought at night.

The defenders dropped the casualties they were carrying and raced back to the confused militia front lines. Reserves were called up in panic and haste. Militia siege weapons were almost out of their ammunition, and struggled to respond.

Fresh enemy troops continued the battle during the daylight hours with grave consequences for the defenders.

The seventh defensive line began to crumble. The exhausted troops there just could not be expected to hold against superior new units and numbers that the enemy sent in.

By the time more militia reserves came on line, the foe had pushed the weary militia defenders halfway back to the eighth line of defense. They could do little but take over and do their best to slow the relentless, grinding enemy advance that punished them at every step.

But Mason could not keep fighting with them. He had to withdraw with his companions and rest.

The defenders had no strategy, no way now to stop the constant enemy advance.

41

David heard that the town council struggled to maintain order, cohesiveness, and cooperation among the various town factions, to plan crops for the coming season, and map the region around them. The leaders continued to learn everything they could. Yet that learning curve kept getting steeper.

They also strove to establish and maintain contact with any other human enclaves still out there. But outside of Mishawaka and Elkhart, there didn't seem to be any others. Michiana was an island in the wilds.

They hoped to eventually meet some other Tharanorians like Jerriel, but from what she told them, the closest city states were around the areas of Chicago, Detroit, and Toledo.

No one had been able to reach any of those places and return to tell about it. The wilds around South Bend were simply that–too wild, and infested with monsters and dangerous creatures from the world of Tharanor.

Each day brought something new and strange.

Jerriel was primarily a wizard and an enchantress. But she understood the principles of how others used magic as well, and continued to test people from the town for magical abilities, and to help translate information about magic into English.

"It's funny," David said to Jerriel and their other friends, "how many of these people who once 'pretended' to have magical abilities before the Merge, can't seem to cut it on the actual magical tests. While absolute nobodies, who never considered having magic talent, test as very powerful."

Jerriel gave the council a regular report on her findings. Even David was surprised at some of the names that popped up.

Stacy Keller, Belle Blackwood, and others showed latent promise at being magical healers. Jerriel could show them the basics of such skills, but her abilities did not go much past first aid: closing, sealing, and cleaning wounds. Higher, advanced healing magic could remove or neutralize toxins, poisons, and infections—even repair damaged blood vessels and nerves, or fix broken bones and torn muscles. Magical healing took various forms, just like all magic.

Jerriel told the budding healers that if they could study under the tutelage of truly great healers, they could learn to heal at the higher levels and do much, much more. A true healer could even replace lifeforce energy in the body of someone dying, and keep them alive.

But even on Tharanor, no known magic could bring back anyone who was truly and completely dead. Death remained permanent. Once the spirit crossed over through the veil of the world—the Prime Material Plane of the living—and passed on into the realm of whatever awaited them thereafter, there was no coming back from that.

Jerriel simply referred to all of that as the Beyond. Even their greatest mages and priests did not know what awaited the soul in the Beyond.

David and his unit leaders sent any mildly injured troops to the budding healers and medics to practice on. Usually, the sessions went as well. Especially during battle drills and sparring bouts during training sessions, where minor injuries and accidents occurred regularly, despite whatever precautions they took.

The budding healers grew in practice, knowledge, and wisdom by dealing with such minor injuries, sharing their progress and tips with each other, while recorders tracked their efforts.

Another of David's MHS friends, Robert Billings, showed promise as a mid-level enchanter. He came over to the house often, and worked closely with Jerriel on several projects, in the wizard's study Jerriel had set up in the sunroom. She even instructed Rob on how to set up his own lab and study at his place, where he could tinker with minor enchantments and continue to learn and experiment on his own, while driving his wife crazy.

Robert started learning Tharanorian, and even borrowed Jerriel's tools and magical implements at times. Soon he was devising his own equipment. Jerriel and he made dry little jokes and puns about magic that they laughed at together while they worked.

Jerriel hoped that one day, they might even be able to either repair or replace her cracked translation gem.

"I have a lot of respect for you, Jerriel," David told her one beautiful day as they walked to their labors. "I know what a burden it must be. You're the only wizard in this entire area. Yet you work yourself into a stupor each day, trying to help me and my people."

Jerriel would smile at him whenever he said something along those lines. "This is where we are, in a dangerous new world, Daeved. We must woork together to survive. How could I doo anything less?"

Each day both of them worked hard, either together or apart. They ate their meals with other friends and comrades, or quietly shared them in their small house together. They still spent time each day laughing and learning to speak each others' languages, both with and without the mindstone.

And every day, every hour, and each minute, David felt himself falling further and deeper in love with her. He was helplessly enthralled by radiant Jerriel, his glorious wizard girl with the gorgeous violet eyes.

At times he worried whether she felt the same way about him. He knew so little about her and her world. Her people. Her culture. What was courtship like for them? What did she expect? What should he do or not do? He hesitated many times, not wanting to spoil or ruin what they did have together, which became more and more precious to him.

Had Jerriel had a lover or a boyfriend before? Most young adults their age had. It would not be surprising.

There was no one to tell him what to do when he had serious, personal questions about their relationship. And some things he definitely couldn't come out and ask her. It was crazy, but sometimes he went for walks alone, and spoke softly to his parents. He'd stare at their picture, which he brought along, or simply talk to them as if their spirits were all around him.

The early days of spring weren't all drudgery. Life went on in many ways. With some degree of order and security back in place, people did what people always do. Older people passed on. Babies were born. Kids went to school and played sports and had fun with their families and friends.

Two of David and Jerriel's new friends were a couple a few years older than them. Brad Daniels and Ellen Stiles moved up the date of their summer wedding to a beautiful spring day. Both of them were young teachers in their mid to late twenties.

Brad taught history and world studies at the same high school where Kevin Policinski taught science. Ellen taught at Christ the King, one of the local Catholic grade schools.

Together they made a pretty, happy young couple.

Brad and Ellen both had served in the militia with Kevin, but all three went back to teaching soon thereafter, once the main threat was gone. Even they admitted that they were all better teachers than soldiers. But like many of the young people in town at that time, they would rise to the occasion and defend their homes and their people if forced to do so, as part of the reserves.

Many had done so, and would again.

Jerriel cried, seeing Ellen in her plain but stunning wedding dress with her few bridesmaids, and Brad in his suit with his groomsmen. With digital cameras no longer working, older film cameras were used by friends and family to take pictures.

Kevin Policinski and the university scientists knew something about photography, and had helped the council set up a few new film labs in town. Hand processing was slower, and the reactive chemicals slightly different now since the Merge, but the modified process could still be made to work. Not all knowledge was lost or incapable of being adapted.

Throughout Michiana, people bartered items, and their time, and donated themselves and their skills to trade for different things.

If there was one positive thing about the Merge that David appreciated, it was the fact that so many people came together to work for the survival of humanity. During the crisis they were under, the focus of many people changed from making money and getting ahead on an individual or selfish level, to looking out for each other and making sure that everyone was safe, secure, and well-cared for. The threat of destruction made some people take better care of one another on a community level.

That part was definitely better. People were forced to work together in order to stay alive, and find some degree of security and happiness therein.

In that respect, the Merge had made many people better people.

But in any situation there were always troublemakers, opportunists, and charlatans who played upon peoples' fears and tried to divide or take advantage of them.

Watching Brad and Ellen cut their small wedding cake at the reception in the high school, with their friends cheering them on, David tried to think positively. No system of any kind was perfect and required constant maintenance and tinkering. Especially when it involved the messy, fallible human factor.

As usual, people could only do their best.

That was all that any one could do.

The town council tried to listen to the brightest minds, the smartest people available to them. Then they came to the conclusion that they thought would work best for the people as a whole.

Someone asked Dirk once what kind of a government they were forming. Dirk merely answered, "Plainly and truthfully, we're creating a Practical-ocracy. Whatever we can find that works best, that's what we're going to do. If we find out that something works better, we'll switch over and do that. And we'll take our lumps and learn from there as we go."

Of course, there were a lot of voices from the past who wanted the old ways back as soon as possible–if not yesterday.

They argued constantly to get their way, but whether some people liked it or not, the old world that they had known was gone.

It really was.

Politically, the two-party system was over, for the simple fact that it did not work. Nothing could ever get done. There was only one party now–the human race, and they were on their own in a dangerous new world with new laws and new realities.

Endless arguing and campaigning between rival factions who were never going to change their opinions anyway just led to paralyzing failure. Nothing could change. Failure and inefficiency would mean death and starvation for tens of thousands, while fanatics from one side or the other argued endlessly about who should be in charge, and why the other side was the greatest evil on the planet. Such zealots would do so, literally until doomsday came.

The people of Michiana no longer had time for such folly.

In a survival situation, people didn't have time for all of that hyper-political nonsense. Actual hordes of monsters crashing through your windows to kill and eat you and your kids made all of that past crap silly and obsolete.

People had to stick together now and discover what worked–or become extinct.

For better or for worse.

David smiled, musing to himself at a table, a little tipsy from one glass of wine too many at the wedding of their friends.

Michiana really was kind of like a big marriage, a wedding, like forming a big family of humanity that took care of itself and looked out for one another. The single-minded, obsessive pursuit of personal gain or power in selfish forms simply could not be tolerated as the primary focus of human life any longer.

Not that there weren't a lot of people out there still trying to go back to that. It was hard for fanatics to give up the past failures.

For the present, at least, as isolated as they were, humans needed to band together in order to stay alive.

All of the other distractions, all of that silly crap from the past was all deception and illusion, smoke and mirrors. Nobody had time for any of that horse hockey anymore.

David danced with the bride and tried not to step on her feet. Jerriel danced with the groom. They danced together into the night beside their friends, holding onto each other.

This was the way it should be with people.

Just dancing with Jerriel and holding her close by themselves were rare and special treats for David.

Smiling at her and looking into her eyes, for him, was a form of paradise.

Young Steven Hayward even got up the nerve to ask Jerriel for a dance, and blushed like a beefsteak tomato all the while. David couldn't blame the young boy for being smitten with her.

In those moments, David felt very much at peace with their new world.

When they all got tired of eating, drinking, and dancing, everyone wished the happy couple well, and went on home to sleep.

David and Jerriel and many of their friends rode their bikes back to their houses, down the middle of the city streets in the cool night air. It was funny to hear so many bikes clipping along down the wide open roads now, with no more cars or trucks to fill them.

A few people in town, outside of the military, were lucky enough to have horses to ride. The town council worked with the area horse owners to greatly expand horse breeding from that point forward.

Brad and Ellen took a long, romantic carriage ride back to their house, to begin their life together as man and wife, in a mixed-up world that was far from certain.

That all took love, and it took guts.

42

Like many of the defenders, Mason didn't like the looks of the new developments at the front one bit. The grueling war was now being prosecuted by the enemy on a 24/7 basis. Fighting continued all throughout that day. At night, the monster hordes swept back in and took over for the mercs, who would rest in turn, and take over once again at the next dawn.

Enemy artillery coordinated their attacks with the infantry and archery units, and no one could forget the enemy mages.

These new tactics forced the South Bend defenders to very quickly rethink and reorganize their own strategies and tactics. First, they needed to switch their units over to also work in shifts, fighting day and night in response to the enemy. The two shifts were formed, but that left very few front line troops in reserve—in case of an enemy breakthrough.

As many feared, second line troops were organized into militia units, brought up, and made active as reserves.

Sadly, these units had numbers, but they were far from effective: older men, women, and young boys and girls ages ten and up. And additional supplies of weapons, armor, gear, and even food and water had to be rationed among them.

Eventually, such secondary reserves would be brought up to help plug holes and hold the line with the regular militia against either monsters, or worse—seasoned, professional mercenary soldiers who knew exactly how to conduct military actions.

No one was looking forward to the casualties that were obviously going to result from such clashes. But the defenders had no choice in that now.

Mason himself informed the militia commanders that the writing was on the wall. They might as well start evacuating what remained of the city, because it was going to be quickly enveloped by the war.

They could not hold the enemy back. They could only delay them.

And, on top of that, Mason's ammunition stores continued to dwindle, although he tried to make every shot count whenever he was on the line.

The word went out.

The evacuation began, and quickly became a panic.

The defenders of Mishawaka were quickly informed that the enemy would most likely be engaging them in their areas—within the week.

Why would the enemy halt its advance once South Bend fell?

Mishawaka would then become the new front line, and then sparsely populated Osceola, and Elkhart after that—until the Urth humans of Michiana were either completely subjugated or wiped out.

That choice would be up to the enemy.

South Bend grimly promised that they would send any surviving forces over to help defend Mishawaka, which wasn't really in any better position than South Bend had been at the start of the war.

The numbers all looked grim, no matter who looked at them.

In response, the defenders grew desperate. They brought about a dozen people up to the front lines who had exhibited fledgling magical abilities.

Some could create or cast fire; a few cold; two, lightning; one smoke; and the final one, an exploding, blasting ray.

Blondie said that they were all sorcerers, just coming into their powers. He warned them that this was a very dangerous time. He warned Major Avery and the new recruits directly that these new mages should not overtax themselves. They could easily burn out their powers in the beginning, or worse.

They could severely damage or even destroy themselves.

They asked Blondie to give them some instruction, and he did what he could, but Blondie was not a teacher, and he still had huge gaps in his own memory still from his amnesia.

"A sorcerer's powers are part of him, and can be affected by his emotions, his mental state, and his physical condition," Blondie attempted to explain. "Sorcerers learn to use, focus, and increase the strength of their abilities gradually, through slow, steady practice with the guidance of experienced mentors. That is why they become apprentices. There are many dangers and pitfalls in trying to develop such abilities on one's own. Such powers cannot be forced, or rushed. To do so can be disastrous, and it far too easy for the ignorant to make big mistakes."

The budding mages still had many questions that he simply could not answer. It was a very frustrating situation for everyone involved.

Blondie still couldn't even use his own former powers at will yet. They only ignited as a defensive reaction, whenever he or his comrades around him were in great jeopardy. And that usually meant in the heat of battle.

That night, the militia tried to have the new mages only cast three times. But the pressure to perform during war made the mages take further risks.

As a result, one mage burned himself out, and might not ever be able to use his abilities ever again. Even worse, a woman in her mid-thirties burst into flames and perished, unable to control her powers when they backfired and went out of control during a fifth casting. Other than dousing her charred corpse with water and finally putting it out, there was nothing else the militia could do for her.

Yet the extra boost from the costly mage castings helped out over the course of three hours, and were used sparingly. But after that, the new mages had to leave the line and find a place to rest and recover.

A line of heavy thunderstorms raged in halfway through the night, with high winds, driving rain, and lightning. Much of the front lines turned to churning mud, and the lightning was truly perilous for both sides. Caught out in the open lifting metal weapons to fight with was very ill-advised during such a powerful storm.

Not only that, but Blondie seemed to have an definite affinity for lightning and lightning storms.

He found a vantage point and directed lightning down on the enemy lines with a furious vengeance. After just half an hour of such punishing effects, the monsters withdrew in panic, leaving many dead and wounded behind them in the mud.

Blondie and the weather had bought the defenders half a night's respite.

The militia did their best to recover and regroup, using the time as wisely as they could. In fact, they were training all of their people to the limit of their endurance each day, attempting to prepare them for the fighting on the front lines that lay ahead. Yet the enemy still seemed to possess almost every strategic and tactical advantage.

"Here's our problem," Mason complained to Major Avery.

Blondie smirked. "Mace, since when did we whittle them all down to just one?" he asked, with a wry edge to his voice.

Mason snorted. "Screw you, Blondie. Bill, on top of everything else, all we can ever do is react. All we can do is defend and wait for them to hit us again, hammer us night and day, and wear us down. We can't attack. We can't break out of this trap they have us in. And we all know that eventually, they're going to wear us down and push us back until all of South Bend is theirs. We're going to run out of defenders, and out of town to defend!"

Messengers raced in to announce. "Major Avery. Pistolero! The new lake you told us about on Allen Street is attracting the lightning from the storm. The waters there are glowing again, just like you said they did in the past!"

Mason felt his own eyes widen and his mouth drop open. "Avery, get all of our inert shooting supplies and gear over to that damn lake. Blondie, Thulkara, we're less than a mile from that location. We need to ride over there fast!"

Their mounts weren't ready, so Mason and Blondie grabbed two post horses from the messengers. Thulkara simply ran behind them as they passed beneath the storm.

An enormous lightning bolt nearly struck them.

Blondie sensed and redirected it onto a huge sycamore tree that exploded in flames on their right flank, going up like a huge torch as the trunk burst and split with loud cracks.

Then the peal of deafening thunder blasted the air around them the next instant.

"Keep going!" Mason tried to yell over the storm's fury. "We have to get there before the effects fade!"

It took them only a few minutes to reach the deep end of the lake that extended out toward the dark woods. But to Mason the time seemed to telescope into an hour or more. They kept riding around the near side.

This might be his one chance to renew his shooting supplies, and he wasn't going to waste it.

The water was indeed glowing more and more with Wild Magic, as Blondie described it.

When they reached the shallow end of the lake where the houses from the broken street were still partially submerged, Mason glanced at the remains of his shattered duplex. The wreckage was in the process of being cleared away from the concrete foundation.

But more amazing, was the ferocity of the lightning hitting the lake, and apparently causing the water to glow even brighter, in rippling waves.

Blondie pointed at the latest strike. "See, the enchanted water is absorbing the energy of the lightning and transmuting it into Wild Magic energy. This must be very similar to the forces that imbued you with your current powers."

Mason looked around nervously, shucking all of his gear that already worked.

"I hear horses and wagons heading this way," Thulkara told them.

"I hope they get here soon," Mason said. "The affects I witnessed right after the Merge only lasted for minutes at best. Otherwise, I would have drowned. They have to get those supplies here so that we can try to charge them up."

"It's a form of enchantment, actually," Blondie noted. "But yours is a very strange case, Mace. You and your gear are symbiotically part of the magic. It won't work without it being channeled directly through you. Good thing you were a strong, latent sorcerer at heart. That's the only explanation. Your unique focus is probably directed by your force of will."

"What does all of that mean?" Thulkara said. "I hate it when mages talk magic."

"He means that my guns are part of me, and that's why they work for me like they do." He stripped down to his boxers again, putting his duster back around him while they waited for the wagons and carts to get there.

Hurry, guys. "I'll tell you," Mason said. "I'm not looking forward to another cold swim in that water."

Blondie looked at him and both his eyebrows went up. "I wouldn't either. And that's Wild Magic, Mace. It's unpredictable. If you can't control it and direct it with your force of will, there's no telling what it could do to you."

"I was in it before. I'll be all right."

Blondie grabbed his arm. "Mace, you don't understand. Every time you go into something like that, it can be different. It could very easily destroy you."

Mason pulled his arm away. "Then I'll be dead, and it won't matter. I have to take this chance."

The enchanted water rippled with a waves of glowing light, as two more gigantic lightning bolts struck it.

43

Someone rapped on David and Jerriel's back door quietly, two nights later. Subdued tapping, but persistent. As if they they didn't want anyone else nearby to hear them but the people inside the home.

What the hell now?

David sighed. Time check on his new watch: 3:35 a.m.

He grabbed the leather baldric with his longsword and tomahawks sheathed on it, and slipped it over his shoulder.

Jerriel came out of her room at about the same time he came out of his. Both of them were in T-shirts and sweat pants. She suffered from a bad case of bedhead, but she apparently had heard the rapping also and held her staff ready.

"Darksight!" she said, casting the spell in English to give them both night vision.

He glanced in a mirror on the wall. Both of them had the same dark band of the spell's energy over their eyes as before.

"Daeved," Jerriel said quietly, keeping her staff aimed at the door. "Who is it?"

The tapping increased, almost urgently.

"I don't know," David said. He slipped one of his tomahawks loose in his right hand and reached for the doorknob with his left. Jerriel covered him.

He pulled the door open, ready to fight.

Steven Hayward crouched down on the back stoop, still reaching up and rapping with his hand.

"Steven?" David said. The boy waddled into the entryway and closed the door behind him. He stood up, a short sword at his side and a dagger on his belt. He was still breathing hard but quietly from running.

He couldn't help staring at Jerriel.

David noticed the boy's arm bleeding from a long gash.

Jerriel saw the wound, too, and tended to it while David looked at him. Steven grinned at having Jerriel fuss over him.

"Steven? What is it? Are the monsters back? Who hurt you?"

"They came to our house. About a dozen of them. They attacked us. I got cut saving Mom."

"Who, Steven? Was it the monsters?"

Steven looked up, still in shock. Tears ran down his face. He nearly sobbed when he spoke. "No, it was people. Just guys from the militia. They turned on us and tried to take us prisoner. Said they'd kill us if we didn't let them gag us, tie us up, and haul us away. They called us traitors. After all we've done—they called us traitors!"

Traitors? To what! The Haywards fought as bravely as anyone else.

Something was wrong. Something about all of this was very wrong.

"Steven, what happened? Your folks, are they—"

He nodded, wiping his nose. "They're okay now. Nobody told these guys that Dad and Mom still had people sleeping over at the house and in the garage. When the trouble started, and the shouting, they all came boiling out armed and ready to help. The intruders got scared and tried to grab my mom and fight their way out." He blinked and his eyes got big.

"That was a big mistake—on their part. I've never seen my dad fight like that, even against the monsters. It was scary the way he cut those guys down; he didn't give them any chance at all."

David knew exactly how good Fred Hayward was with a sword. He had trained with him for years. A third degree black belt, too. Not a man you'd want to cross.

Let alone try to abduct his wife.

Steven shook his head and rubbed his eyes.

"Go on, Steven. You're sure your folks are okay?"

"They got hurt a little, but nothing bad. Dad questioned one of the men before he died. There's a coup going down tonight. Someone in the militia and on the town council is trying take over. My dad sent me here to warn you! They've sent people to kill Dirk Blackwood, and probably some after you, and lots of others. And they'll definitely want to capture Jerriel."

David's blood ran cold in his veins. Then he got get angry.

Bastards. As if things weren't bad enough.

Most likely some power-hungry, greedy jerk or an entire group of such bastards wanted to take charge and set themselves up as petty warlords over everyone else.

Some people hadn't changed very much at all.

In their zeal, they'd kill or capture anyone who might be able to resist them. People like the Blackwoods, the Haywards, and him.

Kill anyone who might oppose their tyranny.

They were after Jerriel, too. Yeah. She'd be a big prize for them. The only known wizard, and someone who knew all about Tharanor.

Jerriel finished bandaging Steven's arm and peeked out the window at the front of the house. She and David pulled running shoes on without socks.

David slipped his padded helmet on. No time for the rest of his armor.

"Daeved!" she said in quiet alarm. "Many peeple are in the street. They're cooming this way."

David wasn't sure how much of Steven's message Jerriel had heard, but apparently enough to know that they were in trouble again.

"Out the back!" David said. If they were lucky, they could make it over to the Hayward's house. By then Fred would have enough militia around him from nearby that were loyal to them.

They just had to get there.

Thank goodness Fred sent Steven to warn them. Although that had been desperate, too, under the circumstances.

They slipped out the back door, out into the cold night air.

They spotted five men with weapons slipping through the neighboring backyard to cut them off.

Two charged David. Two charged Jerriel and Steven.

"They're back here!" the fifth man yelled.

David's tomahawk whizzed through the air and smashed the man in the head, dropping him.

The others attacked.

"Get the girl," a voice shouted from the front. "Kill the others!"

44

An open carriage raced up, filled with one of Mason's four-person reloading teams. They pulled a small cart of inert black powder guns and reloading supplies behind them, along with some modern guns and ammunition that wouldn't function.

They all jumped out and began unhitching the cart.

Mason and his friends went around to help.

"How much does that cart weigh?" he asked.

Cameron Patterson, the leader of the team, jerked the cart free of its hitch. "About two, three hundred pounds," he guessed.

"We might only have seconds to do this," Mason told them. "Help me wheel it up to edge of the lake. The rest of you get some ropes on it. We'll drive it under the water's surface and see what happens. If something goes wrong, or if something happens to me, you'll need to be able to pull the cart back out with the ropes."

"I wish we had thought to have them send some of the new sorcerers over," Blondie said. "Since their powers and their foci haven't solidified yet, they might be able to have focused reactions similar to your—if the process didn't kill them outright. Mace, I hope you don't mind if I don't go in that charged water. There's no reason I have to take a chance on dying. I wouldn't be able to do what you have done, anyway. Whatever my powers are, they're already fixed within me by now. I'd be taking a chance at death for nothing."

Mason nodded as they kept pushing the half-loaded cart closer to the water. "Sure thing, Blondie. You hang back. You're right. Don't risk it."

Blondie dropped back before they reached the edge of the glowing water. By then they had two, bright yellow nylon ropes on the cart, trailing back to the beach.

All four of the loaders kept pushing.

"I can try to wheel it in under the surface myself," Mason told them. "This is going to be dangerous. This Wild Magic power could kill us all. Don't go into the water if you don't have to."

The other three looked to Cam and nodded. "We'll help you push it under and then try to get out and see to the ropes," Cam said. "We all accept the danger, Mace. Like you said, this might be our only chance to get this done. We have to risk it."

They went in up to their knees. The water was still very cold. A few of them cursed. Mason tried to catch his breath and stop his own teeth from chattering.

There wasn't time for the others to shed anything but their coats. They still had all of their clothes on.

Without hesitation, the five of them shoved the cart under water, rolling it forward deeper and deeper.

They gulped in breaths before ducking their heads under the surface.

Lightning struck the water once more and an energy surge grabbed them and the cart and swept them in an arc to the left for about twenty feet.

Strange energies and patterns of light enveloped them. Mason focused all of his energies and thought on concentrating those powers through himself and the supplies in the cart.

A similar haze of disorientation wafted through him, and in his delirious state, he saw the colored waves pulsing through and around himself, just as they had before.

No more lightning struck, and shortly thereafter, Mason shook himself and needed air so badly that he clawed his way up the few feet to the surface.

Even as he caught his breath and went back down, the lights in the water winked out.

301

The Wild Magic had come and gone, even as the other wagons and carts raced up to the water's edge.

Mason followed the ropes. They were slack. Apparently, no one had been able to hang onto them.

He trailed them back and walked out of the cold water shivering, with a rope in each hand.

On the short beach, confusion still reigned. Troops holding the ropes had been yanked into the water when the wagon got swept away.

When the water flashed, anyone still in the water got zapped. The lucky ones were only stunned.

Cam Patterson was the only one to stagger up out of the water before collapsing in the short grass at the edge. He passed out.

Linda Collier was found floating in a strangely shaped block of magical ice.

By the time others busted her out of it, she was dead. She had stopped breathing, and no attempts to revive her worked.

They searched the lake for hours thereafter, but never found any sign of John Wolper, or Marie Purdy.

Major Avery was about to order the other teams into the lake anyway, and asked for volunteers. Many put up their hands and stepped forward.

Mason forced himself back up to his feet and staggered toward them. "Don't bother," he muttered. "The Wild Magic has come and gone, and done whatever it will. The water isn't glowing. Everyone will just get wet and cold for nothing. Am I right, Blondie?"

"That's right, Mace."

It was still raining. The clouds still boiled. Thunder rumbled in the distance.

Major Avery studied the sky. "More storms are coming in. Do you think it will work in the daytime?"

Mason shook his head violently. "We don't even know if it worked this time," he said. "We've already lost three good people. Let's test what we have before we take anymore risks."

Cam Patterson sat down in the short grass on their right, crying into his hands for the loss of his three friends.

Mason picked up the ropes and held them up. "Let's pull this cart out and examine what we have."

Many strong hands quickly pulled the cart back up out of the lake, and Mason asked that the black powder guns and lead shot be dried.

While they waited for that to be completed, Mason tried shooting some of the modern guns and ammunition.

Almost all of them were still duds. And no one knew why.

The only reaction came from a single AR-15, but Mason threw it down after trying to fire it. The rifle grew red hot and hissed, and then melted into slag in the wet grass as everyone watched.

Mason took one of his empty guns and loaded it with the formerly inert black powder, using his own patches, ball, and percussion caps that he knew would work.

He took aim at the wreckage of his old duplex.

The resulting blast shredded a good chunk of it. Despite their losses, Mason could not help grinning and getting excited. "It works. At least we know the powder works!"

A cheer went up from the troops.

Mason felt somewhat relieved. The Pistolero would be able to keep shooting and assisting the war effort in a major way.

Although none of the modern-style guns and ammo functioned properly, they quickly discovered that all of the black powder shooting supplies would work—but once again, only for Mason.

At first they hoped Cam Patterson might be able to use some of the new guns. He had been exposed to the same Wild Magic at the same time.

But none of the guns would work for him.

Blondie tried to explain to them. "For there to be any hope that repeating the process would work, the person exposed would have to be a mage—preferably a new sorcerer whose powers have not fully formed. Unlike wizards, who must learn to cast spells, a sorcerer can use his powers gradually by chance and need, through force of desire and will. But Wild Magic affects even mages randomly. Look at the Shooting Stars. Their focus is very different than that of the Pistolero."

"I honestly don't know if we could get the same reaction twice," Mason flatly said. "But at least now, we do have a way to recharge and replenish my supplies."

"You need to discover as many latent or active mages as possible among your people," Blondie advised. "Especially any who show signs of becoming sorcerers."

"How do we test them?" Avery demanded. "How do we do all that?"

Blondie shrugged. "I don't know. I can't remember."

"We need ten more like the Pistolero and the Shooting Stars," Major Avery said. "Twenty if we could get them."

He grew so frustrated that he punched one of the wagons with is gauntleted hand. "Damn it! We still don't know anything, and we just lost good people."

Mason looked at the cart and tried to calm his friend. "Bill, all of our people were willing to take that risk. They even said so as we took the wagon in together. We barely made it in time as it was. But it wasn't for nothing. I was going to run out of ammunition in about a week. Now we have enough for me to keep fighting on the front for months. That's something."

Avery wiped his cold, sweating face. "I guess you're right. Sorry I wigged out there for a bit."

Mason clapped him on the shoulder. "We're all under a lot of pressure, Bill. Let's distribute all of these reloading supplies and extra guns to the other three reloading teams. You see to Cam and get him some peace and rest off the line. Having those extra guns will help us out, too. And I like the looks of those other black powder shotguns. We can put loads in them that will do a lot of damage up close and far away. I've got a good feeling about all of that."

45

David blocked an ax stroke with his longsword, then slashed deep down the second man's leading leg, through the knee. The man grunted and went down on his knees, thrusting at David with a spear.

David whirled, sliced the spearhead off, took a kick to the side of his leg, and blocked another swing of the axe.

Steven lunged and ran the spear carrier through the chest with one of his short swords.

David rapped the ax guy in the face to stun him, then split his head open, even through the motorcycle helmet he wore.

Jerriel muttered some words quietly. Big spikes shot out from her staff, shredding the two attackers in front of her. They fell at her feet.

One of them clutched a katana in his twitching hand. Steven snatched that up as they ran past the fallen thugs and down a side street.

David looked back. About thirty more attackers swarmed around their house.

The three of them rounded a corner a few blocks later and saw several troops guarding the street. "I'm Captain David Pritchard of the

Blackhawks," he shouted. "Traitors attacked us in our beds. Please, help us!"

The men drew their weapons. Two of them had bows.

"We know who you are," the leader of the band said. He and the others charged at them. "Drop your weapons! Tell the girl to—"

Jerriel cast another spell, a spray of lethal sparks. But two men sprang out of hiding from the right side and threw a net over her. She cried out. They dragged her down.

Her spell shot off harmlessly into the night sky. One of the men dazed her with a blow from a club.

Steven leaped in and thrust his short sword into the club wielder's throat and severed the hands of the other holding the net with the katana.

David dodged and blocked two arrows, deflecting them with his sword. The other men spread out to rush him.

Jerriel tried to get up, and scramble out of the net, reaching around for her staff.

"Steven, get behind me!" David said. "Stay there and protect my back!"

"I will!"

Then they fought, surrounded by seven attackers bent on killing them.

David lashed out quickly. He tried to hold them off, and attempted to wound or kill as many of them as he could. He took a cut on his upper left arm, a grazing jab from a spear to his right leg.

Steven was smaller, but very quick. Even at nearly fifteen, he'd been well-trained by swordsmen much bigger and older than him—including David.

One of the attackers tried to grab Steven and now lay screaming and thrashing with his belly slashed open.

Four of the five remaining attackers were wounded and bleeding by then.

"Get in there and drag them down!" the leader said, the only one not hurt.

"You get in there!" one of them hesitated and taunted back.

"Follow me, then!"

They charged once more.

David cut the leader's arms off just above the elbow. He backcut and ran the attacker on the right through the chest. The man fell back. A spear shot past David's head on the left, just missing his face. He dropped back and held his longsword at the ready in his left hand.

A spear haft struck David in the head from the side, ringing his bell through his helmet.

He pushed the spear aside with his longsword and dropped down low. With a draw cut of his blade, he bent his strength into the stroke and cut the spear man's legs off just below the hips.

The last man facing Steven ran away, vomiting.

But screaming, bleeding, dying men attracted the main group of assassins very quickly.

By then Jerriel had gotten free of the net and had retrieved her staff.

"Run!" David shouted. "Get out of here, Steven. Take Jerriel back to your place!"

"I'm staying with you!" Steven shouted from David's left, a fierce light in his eyes for one so young.

Jerriel took up a place on the right.

"We stay, Daeved!"

No more time. He readied his weapons. "Oh, hell! There's too many of them!"

There were.

At least sixty of them poured around the houses and down the street at them.

Jerriel stepped forward and cried out, with words that hurt the ears.

Several dark, shadowy forms of nameless creatures shot out from her body like exploding shadows and fell upon the advancing attackers, ripping and tearing into them, keeping over half of them busy.

But she collapsed on the ground, apparently spent from the effort of unleashing them on the mob.

David stood in front of her with no ally but a small teenager, however fierce.

Against nearly thirty remaining killers.

"You can run, Steven. Get away. Get help!"

Steven readied his blades and shouted. "I will not run from cowards and scum!"

David laughed and turned his face to their foes once more. What a man that boy was going to be one day–if he survived.

"Then let's face them together!" David told him.

They cut into the first few attackers that reached them.

From every angle possible, arrows and crossbow bolts sliced through the attackers. Defenders poured out of the houses and around the streets.

In moments, the battle ended with most of the traitors cut down.

Few of them reached David and Steven where they stood at bay protecting Jerriel.

And those who reached them did not last long.

The dark, shadowy creatures that attacked the other traitors finished their lethal work at about the same time. Once done, they slipped back like shadows, somehow reabsorbed by Jerriel.

307

She came to a short while later. Troops escorted them to militia HQ, surrounded by thousands of loyal forces.

Attackers from the coup attempt still raged throughout the town in many places. Word went quickly to Dirk and Belinda, to see if they were all right.

But the Blackwoods had sensed something amiss and quietly slipped away that night with their guards around them. They had fled east, and hidden out at Kevin Policinski's house when the coup started.

Yet their house had been ransacked, even worse than by the monsters. Go figure.

By morning, they learned who led the coup—a former disgruntled city council member named Stevenson, denied a spot on the new town council because of his overtly racist remarks. But others had still sided with him, including, unfortunately, a handful of police and National Guard; and some retired military and federal employees, including three militia commanders; and a bunch of goons.

They had all secretly decided that they knew what was best for everyone else. They meant to take over and put down anyone who could oppose them. Three other militia commanders died that night, three remaining town council members, and many other police and National Guard people they deemed as threats to them and their power grab.

Regular people, all murdered; them and even some of their families.

More waste of good people that Michiana would miss greatly, especially if the monsters came back in force.

How stupid it all was.

David still couldn't believe that people could be this dumb. What drove them to do such things?

Just a waste. A stupid, terrible waste.

When it became clear that the coup had failed, Stevenson and his cronies retreated south of town and set up a base in the old 4-H fairgrounds by force. They had about three or four thousand followers from the militia and their families. Lots of other goons and sympathizers also joined them, unfortunately.

They started calling themselves "White Town," of all things, and beat and expelled anyone they wanted to, mostly non-whites. They took up defensive positions and braced for a counterattack from the town council that they had tried to kill.

Martial law was fully reinstated, and militia troops still loyal to the town council protected the south against the betrayers. Stevenson and the rest of his murderers were branded as criminals, with orders to kill them on sight.

But there would be no civil war. That would cost both side more idiotic losses that they could not afford.

Dirk Blackwood and the other thirteen remaining militia commanders decided to merely contain the violent fools, and let them stew in their own juices for a while. They and theirs would not be given any further assistance, and most of their leaders were already marked for execution on sight.

The traitors controlled some parcels of farm land to the south, but not enough.

It would be seen how they liked being shunned and ostracized from the main community come fall and winter. Their many miscalculations would become clearer and clearer to them as time went on.

Especially if the monster hordes returned at some point in force.

Perhaps then the rebel fools would forsake and turn over their criminal leaders to justice for their crimes.

There had been enough senseless bloodshed for one night. Wasting more lives and resources to wipe out several thousand misguided idiots was not a very good option for anyone. Plenty of other important issues and tasks still remained.

But the coup attempt shook up everyone and added to the general malaise and paranoia—already at record levels.

People started to question and look askance at one another where they hadn't before, wondering if their neighbors or the next person down the street was a closet traitor or sympathizer with the traitors.

And who knew? Maybe some of them were.

That growing chaos and uncertainty didn't help things much, either.

Now a lot more time and wasted effort had to be made on internal security, making sure that militia groups and leaders remained loyal to the local populace as a whole, and not just to themselves. Or to one faction.

They didn't need a bunch of petty warlords rising up to cause trouble.

Again, what a stupid waste in almost every way.

David and Jerriel had three dozen, hand-picked troops camped around their home the very next day. A unit of twelve guards went with them anywhere they went.

David did take time to point out to Fred and Rosalyn just how brave young Steven had been in saving their lives. Without him, David knew for certain that he would have been killed, and Jerriel would now be a captive of the traitors.

Fred and Rosalyn hugged their boy with pride. Steven blushed and grew embarrassed. David continued to note the young boy's deep crush on Jerriel.

Steven must have been in heaven when Jerriel hugged him close to her and kissed him on the forehead, calling him her 'valiant young heroo'.

A crush on Jerriel?

That was certainly easy to understand.

David felt much the same way.

46

The relentless day-and-night grind at the front resumed like a machine, as soon as the spring storms let up.

Mason divided the battlefield time of the Pistolero between the day and night shifts. He would rest for four hours, and then fight for four hours. Then he mixed up the four-hour blocks in an attempt to keep the enemy off guard.

The Shooting Stars had to work in tandem, so they could not split up. But they fought for twelve hours at a time, and then rested for twelve hours.

The ten new fledgling militia sorcerers attempted help hold the line during the down times, but they were still limited to only three to five magical blasts from each of them during their shifts. Five mages were kept on the southern line. Five mages went to the western line.

The defenders held the tenth defensive line for three stubborn days.

There were only fifteen defensive lines total, and losing them all would push any remaining defenders into Mishawaka proper.

The militia fought another fighting retreat back to the eleventh defensive line. It seemed to be the only military action they had mastered. They certainly had had enough practice.

In some of their free time, Mason and Blondie both went to the stables to help care for their horses and relax. Today, Mace used a water brush to work out Winger's mane and tail.

Blondie was already finished with Patton, and had started grooming sweet little Ginger. Both of them had a special affinity for their three horses.

Thulkara's big brute Goliath was still a rat bastard to almost everyone but her. He hurt other handlers regularly; if he could bite or stomp on them, or sidle them into a wall, he would.

Further away from their unit, Mason heard a couple of horses scream and grunt in pain. Both his and Blondie's heads snapped up at those distinctive sounds.

"Let's check that out," Mason said, leaving his hat behind. "That doesn't sound right.

Near another stockade for another militia unit, they came around a corner and beheld a terrible sight.

Four or five drunken militia troops, who looked like supply people, were in the process of beating and terrorizing two older, much less serviceable horses.

One horse was an ancient Appaloosa mare with a swayed back, the other some kind of liver-chestnut, farm horse gelding that wasn't much younger. From the whiter hair around their eyes and muzzles, and the length of their front teeth when they screamed, both horses had to be well into their twenties and had seen better days.

Certainly better than this one.

Both horses were not only tethered, but hobbled as well. And the bullies tormenting them—three men and two women, all of them middle aged—passed around a half-empty bottle of Jack Daniels. They cursed and laughed at the poor, terrified horses, left to the tender mercies of these drunks.

One of the women kicked the farm horse hard in the brisket with her boot. The old gelding grunted and almost went down to its knees. It barely caught itself and stood there shivering and shaking with a wide, pitiful look in its eyes.

The biggest, hairiest, and dirtiest of the five sots snatched the bottle away, guzzled a long draught, and then wiped his greasy face as he bellowed. "Aw, that's nuthin. Take another, you worthless nag!"

He swung a length of pipe and cracked the Appaloosa mare right in the cheekbone, where her face and head already looked swollen and bloody from other similar blows.

The old horse screamed and bashed her head into the nearby building, trying to get away.

Mason had to resist the urge to gun them all down right then and there. "What in the depths of hell do you people think you're doing?" Mason demanded.

The drunks staggered back a moment. Then they saw nothing but two angry college-aged guys glaring at them.

Mason forgot how young he and Blondie looked without their hats. And they never really wore militia uniforms or sported any rank.

The big, fat, smelly leader snarled at them. He was hairy and six foot-four, at least, but most of that was flab. "This don't concern you punks none. Mind your own business, and keep walking."

Mason ignored him and looked at the others. "All of you with the militia? With one of the supply units?"

"What's it to you, boys?" the woman who had kicked the farm horse shouted.

"Who's your commanding officer?" Blondie asked.

"Lieutenant Arnold Spelling," another drunk cheerfully piped up, obviously feeling no pain.

"Shut up, Lou!" the others hissed at him.

"Yeah, nobody say nothing," the leader said, smacking the same length of bloody pipe in his dirty hands as he caught Mason's eye. "You need to clear out of here, boy. Afore I gave you the same I'm giving this here nag."

Two of the drunks had loaded crossbows handy, but not in their hands.

Mason grinned slightly. "Oh, mister. I would dearly love to see you try." He flipped the right side of his duster back, displaying his row of steel pistols hanging down his one side.

All five of the drunks nearly soiled themselves right then and there.

"Jeezus! It's the Pistolero."

"He's a killer!"

"Please...don't kill us!"

"Please, we were just having some fun."

"These horses are worthless. We might as well put them out of their misery."

"You can shoot them yourself, if you like!"

The leader dropped his length of pipe in the dirt and all five of them held up their hands in the air as if they were in an old Western movie holdup.

Their faces went pale and their mouths drooped slack and open.

Mason never even touched his guns. He just sat nearby on some crates in the shade and waited for Blondie to fetch Major Avery and tell him what was going on.

Avery came by with two squads and promptly arrested the five drunks and ordered the two old horses confiscated.

Anyone looking at the pair could see that they had been given a rough time.

Avery was red-faced when he unloaded on the drunks. They were almost as terrified of the Major as they were Mason's pistols.

"Drinking on duty when you should be working? Beating horses? You assholes are done working for the militia. Finished. You're lucky I don't have you all horsewhipped. I still might. Do any of you have any idea how scarce and valuable horses are right now? Any horse, even old ones such as these? If handled properly and cared for right, they can still perform valuable service."

None of the drunks had any answer for the major.

Avery turned away from them in disgust. "Get them out of my sight and hold them under arrest, pending notification of their commanding officer in the supply corps. Give them nothing but water, and either crackers or bread. Nothing else."

Mason and Blondie did their best to comfort the two old horses, and helped take them back to the stable for their unit's mounts. Their cavalry people came over to help, and once they saw the condition of the two horses and heard the story, they were livid. For a cavalry rider, a horse could mean his or her life or death.

Later that day, the five drunks were dishonorably discharged and promptly kicked out of the militia camp and told not to come back.

A unit of cavalry troops just happened by, and stomped all five of those morons into the mud. Both Mason and Blondie heard the story and grinned.

"I've always detested bullies," Mason said.

"You know you're just on the razor's edge of becoming one, yourself," Blondie told him. He pointed at Mason's rigs. "Those pistols give you power over others. It's all too tempting to use that power to intimidate others and make them fear you. Isn't it?"

"I want them to fear me. You speaking from experience or something, Blondie?"

"Maybe. Just be careful, Mace. People tend to hate what they fear. It's just too damn easy to become a bully and make others crawl on their bellies for your amusement."

"Why is that, Blondie?"

His friend grinned. "Because it's so damn fun."

Mason thought about the truth of that. He'd those drunks shaking in their shit just by flashing his iron their way. There hadn't been any need to draw. His friend Blondie was right. Power was seductive, and using it came far too easy. War was one thing. Dealing with regular folks was something different. He needed to maintain a clear perspective on that.

Mason had no desire to become the same kind of jerk he despised.

#

Military observers from Mishawaka—and even a few from Elkhart—managed to come online that evening in serious numbers, to get an experience of what they themselves would be facing firsthand once South Bend fell.

Everyone on both sides seemed to see that eventual fact as only a matter of time.

The eleventh line held. Then two nights later, the enemy made a massive push.

This was no longer a grinding assault.

This was an all-out attack.

It became clear very quickly that the enemy was hitting them with everything they had, in an attempt to break the defenders for good and crush them.

All of the remaining defenses were in danger of complete collapse.

As luck would have it, the Pistolero was off duty when the attack began. He and his friends had only slept for about three hours.

Major Avery woke Mason and the unit personally. "Mace, we have to get everyone on the line. We've never seen an enemy attack this large."

Mason blinked and simply nodded.

This was bad.

When they got into position with their supporting and reserve forces, they were poised on the extreme left flank, halfway to the twelfth line of defense.

"We're going to try to cut them off and break their front lines, similar to the way we did once before," Avery said.

Mason had come up through the reserves. Old people, women, and kids, many of them competent archers by now, but not so good in stand-up, hand-to-hand fighting.

This was going to get real bad, real fast.

Everyone was scared, including Mason himself.

"Prepare yourselves!" Major Avery called out.

Mason had his three remaining reloading teams following close by him with their runners and reserve runners. A fourth replacement team was still in the process of being trained.

The massive ranks of enemy forces surged into view. Their numbers seemed endless.

315

Enemy mages, and flight after flight of merc archers and siege engines rolled up, along with hordes of ravening monsters.

They caught up to the retreating militia and slammed into them hard.

"Sortie, forward and attack at will!" Major Avery shouted.

At first, the counterattack sortie did its job. The Pistolero blasted the way ahead, and the new black powder shotguns and their experimental loads were devastating. They cut a wide swath of destruction through the enemy and nearly halted the advance.

The militia and reserve archers kept up a punishing rate of fire.

But the other defenders behind them were still reeling, and some grew confused and kept fleeing.

Not enough militia forces charged back into the staggered foes while they had the chance.

And the enemy had many more reserves to send in and absorb their losses.

Halfway through their counterassault, enemy mages exploded huge craters and pits in the ground in front of the Pistolero and his units.

Mason's forward movement was now cut off.

The sortie, a thousand strong, suddenly found itself trapped, stranded right in the middle of the battle in a sea of fresh enemy forces.

They were in danger of being entirely surrounded and swallowed up.

Mason and his friends took point, Thulkara protecting his left, Blondie on the right, the reload teams in an inverted triangle behind them. Guns kept going back and forth as rapidly as they could, and the Pistolero blazed away with whatever weapon came to hand.

He emptied his guns in all directions, dodging magic and arrows, and negating magic with his blasts whenever he or his spotters could see it coming his way.

Several fireballs struck near them as they tried to maneuver.

They dove under numerous protective archery mantlets.

It had been found that salt and certain other crystals, mixed with silver, negated or lessoned some magical effects.

One of the ponies pulling the third reloading cart popped its head out, rearing and screaming in terror.

It died almost instantly.

"Get up and keep fighting before they drag us all down!" Major Avery shouted.

The enemy rushed in and the fighting grew hot and up close.

The reloading teams struggled to get back in business. Team Three cut the dead pony loose and pulled the cart along themselves.

Only the Pistolero and his blazing weapons kept them all from being completely swept away.

He poured fire into the packed enemy numbers, blasting them to burning bits in the heat of battle.

Finally they got a space to begin to pull back.

Fresh militia forces reached them and tried to draw them within.

But the enemy surged forward, trying to take them all down at once.

Once more, Mason and his units were hemmed in and nearly surrounded.

There seemed to be no limit to the numbers the enemy had to hurl against them.

A militia catapult hurled a spray of sparkling sulfur and silver powder over that entire area.

Mason took up two of the new shotguns, a twelve and a ten gauge, just as targets lit up like magical torches all around him.

He wheeled at bay with almost two dozen enemy mages closing in right on him.

Time for the Pistolero to make his stand.

The shotguns barked white-hot destruction at what was almost the compass points, each barrel sending an obliterating fan of magic power thirty yards at the widest, and sixty yards in length.

Glowing mages vanished as well, or fell flat and tried to protect themselves and survive.

Those four massive blasts kept the defenders alive and gave them all room to fight.

Mason dropped the empty shotguns at his feet, and the runners snapped them back up.

Pistols, pistols, pistols.

First he dueled with the remaining mages, ducking and dodging, negating enemy attacks, gunning down any target he could pinpoint. Fire at will, or at any other enemy bastard charging up to kill him and his friends.

Things got so hot that Blondie's hands began to glow with blue-white magefire.

He froze dozens of foes solid within an arc of a magical ice wall on the right side almost behind them. The enemy soon poured over and around it.

Thulkara laughed and sang and shouted war cries like a warrior goddess in love with the crash of battle, deflecting magic off her shield and splitting faces and skulls with her whirring battle axes.

Even the mindless monsters began to fear her prowess, and with good reason. Thulkara built a wall of death, constructed out of bodies all about her. She kicked it down to get at more foes to slaughter.

When it came to up close combat, it was difficult to beat a Thul in her battle fury. No one on Urth or Tharanor could fight like them.

The first crossbow bolt passed directly through Mason's left calf muscle from front to back.

A second clipped his right shoulder, tearing through flesh and muscle.

He staggered for an instant, then kept firing.

One of the runners shouted at him, "Mace, you're hurt. You're bleeding!"

"Well, plug or patch me up so that I can keep shooting. This isn't a cotillion we're in here!"

He gritted his teeth against the pain. He couldn't bleed out.

Just keep firing. Keep shooting.

A killing ray shot out at him from less than thirty feet away.

He negated it point blank.

The resulting detonation knocked him on his back and punched the wind out of him like a giant fist.

Guns. He dropped his guns.

He drew his Spillers and spun on his back, picking off any foe that came near.

Hands grabbed him.

"It's us, Mace, his runners shouted. "Don't plug us!"

He couldn't stand. He hardly had his breath back. "Up…stand me up. Keep me shooting!"

They jerked him back up to his feet to face the enemy. People worked on his wounds, trying to patch him up.

He fought on in a daze, pistols being shoved into and ripped out of his fingers. His people tried to help him direct his fire.

They also shielded him with their bodies.

Five of them took arrows or bolts or got dragged off him in the confusion of the fight. Others stepped in to take their places.

More arrows. At least the magic attacks stopped.

Then an arrow struck the meat of his left shoulder.

Another passed through his left side. Another hit him in the back.

Major Avery and the militia tried to charge forward and protect them with shields and mantlets.

Mason kept firing until he couldn't lift his arms. People lifted his arms for him and told him to fire. He kept firing.

He couldn't focus his eyes.

He fired when and where he was told.

His vision blurred even more.

Then something changed. He could sense it in the air.

Cries and cheering came from the militia forces up from the south. They sounded very close.

What did they have to cheer about? They were all about to be swept away and killed.

Finally, Mason didn't have the strength to pull his triggers any more, and his head drooped forward onto his chest. Blondie cut loose again with some kind of magic, and there was a bright flare.

Mason's wounds burned and hurt like fire inside him.

But even their pain and everybody jostling and yelling at him couldn't keep him from blacking out this time.

47

Before noon, David and Jerriel met with Danielle, Theo, and the linguists again and did their best to continue developing their working dictionaries of Tharanorian words and grammar. They still focused primarily on Sylurrian and Marandorian.

The effort remained notoriously tedious at times, but vital to many of their survival goals.

And it helped Jerriel learn English faster, and David learn Tharanorian.

They went home in the afternoon for Jerriel to work in her lab. David always had plenty of militia paperwork to catch up on.

His turn came to make dinner that evening. Just tomato soup and grilled cheese sandwiches, but it was one of their favorite simple meals. He went to the family room magic lab to call her to the table around four-thirty.

What he beheld there forced him to step back a moment.

The room radiated with light. Blue, gold, and green orbs of light bobbed around near the ceiling, causing the room to blaze with color. Jerriel floated near the center with her toes pointing down, her posture erect and her attention focused on the center of the room. She chanted, perhaps in her magical language. It did not even sound like Tharanorian.

She looked incredibly beautiful, as always. Her alabaster face burned into his mind, his soul. The alluring shape of every luxurious part of her.

His legs felt weak.

He stepped over, leaned on something, and saw what she was working on.

His faithful longsword floated in the very center of a magic, glowing circle of runes. Sparks flew from a glowing crystal, working its way up and down the white-hot edges of his blade at Jerriel's direction.

With her other hand, she etched flaring runes onto one side of the blade, and then the other, as she wheeled, shifting around to one position and the next. Hot sparks flew.

She noted his presence briefly with a raised eyebrow, a quick wink, and a happy smile, apparently almost finished with her labors.

David stepped into the room to watch. The enchanting came to its crescendo and began to cycle down. His sword still glowed with power.

His palm actually itched to hold the sword, whether the forged steel was still hot or not.

In response to his thoughts, a transparent, silvery line of energy shot out from his hand to the hilt of his sword.

In a brief flash, the sword appeared back in his hands, warm, but not hot.

Was it some trick of his eyes? Lines of force coruscated up and down the length of the blade. The sword pulsed with magic.

He grinned at her. "You really surprise me, Jerriel. I keep finding new reasons to...fully appreciate you." He sheathed the blade. It nearly hummed in the scabbard.

"I hope you always feel that way about me, Daeved."

She floated over to him, descending. Giving him her hand. He shivered just looking at her.

"Dinner's ready," he told her.

Her feet touched the floor. "Thank you. I think there's an impoortant meeting toonight. We should attend."

He rolled his eyes. "There's an important meeting every night."

"Let's eat, and then we can goo."

He followed her into the dining room. She was probably right, as usual.

When they were ready after dinner, they stepped out of their house and walked to the street. Their guards rose to attention. The sky burned with the brilliant lights of a Michiana sunset.

"What's the news of the day, guys?"

One of them handed him four or five pieces of paper stapled together.

"Here's today's paper, sir. First issue with five pages. Talks about the fallout of the coup attempt. Gives a lot of tips and lists of places to go for this or that. Pretty cool, actually."

David looked at it and smiled. "Gets better every day. We're going over to the library."

The trooper nodded. "Part of our detail will go with you and the lady, sir. Others will remain here to protect your home."

"Good work, troops. Carry on."

"Thanka you," Jerriel told them. "All of you. We really appreciate you protecting us."

"Thank you, ma'am. Sir, we could still use some more pointers on swordsmanship, if you have some time. Anything to make us better fighters."

David smiled. "I'll do that. I'd be proud to, but it might be tomorrow, guys. We'll continue our regular training sessions with the rest of the Blackhawks after that."

"That's fine, sir."

At the library, they linked up with Danielle and some of the linguists for a while. Everyone continued adding to their lists of words and their understanding of both worlds through language.

Dinner came, so they ate a second meal. Ham, instant potatoes, and canned peas. Simple, but filling. Extra food wasn't always made available, so people ate whenever they could.

The lead linguist was a short woman in her fifties named Connie, as in Consuela. Connie Ortega was a little rotund and had bobbed black hair, sparkling brown eyes, and a very pleasant disposition. She spoke five languages.

Six or seven now, including her fledgling two Tharanorian tongues.

She counseled them after dinner. "Our language work is of paramount importance, of course, but a group of think tankers and concerned citizens are going to be holding an open discussion forum this evening at the Morris Theater. We would very much like to have the both of you there. I think you'll find it interesting. So many people have questions, and thus far, Jerriel is the only sentient Tharanorian we've met."

"We would love to goo," Jerriel said.

David blinked. That was fast. "Sure," he said.

There was a lot he still wanted to know. David continued to sense the enormous intellect and mind that Jerriel possessed. She would need to be very intelligent to become a high level wizard and an enchantress. He guessed that much. She learned and recalled things more quickly than he did, and was also more driven intellectually.

Most likely she was even smarter than him, but then he considered himself more of a generalist, a Renaissance person. He wasn't a specialist like Jerriel was.

Not that David was a moron. Far from it. His grades were always good in school. A's and B's, an occasional C. In college, he had done well in philosophy, history, and even math and physics. He didn't do so well in chemistry and biology, mostly out of personal choice and because of instructors who weren't always a good match for him.

But of course, things were very different now after the Merge.

Perhaps the meeting would be very interesting indeed.

As they stepped out, a big contingent from the militia walked over to the Morris Theater. They spotted Dirk and Belle; Fred, Rose, and Steven; and Robert, Kevin, and Pete. Many of their other friends were also attending.

Steven beamed at Jerriel the way that only a crushing teenage boy could. Several other militia commanders attended as well, all under heavy guard.

David turned to Jerriel. "Something big is up if they're joining this meeting this late," he said. "Let's catch up with them and find out what's happening."

They called to Dirk. The guards parted and let them get in close once they were sure it was all right. Many of them recognized David and Jerriel. Connie was now over with them, he noticed.

"Dirk, you look worried," David said.

Belinda did, too. Both of them shook their heads.

"We're falling apart fast," Dirk said.

"Four more militia commanders have broken away to consolidate their own enclaves," Belinda announced. "Nobody can believe it. We should be pulling together, not pulling apart! What's happening to us? What's driving all of this?"

"You'd think they would have learned from the attacks," Dirk said. "And its only going to get worse—especially once stuff starts to run out." He sighed heavily. "So this is where we're at, Dave: we've got the traitors from the defacto 'Whites-First' faction setting up shop and barricading an area south of town. West of town is now splitting rapidly between what the factions now call Black Town and Spanish Town. There have even been a few clashes there on the new borders. People who don't fit into either tribe are being expelled from their homes and sent packing. Told to get out and go somewhere else—or else. It's not right."

"What a bunch of crap," David said. "It's ethnic cleansing. Can't they see what garbage this is?"

Dirk shook his head sadly. "People are scared, and scared people do stupid stuff. They know society has broken down on every level, Dave. There's no authority except for that which we uphold and create. They've chosen to splinter off and create their own. Some people are power hungry and driven by that. It's only going to get worse from here, as people turn against each other."

A messenger biked in quickly and handed Dirk a piece of paper. He read it.

"This just in," Dirk said. "There's even a new enclave in the northwest of town now–Gay Town. They're not kicking anyone out, but they say they're forming their own town council and laws sympathetic to gay and lesbian issues. Anyone who doesn't like that can leave voluntarily, if they don't like the new laws."

Another messenger met them at the doors. Another written message to read. "Great," Dirk said. "We finally have word from Elkhart. They fought off a monster attack slightly smaller than ours, but now they're divided, too. They've got their own headaches. One third of their town is overrun by various gangs, who seem to have started a Dragon Cult, worshiping a mated pair of dragons in their area–as gods. There have even been human sacrifices made to the creatures.

"In response, another third has formed a theocracy. The remaining third is still trying to organize, caught between the clashes of the other two."

Jerriel even shook her head. "If I did not know better," she said. "I would think that demoons were at woork, here–driving all of yoor peeple apart. Such madness can be inflamed by demoons. They feed on chaos and discoord. It is like food to them."

David Blinked. "The dragon I met mentioned that a demon was somewhere nearby in South Bend."

Jerriel gasped. "Yoo did not tell me that, Daeved."

"So much has happened, I didn't take it seriously. Demons don't really exist on Urth. I guess I just forgot about it."

"Peeple can be stupid on their own, but demons will be drawn to that hatred and do everything in their power to make it woorse. We will have to get priests and holy peeple to help us banish the fiend. But first, we must locate it."

"Maybe we should go talk to the dragon I met," David said.

"Maybe we should go inside and talk to our own people first," Dirk told them. "They're going to need to hear all of this, including what you know about this new demon threat."

"Not much, Dirk." David said. "The dragon only mentioned it in passing. He just said there was one somewhere in town."

"Well, Dave, at least we still have a bunch of our best minds together. We're going to need a lot of that knowledge and wisdom in the days ahead. And I have plenty of security on hand tonight, in case anyone tries to attack us."

They finally entered the building and shuffled into the theater, which was lit by old-fashioned lamps and lanterns. Chairs and megaphones and podiums were set up on the open stage. David and Jerriel joined Dirk and Belinda up there. Fred, Rosalyn, and Steven took seats up front. The Haywards were extremely intelligent, but awkward when it came to public speaking.

Jerriel and her staff caught a lot of attention, and not just because of her beauty. This was the first time many people in town were getting a good look at the Tharanorian wizard girl in person.

New reports and updates continued to pour in to the town council, even before the meeting got started. More people filed in.

David glanced at some of those reports as Dirk passed them around. A lot of the news wasn't very good.

Wait until Dirk told them all about the demon.

48

Mason opened his eyes, and the pain seemed to flood back into him all at once. It was like suddenly slamming into a solid wall that was somehow shaped like the inside of his body. He gasped, but couldn't move much.

That was probably a good thing, because the more he moved around, the more he ached. He continued to gasp, wince, grunt, and whine at the intensity of the agony ripping through him. Tears flowed from his eyes. Someone dabbed his face with a cool damp cloth.

"Hold him down if he starts to thrash around, or if he tries to get out of bed," Major Avery ordered the medical staff. "Hold his head back gently, then his arms by the wrists and shoulders, and his legs by the ankles and knees. Most likely, he's in a lot of pain from all of his wounds. It's a wonder he's alive after he was hit so many times. We've given him some blood and fresh plasma from donors on hand, but we don't want his injuries tearing open again."

There seemed to be several people working around him.

He was in some kind of medical bed. Except for a thin hospital gown of some obnoxious, purple floral print–lilacs or some such–he was buck naked.

Every part of his body seemed bandaged in some fashion, and he reeked like a hospital ward.

Finally his vision cleared and he could hear properly without his head feeling as if it was under a bucket. "Avery," he croaked. "Bill…water."

Avery nodded. "Give it to him in sips, like the doctor said. A little at a time. We don't want him throwing up."

A tube or a straw came to his dry lips. Mason didn't care which. He sealed his mouth around it and pulled. Cool water bathed his dry mouth and throat. He relaxed and pulled on the tube in sequence. Like a nursing baby he drank and closed his eyes, feeling the soothing relief slipping down his parched mouth and throat until he relaxed.

He opened his eyes again and looked up at Major Avery. "Bill, I figured we were all dead when I went down. What the hell happened? How did we get away?"

Bill Avery smiled down at him and rested a strong hand softly on Mason's right hand. "We didn't expect it, either, but just as the enemy committed all of its reserves, spotters saw thousands of militia sweeping in out of the dark to flank the enemy and hem them in from the rear."

Mason's mouth fell open. "Where in the hell did they–"

Avery grinned. "Mishawaka finally got off their asses and had the gumption to move in and try to help us. They voted to do so just a few hours before, and put their people on the move."

"Well, damn–dip me in mustard like a corndog!" Mason said, quickly regretting his sudden excitement.

Hands pushed him back gasping onto his bed once more. Mason made out five medical corps people hovering around him, not seven. Two men and three women, all wearing the red cross on their arms. He didn't know any of them by name yet.

"Stop moving around, Mace. I know it's tough," Avery told him. "That's an order. Mishawaka sent ten divisions in to punish the enemy as bad as they could. They finally all agreed that it was now better to send their people in to help, and fight the foe in South Bend, rather than to wait for the enemy to march in on their doorstep."

"Wow," Mason said, still having trouble believing it. "They sent ten thousand troops into battle?"

Avery nodded. "Almost half of their frontline forces, with the rest of their people out and on the alert, in case the enemy tried something else. Mishawaka won the battle for us, but not the war, I'm afraid. Too many of the enemy squirted out toward the north and got away to regroup. Our combined troops drove them hard and showered them with every arrow we had. We're still making a full tally of the merc losses—some thousands. We're not bothering to count the dead monsters, but it was a lot. Most of them have dissolved into slime by now, anyway."

Mason nodded slightly. "Good riddance."

"We've captured a few hundred of the mercs, and three more of their mages—including one of those necromancers that everyone seems so afraid of."

"Don't underestimate them," Mason said. "We don't know what their powers are."

Avery grunted. "We might not ever know, as quiet and as tight-lipped as those damn mages are. Even when some of our military people have tried to 'persuade' them to talk, the enemy mages have some way of shutting down and putting themselves into a trance-like state, where all they do is grunt and smile."

"They won't talk to anyone? Even if you put them in a room with some of the mercenary officers and just listen in?"

"Nope. We've tried everything. They won't even talk to each other."

"What about Blondie?" Mason suggested.

"Since that necromancer joined them, they won't even talk to him."

"They talk to each other whenever they wish," Blondie said.

He stepped in at that moment, smiling and looking genuinely glad to see Mason alive and recovering. Blondie had one arm in a sling and was also bandaged up in several places. No one who had fought near Mason had gotten away unscathed.

Blondie continued. "As I've told you before, the enemy mages all use telepathy to communicate. They don't have to talk. They have many disciplines and abilities that you are not used to. You are correct; the necromancer has ordered all of his underlings to ignore me and consider me an enemy."

Blondie folded his hands together in front of himself. "I've been trying to listen in on what they are saying, but I still can't seem to get my telepathy working properly. All I've picked up so far is a few words and phrases here and there. Nothing definite. But I get the impression that they remain supremely overconfident, even as our prisoners and after this recent setback. They continue to underestimate us and see themselves as far superior to Urth people in almost every way. That is an advantage that we can continue to exploit."

Mason smiled weakly and took his friend's hand as Blondie came near. "I'm glad to hear you saying 'us' and 'we'," he noted.

Blondie casually frowned and shrugged. "Major, if you have anyone showing signs of developing telepathy or other mental abilities, I would bring them in near the prisoners to see if they can make out anything."

Avery nodded. "Will do. Thanks for the intelligence, Blondie."

"Free of charge," Blondie said.

One of the aides brought folding chairs up to Mason's bed for Major Avery and Blondie to sit on.

"So, where does this leave us?" Mason asked.

Avery sighed. "Better off than we were. We're back defending the ninth line of defense, and so far, the Mishawaka people are staying with us. Every hour the enemy doesn't renew their attack works in our favor, but we know they're out there. They will regroup and hit us again, as soon as they are ready. And we still can't stop them."

"Perhaps we should attack them out in the open," Blondie said. "That would certainly surprise them."

"We've considered pressing our current advantage," Avery said. "But fighting in the built-up areas of the city that we know gives us many advantages. Out in the open, our forces could be cut off and surrounded far too easily. The enemy still possesses superior numbers by our estimates. At least three or four to one, but that is difficult to confirm. And we can't hold very long without the Pistolero or the Shooting Stars."

Mason's mouth fell open. The girls. "What has happened to—"

Avery held up both hands. "Nothing serious. Both will recover. Hannah Masters took an arrow through the meaty part of her upper right leg—just a flesh wound. She'll limp for a while. Minnie Patterson got knocked down by a chunk of debris; she has a light concussion. Both are recovering, the same as you, Mace.

"We have two other girls impersonating them, walking around at the front in their gear, carrying their weapons. With their helmets on, nobody would know it isn't the real Shooting Stars. Even most of the troops don't know. But all of you need to get healthy fast. We don't know when things are going to heat up again."

"Where's Thulkara?" Mason asked.

Both Blondie and Major Avery burst out laughing at the same time.

"She's bored," Blondie said. "She's helping train our troops how to fight better, and that remains a real eye-opener to watch."

Avery grimaced. "And when she's not busting heads, she has taken up a new hobby."

Mason blinked. "A what?"

"A hobby. She likes to paint."

"Shoot me dead right now."

"Serious as a heart attack, Mace. She's taking lessons at the art museum. At least it gives our troops a rest. Our people have gotten tougher, but they sure aren't Thulls. We've had to repeatedly ask her to tone down her training so that our people aren't getting banged up too much. That woman is a menace—the greatest single fighter I have ever seen."

"Wait until she locates this prince of her people that she keeps bragging about," Blondie said. "Thulkara says that he's the best of the best—that he puts all of the other Thulls to shame."

"Now that, I would like to see. What I wouldn't give to have an army of those big buggers fighting for us," Avery said. "But we don't. Yet I am glad that she is on our side, that's for sure. When you fell, Mace, Thulkara scooped you up and fought off all comers. Blondie blasted that necromancer and his goons close up when they tried to go after you. He zapped them with a spray of what looked to be some kind of red, glowing needles that struck everything in front of him and then detonated. The blast cut down or stunned the enemy front wave and broke them. That's how we captured the enemy mages. We trussed them up, gagged them, and dragged them back with you."

Mason smiled and shook Blondie's hand again. "Thanks, my friend. Give my thanks to Thulkara, as well, or send her in to see me."

Blondie grinned again. "I'll do both. You keep healing, Mace. We need you up and around again. I'll come back and sit with you from time to time, as you heal. I'll bring you any news I can."

"Well, I don't want you take too much time away from your gals that are always chasing you," Mason told him.

"Yeah, I might have to slack off a bit for a few days. I got banged up a little myself, as you can see. But at least I won't be bedridden like you are—in your way, at least."

Everybody in the room had a good chuckle. Blondie had his reputation for being a major player to maintain. He seemed to derive a great deal of personal pride, satisfaction, and pleasure from that rep. Blondie loved the ladies, and a certain slice of them were more than willing to love him right back.

He always seemed to have his choice of eager dance partners to take a stroll with at night, or during the day, even when there wasn't a dance anywhere.

49

Two council members were delayed. The big town forum was therefore held off for one more hour.

During that time, David and Jerriel went off to an adjacent meeting room and held another debriefing and discussion session with Dirk, Connie, and members of the Research and Advisory Council. With the coup attempt and everything else, there hadn't been enough time before that point.

They continued to get as much information out of Jerriel as time and scheduling permitted.

For the first time, David told them what the dragon mentioned about the demon in town. He went over his ordeal of falling into the glowing pool, and then his out-of-body experience immediately thereafter, during the battle on Jefferson Street. He described what he both saw and overheard in the enemy camp during that vision.

Jerriel laughed. She apparently had a perfect explanation for what occurred. She tried to explain it to them all as best she could.

"Yoo were not dead, Daeved."

But his physical body had been left helpless while his spirit was away from his body in astral form. His physical body would have been at the mercy of any foe that stumbled upon it.

Much as the dragon Shavalkathar had told him, the enchanted pools were random, Wild Magic of varying types.

In short, he had fallen into a glowing pool that had separated his spirit from his still living body and released his astral form, which then had been able to zip around–invisible and insubstantial–much like a ghost. Once up in the air, his thoughts had directed him where they would, finally drawn to the lights of the observation camp of the enemy, up on that nearby hillside.

And he had been able to understand what they said because, in astral form–much like dragons–he understood the pure language of sentient thoughts.

The account of his adventures intrigued Dirk and the others.

"Can such an experience be duplicated under controlled conditions?" Dirk asked. "The possibilities for intelligence, communications, and scouting alone would be...staggering."

Jerriel shook her head. "My magic does not woork that way. I am not a traveler. I can not travel in ethereal or astral form, oor blink, or telepoort. Soome wizards can. It is a rare gift, like mine for wizardry and enchanting. I inherited them from my mother."

Dirk leaned forward eagerly. "Yes, David also told us how you might enchant some of his weapons to work better. Can you do so for others?"

"It would take some time. I would gladly do so for you, Dirk. Perhaps we can find others among yoor people, like Rob-hert, who have my talent as well. That would help."

"What do you have in mind, Dirk?" David asked.

"I want an edge. As much as we can get. I'm picturing a strike force of a few hundred to a few thousand troops ready to go anywhere, any time, and face down any threat. Led by you two and any others that you hand pick. Elite fighters. Best of the best. Weapons and armor enchanted to the hilt, if we have time to do so."

"A shock force," David said.

"Pretty much."

Someone handed Connie a note.

"Gentleman, I'm sorry," Connie said. "I know we're breaking new ground here, but we don't have much time left before the meeting."

"Wait!" David said. "What about those people I saw? The enemy leaders, those wizards in the black masks and robes? They were directing the assault on our town. They seemed pretty pissed off that we were somehow managing to win against the forces they sent at us."

"Intriguing," Dirk said. "But they're gone now, and we don't know where they went, why, or when they'll return, if ever. We can watch for them, but it's not a lot to go on. Jerriel, any thoughts?"

Her face turned pale and took on a very grave expression. "Sounds like the woork of mages from the Dark Khabal. Something as cataclysmic as the Merge woould be the perfect chaotic oppoortunity for them to may-hake a grab for power in the coloonies, oor anywhere they think they could subjugate others to expand their control."

"What is this cult?"

She bowed her head. "The Dark Khabal is a plague on my woorld, and now upon yoors, apparently. A secret league of wizards. Criminals who practice the darkest, moost forbidden and destructive magicks. They are in league with assassins, and demoons, and oother vile creatures from the Shadow Worlds and the negative plane dimensions. Their goal is to dominate or destrooy all life, accoording to their oown tyrannical whims, and woorse—the dicta-hates of their real masters: the Old Ones, the Fallen, The Dark Ghods."

She paused and lifted her clenched right fist. "I think that they may have had a hand in the deaths of my parents. We coould never proove it. Befoore they died, my parents were among the Khabal's greatest foes."

David stared.

Oh, joy. More bad guys.

Clearly these were enemies more powerful than the mortal insects living in South Bend. The leader even said something to that effect. To the enemy, David's hometown was just another worthless little Urth hamlet to be wiped out in the course of their grand quest for power.

"To hell with them," David said. "They wanted to annihilate us! They even sent more forces than they thought it would take, and we still beat them. We beat the hell out of them, and we beat the odds. We defeated them all and crushed them! They must be really pissed by now."

Dirk wasn't so happy. He leaned back in his seat and rubbed his temples. "It's not just the monsters, now. We have powerful, intelligent enemies who tried to destroy us—as an afterthought. They even stated that more important matters were calling them away. They seem to know a great deal about us and our world. Yet we know next to nothing about them and theirs. Jerriel, we need everything that you have on this cult."

"My father and mother opposed them most of their lives," she said. "Not I." She held up her hands. "They act in secret most of the time. I spent my years studying magic and enchanting. I have my father's journal, but it was written in his magical, coded scripts. He did so with all of his writings and notes. Even my older brother could not understand it. Wizards in general are a secretive lot. Given time and research, I might be able to unlock the journal's secrets. My father must have kept notes on the Dark Mages, as many times as he helped thwart their evil plots."

"Keep working on that," Dirk told her. "Inform us immediately about any progress. I don't think we have anything definite that we can tell the public yet, so we'll keep this under wraps until we do. Everybody's scared enough right now."

Connie rose up, after a messenger zipped in and whispered to her once more.

"My friends, we're out of time. The missing council members have arrived. The main public forum is being reseated as we speak. I'm sorry, but we must break this discussion off and attend. I'm presenting our findings so far in a matter of minutes."

"But the demon must be—" Jerriel began.

"We'll discuss that threat and how to deal with it at the meeting," Dirk said. "You'll get your chance." He rose up and headed toward the door. "Connie's right. We have to go in."

50

Suffering from several wounds, and remaining still and bedridden for days at a time, was a terrible, torturous thing.

And it was so incredibly tedious; there was nothing to do.

Major Avery sent people in to read books to Mason, even play music and sing songs to him. They offered to play games, but he couldn't sit up yet. Lying on his back all the time quickly became a form of torment. He got cramps at the worst times and had to beg with tears in his eyes to be massaged.

He worried about getting bedsores.

Did anyone enjoy using a bedpan and being cleaned up by others like an infant or an invalid? Not Mason, that was for sure. Even if some of his nurses were pretty, that was not at all the point, or any comfort to him. It was still fricking embarrassing and humiliating, no matter how much they told him it was all "no big deal."

In the end, Mason was saved…by sponge baths. Sponge baths were incredibly nice and warm and slow—and he could have them three or four times a day and night. Those soothing baths kept him from losing his mind and going insane.

And they were was far different and much more enjoyable than simply having your nether regions wiped off in haste and leaving you cold and humiliated after using the damn bedpan.

Maybe there was still a god out there somewhere. Sponge baths were definitive proof of a benevolent deity, at least to Mason's mind.

A middle-aged black nurse named Donna had the gentlest hands Mason had ever been touched by, outside of his sweet lover, Tori.

Donna gave the greatest sponge baths this side of heaven. They never failed to soothe him and put him to sleep. Mason made a point of asking Major Avery to reward the nurse as much as she could be rewarded. They both thanked her profusely and told her how much they appreciated her kindness. Donna became Mason's favorite, and he perked up and went on his best behavior whenever she came around.

Even the prettiest nurses grew jealous.

Mason even got up the nerve to ask Donna in private one day if she'd let him kiss her small, strong hands. She graciously did so, and the both of them sat alone together in that room, held hands, and quietly bawled like little lost kids together.

It had been a rough few months for everyone in Michiana. Both he and Donna the nurse, and so many others, had seen far too much death and destruction over the course of that horrible time. And it wasn't over.

Finally Mason's appetite returned, and that damn metallic taste in his mouth went away. By then he could eat anything he wanted. Nothing too spicy, perhaps.

Blondie brought him special snacks and desserts.

Thulkara wasn't usually a good one to send out for meals. Being a voracious Thul, who naturally inhaled food by the tableful, she often ate Mason's chow herself and then had to send someone more reliable out for another helping.

A little more than a week later, Mason could sit up.

Ten days, and they began massaging and working his muscles a great deal more, and at first that was stiff agony. But they could lift him into a wheelchair and push him around.

By two weeks, they got him up and he could stand. Then he could shuffle and move around his bed, hand-over-hand. But at least he was back on his feet.

And triumph at last, they could sit him on a toilet and close the door behind him, so that he could do his business in private. He'd knock to let them know when he was finished. Once he even leaned against the cool wall and took a nap for fifteen minutes, before they woke him up with a knock on the door.

He could shuffle about between two people. As he and his arms got stronger, he tried crutches and then a walker.

He fell and slipped less and less. Usually he had two experienced physical therapists on him in any case, and they caught him before he ever hit hard.

But soon he was catching himself from falling or losing his balance. They got him back up pretty fast, and his injuries were such that his muscles did not atrophy that much.

But he was still looking at a long recovery of at least four or five more weeks—well over a month.

The enemy attacks started up again. Slowly at first—skirmishes, probes, and feints to test the defenders. Increasingly heavier raids and monster attacks were soon on the rise.

But everyone knew what was coming.

And Mason was still in no shape to fight.

With no Pistolero to help out, the war was going to be over before he could even do anything. Even with him it probably wouldn't end well.

How many more people were going to die now? How bad would it be?

Then Major Avery brought word that a score of captives had been rescued from the enemy. The Urth people confirmed reports that anyone captured by the mercenaries were made slaves. Many were being taken far south somewhere. It was widely reported that the mercs had seized control of extensive areas of farmland down that way, and were making Urth people work the fields.

Any captured Urth women with any looks were offered better food and treatment for them and theirs—if they agreed to pleasure the troops as comfort women.

Anyone who protested or caused too much trouble, whether by being too mouthy, or old, or sick, or useless—was given over to the monsters for disposal as slaves for both amusement...and food.

Amusement meant torture. The monsters delighted in tormenting the weak and the helpless. It made the brutes laugh until they choked.

It was their only form of entertainment.

The monsters had their own pens where they kept their human livestock. Captives there didn't last very long, and sought to take their own lives whenever they could. There were many stories of civilian parents strangling and cutting the throats of their own children rather than letting them fall into the hands and fire pits of those vile creatures.

A quick death was better than being skinned alive or slowly burned to death, feet or head first. The monsters were very creative, and could keep their captives shrieking and screaming for many long hours.

Tales of such horrors did not fall upon deaf ears in Mishawaka and Elkhart. Such horrors and atrocities would fall upon them next. And everyone knew about the eight merc-run slave camps surrounding Elkhart.

The only thing standing between all of them and the enemy were the last, dwindling defenders of South Bend.

Mason couldn't endure feeling so helpless.

He went to a shooting range, and practiced as much as he could with his dry guns to keep up his skill. But he still grew tired too quickly.

Fighting from a walker or wheelchair wasn't going to be possible.

He'd be a sitting duck.

The enemy would take him out in a matter of minutes.

At least he heard that the Shooting Stars were back up and around. That was good news.

But that didn't help him, or the western front.

Mason sent for Major Avery.

"Bill, isn't there any way to get me back into this fight? I'm healing, but it's going too slow. It's going to take too long. Both of us know that. Help me."

Bill Avery sighed. "I've already sent for this woman from Elkhart, Mace. They say that she can heal people faster, over a few days instead of a few weeks or months."

Mason felt better already. "Get her here as soon as you can."

"We're trying. Elkhart didn't want to let her go. They've been keeping her a secret, but they understand our need. There's a problem, however, Mace. A danger, really."

"What's that?"

"The process is said to be very painful, and in some cases, even fatal."

Mason didn't hesitate. "We don't have a choice. Get her here and let's try it out. I don't care about the risks."

51

The main stage in the heavily guarded Morris Theater filled to capacity. Crowds of worried thousands who could not get inside waited outside in the cold.

Handwritten transcripts taken from the meeting would be brought out periodically in chunks, and read to the crowds standing out there. With all of the uncertainty, above all else, people demanded information.

Connie Ortega welcomed and addressed the assembly.

Then she got down to her presentation.

"Here's what we know about Tharanor and Tharanorians, thus far..."

At her signal, aides flipped a big pad of paper over with sketches on it, drawings Jerriel had advised them on. "Keep in mind that our current information is sometimes sketchy or incomplete. We're adding to our pool of knowledge every day." She took a deep breath.

"As we guessed, the world of Tharanor is indeed an alternate Earth in many respects. One that our world has become merged with: half mixed up in our dimension, and half mixed up in theirs, through some kind of cataclysm that we do not, as yet, fully understand. Most likely, Tharanorians are experiencing the same massive disruptions that we are."

"Is that why Jerriel is the only Tharanorian that we've met?" someone said.

"We think that is going to change, very shortly," Connie noted. "They won't all be wizards. They won't speak our language or look like her, so we have to be very careful in our dealings with them. Report any contact with other Tharanorians to the militia or directly to the town council immediately. Don't antagonize them or try to restrain them in any way.

"Now, Tharanor has the same continents we do." She pointed to them with a wooden pointer. "One interesting point to note: they see our South Pole as their North Pole."

"That sounds about right," someone quipped. "Everything is backwards." There was some laughter at that.

"And most of their nations are located on what to us would be the Old World: Europe, Asia, and Africa. But just within the past century years, they have discovered and colonized this continent. The New Worlds that they found, like during our discovery and early colonial historical periods, are in similar areas: North America, South and Central America. Australia, Pacific Rim Oceana, and Polynesia.

"Unfortunately, these new worlds on Tharanor were and are still mostly wild places, overrun by savage, dangerous creatures: dragons, and torgs, ka-torgs, and who knows what else. Next page please."

The page flipped, showing closer maps of Europe, Asia, and Africa.

"Jerriel instructed us that on her world, there are six major nations of people. Thulldor, for example, is a nation of tall, powerful warriors, sort of a cross between Vikings and Mongols, culturally. They are the Thulls. Theirs is a warrior culture, proud, stubborn, but honorable for the most part, keeping to many traditions. They are accomplished mariners and fierce explorers, who dare to go anywhere in the world."

"Let's get some of them on our side," a woman suggested.

"That might be possible. Jerriel says that a colony stronghold from Thuldor has fortresses and towns set up around what we would call the area in Michigan around Detroit. I'm sure the Urth humans in those areas are learning firsthand about Thulls and their culture. We hope to make contact with them all in the weeks and months ahead."

"Why was Jerriel in this area, and is there anything or anyone else around us besides monsters?"

"That's a good question. Unfortunately, in the New World on Tharanor, our area is still a mostly wild region, unsettled by humans, just by monsters and other creatures. All that we know is that Jerriel had been traveling through this region at the time of the Merge. She used magic to avoid detection, but those protections failed when the Merge occurred, and all magic and technology were disrupted.

"All of this must have been a big surprise to her as well. Especially finding herself stumbling into one of our strange towns, which then came under attack from monster hordes."

"It was," Jerriel said. Some even managed to laugh at that.

Connie pointed to the map again. "Jerriel's people come from a nation called Sylurria: a nation of sorcerers, wizards, and magic users. Their magic is as advanced as our technology was, and they relied on it every day in many ways as we did on our technology. The Sylurrians are determined explorers as well. In fact, Jerriel says they have a colony set up in the mountains we see in the distance, near where Chicago is, or at least was. We haven't heard back from the scouts sent that way, and all reports are that it is a very dangerous region.

"Many of the monsters are superstitious of any type of magic and or power, and greatly fear the mighty Sylurrians and their powerful magicks. Some of the tribes have even taken to serving and helping protect them. But they are said to be fickle allies at best."

A minister stood up. He shook a bible in his fist. "I knew it. I knew it! These creatures are not monsters. They do not look like us. But this proves that they are not all mindless beasts. They can be reasoned with. They must have souls! I propose that we immediately send missionaries among them to try to reason with them and preach the Word–make peace with them–even convert them to the Lord and out of their heathen darkness."

Jerriel shook her head at the man's words. She looked at David and widened her eyes.

"I would strongly advise against that any time soon," David said. "They're more likely to eat you than listen to a sermon."

"With God, all things are possible," the minister insisted. "I insist that we be taught their language, or a language that they can understand. Then we can begin to communicate with them. I will go myself if I must."

This caused a commotion as well. A call to general order followed.

"The theological ramifications can be discussed later," Connie said. "Please allow me to continue with the overview. We have a lot of ground to cover, and new reports continue to come in. An information sheet has been printed up and will be given out later tonight. It will also appear in tomorrow's paper. Updates will follow."

Everyone sat back down. "The next Tharanorian nation, Khairun, is a land of mercenaries, battle wizards, and elementalists. Like the other nations, they have explored the New World as well, making their fortunes mostly by selling their military services to the highest bidders.

"Thus they have flourished as well, and can be found woven among nearly all of the other nations and colonies. Jerriel says that they can be greedy, and tricky to deal with. But usually they stick to a blood contract once it has been made—even to the death. In the New World of Tharanor, the mercenaries of Khairun stick mainly to the east and west coasts, and venture inland as needed, and as hired."

Connie stopped and sipped some bottled water before she continued.

"Jattar is another fierce nation of wizards and warriors, feared far and wide for their superb cavalry, lancers, and mounted archers. Jattarans are stoic and shrewd, who adhere to strict codes of personal and family honor. They are superb sailors and traders and merchants as well. Most of their colonies are in what we would call South America. But some adventurers and outcasts can be found in the Mercenary Bands and among other explorers.

"The next nation is Darshia, famous for its swordmasters, crossbow units, and armies of pike units. Their wizards specialize in being conjurers and illusionists. Jerriel even says that the greatest among them can create new things, creatures—even people—and alter reality itself with their unique powers. They are present in the New World, but they are far more active in what is to us South America and Australia, as well."

"Forgive me," a member of the crowd said. "But all of these cultures sound primitive, medieval, and warlike."

"You've noted the pattern as well."

More nervous laughter.

"Tharanor to a large degree, appears to be just such a world," Connie said. "As we have already seen, firsthand. But it is encouraging to think that there are other sentient humans similar to us—like Jerriel—who we can ally and negotiate with. Most of them value peace and freedom as much as we do. As much as any people can in a dangerous world."

Connie cleared her throat. "One last nation to go. Marrandor is a feudal monarchy state of kings, queens, and loosely allied city states. They have a colonial kingdom set up in what was once Toledo, Ohio. They call the Great Lakes and the Mississippi River, the Inner Seas. Like the Thulls, we hope to make contact with them soon. Jerriel was trying to reach them when the Merge interrupted her travels. She is related to them on her mother's side.

"The Marandorians at times quarrel and war amongst themselves, but these are all complex cultures with their own values, knowledge, and ideas. Marrandor is famous for its heavily armored champions what we would call knights—their deadly longbow archers, and expert spear units. And their enchanters and wizards are as advanced as any of the other nations. Most of the six nations use magic to a very high degree, as stated. Jerriel's mother, for example, was a very famous and accomplished enchanter, and passed that skill and talent on to her daughter.

"That is the update on the extent of our knowledge thus far. I believe General Blackwood and the remaining militia leaders have some important announcements to make, now that this general presentation is over."

Connie took her seat. A militia spokeswoman informed everyone about how the town was breaking down into tribes and rival factions.

That news caused another uproar among the gathering, although many had already heard the rumors.

"We can't let this happen," one of the professors said.

Dirk went to one of the megaphone podiums.

"Listen, everyone. Listen up. In the chaos and anarchy that we now live in, people in fear will sometimes splinter off into tribes and groups that they feel safer in. Right or wrong, we cannot stop them," he said. "If they want to waste their time on such foolishness, let them. We could only change their minds with force, and that would simply play into their hands and their paranoia.

"We've discussed these situations at length with the town council, and we believe that we should hang tight. The worst thing that we could possible do right now is engage in several small civil wars amongst ourselves, over ethnicity or orientation. We would literally destroy ourselves from within. There are many other things for our hands to keep busy with at the present time.

"We still control roughly sixty percent of the remaining Michiana area and its population. Our standing policy is to accept working with anyone of good will who abides by the law, and try to help them if we can. Their refugees are already flooding to us, depleting their numbers— not the other way around.

"We will defend our areas and prevent these other groups from committing raids against us as much as we can, but we will not attack them unless provoked. Let another monster horde invade, and we'll see how well their stand-alone, isolationist policies work for them. Then they might very well change their minds and rethink their current, political strategies."

Dirk sat down. A large number of people applauded.

David had to admit, he himself was too young and hot-headed. If it were up to him, he might have used force to bring the others back in line.

Dirk and the other town leaders were older, wiser, and more level-headed. David still had a lot to learn before he could even become half the man and half the leader that Dirk and some of the others were.

The discussion group went on to speak about several related topics at length. A representative from the scientists stood up.

"Our greatest problem remains a lack of electricity. Try as we might, we can't get motors, engines, or generators to produce and create electric power. Without a consistent source of power, our society is greatly crippled. There's something we're missing completely. Something unfathomable about the effects of this dimensional cataclysm has fundamentally made changes in reality and scientific principle that won't allow our technology to work."

Other experts shook their heads. "It has only been a short while," the scientist said, "but until we discover that solution, we still must plan ahead for the worst and mobilize our people to produce food, clean water, and modify our existing buildings and technology to survive the next winter. Otherwise, there will be mass starvation and people freezing to death in their homes. Not to mention surviving the hottest parts of the summer without air conditioning. These are not minor concerns."

"There have already been casualties from exposure, among the very young and the very old, and sick," a doctor noted. "Modern medicine has been greatly reduced without electrical energy and technology, and many people who would have normally survived, have perished. There is a limit to what we can do these days. And after the battle, we have many people who are crippled and others who will take months to recover."

A woman stood up. "What about the ghosts? Hundreds of people have reported seeing spirits, apparitions, and ghosts of the dead moving around or seen in familiar spots."

A spokesman from the religious community rose up. He looked to be a Catholic priest. "We don't know what to make of these reports. They have definitely increased, but so much of all of this is new and abnormal. Priests, ministers, and lay persons have formed units with the authorities to investigate these phenomena, and will report back to our leaders and the community."

The woman was persistent. "Do we have anything to fear from these spirits, Father?"

The priest shook his head and lifted his hands. "We just don't know at this time. As with all of this, we advise people to use caution about anything strange, and alert the authorities concerning anything unusual."

Then Jerriel stood up and dropped her bomb on everyone. "Yoor holy men and women will need to use their powers of faith verry shoortly. A demon is nearby, hiding in your town, using its powers to add to the growing hatred and chaos. This is no accident. It feeds off terroor and violence like food, groowing stronger and doing what it can to cause moore. Together we must find and defeat it. It will use all of its abilities to turn you all against each other."

"Demons?" someone said, reacting with alarm like many others as the crowd murmured. "Now we have to fight demons?"

Jerriel turned to David and looked puzzled. "Yoo do not fight demons in your world, Daeved?"

"Maybe not as often," David said. "Or as openly. It's not like it happens all the time."

"We will hunt down this demon and banish or destrooy it," Jerriel assured them. "Bring yoor holy peeple with us. Demons can be very tricky, and dangerous, depending on what kind it is. Yoo cannot defeat them merely with normal weapons. Demons are creatures of power and supernatural evil, and are vulnerable to both faith and magical energy."

She put her hands behind her back and paced across the stage. "This raises another issue. We will need to begin training wizards among yoo. I have tested some. I can test others. Without wizards, yoor people are at a verry big disadvantage. Then they can tap into the strange sources of magic essence we coontinue to find. But first, we must eliminate the plague of this demon."

Connie stood up again. "In truth, we have received reports that some people have been demonstrating strange abilities. We will continue to investigate and ask Jerriel's help in determining how to proceed in these new directions."

All of that only raised more questions, and the consulting group once again came to the point of uproar.

The council called a recess to give everyone a chance to calm down.

Minutes later, Dirk caught David and Jerriel back stage.

"I had a hasty discussion with the town council," he said. "I'm putting you two in charge of this demon threat as of this moment. Do what you must to take care of it."

David nodded. "We will hunt this thing down and eliminate it as a threat."

"Good," Dirk said. "The religious people are sending a group of their folks to meet with you. Tonight. Not all of them are hip on pursuing this demon angle, especially the Baptists, for some reason. But the ones who go with you will need some guidance. Things are very different after the Merge. All of this weird stuff is now commonplace, and we're constantly playing catchup. I'm sorry to burden you two like this, but that's just the way it is. We don't need any outside forces, supernatural or whatever, making things even worse around here."

"We'll do whatever we can," David said. Although at the moment, he didn't know what exactly that was going to be.

"Demons are cunning personified," Jerriel tried to explain. "They will always try to twist everything to their advantage. It is a great misfortune to be foorced to deal with them directly, but it is woorse to do nothing and let them spread their hatred and destroy yoor town from within. And there are many different kinds who woork in different ways."

Dirk shook his head. "Let us know if we can give you any further assistance. Dave, keep forming that strike force we talked about. Assemble what you need. I know everyone has more than enough to deal with right now after the coups. I'm counting on you."

They said goodbye and left the auditorium. David admitted to her right up front. "Jerriel, I've never confronted a demon before, and I don't think any of these religious people have either, if I'm guessing right. You will need to tell us exactly what to do and what not to do. We aren't going to know."

Jerriel sighed and shook her head. "Verry well. Then you'd better get yoor peeple together, and you'll all need to start learning fast."

"Is there some kind of hurry? First thing in the morning we'll—"

She stopped him with her slender fingertips on his lips. "You still doo not fully comprehend the serious nature of this threat, Daeved. There is no time. We act this night, and we do not stop until our foe is defeated and destrooyed. We hunt it down, and banish it or destroy its physical form—oor we die trying."

She walked fast. David stopped a trooper and sent word back to Dirk for the religious people to join them at the Madison and 933 militia garrison station. He had to jog to catch up to Jerriel. "All right. I'm with you. They'll meet us at the station shortly and we can proceed from there."

52

Mason studied the healer woman from Elkhart. Marisol Gallegos was about twenty-seven years old with long black hair and dark eyes. She was quiet, small, and plump—about five-foot-one. She had a nervous smile, slightly coffee-stained teeth, and she looked around a lot.

Mason's initial impression of Miss Marisol was that she was skittish and a bit jumpy.

But they had just transported her from Elkhart across a war zone in a dusty, bumpy carriage, to bring her to a South Bend under siege.

Major Avery welcomed her.

"Where is the Pistolero?" she asked, impatiently. "I was told we were in a hurry. If so, then let's get started. This is going to be bad enough as it is. I don't like being here, and I want to go back home as soon as I can."

She looked Mason in the eyes, as if to silently say to him, Yes, it's you. You're him. The one with all the pistols that still work like magic. You're the one with all the wounds that I need to heal, with the magic I now control.

Everything about Marisol looked and seemed Hispanic in some general way. Even her simple clothing and the way she wore her hair. But her voice barely had the hint of an accent.

None of that really mattered. If she could heal him and get him back to the front, she could look and sound like anything or anyone under the sun.

When Mason looked back at her, his eyes told her that she had guessed right.

She put down her green leather purse and came to him where he sat up in bed. "You need to lie down. Give him something tough to bite down on that won't break his teeth."

That sounded encouraging.

"I'm letting you know up front that this is going to hurt both of us, Mister Pistolero. It's going to hurt both of us like hell itself. And I want you to know—what you feel, I also feel. That is why we cannot use drugs for pain. If I dulled my senses, I would certainly kill you."

She did not look exactly happy about that, either.

So, she suffered, too, whenever she healed someone. Interesting. Magic always seemed to work in funny ways.

"I want to thank you, ahead of time," Mason told her.

Marisol glared at him and frowned, the corners of her mouth sinking down. "You'll be cursing me over the next few days, every time we do a treatment together...and I'll be cursing you."

She looked to Major Avery. "There will be two or three treatments each day. Didn't they tell you? At the very least, your people will have to hold him down. But I strongly suggest that you wrap his ankles and wrists in foam and strap him down to the bed. Hospital restraints work well. This will all save time."

Avery was about to protest, but Mason barked, "Do as she says, Bill. Get on with it. If the pain's that bad...it's that bad."

Marisol grinned for the first time. "I like you, Mr. Pistolero. But I don't want you hitting or kicking me, or spitting on me—or trying to bite me or butt me with your head. If you tie him down good, as I say, you only have to hold down the head. That makes everything go much faster."

"How long is each treatment?" Mason asked her.

The medical people were already restraining him.

"Too long," Marisol said. "Ten or fifteen minutes that will seem much, much longer. Afterwards, we will both need to drink water and sleep. I don't advise eating much until after the third treatment of each day. You'll probably just throw it up. I do not like being vomited on."

"Very well," Mason said. "I've already skipped breakfast and lunch. They told me that much."

Marisol gritted her teeth and her face went hard. "Then let's get started."

"How much down time between treatments?" Major Avery asked.

She began examining his wounds and his body with her firm hands, wincing and sucking in a breath whenever she touched or passed her hands and fingers over his injuries. "Two to four hours between treatments. We'll both feel like sleeping in between. Prepare yourself, Mr. Pistolero. Know that the first day is always the worst, by far."

Major Avery gave him a thick swatch of leather over a chunk of foam rubber to bite down on. Then he pressed Mason's head back.

"Do your best to try to think of something else," Marisol told him "Looking and watching won't help. Close your eyes and try to think of something nice."

Mason instantly thought of his beloved Tori. The smell of her soft red hair. The feel of her lying next to him with her head on his chest while he smelled her hair and kept his arm around her.

Mason's eyes suddenly bulged and his body jerked against the restraints.

Someone had just rammed a red-hot harpoon up through his body and out the top of his skull. He bit down hard, and then gasped, and chomped again.

The pain was not only blinding, but it seemed to come in waves and burn from within.

He wept; he sobbed and moaned. His restraints burned his wrists and ankles as he tried to get away.

Within seconds, he was shuddering and drenched with sweat.

Shooting jolts of agony continued to rip through him, as his hips and spine arced up into the air again and again as the pain transfixed him. It was like slowly being electrocuted, but not dying.

The pain and the terror of the next second of the pain seemed to last and linger for hours.

Then the pain subsided without warning and mercifully began to fade.

Through his blurred vision, he saw Marisol, sweating and disheveled as well. She collapsed and fell back into the arms of two medics. The whites of her eyes rolled back up into her head. They laid her out on a stretcher cot and carried her out of the room.

Mason wanted to crawl off his hospital bed and throttle her to death. He cursed her through the gag in his mouth, which he had chewed to bits by then. He wanted that little woman dead and bleeding at his feet for what she had done to him.

It wasn't rational. Nor feasible. He could barely move and he was close to passing out. He could sense that he was seriously dehydrated.

The medics put him on an IV and gave him sips of room-temp water until he drifted off to sleep. He felt them gently cleaning him up, but he was too far gone to care what they did to him.

As long as those waves of pain were gone.

When they woke him for the second treatment of the day, four hours later, he begged and pleaded with them not to go through with it.

Major Avery gritted his teeth and ordered a new gag put in Mason's mouth. Mason cursed his friend Bill as well, while he was able.

Marisol came in, her grim face set. She brought hell back with her touch.

She must have learned these techniques from demons in Tartarus itself, tormenting the damned. Damnation. If *that* was what he had to look forward to for all eternity in the nether regions of the universe, then he'd best get himself some religion, and stay on the better side of it pretty damn quick.

Mason blacked out three times during the second treatment, but was brought back screaming each time as the torment continued.

It did not matter how long the treatment lasted.

One second was too much, and telescoped out into what felt like an eternity.

The only thing that mattered was the sweet cessation of the pain when it suddenly and abruptly cut off.

Ahhh…the mere absence of that pain was heaven itself.

Mason took in more water and slept again.

Three hours later, it was time for the third and final treatment of the first day.

Then the first day would be over.

Oh, hell. There were still two more entire days of this nightmare to go.

If he had one of his pistols, he would have blown his own head off his neck right then and there. Something he never thought that he would ever do.

Miss Marisol was wrong. He couldn't think of anything pleasant during that kind of agony. Even his love for Tori didn't help him when he was in that much pain. Nothing helped.

Just make the pain stop.

Make it stop.

All he could do was beg, scream, and whimper.

Then, it ended. Somehow, it ended.

He didn't even take water this time.

Exhaustion and sleep rocketed him away from the pain into darkness.

Mason woke up that night when it was dark, overcome by hunger and thirst.

They brought him all of the soup, and stew, and toast, and fruit gelatin that he could eat.

He ate a lot.

He felt some of his strength returning. He flexed one arm, then his legs.

It was so good to be out of those damn restraints.

He considered running away that night, but Major Avery had a score of strong guards posted around the room, inside and out, including Thulkara.

Mason wouldn't get to a door or a window before she nabbed him.

He dozed off again, and then someone came in. He heard a soft, familiar humming.

He looked up at Donna and smiled. He nearly burst into tears.

His beloved Donna gave him a sponge bath that was as gentle and as soothing as the touch of a thousand angels. Her hands seem to draw even the memory of all of that pain right out of him.

In his mind, Mason felt so great, he could leap out of that damn bed and lick the entire enemy force and all of its mages and armies, with his good right hand tied behind his back.

When she was done, she patted him on the head as if he was a little boy.

"You'll sleep well now, Mace," she told him. "I'm so sorry you have to go through all of this."

Mason licked his lips, very sleepy. "It's okay, Donna. I want you to go...give Miss Marisol one of your sponge baths, too. Tell Major Bill...that I insist on it."

"Okay, I'll tell him, but she didn't request one."

Mason smiled. "Tell them...I insist."

With that, he was sleeping.

53

Four members of the local religious community joined their band, as well as a handpicked platoon of thirty militia troops from David's Blackhawks. A young priest, Father Michael Petrowski led the religious contingent. The priest was thirtyish, tall, slender, and dressed all in black except for his collar. He wore a long, black wool coat and leather gloves. His dark brown hair was trimmed short, and his gray eyes in his angular face gave him a hard but intelligent look, slightly disarmed by an occasional grin.

"Yoo are a holy man?" Jerriel asked him directly. "What do you know about demons?"

"I have never encountered one directly, but I have studied some of the Church's extensive lore on demonology and methods of exorcism."

She flashed a puzzled look at David. "I do not understand?"

"How to defeat and banish demons," David said.

"Oh, verry good. We will certainly have need of yoo."

A little, short chubby man in his forties, with gold-rimmed glasses, steel-gray curls, and a black kippah butted in and took Jerriel's hand. "A great pleasure to meet you, mademoiselle. I am Rabbi Yosef Bergman. My good friend Michael asked me to accompany this group and help out if I may. Will we really confront an actual demon? It all sounds so impossible."

His blue eyes twinkled merrily. Jerriel studied the man intently and stared at his hand in an odd fashion.

"I fear it is soo," Jerriel said.

"Excellent!" The rabbi was clearly excited.

But David had the feeling this was not going to be a very fun game at all. "Father Michael, who are the other members of your team?" They were both young and wore helmets, armor, and even swords at their sides.

"These are our friends as well as our bodyguards. Jason Inada is a devoted Japanese-American Buddhist, as well as a practitioner of Iaido, the Way of the Sword."

David bowed briefly to the intense-looking young swordsman. His daisho appeared to be of the highest quality, and the athletic, mid-sized man looked as if he could handle himself well.

The other man was both young and huge, wearing what appeared to be a full suit of field plate armor, complete with chainmail, and two swords. He actually had an elaborate red cross painted across his breastplate and on his battered shield. Father Michael introduced him.

"Pastor Bryan Doran of the Methodist Church just joined his parish recently, and is also a student of the middle ages and their combat styles. He successfully led the defense of his church against the monsters that attacked his area."

Doran's short red beard and hair and green eyes added to the fierceness of his overall appearance. He looked like Barbarossa reborn.

"Well met," David said, and extended his arm.

Pastor Doran took it and grinned. "Well met, milord." He had a slightly southern accent, maybe Tennessee or Kentucky. "Medieval Historical Society?" he asked.

David nodded. "Yep. Good old MHS. Good thing we learned how to fight there."

"Good thing," the pastor agreed. "I'm just not sure what use fighting will be against a real demon."

"Sometimes it is necessary," Jerriel said. "They are inpredicatable, and may decide to attack you directly if they think they can. Yoo must bee ready for anything."

David readied his weapons, just in case. "So, how do we hunt a demon? How do we find it?"

"First," Jerriel said, "yoor holy people must give us their blessings, and bless and anoint our weapons with holy water, incense, oil, or by touch, amulets, relics, or chanting. That part is up to them. But we all must empty our minds of negative or impure thoughts and doubts. In the face of a demon, yoo must find yoor own way to stay focused and ignoore their many tricks and deceptions."

David turned to their platoon. "All right everybody. You heard the wizard lady. Present arms. Hold your weapons up to be blessed. C'mon, don't laugh or argue about it. This is important." Father Michael and the others went up and down the ranks, praying, chanting, sprinkling their armaments with holy water or dabbing them with blessed oil. Jason Inada chanted and rang a small clear bell. The very tone of it sounded beautiful and serene.

Finally, Jerriel and David received their blessings. Jerriel's staff glittered with a blue aura for a moment, then faded. She had added a long curved fighting sword and a matching dagger to her belt from Dirk's sword collection—as gifts.

One by one, David drew his weapons and received the blessings of their band of holy people. When he drew his longsword, the runes Jerriel had etched on it each shimmered in turn a different color, like numbers going up on an elevator. And the magically honed edges of the blade glowed white-hot.

Even the holy people looked a little surprised at that.

David turned to her. "We haven't had time for me to ask, but what did you do to my sword?"

"Simple enchantments, really. I can put similar ones on yoor other weapons when we have time. The blade will remain unnaturally sharp, and will be more effective against magical creatures, even dragons and demons. It will return to your hand at will should you drop it. The runes can detect enemies if they are near and will glow red, brighter as your foes or anyone who means you harm draws closer. Powerful beings will cause the edges to glow darker and darker, even to black in the presence of demons, shadows, or other negative plane creatures."

"Wow. All of that?"

She smiled and nodded. "If you are going to face down dragons for me, I thought maybe yoo should have weapons worthy of your bravery. That was very foolish, by the way, but exceptionally brave."

He held his longsword up and studied it. "These runes are Tharanorian magic?"

"Yes. As powerful as I could make them."

"What do they say?"

"They do not speak anything. They are signs of power. I will teach you their meaning and how to invooke them, alone or in combination. The first on this side is 'Shi,' or Spirit; next is 'Vae,' or Air; then 'Doru,' Earth; 'Zae,' Water; and 'Kal,' Fire." She suddenly looked at the sword and blinked.

She touched her staff to it. The blade suddenly flared brightly.

She drew back in surprise.

"Verry odd," she said. "The sword has gotten even stronger than I made it. It is filled with power." She went to touch him with her staff. Energies crackled between them.

She drew back again.

"Daeved. You are filled with magic essence. It is pass-hive, but you are conducting it in a very raw, intense foorm. This is not norm-hal. Even foor mages."

As if anything about magic were normal to him.

She patted his shoulder. "This could be dangerous. We will study it more when we have time."

Whenever that would be. Each day they barely had time to sleep and eat or catch their breath before running off on some new mission.

Now they were hunting a dangerous demon.

Again, the intense rush of frustration. So much they didn't know. So many growing threats and so little time. But they had to keep going forward anyway. No choice.

They left the station with their new, merry band of holy men and their fledgling strike force in tow. David turned to Jerriel once more.

"So, how do we find this demon?"

She turned to the holy men. "None of you can detect it in the area?"

They all looked uncomfortable and shook their heads. "We currently have no means to do so," Father Petrowski said. "Is there anything that can help us?"

Jerriel reached into one of her belt pouches and pulled out a small, clear sliver of either crystal or gemstone. She held it up between her right thumb and forefinger. "This is an Illigixxian crystal—an ancient spiritstone of great power that I have from my mother, and all of my mothers before them. Some call it a soulstone—which may mean nothing to yoo. It is verry rare. They are found sometimes along primary ley lines of power at prime nexus points. They grow very slowly over eons, absorbing the residual interdimensional energies that leak out from the endless realities—the myriad universes."

Dead silence.

"Jerriel," David reminded her, "none of us are wizards."

Jerriel smiled at Rabbi Bergman. "I'm not so sure about that."

She handed Bergman the enchanted crystal. He took it in his fingerless gloves. It flashed white-green as soon as he touched it with his fingertips.

"This man," she said, "has a strong talent somewhere in the white and green aura spectrums. I sensed it almost immediately; it is raw and undeveloped, but I don't know what it is yet. But he certainly has one. Josef, you are a mage."

"I am a rabbi," he said. And quickly handed the soul stone back to her as if it were white-hot.

"You are a teacher. I understand. Know that being a mage never makes you less, only more. But you have been blessed with a magical gift as powerful as any I have ever seen—and that is saying something. Whether you deny or accept your gift, whether you choose to develop or ignore it." She clenched the stone in her fist and spoke a few mystical words.

The stone and her hand holding it glowed bright blue, with a radiance that lit the entire area.

"A soulstone reveals, exposes, and detects power. All kinds of power. My aura is blue. My primary talents are spell casting and enchanting. My minor talents are conjuring, healing, and illusion."

"What about the demon?" Jason Inada asked.

"I was getting to that. Were we close enough, David's sword that I enchanted would detect its vile energies. But we are not close enough for that to work yet."

David drew his sword and looked at it. Nothing.

"The spiritstone can help us. But it is only a tool, and must be focused and directed. Spells, meditation, even prayers can help focus the effort. Demons are beings of intense, negative power, and that malignant power can be detected. Once we home in on it, the stone will glow more intensely as we draw closer."

Jerriel slowly turned in place, holding the crystal before her while she chanted. Surprisingly, the stone glittered and flashed several times in several different shades of color as she completed her circle, even when she passed David and the rabbi.

She dropped her arms and shook her head.

"Nothing. My skills are not attuned enough by themselves. Yoo must all help me. Form a circle about me. Focus yoor thoughts, yoor faith, all that yoo are, into detecting the demon and its evil power. Will it so."

David and the holy men gathered around her, lending their thoughts and prayers to her efforts.

She made another full circle.

The crystal suddenly turned dull gray and pulsed ominously as it pointed in a certain direction.

"We're getting something, but it's faint," she said. "Stay foocused! Everyone draw closer. Touch the crystal with yoor fingertips."

David emptied his mind and tried to picture the creature in his mind while the holy men chanted and touched the stone.

A shot of pain went down his arm. In his mind's eye, he had a brief vision of a bizarre, twisted creature, sitting intently...in front of a mirror, of all things. But it was only for the flash of an instant.

"We've loocated it!" Jerriel said.

They drew back.

Jerriel held the soulstone before her. A small black imperfection smoked within it. It smoldered strongest when she turned due west.

"That way," she said. "We need to seek the demon that way."

"Then let's head out," David said. "Let's find this vile thing and put it down."

The spiritstone's focus signal slowly grew stronger as they followed it west through town. They passed checkpoint after checkpoint. The night was cold. Early spring winds wailed through the skeletal trees. Clouds came in. The troops lit oil lamps to keep going in the deep darkness.

"Sir," one of the troopers said, "we're less than a mile from Black Town. We'll reach their lines starting at Chapin Street. What do we do there, if they don't let us pass?"

"If it comes to that, we'll ask for their help and try to negotiate something. Hopefully they'll listen. This thing is a threat to everyone."

Pastor Bryan Doran rubbed his red beard and pointed at the soulstone. "We must be getting closer," he said. Black wisps of some kind of magical ichor or vapor curled off the stone and vanished in the breeze.

David drew his longsword. The edges of his blade turned from gray to black. He moved the sword and found that at this range, he could also track the demon.

"Looks like we're going the right way," he said. "Jerriel, what do we do when we get there?"

She continued following the stone. "We're close. If we can coorner it, we can try to destroy or banish it. It will try many tricks and attempt to get away. Or it may attack. Yoor holy men must try whatever rites they have to dispel demons and break their power. Who knows what will woork after the Merge."

As they went forward, the night darkened noticeably. Some of their lanterns went out and could not be re-lit in the harsh wind. David felt as if a cold hand scratched lightly all over his body. He found it both annoying and very unnerving, making it hard to think or concentrate.

They weren't to Black Town yet. At least they didn't have that issue to deal with.

From what he could see, the block up ahead of them looked to be a total wasteland. Burned houses; scorched, bare trees. Dead bodies.

Bones—from humans and animals. The entire place stank of death, smoke, and ash.

"This looks like hell itself," Jerriel said.

They came to a big, skeletal, white oak tree, lifeless, scorched, and blackened from house fires. The corpse of an old man hung from one of the remaining high branches. His body and bones had been horribly shredded.

David's blood locked up cold.

Just like the bodies in that serial killer's basement.

At the same time, Jerriel held up the spiritstone. David held up his sword. Weird black flames curled off of them both...

In the exact direction of the last house standing.

That dwelling was a bleak, collapsing, three-story brownstone. The dark red brick had been scorched with ash from the house fires, like black bloodstains on rotten flesh. It looked like a gigantic, charred skull half-buried in the ground. A skull that leered at them.

"There. The demon lurks in that defiled place," Jerriel said.

All of their lanterns went out.

54

Mason fully intended to rise up early the next morning and somehow sneak away.

But when he woke up, the medics already had him in his restraints, and Marisol walked into the room, the same resigned look on her grim face.

He felt his own eyes widen like searchlights.

Marisol came to him and whispered briefly. "Thanks for that sponge bath, Mr. Pistolero. I tried to beg off at first, but I'm glad that nurse Donna insisted. Talk about magic. I have not slept like that in weeks!"

Just like before, she examined his body and his wounds first.

Mason tipped his head back and tried not to look at her as a fresh gag was stuffed between his teeth.

Marisol didn't look at him directly, either, but he heard her voice. "Shall we begin?"

No!

She wasn't really asking him.

The pain was just a terrible as before, but the strange thing was that Marisol was right.

The first day was the worst, somehow.

It wasn't as if anyone could get used to pain such as that, but today, it somehow seemed…less.

Nor did the treatments seem to last as long.

He didn't sweat as much, either. He wasn't as exhausted. He didn't need as much water, or sleep.

He was only out for less than three hours, and then the next thing he knew, they were preparing for the second treatment.

Each treatment was still excruciating while it lasted, of course, but now he could keep telling himself that it was going to end.

In the end, all three treatments on the second day took less than nine hours, while the first day, they had taken almost fourteen hours.

Only one day to go.

He could do this.

He was very hungry that night, and ate several helpings of chicken soup with carrots, celery, and chunks of real chicken…from a can, he was told. He had a baked potato and ate the skin. Then apple cobbler for dessert, fruit juice, and applesauce by his own request.

Another sponge bath from Donna and he was ready to sleep.

He thought he heard sounds of fighting outside that night.

That wasn't a dream.

When he woke up, Major Avery had the troops evacuating that building and the entire area, pulling back before an enemy advance.

No matter how badly Mason asked, Bill would not tell him how tough things were.

Mason feared the worst.

They got him settled and secure in a new building. He went to sleep, but woke up several times, filled with worry and doubt.

The war continued, while he was living high on the hog and getting sponge baths.

He felt guilty and worried about Blondie and Thulkara, and the rest of his friends and comrades.

Before dawn, he told the medics that he felt great, to strap him in and go fetch Miss Marisol for his final treatments.

The healer was with him within a quarter hour.

The first treatment took twelve minutes.

Not one bit less painful than all of the others. Mason and Marisol were sweating and exhausted, but it was all nothing that they did not expect by then.

They both slept for two hours.

The second treatment lasted eleven minutes, followed by two more hours of rest.

Marisol came to him without a word for the third and final treatment.

Ten minutes.

Mason drank some water and went to sleep.

Four hours later, he got out of bed without hesitation. He dressed without any assistance, pulled on his boots, and even called for his guns.

Once he strapped on his steel and iron, and put on his outlaw hat, he felt like himself again.

He felt healthy. He felt good once more. No stiffness, no weakness—ready for duty.

Ready to do battle.

He checked the locations of his wounds.

Not even any scars.

He went directly to Major Avery, even though he wanted to hit the nearest mess hall and eat everything in sight.

At that moment, he could probably even out-eat Thulkara.

Bill stood up when the Pistolero walked in.

"It worked," Mason told him. "I'm back. I'm fit and ready to return to the lines—right now, if need be."

Major Avery nodded. "Good. We need you."

Mason looked around. "Is Miss Marisol here? I...I'd like to thank her."

"That's not necessary, Mace. I've already done so, and in any case, she already departed—over an hour ago. She said that from her experience, that was best for everyone."

Mason nodded. "Perhaps she was right. I didn't know until just now, if I was going to thank her, or attack her."

"She said that she was as anxious to return home as you were."

"Home?" Mason said quizzically.

"The battle, Mace. The front lines are your home."

"No, I wouldn't call it that, exactly. The war is not my home, but you, my friends, and our unit are my family. So, I guess it's not that far off. But there's a pretty, red-haired girl out there somewhere. She's my home. And I won't be home again until I find her. I just hope she's still alive...somewhere."

Bill clapped him on the back. "I hope she is, too, Mace. And if we can find a way out of this mess, I hope you do find her."

"Tell me how the fight is going, Bill. Get me up to speed."

Avery sighed as they paced side by side down the hallway to the stairs. "Not very good, Mace."

"Oh, I was guessing not. What else is new?"

"We've had to drop back to the eleventh line of defense once more."

"Back to the eleventh...already?"

"On a better note, we now have four reloading teams again. And, we want to try out some new experimental loads mixed with gemstones...and uranium."

Mason sucked in a breath. "Atomic bullets, Bill? We don't want to blow up the enemy and all of us with them."

"Why do you think we need to test them? Oh, and something else. We've fashioned a suit of armor for your to wear that will protect your torso and your extremities—even your neck and head. There's even an insert cap for your hat."

"I appreciate the thought, Bill. But my guns are heavy enough. I still need to be able to move around. I can't wear fifty or sixty pounds of armor."

"Try twenty-two pounds, and it's coated with silver and a mix of diamond and crystal dust to resist magic."

"Seriously?" Mason said. "How did you make it so light?"

"Our main threat seems to be crossbow bolts and arrows, so we're using protective plates made of a light, high-strength plastic. We've already tested it. Crossbow bolts and arrows mostly bounce right off the padded plates."

"All right. Suit me up and I'll try it."

"We have troops testing the plastic armor as well. It's a lot lighter than metal, it protects almost ninety percent of the body, and we don't have to worry about stopping bullets—just arrows and spears and such."

By the time he had the armor on under his clothing and rigs, the sun had set.

The Pistolero returned to the front lines. There was even some cheering.

Then the monsters began to advance on the western line, just like old times. The night shift had arrived.

Mason turned to Major Avery. "Bring me some of those new uranium rounds. What do they have them in?"

"Your 1858 carbine."

"Ooh...good choice."

The runners handed it up.

Mason took aim at the center of the mass of shadowspawn marching toward the front lines.

The single shot lobbed up into the sky like a bright star or flare, illuminating the sky and the area so brightly that the monsters hissed and would not look at the bright, blinding light.

Then the round detonated thirty feet above the ground as the star arced down more than a quarter mile away.

A ball of fire erupted, enveloping the monsters in a dome of destruction, a hundred and fifty yards in diameter.

All that remained within the fiery crater were a bunch of glowing skeletons, reducing to ash.

The blast wave flattened friend and foe on their backs within a mile, and took down weakened trees and buildings, setting anything flammable on fire.

Mason swallowed, and turned to Major Avery.

"I think the team got that load just right," he said. "I sure as hell wouldn't make it any more powerful. I don't have anything that will shoot much farther away. We sure can't use those rounds up close."

He checked his carbine.

The steel barrel was still red-hot in places. "Check it. That's not good. It'll be a while before we can fire another one of those rounds with this weapon, and eventually, those shots are going to wear out the barrels we shoot them through. If we can only shoot one round at a time, maybe we should try the St. Louis rifle, or the shotguns with slugs. We might be able to use the shotguns like mortars."

"They really would be like artillery, then," Avery noted.

That one blast and the losses inflicted by it staggered even the brutes, and caused them to withdraw in terror, at least for the moment.

"Saddle up," Avery told Mason. "We need to unleash another of those surprises on the mercs at the southern line. Give them something to think about. Blondie and Thulkara will join up with us."

Mason smiled. It was good to be back. And it would be good to ride Winger again and fight beside his friends. Avery had even made armored plates for their horses out of the same plastic.

They held the eleventh line of defense throughout that night, and for hours into the next day.

The enemy adjusted their tactics and no longer exposed large numbers of their forces in the distant killing fields.

Now the Pistolero rode again.

55

Sergeant Blaylock staggered up front. He moved sluggishly and looked bewildered. "Major. Half of the platoon has...wandered off, sir. We're having trouble getting the other half to go forward. The troops are pretty scared. Some of them even terrified."

David nodded. "I feel it, too. We all do." He looked to Jerriel and the holy men.

"An aura of fear and confusion," Jerriel said. "It will get woorse as we go closer. We will need blessings and prayers to bolster our spirits. Positive energy. Good will. That is all that can counter such evil."

Father Mike and the others went among the remaining troops, blessing, praying, and encouraging. Even David felt the pall of terror and its oppressing weight lift to a great degree. It was encouraging.

The troops could focus and take orders once more.

"Who says prayer doesn't work? I want that damn house encircled," David said. "We're going in. After we do, nothing comes out without getting doused with holy water and destroyed if need be. This thing we're after must not escape, even if it takes all of us to drag it down and rip it apart. Do you understand?"

They nodded. "We do," Blaylock said. "Good luck, sir." The militia troops held their ground, but they looked happy that they could stay outside.

Jerriel reached over and took David's hand for a moment. Even she trembled slightly–she who had never shown any fear. She leaned in and kissed him on the cheek. The darkness and the fear oppressing them lessened greatly.

She smiled at him. "Love works, too, sometimes. Evil can neither understand nor withstand it."

The holy men flanked them, two on either side.

"We will try to slip inside quietly," Jerriel said. "If the demon is at work, as they usually are, it will be committing some deviltry. It may become completely absorbed in its dark work, unaware of our pres- hence until we attack or make ourselves known. That would be moost fortunate. But even its passive defenses can be very formidable, as we have already seen. Prepare yourselves. Shield and boolster your mind and spirit as best you can."

They entered the house through the open front door. It was even darker inside, if that were at all possible. Only the weird light from the soulstone and David's blade guided them.

Then that light went out as well.

To plunge into that darkness, that nest of palpable fear and terror, took every ounce of courage David had. He didn't know if he could have done so on his own.

He quickly felt as if he sleepwalked into those deep shadows. He did not know for how long. At first he wondered where the others were in the darkness. Then he even had trouble recalling who the others were.

Jerriel. He knew she was there.

Something powerful affected him–disorientation, grogginess, and a mindless stupor. If it affected him, the others suffered from it, too.

Jerriel. Where was she? He struggled to clear and shield his mind, just as he had when talking to the dragon. Yes. Shield his mind. That's what the dragon said. Jerriel said something similar. He needed to shield his mind from the evil influences around him.

A barrier of clear steel. He pictured it in his mind and made it real once more.

He took in deep breaths, he emptied his thoughts. He remembered a trick from martial arts and kendo: the concept of no mind.

No mind. No thoughts.

No mind that another could control or deceive.

His efforts paid off. His head cleared somewhat.

David reached out into the darkness. His sword. It glimmered faintly at his touch, ringing an electric chord of energy throughout his body like a jolt that shook him, made him gasp and stare, wide-eyed.

His sword knew his touch. He sensed it. It knew him somehow. He had been around blade weapons all his life. Instinctively he avoided cutting himself, despite the perfectly honed edges.

He could bleed if he forced himself to be cut.

It was all his choice.

That was the key. He had to focus on his choices, instead of stumbling through all of the distractions and illusions, the psychic miasma they moved in.

Light.

They needed light. Darksight did not work. Not in this evil place. He focused on his sword.

Something ignited within him, like an inner fire.

Instead of his sword, his skin began to glow. Just barely, but enough light to see by.

Pastor Doran, Jason Inada, Rabbi Bergman, and Father Petrowski. They all followed Jerriel, struggling against the invisible forces all around them, trying to hold them back.

They headed upstairs into the house.

David checked his sword.

According to that, they should go downstairs—not up. The demon was downstairs. He tried to open his mouth to tell them, but no sound came out. He tried to move, but it became a struggle to go after them. Exhausting.

Just as they exhausted themselves trying to climb the stairs.

They were going the wrong way.

The demon's power deluded everyone. It was winning.

He managed to reach Pastor Doran and had to catch his breath.

He grabbed at the big man's armored forearm, and finally got it.

Slowly, Bryan turned and blinked at him.

Why did they all feel so weak? His hand dropped to his belt, and rested on a small plastic bottle filled with holy water.

It couldn't hurt to try that.

With effort, he poured some in his hand and splashed it in his face. The water was ice cold and tingly.

It did help. His mind cleared. He moved more freely.

David rubbed his eyes, his chapped lips. He wetted his fingers and unplugged his ears. Outside, he heard the howling wind again.

He splashed some in Pastor Doran's face. The big man spluttered and shook himself.

"What? Upstairs...the demon."

"Wrong way," David told him. "We're in...some kind of delusion. Splash holy water in the face of the others. Snap them out of it." He pointed at the stairs going down into the dark basement. "The demon's down there. Not up."

Pastor Doran nodded. "Got it. Will do." He moved a little faster, pulling out a canteen of holy water to douse the others with. They still floundered on the stairs. David poured the rest of his bottle of holy water on his sword.

Time to confront this thing. Time to put an end to the threat.

He crept downstairs, every hair on his body tingling. Like struggling to walk through a high surf. Yet the breakers weren't water, but raw, intense waves of solid fear.

Eerie lights flashed below out of the basement's pitch darkness.

An oily voice echoed and shifted, changing in both pattern and manner of speech every so often. He'd heard that inhuman voice before. It creeped him out exactly the same way.

He reached the floor of the basement. He spotted bones, pieces of shredded, rotting bodies—there was filth everywhere. David looked up.

Before him were chairs, crates, small desks, nightstands, and boxes that ringed the basement.

Propped up on all of them was a multitude of shining mirrors of various shapes and sizes. Images of people's faces flashed in and out of the mirrors. Every age and race, men and women, even children.

In the center of that morass, a dark, shifting form moved.

A vile and hideous thing.

56

The dark, cloudy night turned warmer and the air grew very still. Everything around Mason and his friends seemed too quiet. That wasn't normal.

"Something is wrong," Thulkara said aloud.

"I agree," Blondie added.

Mason felt it, too. But what could it be?

They had just held off the enemy for another eight-hour shift at the front. But this time, they didn't even have to resort to any of the new uranium-laced rounds.

They never had an opportunity to use one, and they didn't want to level another part of their own town and its buildings for no reason.

That was only worth doing it if they could take down a thousand or more of the enemy all at once, from a safe distance. Those deadly rounds weren't safe to use up close. They'd take out themselves and their own people as well.

The monsters still gathered to attack, but they filtered in along multiple attack lines in the dark and came together up close. Very clever.

The three friends reported their gut misgivings to Major Avery. Where were the mercs and the mages? What were they doing? Why had the enemy attacks decreased in this manner?

All of that remained a major concern.

"All of you get some rest for the next shift," Avery told them. "Your current shift is over as of right now. Unless you have something specific to tell me or warn me about, there's nothing for any of us to consider further or act upon."

"How about this," Blondie said. "Their mages haven't hit us for three days in a row. Now the mercs fall back."

"We don't know," Avery said. "The spotters can't see anything. Maybe they heard the Pistolero's back, with new abilities. Maybe they're plotting how to counter them. I wish we knew. But until we know something definite, we will follow orders and keep doing what we are doing. Your unit is dismissed, so get the hell off the line."

All of them were tired.

All of them could use the rest.

Three hours later, Bill woke them up in a hurry once more.

"Suit up. All available reserves are to race to reinforce Mishawaka along their southern defensive lines."

"What's happening?" Mason asked.

"The enemy has gone for broke, Mace. All of their mages and most of their reserves are apparently pounding Mishawaka as we speak. The defenders there don't have anyone like you or the Shooting Stars, yet. It's a goddam bloodbath."

"How bad?" Blondie asked.

"Very bad. The enemy's all out-attack in that area came as a complete surprise. No one can stop the enemy right now, and with the explosion of panicked refugees, almost no one can maneuver or get in there, either. Anyone who tries to get in the enemy's way and stop them, gets taken down by the concentrated firepower of the enemy mages. If the enemy keeps driving like this, they can destroy all of Mishawaka in a few days or less. Our allies will be crushed, and South Bend will be cut off and surrounded by superior numbers."

Mason blinked. "Then I guess we'd better hump it over there; good thing it's not far."

It took them slightly over an hour to make contact with the enemy on the west side of Mishawaka around River Park.

Forward scouts and spotters from the rooftops and other vantage points reported that most of the enemy mages were still about a mile and half away, spread out on a line, supporting the main thrust of the enemy advance at the center.

369

Major Avery sent word to have that entire area of the battlefield evacuated.

The Pistolero and his unit rode hard all that way, guns blazing, in an attempt to cut off the foe.

When they barely got close enough for Mason to engage, the spotters reported that the enemy mages were already scattering in all directions.

A catapult canister of silver and sulfur dust exposed many of the fleeing mages, glowing like beacons in the night.

"Gotta chance it now," Mason said, from up on a high rooftop, three stories up. "Before they all get out of range."

His runner handed him his carbine.

The Pistolero aimed his arc of fire for the best trajectory he could manage.

The star shot out, leaving the barrel red-hot.

A bright dome of destruction blasted everything within a hundred and fifty yards, including the enemy mercs and numerous enemy mages who didn't move fast enough.

Mason knew that was his only shot like that. They couldn't use any more of those annihilator rounds on the local Mishawaka population. All of the other areas were far too populated.

No doubt some innocent civilians had also died in that blast as well.

But the enemy advance had to be stopped, no matter what. More would die by the thousands if it wasn't.

For a few precious minutes, the devastating results of that one blast stalled the juggernaut of the enemy advance. The Pistolero and his unit raced back down and charged in to help hold the broken front lines, and the defenders of Mishawaka rallied behind his blazing guns.

They fought the regrouping invaders point blank and up close, house to house, and street to street.

Enemy mages still cut down defenders in droves at will, all along the line. Even the Pistolero could not be everywhere at once to counter them.

The defenders had to tough it out, absorb such losses, and keep fighting. There was no other choice.

The lines fluctuated back and forth during the battle that raged to decide the fate of Mishawaka, South Bend, and perhaps all of Michiana.

If both of the latter fell, Elkhart would stand alone and surrounded.

Three more brutal hours passed, and there were still hours of darkness before dawn. And because they were fighting mercs and not monsters, the battle would only continue throughout the following day.

Both sides were all in. They had committed the last of their reserves. All of their forces wound up fully engaged.

Try as they might, the Michiana defenders were still slowly getting pushed back and rammed into the earth.

Once more, the abundance of enemy mages remained the telling difference, the one gross advantage in firepower and destruction against which the militias had no practical countermeasure.

Mason and his friends held their ground, an island within a typhoon of magic and fire. The enemy saw their chance to destroy them, and closed in for the kill.

The Pistolero negated several deadly spells swooping down upon them, dueling with almost two dozen mages at once. Thulkara whirled like a dervish in her dance of battle fury, her red axes buzzing through the mercs like a gigantic, death-dealing saw. Blondie cast scarlet lightning into the faces of enemy attack waves, roaring in to sweep them away.

They fought with a sea of dead bodies in front and behind them.

They were almost surrounded and cut off.

At any second, the fiery maelstrom could annihilate them.

Several mighty blasts of magical fire suddenly hit the enemy's exposed left flank.

The Shooting Stars raced in, at the front of fresh militia forces. Side by side, the two valiant young girls advanced, rapidly firing their shining energy bows. Fearless, they sent glittering arrow after magical arrow into the enemy ranks and targeted several mages.

Enchanted flame, exploding ice, and lightning blasted the enemy's left flank.

From the right, the remaining sorcerers of South Bend arrived, and concentrated their own magic blasts on the enemy's forward advancing lines on that flank. They opened a breach on the right, and some of the surviving Mishawaka units saw they chance and poured into that gap to exploit it.

An hour before dawn, dismay suddenly took the driving, overconfident mercenary lines.

Elkhart forces had broken through at last, and attacked in waves of large numbers of fresh troops.

All of the forces of Michiana had learned their lesson.

If they were an island of Urth people cut off from the rest of the world, they had to stand together in order to assure their mutual survival.

They couldn't just stand by while the foe destroyed their neighbors, and simply wait for themselves to be next.

The enemy quickly found themselves at a severe disadvantage, cut off on three sides. They were swallowed up in many small pockets and wiped out, or forced to surrender outright. Enemy mages attempted to escape. Some did so. Some did not, and became prisoners with the mercs, shocked and silent.

By noon, the combined forces of Elkhart, Mishawaka, and South Bend pushed the enemy's main forces out of Mishawaka proper.

It wasn't a rout, but it was the next best thing.

Even the disciplined mercs retreated in full flight, taking cover behind their South Bend lines, which had also pulled back to less-exposed, more-defensible positions close to the old tenth line of defense.

The enemy knew when they were licked.

Mason and his friends collapsed where they were and rested on the ground, completely spent.

But the war still wasn't over. The odds were simply even now. At least that's what the spotters and observers estimated. Even with the monsters at night, the enemy no longer outnumbered the defenders. Not even two to one.

Back in Elkhart, the eight enemy slave camps were cut off and contained. Once the war was decided, they would be dealt with and liberated, but not until then.

There was no time to celebrate anything just yet, and losses on both sides had been appalling.

A great deal of fighting still remained.

But now, there was at least a chance of victory for the defenders.

57

The demon-thing surged in several directions, murmuring to this mirror, then whispering into another as the faces continued to flash and fade in and out.

The demon wasn't shaped like anything human.

Nothing sane should look or move the way it did. It literally defied description. Just staring at it while it shifted and writhed this way and that threatened to drive David mad. He couldn't focus on it, and yet he could not look away.

David shuddered to his core.

Terrifying.

The demon was raw terror itself—horror personified—given an obscene form.

David's hands shook. He gulped air and struggled to breathe, to keep his eyes from rolling up into the back of his head and to prevent himself from fainting. His sword would clatter to the ground. He would be lost.

Lost to join the bones and festering pieces of corpses on that dark floor.

Not knowing what else to do, he gritted his teeth and gripped his sword tight.

This...thing. This demon was an enemy. Of that there was no doubt. He had to master his fear. Face it and defeat it–any way possible.

David thought of Jerriel. He thought of his mom and dad. He tried to picture their faces.

And scarier than anything else...the demon exuded fear, power, and despair like an odor–like crippling waves of energy.

Get over it. Get used to it. Beat this thing. Destroy it.

All this while it acted totally oblivious to his presence. Jerriel said it might be that way. So absorbed in its dark work. David was no threat. It was so powerful it did not even need to notice him.

What was it doing? The thought suddenly occurred to him. He inched forward, ready to fight for his life, trying to find out.

The demon's head, if one could call it that, seemed to be a blob of dark pus or vitriol or nasty ooze that surged and stretched beneath the undulating dark flesh, bulging with various lidless eyes, pustules, sores, and boiling, smoking orifices.

The foul wisps and weird vapors the thing emitted at times made it look like a multi-limbed, amoeboid octopus covered in boiling, charred, scrambled, black, rotten eggs–with a bunch of dead eyeballs thrown in.

This abomination was the most unpleasant thing David had ever seen.

At last, he heard what it said.

The oozing head lurched in several directions, whispering and babbling to the faces in the mirrors.

Its limbs, tentacles and pseudopods–some like those of giant insects–scratched and clicked, and writhed greedily.

Then he saw its profile for a few instants.

The primary face shifted in a flash into a distorted attempt to match or mimic whatever face it viewed in the mirror.

Like that of a young black girl, maybe eleven.

"Yess, yes, there will not be enough food for you and your mother. You will starve. Your baby brother is already sick. Better to get rid of him now. Stop resisting; stop putting it off. Each night you hesitate means more starvation.

"Do it tonight, just like I tell you. While you huddle in the dark to stay warm, cover his mouth and nose. Put all your weight on him until he goes still and cold. Then shove him close to your fat mother while she sleeps. When she wakes she, she will think she crushed the life out of him. She will not blame you..."

Lightning fast, it shifted its head to another mirror and the face changed again.

This time to that of middle-aged white woman.

"You did well speaking before the White Town council. Inflame them to action. That young black couple down the street, just across the border. They need to be gotten rid of one way or another. So what if they helped you during the attacks and took you in? They're not like you. Burning that cross in front of their house won't be enough. Burn them out. Drive them out. Burn down their house with them in it if you must, but get rid of them.

"Go to the skinhead defense force. Tell them the husband raped you while you were with them. You were too scared to say anything until now. He laid hands on a white woman. String him up and burn him while he jerks on the end of rope. Have them do the same to his wife and kids while he watches, before his turn. Do it. Stop holding back. Make an example of them!"

The demon's face shifted rapidly to another mirror, taking on the face of a young Asian boy.

The boy stared into the mirror, blubbering and crying, wiping his face and runny nose.

"I don't like this anymore," the boy said. "It doesn't feel right. I won't listen to you anymore. You're scaring me!"

Several demon limbs shot through the mirror and ensnared the boy, who gasped, completely terrified.

"You listen to me, you little shit! I will come through our portal and slowly rip you into little pieces and splatter you all over your room for your family to find. You thought it was fun having me work for you and make things happen? How I sent those monsters to your neighbors next door and barbecued that bully and his family in their own backyard–while you secretly watched? Well now it's *my* turn for fun. You're mine, now. From now on, you do what I say. That skinny young priest at church? You tell your parents and everyone else how he can't keep his hands off you. You got that? Good!"

David gripped his sword with both hands, feeling his wrath begin to overtake his fear. This creature was utterly detestable–playing on people's weaknesses and fears, driving them to commit evil acts, sowing discord and hatred.

Destruction and death.

An older man's face appeared in another mirror. "Judge Moran. A pleasure as always. Good that we can finally join forces. Maintain your secret contacts with former councilman Stevenson. Continue jerking around your various docket cases as you see fit, but certain cases and trials will need our careful attention. Remember, the goal is to continue to undermine the local authorities and remove key persons we want neutralized."

Next, a young black man. "Hey, K-J. You're doing all right in Black Town. Keep the drugs and the girls flowing to your thugs. When it's time to make your move, you'll have enough muscle to take over your area and become one of the new warlords. Then you can go house to house and take whomever and whatever you want—whenever you want it. You can raid any area you like after that. Take down anyone you want. No one will ever mess with you again."

Then a young woman, college-aged, plain, with sandy blond hair.

"Hey, Kelly. Wow, you look great today. Keep up the good work tracking all that information on the militia, its leaders, and their locations. It all could be very handy someday. Trust me, gal. You know I wouldn't steer you wrong. That's it, you need more and more face time in front of your special mirror. Someday soon you'll find out how special it really is—once we get a little closer. That's it. Get out your makeup and try something new. That hot guy Jake who helps guard your office doesn't know your name yet...but he will. Wait until you take him for a ride and make him suffer. Just keep listening to my voice in your head."

David lifted his sword and was about to strike when a single, intensely angry face filled all of the mirrors. A powerful, dark man's grim, handsome face. Black hair, beard, and deep black eyes. He looked murderous and angry.

The demon writhed and cried out in fear, cowering away.

What could make this thing afraid?

Blue-violet electric jolts of pain coruscated out of the mirrors, shocking the demon repeatedly.

"Deceitful wretch!" the dark, angry man snarled. "I should destroy you. We have just learned of your many failures. My masters punished me, severely! I nearly perished. The hordes we sent you to secure your area were defeated and destroyed by the local weaklings and fools. How could you suffer such a defeat? Nor have you captured or killed the traitor. Now all I find is you glutting yourself—feeding constantly off your various Urther hosts!"

The demon abased itself and wailed and pleaded.

"Master, Master. Please listen! It was not my fault. The creatures you sent me to do your bidding were too stupid. They would not listen to my directions! I told them that an all-out, direct attack would only alarm the natives here and pull them together."

"Fool! I should have known better than to trust a demon. The thousands we sent should have been more than sufficient to crush that entire region. Admit your base incompetence. You bungled it!"

"Master, no! Please. I wanted to weaken and divide them more first, before the final blow. The leaders of the horde would not listen. They were certain of victory over the soft humans here. But these detestable mortals have proven much more formidable than any of us imagined, and the traitor—she is helping them!"

"Prepare to be destroyed, foul creature. My wrath is upon you! You have failed me for the last—"

"Master. No. I beg of you! I can make amends. I have set many plans in motion. I am sowing chaos and discord day by day. I can still destroy them from within!"

"Enough of your lies!"

"I...I can get you the wizard girl—the daughter of your hated enemies. I know exactly where she is!"

58

Major Avery eagerly rubbed his hands together, pacing in front of Mason. "At long last, now the task at hand becomes driving the enemy out of South Bend and retaking the city. For good this time."

Blondie wasn't the only one who wasn't too sure about that. "Sir, I think the enemy still has more than a few nasty tricks up their sleeves, and is just waiting to spring them on us."

That turned out to be more than true. Mason, Blondie, Thulkara, and their unit were among the first to witness the widespread use of civilian Urth captives by the enemy as human shields. Captives of all ages.

It was a terrible sight to behold. Normal people, tied up across picket lines and on the front of archery mantlets. Urth people staked out among units of enemy forces, like orchards of strange fruit trees.

The enemy used the human shields to discourage forward movement by the militia, and to limit the use of the Pistolero's wide effect blasts. Any such further attacks would now kill scores and hundreds of Urth people, along with the enemy numbers.

Mason put away the uranium loads and picked his shots carefully with more conventional combinations.

But there were still times when he was forced to fire, no matter the cost to the human shields. The defenders could not hold back and let themselves be overrun.

The enemy forced such choices upon the defenders.

Sometimes the militia forces could flank pockets of the enemy and sweep in fast enough to rescue at least some of the human shields.

But all too often, the foe would simply slit the throats of the helpless captives as they pulled back, or before they themselves were cut down.

The captives often seemed doomed either way.

If the enemy gained or held a position, they died.

If the enemy withdrew or were killed, they also died.

Word came down from the militia high commanders: As long as the enemy continued to use human shields, there would be no quarter— no mercy for any captured troops. This included both the mercs—and the enemy mages.

This decision did not affect the monsters either way. The darkspawn could not be reasoned with, and would do what they would, no matter what. They were already routinely put down.

But the mercenaries and especially the mages took notice, as any of them who were captured now—including any wounded—would be executed. No further prisoners would be taken.

All new enemy prisoners were summarily killed or hanged from trees, and poles, and buildings, and out of windows.

The defenders hanged the invaders like war criminals by the hundreds, for all to see. To rot in the heat and to be pecked at by crows and seagulls.

After the second day of such retaliation, the mercenary leadership itself—not the enemy mages—called a brief, rare parlay, and ended the practice of using human shields.

The Michiana defenders agreed to take prisoners once more.

And the battle promptly resumed.

The enemy tried everything they could think of to reverse their slow, steady retreat through South Bend.

They set parts of the town on fire to delay the advance.

They used arrows and siege engines. The enemy tried massed firebomb attacks. They used magic.

But the defenders had mostly seen all of their tricks and ploys by that time, and could quickly shift to counter each one whenever and wherever they erupted. Spotters and observers had become experts at reading the signs and predicting what the foe was going to try next.

The militia knew their enemies, and fully understood exactly how to match and fight them.

Without superior numbers to press their advantage any longer, the enemy had lost any hope at surprise in any form to out-maneuver the Urth defenders, or to otherwise reestablish and regain their own forward momentum.

The enemy even tried to withdraw and go back to fighting only at night.

But the defenders would now have none of that.

They advanced and continued to press the attack, keeping it up 24/7.

This issue had to be decided.

This war had to end.

More budding mages and sorcerers were being discovered among the Urth population. The Merge had awoken magical abilities in some.

Of the ten secondary mages in the militia, the surviving six began teaching the newbs what they knew in small groups.

By then, the six were up to eight or nine blasts of sorcery per battle shift. They continually strove to achieve more. But they did not want any of the newbs to burn themselves out, or be inadvertently destroyed by their awakening powers.

As the foe continued to withdraw, people began to see just how devastated large portions of South Bend now were—both from the fighting and at the hands of the occupiers.

The full extent of that devastation would not be tabulated until the war was finally over.

An end to the war became a hopeful thing in itself.

Now the defenders of Michiana had hope that the war could and would end, and most likely in their favor.

It was possible for people to consider what they could and would do after the war's end.

And that made some troops eager, and some few careless.

Mason knew very well that carelessness was never a good thing on the battlefield.

The experienced enemy pounced on any opportunity to make the defenders pay a high price for not keeping their minds fully fixed and focused on the task at hand.

Militia commanders reminded their forces that the enemy was not yet driven out, nor had they been defeated.

Mason began to see himself and his unit as more or less a machine with a task at hand to perform and complete.

Later that day, while the campaign continued, the sky clouded up very quickly. Yet the approaching storm looked unusual somehow. The storm clouds were black and gray, but with a sickly green light to them. Very strange.

Blondie started watching those clouds form up as well.

He rubbed and stroked his throat as if it suddenly went dry and tight.

Mason took careful aim at a big, three-story house full of merc spotters and archers.

More archers and two enemy mages were using that large, sprawling house for cover, and launching deadly attacks from it.

Not for much longer.

Six rapid-fire, devastator rounds should pretty much demolish the house.

Another four to six more rounds should take out or scatter the knot of enemy troops and the mages around it.

Fire for effect.

The storm clouds cut loose right as he fired.

A visible sheet of foul-smelling rain walked in over the militia.

Black and green lightning struck among the defender ranks.

"Get inside!" Blondie screamed, already choking.

When the rain hit Mason, it seemed to burn and sting, as if it were acidic. His weatherproof duster protected him somewhat, but the very smell of the rain was rank and terrible. It made him want to vomit.

"Poison rain. Poison rain!" Blondie kept shouting, and coughing.

A sickly, greenish mist began to rise up from the ground where the rain struck and hissed.

The fighting ended and the militia struggled to take cover under the nearest shelter they could find. Trees were not a good choice. Prolonged exposure to the poison rain burned the leaves off the trees, withered, and killed them. The grass scorched and turned first to gray-green dust, and then to acidic mud that burned flesh where it touched.

It ate through shoes and corroded and pitted metal weapons.

If there was no shelter at hand, the troops retreated, trying to get out of the burning squall.

Strangely enough, the destructive show seemed to hover exactly over the front lines.

Inside the nearest house, Blondie, Mason, and others threw up, and struggled to get the rain off of them, wiping it off on curtains, towels, blankets—anything that came to hand.

Blondie guzzled some fresh water from his canteen, and coughed and choked. "That poison rain was no accident. It is a powerful magic that was prepared for days and directed against us."

"You don't say," Mason said, still trying not to gag. "How long can they keep it on us?"

"Not long, I think. But they must have had a reason for doing so. It takes many mages working together in concert for three or four days to unleash such an attack. Or one very powerful archmage. But the effects will pass in about half an hour. A normal rain will wash it away, and we can continue our attacks."

"I wonder what they are doing while we hold back."

"We'll find out shortly," Blondie said.

A regular rainstorm did come in on the heels of the poison rain. In less than another hour, the rain swept away the effects of the magic.

When they emerged from their shelter, the enemy lines were nowhere in sight.

Major Avery reported to them twenty minutes later. "Mace, we're advancing to the old seventh defensive line. Our visiting friends have regrouped and prepared their new defensive positions there, complete with trenches and all of their remaining siege engines. They have some new kind of magical traps set up that go off when our people get too close to them–fire, explosion, ice, lightning. We'll need you to clear the way for us."

"What does all of this mean?" Mason said aloud.

Blondie grinned. "It means the enemy is scared, Mace. They know we're going to beat them now. They want to slow us down so that they can try to get away. These are acts of desperation."

Thulkara grunted. "I agree. They'll keep fighting us until they're ready. Then they'll pull some other kind of trick, and the bulk of them will make a run for it."

She spat on the ground. "Cowards."

59

Dark vapor and ichor boiled and curled around the mirror. The demon's master hesitated, on the brink of destroying the thing.

The brief pause of silence filled the dark room. The demon clung to any thread of hope that might save its foul skin.

It pressed its last bargaining point. "I know where she is, Master. The traitorous bitch is helping them! I alone can capture her for you."

"What? Lie to me again and your torments shall indeed be long before you perish!"

"No lies, Master. Hear your faithful servant out. I can deliver her to you. She beds with a militia commander. If we plan it right, we can take her easily."

"You may just need to kill her outright," the man said.

Jerriel? That had to be who they were talking about.

"Would you not rather bring her back bloody and in chains, as a prize to our masters?" the demon said. "Think of the fame and the rewards you would win. The daughter of their hated enemies, a blood offering to the Dark Ghods. She is in our grasp, even now!"

"Do not attempt to deceive me, you gutless wretch."

"Aaiee! Stay your mighty hand, Master. Venting your rage on your poor servant will only cost you this golden opportunity."

The wizard paused once more. "You survive, filth. For now. Only until you succeed or fail in securing the girl. That shall decide your fate. Make it so, or your punishments shall be even worse before I crush you. I expect constant reports. None of your deceptions from this point on."

"Of course not, Master. I wouldn't dream of it. I shall not fail you."

The face went out and the mirrors went dark.

The demon reeled and shook with fear and rage all its own.

One by one it began to reconnect with the mirrors.

Then David realized: the creature fed off of its victims and the chaos it helped cause.

This foul thing was nothing but a sickening, disgusting parasite. It had to be stopped.

Movement behind him. The others finally made their way down the basement steps at last. Good. He would need their help once the thing became aware of them.

They had to do something. The demon grew stronger all the while.

David lifted his sword and sprang at the thing where its vile head bulged up in front of one of the mirrors once more.

His sword stroke cleaved right through the noxious goo that made up the demon's physical form. The bulbous head splattered, reabsorbed by the rest of the body. David found himself stuck up to his ankles in the puddle of the thing as it convulsed and shuddered.

The head swelled up again and took shape with a face trying hard to be like David's.

It had a hissing quality to its voice when it spoke, like snakes and hot steam. "Well, well, what do we have here? A pack of fools sent to 'take care' of me?' Begone! Before I destroy you. None of you have the power to harm me." It laughed insanely just before David destroyed its head once more.

It popped up again on his left.

"You can do that as much as you like, meatbag. You won't defeat me that way. I'm going to slowly suck the flesh off your bones while your friends watch."

Jason Inada rang the bell he carried, once. The clear tone made the demon tremble and cry out for an instant. It turned toward the Buddhist, trying to assume the man's face.

But it couldn't.

"Idiot. You'll have to do better than just an annoying bell!"

Jason reached into a pocket and pulled out some type of beans and cast them to the four directions.

"Enter good fortune! Demons depart!"

The demon drew back slightly and rolled its eyes. "Amateurs. What a waste of my precious time."

Jerriel nailed it with a lightning bolt.

David felt an agonizing jolt of power go through him, although much less than what the demon endured.

"Do not listen to a word that deceiver says," Jerriel told them. "It only lies or speaks in half-truths at best."

"Traitor witch!" the demon shrieked. "When the Masters finish with you, my brethren and I will torment your soul for centuries before we devour it. Just as we have the souls of your sweet, murdered parents. Their screams still echo in the lowest hells where we ravage them!"

"You lie," Jerriel said. Blasts of magic punched gaping holes through its flesh. "Keep at it–it will say anything to distract you!"

The demon surged in several directions, absorbing the damage. It turned again at Jason Inada, the next closest, who fingered some prayer beads and recited a chant of some kind.

"Stupid priest. What's that nonsense you're babbling?"

Jason smiled. "The Heart Sutra. Enjoy its wisdom." He went on chanting.

"Hah! All it's doing is pissing me off! Is that the best you fools have got? Poetry?"

"Keep it up," David said. Jason nodded.

Rabbi Bergman stepped forward. "I know not what you are creature, or from whence you came. I only put my faith in the power of prayer and the might of Yahweh."

The thing drew back again and moaned. "A thousand curses upon you and yours, old man. This is a test of will. Your weak heart will give out before I do!"

Bergman began to quote from the Psalms.

The demon cursed and swept a heavy tentacle at the rabbi, the appendage covered in broken glass.

Rabbi Bergman squinted his eyes shut.

And vanished.

He reappeared, wide-eyed, gasping, in the opposite corner.

Father Michael Petrowski and Pastor Bryan Doran closed in on the demon from the other flank. Doran held his sword before him as if were a cross. Father Michael swung a smoking censer back and forth.

Pastor Doran shouted out. "I cast you out, unclean spirit, along with every Satanic power of the enemy, every specter from Hell, and all your fell companions; in the name of our Lord Jesus Christ."

The demon wailed again. And drew itself up to a menacing height where its presence cracked the already broken ceiling even more, and towered over them all. A tendril or some part of it stayed connected to each of the mirrors in some way.

First it yawned as if bored. Then it laughed again. "I have heard rumors of this dead dreamer nailed to stick, whose name you sling at me like dung. His feeble power will not avail you!"

"Don't listen to him." Jerriel said again. "It is all woorking. Keep it up. All of yoo. He's weakening."

Father Michael strode forward, emboldened. "Depart, then, transgressor. Depart, seducer, full of lies and cunning, foe of virtue, persecutor of the innocent. Give place, abominable creature, give way, you monster, give way to Christ, in whom you found none of your work. For He has already stripped you of your powers and laid waste to your kingdom!"

The demon gave up a terrible cry. David and Jerriel covered their ears and brought them away bloody. Blood seeped from their noses. Then their eyes.

They struggled to wipe it away.

"Do your worst. I'm not going anywhere!" the demon raged.

Black tentacles swarmed and rushed forward like a tide of snakes and enveloped Pastor Doran.

The big man struggled to lift his sword to hack at them, but they ensnared him too quickly. Yet the silver crucifix in Bryan's other hand burst into white flame and dissolved the demon wherever it touched, causing the monster to shriek again.

It knocked the cross from the pastor's hand and flung it across the room.

But instead, the cross bounced back and fell right into the demon's body.

The blinding blast that followed flattened them all.

60

Now that the tide had finished turning, Mason and the defenders kept on the offensive.

Backed by reinforcements of troops from both Mishawaka and Elkhart, the Urth people of Michiana fought together as one to take back the rest of South Bend.

And the Pistolero and the Shooting Stars were right there with them at every step of the way.

For six solid days of fighting, the defenders kept up the pressure and pushed the mercenaries back, fighting around the clock—both day and night. The mercs fought a disciplined, textbook fighting retreat—nearly in imitation of the much longer, drawn-out efforts of the original South Bend forces. They continued to use the monsters as shock troops and distractions at night.

All obvious tactics of delay.

The mercs proved once again that they were skilled, professional soldiers, holding positions for as long as they could. They forced their foes to pay a price in lives and supplies for taking back every foot of territory the mercs gave up.

They used nearly the same defensive points and lines as the militia, but, of course, in reverse.

On the night of the seventh day, the enemy suddenly unleashed a massive counterassault without warning, made up entirely of monster hordes, surrounding and attacking the defenders almost from all sides.

But the Urth forces had earned their stripes after months of difficult fighting that tested and honed their instincts and abilities. Despite all of their many losses, the Michiana forces were now competent and determined soldiers in their own right, who did not easily stumble or yield in the face of any hostile force, great or small.

They knew how to match and outfight the monsters, and knew all of their cunning little tricks and ploys.

Two hours before dawn, they put the rest of the monster hordes to flight. Then, as best they could, they pursued and continued to cut down the monsters at will, in a complete and total rout.

Not many of those brutes escaped before dawn came up.

The remaining mercenary forces, still believed to be quite formidable, numerous, and dangerous, had not only voided the field of battle, but apparently had also marched quickly out of the region entirely.

All signs pointed to them passing either south or west, in full flight.

The Michiana defenders had given them a bellyful, and it was most definitely not to the enemy's liking. The foe had suffered grievous losses.

For all intents and purposes, the war was over.

Not that there would not be others, but the people of South Bend and Michiana had won this conflict. They had proven their right to survive and exist, against terrible foes and odds, and at great costs.

Much of the southern and especially the western sections of town were completely devastated, systematically burned, torn down, and reduced to utter ruin. Few buildings remained, and any of those that did—in the monster areas—had been so defiled by the darkspawn that they, too, would need to be demolished.

Yet despite the heavy losses, life and a chance at survival was always preferable to the brutal finality of death and defeat. With August only weeks away, after the heat of summer, the weather would grow cooler all too soon. Then fall and winter would quickly follow.

It would be the first winter since the Merge, and everyone would need to band together to make sure that as many as possible could survive.

The victorious armies of Michiana could now explore and map the wilds properly, and seek out and pull in any other Urth human survivors that they could find. Any kind of crop or patch of crops had to be located and protected for the coming harvest. Any kind of livestock or game had to be managed and controlled. If there were further tribes of monsters, or other dangerous creatures or enemies nearby, that had to be known, as well.

Perhaps they could even push east and north to reach the Tharanorian colonies at Kellendra and Tornhold before the winter. Such journeys through the treacherous wilds would be major adventures, and perhaps battles within themselves. But all of it must be attempted.

There still might be many pockets of Urth humans hiding out and banded together in remote places for survival.

There was no talk of going to Vaejan, since the mercenaries and the dark mages who hired them were thought to be from there. That was their apparent stronghold.

And eventually, an attempt would need to be made to see if any Urth people had survived around former Indianapolis. There was no Tharanorian colony there, so the Urth people would have been on their own all this time. But they would have numbers, at least, to hurl against the threats of the monsters and the Wildlands.

If Michiana could survive, perhaps other pockets of Urth humans could as well.

The first tales and sightings of dragons came from travelers and refugees who somehow managed to survive, and come up from the southeast.

Many refugees wished to return to South Bend and rebuild. The militia wanted to hold back the tide for a few days and make certain that everything was safe enough for civilians to return.

And the authorities wanted to keep the roads clear for the forces from Mishawaka and Elkhart who would also be marching home.

There remained the final matters of liberating the enemy slave camps.

The South Bend militia promised to assist.

And Mason needed no other reason to return to Elkhart, now that there was going to be peace for a time.

He could finally try to locate any sign of Tori, and either find her or discover what had happened to her, once and for all. He needed to know.

Now that the main fighting was finally over, at least for the near future, Mason took an entire day and slept. For another day after that, as they traveled, he kept to himself, and bathed, and ate, and slept as much as he wanted.

He located Donna and had sponge baths each and every day. What a blessing that was.

He took off all of his guns and armor and didn't go near any of them the entire time, feeling a tremendous weight and responsibility lifted from him.

Blondie and a very hot girl named Jennifer spent two days destroying a hotel room together and had to be chased out when the owners returned by surprise to evict them and other squatters.

After making good their escape through a sudden cloud of sorcerous smoke—and without their booze stash or much of their clothing, for that matter, both of them promptly threw up.

Then they took a naked, dancing shower in a pouring rain together. After that, they proceeded to sleep most of the next thirty hours in Blondie's old tent. Their militia guards assigned to them continued to keep watch over the couple from a safe distance.

Thulkara seemed to have her own personal eating contest and feast at all of the nearby militia mess tents, until no scrap of chow remained at many. Then she also proceeded to sleep for nearly two straight days, and then took up her training duties and painting lessons once more.

Mason sat up with Blondie one night, looking at the stars in the warm night air. It was still hard to get used to not having a moon up in the sky.

"Blondie," Mason said, "answer me this. Why do the Dark Mages of Vaejan and Sylurria want this part of Michiana so badly? What could it possibly mean to them, that they would go to all of this trouble?"

His friend shrugged. "That, my friend, is an excellent question. But none of the captive mages will talk to us now. Not even to me."

"It must be something important."

"It must surely be, Mace."

"I mean, it's got to be something really big, right? They went to all of this hassle to control those monsters, hire those mercenaries, and attack us full on like they did and try to wipe us all out. They wanted to make the rest of us their slaves. But that can't just be it. They fought an entire war against the Urth people in this area, and for what?"

"Mace, I'm agreeing with you. They must be after something. We just don't know what it is yet."

Mason hissed. "Well, whatever the hell it is, it must be something awfully important. And we need to figure that out."

"Yep," Blondie said.

61

The destruction threatened to topple the house down around David and his friends.

But the demon held its ground, clinging to the fixed circle of mirrors.

Pastor Doran rose up mechanically, and lurched forward, swinging his big sword wildly. Black tentacles enveloped his entire head and face, joining him to the demon.

Jason Inada barely blocked one blow from Bryan with his katana, he ducked another, and pulled Father Michael back.

"Look out!" Jerriel said. "The demon controls him now. Sever the connections between them to set him free!"

David engaged the possessed man, deflecting his sword strokes. He charged forward and knocked the pastor off his feet.

They crashed into the mirrors, destroying two of them.

The demon wailed and shuddered in a convulsion of agony. It flew into a furious rage. "No, no. I'll rip you apart for that!"

Father Michael sprang forward and dumped a large-mouthed container of holy water all over Pastor Doran's head and shoulders. The demon's connection boiled and bubbled away. Doran spluttered and cried out for help.

David and Jason hacked at the remaining tentacles.

"CURSE YOU MEAT SACKS! PERISH IN HELLFIRE, MORTAL WORMS!"

The entire room burst into flame, roaring up all the walls.

"We have to get out of here!" David yelled. He grabbed Jerriel's arm.

"No, wait," she said. "No smooke, no fumes? It's an illusion of fear to make us flee, just as we're winning. Keep attacking!"

Jerriel blasted the demon with magic ice shards.

Pastor Doran came back to himself. "Thank you!" he shouted. "Come, brothers. By heaven. Let's finish this accursed thing!"

Together the three of them charged into battle, Jerriel right behind them. The illusion of flames vanished, but the demon went mad.

One by one, it clobbered them, taking damage, but flinging them away until all four of them lay stunned and in agony.

"FOOLS! NOW I WILL CRUSH YOU ALL. I WIELD THE MIGHT OF FALLEN STARS! YOUR POWER IS AS NOTHING TO MINE! YOU CANNOT STAND BEFORE ME AND LIVE!"

Father Michael stepped in front of them, just as the monster fell upon them. The priest stood fast, Pastor Doran's flaming crucifix in his hand as he advanced.

"Yield, demon. Not to my own person, but to the ministry of Christ! For it is the power of Christ that compels you, who brought you low by His cross. Tremble before that mighty arm that broke asunder the dark prison walls and led souls forth to the light!"

The demon drew back, trapped and uncertain before the blinding light the priest wielded.

"You are *not* the one you invoke!" the demon argued. "You are not He! You are a weak, mortal insect of mere flesh. You are nothing!"

Father Michael pressed forward without relent. "Do not think of deflecting my commands with false words, foul spirit, just because you know me to be a great sinner. It is God Himself who commands you; the majestic Christ who commands you. God the Father commands you. God the Son commands you. God the Holy Spirit commands you. The mystery of the cross commands you! Depart, for you are defeated. Your power is no more. Without the Love of the Creator, it is you and your kind who are void and nothing!"

The demon opened its mouth to roar again.

Father Michael plunged the shining cross directly into its dark maw. Both of them cried out in agony.

Another detonation. The demon's head burst. A pillar of fire shot up through its body, enveloping both it and the priest.

Weird glowing circles of power and lines and symbols of force flickered throughout the room and across all the remaining mirrors. Some of them cracked and splintered.

The remains of the demon shuddered in agony and terror.

Jerriel rose up and pointed. She staggered forward with her staff. "Destroy the mirrors. They are sources of its power–every one of them. Do not let him feed off of them!"

She shattered one with her staff.

Father Michael toppled to one side. Roiling, black ichor rippled off him like gouts of streaming smoke. Rabbi Bergman flashed over to him, caught him, and doused him with holy water.

David broke another mirror with his sword.

The remnants of the demon had great difficulty reforming.

"Jerriel's right. It feeds off its victims through the mirrors. Break them all!"

Jason and Pastor Doran lurched forward, swinging at the remaining mirrors with their swords.

Glass shattered everywhere. The demon shrank and weakened.

Gibbering mouths appeared on the demon's convulsing, shrinking form, crying out in fear with many fell voices.

Jerriel gasped and leaned on her staff, exhausted. "We've beaten it down. Now...we must...finish destroying its material foorm. That will banish it from this world...sending its foul spirit back through the Void and into the Abyss once moore."

"How? How do we do that?" Jason demanded.

"Holy water." Jerriel said. "Make a circle, a circle of power around it with holy water soo that it cannot escape."

"Do it!" Pastor Doran said, dragging back the stunned, scorched form of Father Michael.

Rabbi Bergman and Jason Inada poured a circle of holy water around the demon's convulsing remains.

Jerriel doused David's blade with more holy water.

"Pin down the core of the demon! Fix it to one spot while we dissolve it all. You must be strong, Daeved. Stand fast. Do not move, whatever tricks and illusions it tries on you. It will be desperate. If one part of the core man-hages to escape, we will have to track it down and fight it all over again."

To hell with that. Literally. They weren't going through all of this crap again.

David did not hesitate. He charged forward and impaled the demon to the spot with his sword. The runes upon his blade glowed white-hot. Foul, dark vapors, smoke, and fumes enveloped him, clouding and confusing his perceptions.

Immediately, his senses went fuzzy once again. He reeled drunkenly and fell to his knees. But he clung to his sword and kept the demon nailed to that one spot so that it could not escape.

His friends shouted to one another. Jerriel told them what they must do.

The demon wailed, and drowned out everything else.

David gasped and struggled to remain conscious. He wanted to sleep so badly, but he couldn't. If he was weak, they were all lost.

Then he heard the sounds. His friends crying out in terror as the demon stalked and killed them, and mocked him all the while.

Finally Jerriel screamed, shrieking for him to come save her, as the demon tore her apart. He wept, but he clung to his sword.

It couldn't be real.

"You could have saved her," the demon mocked. "You let them all die. Now I'm coming for you. Flee before me!"

"I...will...not!" he shouted. "Liar. Deceiver!"

Through a vision, as if through a shining mirror, he saw himself, walking down from his old apartment, going out to his faithful old car, and driving to class. All as if the Merge and everything that followed had never happened.

In a way—that was everything he wanted. To simply go back to the way things had been before the Merge.

Or was it? Did he really want that now?

"There...see...human—that is an alternate dimension, a reality apart from this one. Everything there is back to the way it was, because nothing there has changed. Nothing has gone wrong in that version of your world. There was no Merge. You can have your little life back...go back to being a simple nobody...anonymous...nothing.

"Live your empty little life, human. Live to the end of your days without all of this strife and chaos. But hurry. Just let go of the sword. Rise up and enter that reality while you still may. I offer it to you freely. All of this trouble will be gone. It will vanish like a bad dream. Isn't that what you most want?"

Jerriel. He thought of Jerriel and all of his friends and his love for them and their world.

Their world. Whatever world that was now, no matter what it had become. It was precious to him now for the simple fact that they were all in it together.

And not only that.

In the past, there would be no Jerriel.

Nothing mattered, in any case. The demon was an abject liar. It offered what it could never give. It would say anything, try any trick or deception in order to escape.

He laughed. David looked up and laughed into the demon's cowardly face.

"No. Not at all," he said. "You're a total moron, you filthy, wretched, gutless thing. I see you for what you truly are now. You're nothing. How could you possibly know what I desire? What I really want—more than anything else right now—*is to destroy you!*"

With one weak hand, he reached into a pouch on his belt and sprayed himself in the face, eyes, nose, and ears with holy water.

The dark mists and illusions parted around him.

He spoke the words of command Jerriel taught him, and the runes on his longsword flashed rapid-fire in bursts of magical force.

"Kal!" Fire engulfed the demon.

"Zae!" Holy water blasted it.

"Doru!" Earth and rock smashed it down.

"Vae!" A fierce vortex of wind wore it away.

"Shi!" Blasts of spirit energy annihilated the fragments.

With a fading cry, the demon shriveled up beneath his sword.

All illusion vanished.

His friends stood beside him, battered but hale and triumphant. They doused the fragments of the fiend with more holy water. Chanting and praying, even Father Michael stood on his feet once again, lending his aid.

He placed the shining crucifix on the dark, squirming remnant of the demon squirming beneath David's sword—still pinned to the ground.

White flame spurted, incinerating the last pieces of the demon's core to ash.

The ash scattered, dissolving into nothing on a spurt of putrid air.

Jerriel put her arms around him. "You can let go," she told him. "It's all right, Daeved. We've beaten and destroyed it. We've won."

David fell back into her arms, exhausted. "Thank goodness," was all he could mutter.

Pastor Doran thumbed his sword and nodded around them. "There are still a few mirrors left intact," he said. "Should we break them, too?"

Jerriel shook her head. "No, not now. The demon's powers are broken forever. But have the troops bring the mirrors with us. We might be able to use them to see what the demon saw through them and who he was feeding off of and working with."

After he regained his strength, David would tell her about all that he had seen.

They gathered the few remaining mirrors, just as the ruined house started to collapse in on them.

"Gather around Rabbi Bergman," Jerriel commanded. "Embrace him. Yosef—get us out of here."

"I-I...I don't know if I can!"

"You can and you will. Focus on taking us somewhere else. Make it close by. Do it! Anywhere but here."

"I'll try—"

They encircled him with their arms. The house collapsed inwards upon itself, and on them.

"Do it now, Rabbi. Or we all die!"

A flash of light. A wave of cold energy swept through them all.

They fell out of the air outside the crumbling wreck.

They appeared several feet above the ground.

All of them crashed on top of each other—painfully.

Rabbi Bergman lay stunned when they all rolled free.

"He saved us," David said. "Is he going to be all right?"

Jerriel felt his forehead. "He's just exhausted. He's gooing to be fine."

"He's...old."

Jerriel smiled. "He has the heart of a lion. He's a traveler, Daeved. A natural adept at it. Once he trains himself, he will knoow few limits."

David looked around as the troops rushed in to help them. The ruined block looked less bleak now. The sky cleared. Stars winked overhead, and the moon rose.

The demon's power was finally broken—another grim threat to Michiana had been vanquished.

So weary, David sighed to himself. Everyone was, after all of that.

All he wanted to do was get home, drive the darkness from his mind, and sleep peacefully.

62

With the help of forces from Elkhart and Mishawaka, Mason and his comrades, and the Shooting Stars, undertook one final task.

Together with the forces of Michiana, they hit and raided all eight of the mercenary slave camps all at once, on the same night.

They very nearly struck at all of the camps at the same exact time.

They attacked and defeated the mercenary guards, or accepted their ready surrender. They captured hoarded supplies and contraband, and, most importantly, freed tens of thousands of people at each location.

The Pistolero helped the militias surround Slave Camp Number 4 and led the charge against its gates, cutting down the guard towers on either side of the main gate.

Blondie the sorcerer blasted those gates right off their supports and blew it to shattered bits with exploding force from his bright, glowing hands.

Some pockets of mercs formed up and tried to break out in an attempt to get away.

Thulkara leaped forward, bellowing her war cries, and swinging her deadly weapons. She led the charge that drove the mercs back, and cut many of them down. In open battle, she remained a premier force to be reckoned with—nearly unstoppable.

In less than and hour all resistance had been beaten down, and the camp and its former slaves were finally liberated and safely in defender hands.

For a few brief minutes, everyone celebrated the victory, and the return of liberty to so many. They would learn later that all eight of the slave camps were liberated in that same hour, and the siege and containment of the City of Elkhart was also brought to an end.

But confusion and chaos instantly ensued thereafter, as it often did with fallible humanity. Problems quickly mounted.

First, the comfort women had to be freed, separated, and protected under heavy guard. Despite all that they had endured at the hands of the enemy, there were many angry slaves who insisted vehemently that those poor women and girls should be beaten, stoned to death, or hanged as traitors.

The militia declared that they and all of the slaves had already suffered more than enough during their captivity.

After that debacle, many captives insisted on leaving the camps in droves on their own, regardless of their condition. They clogged the roads with new waves of sick, weakened refugees.

Some people who might have survived went forward heedless, and later collapsed and even died at countless places along the roads where no help could reach them.

This scattering madness hampered travel on the roads in the region, even for the military, who were still trying to pursue and stamp out any lingering pockets of the enemy. Small bands of bandits and monsters remained stubborn raiders, always hunting for anyone weaker than themselves to attack. The isolated roads at night remained unsafe for small groups or individuals.

A monumental effort was made to try to get all of the remaining, former slaves to remain in the camps for a short while longer. There they could be fed properly, healed, and strengthened. People could be identified and reunited with lost family or friends. And finally, they could be systematically relocated to a choice of places where they could find reliable housing, relative safety, and local support.

Many of the places they insisted on returning to, especially in South Bend, were no longer there.

There was also an exploding demand for much work to be done in general, in order to help the isolated population of Michiana find a way to survive what everyone expected to be a very harsh winter.

This was going to be a winter without the protection of electricity or modern heating. Not to mention the dwindling food supply.

Summer passed with each day. Every field available that could be planted with short growth crops of any kind needed to be put in. There was much to do, and it all became overwhelming.

With the war over, Blondie still felt torn and confused. He knew his name, of course, for all the good that did him. But he still knew very little about his family, his past, and who he had really been before the Merge. Much of that still eluded him.

The few memories that did return to him were disturbing and, from what he said, not at all helpful.

In many ways, he remained a lost and broken young man, without purpose.

Yet all the slim evidence they possessed pointed to the fact that he had most likely worked very closely with the enemy, as one of their elite mages and spies. Perhaps he even played some kind of role in causing the actual Merge itself, or–at the very least–he had worked closely with those who did.

For the time being, at least, he still felt very loyal and obligated to his new friends and allies. He was in what he himself called an intensely satisfying, very physical relationship with his smitten but often bitchy girlfriend, Jennifer Gilbert.

But both he and Mason often spoke together about what might happen to him and his current allegiances, once he recalled more of who and what he was–or had been.

What would he do if he didn't like who and what he had been before? Could he truly change? Could he remain who he was becoming now, as he went forward?

What would happen if he actually chose to go back to being who and what he had been in the past? What then?

Would he rejoin the enemy? Would he turn on and betray the people he professed to care about now?

Could he turn against them? Fight them–even injure or kill them, if need be? Could they do the same to him, after they had all lived, and fought side by side with each other as friends and faithful comrades?

All of these issues and potential issues caused Mason and Blondie no small degree of worry and distress. It weighed heavily on both of them, and served as the grist for many discussions that went long into the night, with or without strong drink.

Blondie labored, impaled on the horns of his personal dilemma.

Just who was he, and what was real anymore? What did he want to be now, and would that change drastically once he fully recalled his past and his old allegiances and patterns of behavior?

His memory was going to return at some point. Each day that passed after the war, he recalled a little something more. And the cascade of thoughts, memories, emotions, and images only continued to trouble him.

Some he shared openly with his new friends.

Some he most likely kept to himself. Mason felt sure of that.

But Mason had his own ghosts and demons to track down and finally put to rest. He couldn't spend all of his time on Blondie's problems.

Now that things were more stable, Mason spent the better part of five days in Elkhart, searching locations, talking to people who might know or recall something, and tracking down official accounts and reports.

The gray sky above him threatened heavy rain on that third day.

He went to yet another city records depository and sifted through a bewildering number of hastily scribbled record sheets and accounts of casualties and dead bodies that were found and taken care of at that time.

When his eyes bugged out from the strain, he even took a break and visited the house of Tori and her family.

It had been cleaned up and repaired. A new family with younger children were living there now. When Mason explained the reason for his search to them, they allowed him inside.

None of the Nelsons had returned home to the house thus far.

The adults quietly told him about the various old bloodstains they had cleaned up or painted over, prior to them moving in. They said that the house had been ransacked a couple of times before they took it over.

Mason found the spot, less than two blocks away, where a body matching the description of either Tori or her younger sister Tanya had been found by the burial details.

Then, at long last, with the help of some elderly clerks back at the next closest depository, he located the actual document made by the burial detail recorder in that exact area in question.

Mason sat down in the dusty clerk's office, keeping the paper turned facedown, staring at the back of it with its stains and wrinkles.

This was it.

This lousy piece of paper that no one else even cared about—that had been misfiled in some box of documents—was going to tell him whether the woman he loved was alive or dead. Period. Forever.

Mason sat there for a long time, staring at the back of that piece of paper. Afraid to know. Afraid to not know.

One of the elderly clerks, doddering like any blue-haired great grandmother, knew what he was searching for, and brought him a steaming cup of herbal tea and patted him on the arm without saying a word. He thought he smelled rose hips and orange peel.

Mason hated herbal tea, but it was the only comfort he had.

He took the time to hold that warm tea cup in his hands and drink it all down over the course of a few minutes.

He set the cup down, well out of the way, and took in a deep breath. He struggled to stop his hands from shaking.

Mason exhaled, and flipped the paper over. He read.

The document described the corpse of a young woman, aged approximately sixteen to twenty, with a major head wound. She had either fallen on her head or suffered a heavy, fatal blow. Part of her skull was obviously crushed. That was the apparent cause of death, and noted as such.

Mason closed his eyes for a minute.

Regardless of whether it had been Tori or her sister Tanya, at least the young woman had probably died quickly from a major injury such as that. He hoped she didn't suffer in pain for a long time, without anyone to help her or comfort her in her last moments.

He thought he might be sick, but he had to keep going.

From the signs, the body had apparently been dragged from one of the houses nearby. Then, horribly, the report described the well-known signs that the monsters raiding that part of town had partially devoured the corpse.

Mason prayed that she was already dead by then. He had read the same description on countless casualty and burial reports, and seen them firsthand for himself.

The monsters ate or hacked the meat off the body, and left the rest of the mutilated corpse behind. That was simply what they did. They gulped the meat down right then and there like ravenous wolves at a kill, or they stuffed it into a sack to save for later. If it spoiled and turned rank, it made no difference to them. The monsters even seemed to prefer decaying carrion.

When searched, many of the monsters were found carrying such grisly meat sacks.

Then Mason read the rest of the description, and it hit him between the eyes like a hammer.

The female victim had red hair, freckles—and brown eyes.

Brown eyes. Brown eyes.

Tanya had green eyes.

Tori had brown eyes. The most beautiful brown eyes that he had ever...

It was her. It was Tori. The dead girl had been Tori.

Tori was dead.

Mason's mind raced out of control, and he seemed to have dropped down into a dark abyss.

The girl he loved was rotting in a nameless grave somewhere and he would never see her again. Never kiss her. Never touch her, hold her in his arms and hear her laugh, feel her breathe. Never have everything he wanted to have with her.

She was gone.

He had always feared and known that this could be the answer. But he lied to himself for as long as there was hope.

But nothing could actually prepare a person for such a thing itself.

He went into a daze of shock. Mason rose up from the table and left the paper there. He had read most of it. No reason to read anymore.

Brown eyes.

He didn't say a word to the old ladies. He didn't even look at them.

Mason walked out, and kept walking.

As if on cue, the Michiana sky opened up and pelted him with stinging cold rain. His eyes rained down on himself as he kept walking.

Screw it all. Screw everything.

63

David and Jerriel slept in the next day, recovering from their ordeal in every way that they could.

In the early afternoon, they biked over to the library under a threatening, dark sky and made their report to the town council recorders and Dirk on defeating the demon. They gave special thanks to Father Michael, Pastor Bryan, Rabbi Bergman, and Jason Inada—the local holy men who greatly assisted them in completing that vile and difficult task.

A stirring, edited account of the confrontation would appear in the newspaper the next day for all the public to read. The people needed to be warned about the potential of such supernatural threats. But the council didn't want to completely panic the general public, either. Or have everyone rush out and, say, break all of their mirrors in fear of demons.

Based on what they had learned, the council moved quickly and quietly to locate and help any of the demon's victims who could be identified. Anyone willing to come forward on their own would be helped as well.

A warning would also be included for everyone to beware of, and not to give in to, the pull of their darker sides. Especially since demons apparently fed off of them and only grew stronger.

Those actively working under the evil influence of the actual demon who had committed actual crimes also needed to be dealt with.

The town council immediately removed Judge Moran from the bench and advised him to take an early retirement. And re-think his own choices.

Moran quickly fled to White Town.

The Black Town militia commanders would get a warning about K-J's aspirations to become a petty warlord in his area.

David and Jerriel pooped out early that day, and went back home early to continue their recovery. Fighting powerful supernatural beings, as it turned out, was taxing and distressing work.

After another good night's rest, David and Jerriel went back to work as normal. Work that continued to mount as the summer days passed. The same ever-present threats continued hanging over them and all of Michiana.

Where had the enemy gone? What were they planning?

When and where would they strike next?

Each morning, David and Jerriel met with the town linguists, furthering their language studies.

In the afternoons after lunch, David helped train troops and select more troops for his strike force, and he also helped train the other militia forces.

On breaks, he often took a walk, or went with Dirk Blackwood to review various projects.

Like the one day they inspected the new weapon and armor smithies nearby. They had just started processing metal, leather, and cloth—and even high-strength plastic, to crank out good, assembly-line-quality armor, weapons, uniforms, and various gear.

David hefted some of the new militia spears and pikes. "Looks like good gear, Dirk."

"Our troops will need the best equipment they can get their hands on if more invaders hit us. Those foes were sent here from somewhere, and seemed to be supplied pretty well. And that means there's more of them out there where they came from. And these sinister Dark Mages of the Khabal leading them have yet to directly show themselves. But I think that they will eventually do so.

"Nor am I forgetting that our foes also sent that evil demon to command those same monster hordes to crush us and turn us all against one another. And from what you said about that head mage in that enemy camp and again in the demon's mirror, they're also after Jerriel for some reason. Has she said anything about all that?"

David shook his head. "She doesn't know much for certain. She thinks that the Dark Mages want revenge on her because her father and mother opposed them for so long. Remember, she was in the process of fleeing Vaejan/Chicago when the Merge struck. She had just discovered that the Khabal was, in fact, secretly in charge of the colony there. And that they had played roles in both of her parents' deaths. What was worse, her older brother had also sided with the enemy, it appeared, and was after her. But with the Merge, she had managed to escape all of that, at least up until this point. Now look at her. Jerriel spends all of her days testing and training our new mages."

Dirk crossed his arms, and then reached up and stroked his jaw. "We're incredibly fortunate to have her helping us. We might not have made it this far without her. Under the circumstances, I think we need to increase the number of guards we have protecting both of you, Dave."

David nodded. "I agree with that assessment. I'll pick them myself."

"Hey, I like that new unit symbol you sketched for your strike force," Dirk held up David's insignia design of a black hawk's head set within a circle. "It's going to be on all of your shields, and on your uniforms."

David smiled. "Yeah, the Blackhawks."

"I never knew you were a hockey fan, Dave. Or did you also collect old comics?"

"Comics?" He gave Dirk a blank look.

"Forget it, Dave. Way before your time."

"Dirk, hawks in general are a Native American symbol throughout the Midwest. Hawks are always good medicine. Hawks are warriors, hunters, explorers–they're adventurers. That's why I chose the Blackhawks as our elite unit symbol; there's more to it all than just a hockey team."

Dirk clapped him on the back, "You got it, Dave; whatever you want. It's the least we can do. You and your people have done everything we've asked of you...and more. Much more."

"Dirk, tell me true. Are we gaining any ground?"

His friend sighed heavily. "Well, the troubles around town have dropped off a lot with that demon out of the way. But there's still more crime than we expected. A looming food shortage and rationing is coming, no matter what we do. We'll see how well all of that goes over, especially with the self-imposed outcast groups.

"The surviving Amish and other farmers in the area are helping to organize our people into labor teams out in the fields. The seed company folks are working closely with them and our scientists to ensure that we have seeds for the future for various crops. We have greenhouses popping up all over the place. Notices are going out to help everyone plant old-style victory gardens in their backyards, if they don't already have one. We're posting public info on raising chickens, pigs, goats, sheep, cattle, horses, and any other livestock. Those numbers are exploding."

They moved on to the shops where bowyers and fletchers fashioned bows and crossbows, bolts and arrows.

"I need some more bolts for my crossbow," David said. "Can I get some today?"

"I'll sign a requisition and have four dozen sent to your house. Is that enough for now?"

"Plenty. Thanks, Dirk. Well, I'd better get back to the training grounds."

"Hold on. There's a new training area I wanted to show you. It's a surprise. It just started up today, in fact. Follow me out back this way."

They emerged from a back door.

There stood Jerriel and Danielle Callahan, one of their linguist friends assigned to her, a young grad student with short black hair and eyes and olive skin.

They both helped lead a class of over a hundred people. Everyone held a basic quarterstaff, the ends banded in metal—just like Jerriel's.

"A wizard's staff is the first focus for their powers," Jerriel said. "Some may outgrow it as a focus or move on to something else. Others will stay with it, if they choose. Some prefer wands or orbs as a focus. Some will just use their hands." She stamped her staff on the ground. "As you can see, I actually prefer the staff." She grinned at David. "It's a personal choice."

A chuckle from her students.

Correct that. Not quarterstaffs.

Wizard staffs.

Geez, check out all those recruits. Jerriel looked so ecstatic.

She winked at him while he still continued to stare. He turned to Dirk.

Dirk shrugged. "If there is magic out there, we need to be able to both use and defend against it. The new Institute of Magic is her idea."

"Any of them any good?"

He laughed. "We'll see. Half of them might wash out. Jerriel said only eight or nine of them are strong prodigies thus far, with amazing natural abilities." He nodded toward Yosef.

"Like the good rabbi there, and your enchanter friend."

Yosef Bergman. Robert Billings. David walked right up to them through the ranks and shook their hands, patting them on the back.

Rabbi Bergman smiled back, still looking a little nervous holding his freshly fashioned wizard's staff.

"Come on, Dave," Dirk said. "We don't want to interrupt her class too much."

"No, we don't." He smiled back at Jerriel. She beamed and went right on teaching.

"Picture focusing your energies into your staff and storing them there..."

David and Dirk left the mage training area and closed the door.

"That's great," David said. "If anyone can train them, Jerriel can. We do need wizards, about as bad as anything, I'd say."

"Don't forget sorcerers, conjurers, and illusionists," Dirk said.

David smiled. "We can trust Jerriel to sort it all out. She's a natural teacher and instructor. I need to be the same for my fighters."

"Have a good time training the troops," Dirk told him. "I know you enjoy working with the other fighters and warriors. What, about two hours more today on the practice fields?"

"Yeah, probably. If I get my lazy butt over there."

"Good. Jerriel's class should be done about that time. You can go home for dinner tonight, together. Did you hear there's a big dance at the Morris Theater tonight? You know how Belle likes to dance."

David smiled. "Then we should see you both there." Jerriel loved to dance as well, and David didn't know what was better: watching her move and dance, or dancing with her. Each was fantastic in its own way.

Dirk went on talking and David snapped out of his daydream.

"I have to go around and tour the fort construction around town. We're creating guard towers and hard points. We even have plans for a few strategic forts, walls, and castles. Some of our current structures lend themselves to that, with a little modification."

David said, "I'd like to see more of that."

Dirk grinned and clapped him on the shoulders. "You will. You and your troops will still have guard duty around town. Get used to it."

"Can't wait." He checked his watch. "Gotta go. The troops are waiting for me. See you, Dirk."

David was walking back to the practice fields when voices shouted out to him eagerly from somewhere nearby.

"David...David Pritchard! Thank God, we've found you at last!"

He turned and held up his hand over his eyes to shield himself from the bright glare of the sunlight.

A handful of Blackhawk guards led what appeared to be a young man and woman, all dressed in patchwork militia armor and wearing battered lacrosse helmets and masks. They carried banged-up spears in their gloved hands, and hatchets in their canteen belts.

David couldn't make out their faces.

When the man and woman got close enough, they tossed their spears down to either side and took off their helmets.

He looked at them both, and didn't recognize either of them. "Do I know either of you?" David asked.

Both of them shook their heads. "You are Captain David Pritchard of the Blackhawks, right?"

"I am. Who are you?"

"Marie Purdy," the woman said.

"And I'm John Wolper," the man added. "We were in a magic glowing lake and somehow crossed over from the other side. Then we spoke to others here, and heard about you. Then we remembered the Pistolero talking about you as his friend."

What were these people babbling about? Guns didn't work anymore. "Who in the heck is the Pistolero?" David asked them

Marie Purdy jumped in. "Captain, he's your friend, Mason Tyler, helping defend the other side. We worked with him."

Mace was alive.

And there was another side.

David grinned and offered them his hands. "Well met, Marie and John. Come with me. It sounds like we have a lot to talk about."

THE END

Please Post a Book Review Right Now

Please post a review of this book if you enjoyed it. Twenty little words are all that is required. Twenty words that say what you liked about this book while it is still fresh in your heart, mind, and soul. Please do so now before something else makes you forget.

Here is the link for Mergeworld 1, if you purchased it on Amazon:

http://amzn.to/1wjpysT

Please click on the link and post your review now.

Done? The authors would personally like to thank you very much.

In this busy world, everyone is pressed for time. Our time is so important, no doubt. It has reached the point now where authors of nearly every stripe compete not only for sales, but to garner reviews from their readers. Some authors even stoop to "purchasing" reviews in social media that some services now offer in bulk.

In the publish or perish work of competitive fiction, book reviews from readers are golden, they have now become a commodity even.

Many in the business even consider book reviews as important, or even more important than book sales in some ways. As crazy as that sounds.

So therefore, trust us in this. If you have authors whom you adore, and you want to read more of their books in the future, please post as many reviews for them as you can in all of the forms of social media that you use.

Doing so will help your favorite authors in numerous ways that you cannot even possibly imagine. Never forget that fact. Book reviews matter a great deal.

And if by chance, if you find that there is something about this book that you don't like, and you really do want to help authors, before you slam them with bad reviews, try briefly contacting them instead with your concerns through their contact info that is always readily provided, or through their publisher. Most authors, especially new ones, are usually happy to get constructive criticism that will make their books better. Only hating, online trolls slam authors with bad reviews without giving them a chance. Real pros and fen contact authors directly with any valid concerns. That is the current, accepted etiquette. Please don't be a troll.

Amazon Kindle Review Link for Mergeworld 1:

http://amzn.to/1wjpysT

Barnes & Noble Review Link for Mergeworld 1

http://bit.ly/1vZCLHt

Smashwords Review Link for Mergeworld 1

http://bit.ly/1pGWQBx

Other Review Sites

Good Reads

Share on Google+

Pinterest

Reddit

Delicious

Stumble Upon It!

Please post one or more reviews for Mason and Garan for each of their books, everywhere that you can.

Thank you once again.

Cheers,

Mason Elliott & Garan R.R. Faraday

SF Author Mason Elliott's Contact Information

Please Join Mason Elliott's New Releases Email List

Use either of these:

Mailchimp email listserve sign up Bitly link:
http://bit.ly/1L2QpUL

Direct Mailchimp link to listserve sign up:
http://eepurl.com/FgQzv

Be among the first to learn about my writing projects and new releases. I promise that I will not share your info or spam you. I will use the list only to inform you about matters directly connected to my writing projects.

About the Author

Mason Elliott grew up loving Science Fiction and Fantasy in all of their myriad forms. That love has transferred into his dedicated writing. Like most writers he lives a spartan lifestyle and yearns to devote his life even more to his writing, and someday retire on the Pacific coast. So be a fan, buy his stuff, and enjoy!

Like and follow Mason on Facebook, where he does most of his blogging at:
https://www.facebook.com/masonelliott731

And on Twitter at:
http://bit.ly/1nsqOSs

Visit Mason Elliott's website at:
www.masonelliott.authorcontacts.com

And for even more information on Mason Elliott and his works, visit High Mark Publishing online at:

www.HighMarkPublishing.com

Fantasy Author Garan R. R. Faraday's Contact Information

Please Join Garan's Publishing Update e-List

Garan's Publishing Update e-List sign-up form link:

http://eepurl.com/YHOS5

I promise you that I will only send you emails connected to my writing projects and new releases. I do not spam.

About the Author

Garan Reginald Remington Faraday was fortunate to be the child of loving parents who adored all things Fantasy, and passed that love onto their son. It has been said by some, that with such a name, he was born to become a Fantasy writer. Garan, or 'Reg' to his closest friends, has written Fantasy stories since the 7th grade, and completed his first Fantasy Novel at the age of sixteen. If you enjoy anything Fantasy, you most likely have something in common with Garan. His lifelong dream has always been to publish as many Fantasy novels and stories as he possibly can.

Garan's Facebook fanpage link:

http://on.fb.me/12WJYfL

Garan's FB friends page link

https://www.facebook.com/GaranRRFaraday

Garan's Twitter Link

https://twitter.com/GaranRRFaraday

Garan's website and blog link:

http://garanfaraday.authorcontacts.com/

And for even more information on Garan R. R. Faraday and his works, visit High Mark Publishing online at: www.HighMarkPublishing.com

Mason's Acknowledgements

This amazing collaboration to create this book has been a true labor of love. First, I must always thank the staff at High Mark Publishing Fantasy. Working with a virtual press has not only been a dream come true, but a complete joy.

Next and foremost, I must thank my fellow author, and long time writing group friend and life long pal. Reg, I know how much this book means to you, because I know how much it means to me. I could not have written it with anyone else.

We are indeed boon companions through many high adventures, including our writing geek lives, none the least. I am honored, proud, and happy to be the co-author with you on your first published Fantasy novel. I am Gimli to your Legolas, and I know how much Fantasy means to you, as much as you know SF means to me. I know full well that this will be the first of many great works of Fantasy from you, because I have been fortunate to read them in our writer's group for years in advance, and I am one of the blessed to know what is coming. And it is going to be amazing.

Reg, you are going to take the Fantasy World by storm, sword, fire and passion. And I will cheer you all the way. Mark my words, folks. You haven't seen anything from this author yet! Reg has the heart and soul of an elf, the cunning mind of a wizard, the heart of a dragonlord, and I know for a fact that he secretly wishes that he had been born a Stark, with his own dire wolf. There isn't anything about Fantasy that Reg doesn't know about or adore.

And yes, as you will all soon see, he was most definitely born to be a Fantasy writer!

And finally, let me give a cheer to my own Shooting Stars, the real-life Melinda and Hannah, and thank my Beta readers and the rest of our wonderful writer's group, as always.

Garan's Acknowledgements

First I want to say what a pleasure it has been working with High Mark Publishing. For my first publishing experience, working with a virtual press has been painless and enlightening in many ways. Jennifer and Josh, you guys are the absolute best.

I would also like to thank my writer's group and my many friends and family who make up by readers. I have so many great people who love and support me and my madness, that I simply don't deserve it all. I cannot love them enough.

And finally, I cannot thank my good buddy M nearly enough. For the past few years I have cheered and watch my long time, good friend Mason Elliott become a bestselling ebook author in SF with his amazing Naero's Run books. M, so many congrats. You did it, pal. My friend, you were the pioneer. You were the first one of us in the group to break out, and make it, and live your dream. I love your Naero books. Naero is one of the great new characters in all of SF, and you make me and everyone else who reads them want to be a Spacer in your amazing, futuristic universe.

And now, with this collaboration, you are helping me get my start, and launch me on my way to begin to live my own dream as a Fantasist. My brother; it was a great honor to write this book with you, and it was also a lot of fun, too. We are Legolas and Gimili. And when I do finally take my boat to the Undying Lands, I want you right there beside me.

But until that day, let's have all of the fun we can, writing as many great books as we can. The next cider is on me, my brother. Like you always say, Cheers! To the both of us!

Please enjoy the following teaser from the first Spacer Clans Adventure, Book 1:

NAERO'S
RUN

NAERO'S RUN

by Mason Elliott

"We've got more than enough to consider here," Aunt Sleak said. "We'll post our final decisions on the Spacer ClanNet. All crew, take a breather. We're out of jump in less that two standard hours. Everyone on duty needs to be at their ready stations. Dismissed."

Naero went back to her quarters to do some laundry and a little more reading before they emerged. With regular effort, her quarters were less of a disaster than usual. She'd kept her bunk and her floor more or less cleared off, and slept in her bunk regularly now, instead of on the floor or in zero-G or a float bag.

And definitely not in her flex chair, as she had for years because she either couldn't get her bunk panel out or it was too piled up with crap.

Being small had its advantages. She could curl up like a cat and get comfortable almost anywhere for a snooze.

But keeping her quarters in better shape was a promise she made and kept–to herself–and her parents.

They emerged from jump with the customary shuddering of the ship. The fleet spread out into is standard formation, emerging back into real Space-Time.

Naero punched up their positions on one of her screens, even though she didn't have bridge duty for several hours.

The Shinai flanked *The Dromon* on the port side, with *The Slipper* posted starboard. Their two smaller ships, *The Nevada* and *The Ardala*, brought up the rear this time.

A red hot scarlet particle beam, 60mm in diameter, lanced through Naero's walls like they were paper, disrupting her wallscreens.

A direct hit from a big gun.

At the very least, from a heavy destroyer.

Warning lights flashed immediately.

The rupture in the hull led to an immediate explosive decompression.

Naero held on tight to her bunk and went flat on the floor as the hull sealed itself.

All ships were vulnerable coming out of jump. They couldn't activate their shields until right after they emerged.

Someone had been waiting for them.

The Dromon continued getting rocked by multiple hits from what felt like several spinal guns and secondary batteries.

But the big planetoid could take it and give back plenty, her quad main guns humming and whining to life, coming online.

Naero hit her wristcom. All her screens down.

"Bridge. Status?"

"We stepped into it. They were waiting for us. We're under heavy fire. Multiple bogeys."

The general alert sounded.

"Battle Stations. Battle Stations."

Aunt Sleak cut over the com. "All hands. All hands, to your stations. Prepare for battle. All ships, all batteries, return fire. Launch all fighters."

Naero suited up and raced to the drop bay of her fighter. She met Jan along the way.

More intense fire. *Dromon* reeled and fired back.

She and Jan almost got rocked off their feet again.

A security team intercepted them at the launching bays.

Their fighters had already dropped with their backup pilots.

"The fleet captain wants you two at your secondary defense stations, not out in the mix."

Jan started to protest.

"Orders are orders. Get to your stations."

They ran to their remote gunnery stations, small secured cubicles with a chair and a console, operating triple pulse turrets on the hardpoints above them.

Naero brought up her autotargeting displays, weapons already powered up and humming.

The secondary battery gunnery stations operated independently and were well-protected. They were also fully automated, but they still functioned more effectively with a human interface.

Coordinated targeting profiles came online as she watched.

Jan operated a torp turret nearby.

Directly ahead of the fleet. Twelve elite Matayan destroyers, each with a dozen escort fighters.

Half of their number pursued and attacked a convoy of two dozen independent mining freighters.

Aunt Sleak's fleet scrambled, launched, and deployed a total of threescore fighters in a standard Alpha-Charlie-1 defensive screen.

They were outnumbered two to one.

"All batteries make ready. Incoming torps," the bridge com sounded.

Countermeasures took out half of the blips heading their way.

Spacer fighters and the forward defensive batteries blasted the rest.

"That attack's a diversion," Naero muttered.

Shinai's fire control and com computers fixed on and monitored all channels—including those between the hapless freighters and the corsairs.

"Mayday, mayday, we are under intense corsair attack. All ships. Assistance, assistance. Heavy damage and casualties."

"What do you want?" another panic-stricken voice cried out. "We'll surrender. You can board us. We have no goods and few supplies. Please, stop firing. Our ships are full of workers—full of people. You're killing civilians. We're on fire!"

Scanners displayed an awful, one-sided battle among the transports.

Most of the old bulk freighters didn't even have weapons.

Each of the heavily armed Matayan destroyers was more than a match for them or most of the ships in Aunt Sleak's fleet.

Except for the 6m quad spinal guns of *The Dromon*.

One crippled freighter broke apart and exploded under concentrated fire from three destroyers. It didn't have any shields, and only minimal armor. Its two turrets either didn't work or had been taken out already.

Static and Matayan battle language rang out in triumph.

Dromon's four primary guns cut loose, lighting up the entire sector. Its blue-white blasts ripped into the lead corsair flagship and its wingships, disrupting their shields.

The starboard wingship took two hits and listed to one side. Its aft section exploded.

"This is Captain Sleak Maeris of Clan Maeris. Enemy vessels, be advised: Cease hostilities and vacate this system or be destroyed."

Matayan curses and laughter her only reply.

"Clan Maeris," one of the freighter captains cut in. "This is Captain Philsen of *The Botaru*. Help us! Our situation is desperate. The corsairs are trying to destroy us. We don't know why."

"Acknowledged. We're coming in. Disperse if you can. You're still too bunched up. Scatter and concentrate on defensive actions. Jump if you're able. We'll try to draw them off. We're boosting your distress call."

Three more corsairs turned on the fleet, with all twelve dozen fighters full front on intercept.

The other trio of Matayan attackers kept after the freighters.

Naero heard the pleading and the screams on the open channel, just before another freighter got blasted to oblivion.

Naero realized she had tears on her face.

Was that how her parents went? Blasted to death by Matayan guns?

The rage she felt nearly overwhelmed her reason.

She checked her systems, gripped the controls of her gunnery station, and forced her emotions to go cold.

Against superior numbers, Naero and her Clan Fleet closed for battle.

Amazon Link to Naero's Run: *http://amzn.to/1eRKCOb*

THE CITATION SERIES: BOOK 1

MASON ELLIOTT

NAERO'S WAR:

THE ANNEXATION WAR

NAERO'S WAR:
THE ANNEXATION WAR

Annexation War Amazon Link: *http://amzn.to/1gmxGQk*

by Mason Elliott

Naero's flagship, *The Hippolyta,* was one of the latest, Dromon Class dreadnaughts. These warships were fashioned out of dense, iron-nickel planetoids, not less than half a kilometer in diameter. Incredibly tough and rugged on their own.

It took the most powerful mining plasma-borers–working in precise conjunction with construction fixers and an army of teks– months to hollow out armored crew quarters, lift and transport tubes, launching and loading bays. Next came space for power cores, sublight engines, jump drives, backups, gravitics, life support, sensor arrays, communications, navigation, weapons, main bridge and backup bridge.

Set in the exact heart of *The Hippolyta* were its signature big guns. A quad of the largest production guns ever constructed on any ship of war: Four, *16 meter*, rapid-fire, particle beam cannons.

Cannons any larger than that exploded, melted, or otherwise were not feasible within the limits of current tek and materials. Thirty-six secondary batteries, assorted specialized weapons and gun emplacements, and forty-five advanced fighters.

Seven hundred and forty able crew, including a full Rifle Company of two hundred and forty Spacer Marines, and all of their equipment, vehicles, and gear for ship's security and rapid response deployment. Strike Fleet Six's Marines came from the 3rd Spacer Marine Division–known as *The Death Eyes*–because of their superb snipers and their overall, excellent marksmanship ratings. Marines made up a third of the warship's complement.

Their motto: *If We Can See It...We Can Kill It!*

The main bridge was a massive armored dome constructed on top of the dreadnaught's big metal, rough-hewn orb, protected by heavy blast doors, and the latest, most advanced shielding in the fleet. Within, the circular bridge was laid out in four levels under the huge dome, a dome sixty meters high.

Each bridge tier was separated by the height of a few steps from one to the next. The inner three levels could rotate in any direction, independent of the others.

The fleet captain's command nanochair and station occupied the highest tier. Each bridge station had its own secondary shielding, in case enemy fire penetrated the shields, the blast screens, and the hull.

In combat, bridges were routinely targeted, for obvious reasons.

From that primary vantage point, the strike fleet captain could direct battles in three hundred and sixty degrees, through an advanced, battleholo display surrounding her, full zoom data-feeds, constantly updated by battle AIs. Naero could manipulate the displays by nanosensors programmed into the fingertips of her nanosuit gloves.

The battle display system also recognized her voice pattern, and would respond to voice commands, or commands punched in manually through pads on her command chair, or via other backups.

The next bridge level down from hers held the secondary bridge stations: Helm, Weapons, Communications, Navigation, and Scanning, spaced out equally along their ring.

The third ring held all of the twelve tertiary bridge stations, that monitored, controlled, and coordinated all of the ship's other important functions:

Engineering
Gravitics
Life Support
Power Supply
Security
Shields
Medical
Jump and Sub-light Drives
Damage Control
Alliance Fleet and Intel Communications
Main Computer
Launching Bays

The fourth ring went to the two powerlifts, leading from the bridge to the other movers, decks, and levels of the ship. All lift and access points throughout the ship were constantly guarded by two battle-ready Marines, stationed on either side.

If a warship was boarded by enemy assault craft during a battle, invaders could be cut off and eliminated between decks, before they could reach a vital area.

Today, Strike Fleet Six had a mission—a simple one.

Captain Naero Maeris and her fifty warships proceeded to probe the next system on the outer, port arcwall of the Alliance advance at Beleron-4.

A routine run. Current intel assured them to expect little or no Triaxian presence or resistance.

By any stretch of the imagination, Beleron-4 was a nothing world, in the middle of nowhere, with zero, nacha—absolutely no strategic or tactical value whatsoever.

Checking it off the list on the pacified worlds of the Alliance system-hopping schedule was more-or-less just a formality.

But it still had to be done. And Naero and her lot drew the duty at random.

So why did Naero's sense of warning go bonkers?

After they jumped in, simple three-stack, Delta-India-3 formation, the reasons for alarm grew perfectly clear.

They came in right on top of twenty Triaxian fleets of the enemy's latest warships.

And a gigantic new flagship—as huge as *The Hippolyta*—the advanced design of which did not even register as existing.

It had never been seen before.

Naero shot to her feet, kicked her command nanochair back out the way and sent it down into the nanofloor of her top-tier bridge control station.

She instantly called her battle display holos up in spinning, horizontal glowing ribbons and rings all around her.

Data relays went wild. Her fingers flashed among the highlighted screen arcs, taking control of them and their parameters.

Multiple warnings sounded, and with excellent reason.

Nothing about this was good in any way.

Haisha! Twenty enemy fleets could chop them into confetti—well before any other Alliance forces could even jump in to help.

No strategy, no formation could possibly save them against superior numbers such as these.

"All ships, full withdraw. Emergency retreat on this vector, in Charlie-Romeo-7, cone-ring formation. Shields and all weapons full front and hot. Maximize all targeting profiles on the lead attacking enemy elements—they'll be on us in seconds. Whatever happens—we fight until our carriers and some of our ships can break free and jump out behind us. Get the carriers out first!"

For a split second, everyone braced for the sheets of flame that would quickly overtake and overwhelm them.

Annexation War Amazon Link: *http://amzn.to/1gmxGQk*

Please enjoy the following teaser…an excerpt, from the next Spacer Clans Adventure, Book 2:

NAERO'S
GAMBIT

A SPACER CLANS ADVENTURE

NAERO'S
GAMBIT

MASON ELLIOTT

NAERO'S GAMBIT

Naero's Gambit Amazon Link: *http://amzn.to/1lx5Tyy*

by Mason Elliott

Klyne set the huge Mystic testing room on board *The Kathmandu* to muted gray. Smartwalls, floor, and ceiling, Naero saw no equipment, no padding.

The lights were set low.

From experience, Naero knew that in a training room, just about anything could pop up out of anywhere.

She wore nothing but her black Nytex flight togs.

To her surprise, Klyne and his two adepts wore dark gray Nytex togs also, but with hoods and masks pulled up over their heads. Only their keen eyes showed.

All three of the Mystics appeared to be in top physical condition, including Klyne.

One of the adepts was female, with huge green eyes and light freckles across her nose. The other was male, with the black slanted eyes of the Lii-Kim Clans.

If black was the color of Spacers, the Mystics traditionally wore gray.

They all sat with their legs crossed in lotus fashion, focusing their abilities through meditation, and mental discipline. They formed a triangle, each side about three meters apart, with them at the points.

"Follow our instructions," Klyne said. "Take your place among us. Sit in the center; sit as we do. Face the instructor."

A circle of white light appeared at the center of the triangle. Naero walked over and sat down in it, facing Klyne. Her skin barely began to tingle.

A wider ring of similar light appeared, including the instructor and his two adepts.

Every hair on Naero's body went stiff with electric force.

"You have chosen to come before the circle of Spacer Mystics to be tested for Mystic training. Speak your name."

"Naero Amashin Maeris."

"You agree to be tested?"

"I do."

"I am Klyne, the instructor. My assistants are Adept Iselle, and Adept Makita. We shall refer to you as Adept Candidate Naero. Follow our instructions. Respond only if asked to respond. If you require any medical attention, it will be administered at the end of the testing. Until then, you are expected to endure and continue to do your best. If you understand, say yes."

"Yes."

"The training will begin. Defend yourself."

Without warning, Makita's attack smashed into her.

She blocked one or two out every four or five blows.

A snapwheel kick sent her flying twenty meters, nearly winding her.

The only things that saved her at all, once again, were the experience and knowledge she gained from her training sessions with Baeven.

Makita proved stronger and faster than her, but he still paled in comparison to the outcast's terrifying prowess.

Makita charged her.

Naero met him part way.

She took several punishing strikes, but flipped him hard to the ground.

He swept her legs.

They tangled on the ground, wrestling, slipping out of holds, twisting like snakes. They pummeled each other all the while.

They broke, crouched low, and launched themselves at each other again, like Telurian fighting blue cranes.

Naero landed a whipkick on the side of Makita's head.

He clipped her under the chin, grabbed her leg and ankle and swung her hard into the floor, stunning her.

She struggled to get up.

For a few dizzy moments, she couldn't.

She rose up and staggered back into her fighting stance.

She half-smiled.

"Come on."

Makita bowed his head, just slightly, and drew back.

"Defend yourself, "Klyne said again.

Naero whirled to face Iselle.

Too late.

An invisible force slammed into her arms and torso, flinging her back.

She rolled with the strike and came back up into her stance.

Iselle fought her from a distance, punching and striking with her hands in rapid combinations.

Naero struggled to advance, to close the distance between them, while heavy, unseen blows rained down on her from every direction, knocking her one way, and then the other.

"Telekinetic combat," Klyne called out. "Try to sense and block the blows. You cannot see them. Reach out with your battle senses, with your mind. Feel them coming. Counter and deflect them. True masters can fight thus, without even moving, simply by concentrating."

At least Iselle still had to physically move in order to project her attacks. That was some help.

Closer. Get closer.

Iselle thrust both hands forward violently.

A wall of force drove Naero slowly back. She pushed against it, slowing it even more.

"Resist. Focus on the energy before you," Klyne told her, "before it smashes you into the far wall. Fight back. Defeat it."

She rolled to one side and then the other. The barrier felt solid.

Naero leaped up four meters, felt the top, and flipped herself over it.

Iselle withdrew a step, cupping both hands loosely on the sides of her face.

Spinning orbs of pure telekinetic force shot out, rapid-fire.

Naero barely perceived them where they warped through the air; they made explosive popping sounds.

She tried to dodge them. One whirred past her head like an invisible ball at high speed.

The next clipped her left shoulder, spinning her aside.

Another knocked one leg out from under her.

She kept her feet and ducked, weaving to either side in turns.

Iselle directed her attack at Naero's feet.

Naero lost her footing, slipping and sliding on what felt like a bunch of invisible ball bearings cast beneath her.

She tried to roll back to her feet, but panes of force battered her from all sides, keeping her off balance.

It felt like being a rubber ball, bouncing around in a box that someone shook.

The sides of the box rapidly closed in.

They tightened all around her, threatening to crush her.

She couldn't breathe.

Iselle released her without warning.

Naero sprawled, gasping, face down on the floor.

"I'm somewhat surprised," Klyne noted. "Preliminary tests demonstrate no psyonic aptitude or innate talent to my trained senses whatsoever. That in itself is very rare. After your battle with the former Danner entity, we simply assumed that you would exhibit some kind of psyonic ability."

"I burned myself out dealing with the entity. I burned both of us out. I'm a nud once more." She admitted it openly. "None of my former abilities have returned."

So she wasn't psyonic anymore. Not even a teknomancer. Disappointing, but not the end of the universe.

"Yet I sense something incredibly strange within you," Klyne said. "What could it be?"

Was it Om? He was still inside her somewhere. He had not emerged again either.

"Take your place at the center of us once more. Face me again."

Naero did so, resisting an urge to massage several bruises.

Klyne positioned himself directly in front of her, sitting lotus fashion just like her and the others.

"I'm going to attempt to merge directly with your mind telepathically, one of my gifts. I'm also an Auralcognitor. Once I link with your mind, I can sense any type of psyonic energy field you might have, active, passive, or latent. I might even be able to trigger or bring them out to the surface. There might be some discomfort. Shall we proceed?"

"Sure."

"Do as I do. I will show you how to place your hands to effect the mind merge."

Klyne cupped his left hand firmly behind the base of her skull.

Naero followed his lead.

He placed the fingers of his right hand on precise spots on her face.

Thumb on her forehead, directly between her eyes.

Index finger on her left temple.

The next two fingers curled slightly in front of her left ear. His smallest finger hooked at the point of her ear and jaw.

As soon as Naero placed her right hand the same way, she gasped slightly.

Thin hairs of what felt like burning hot energy threaded their way slowly through the layers of her awareness.

She could feel Klyne connecting with her thoughts, joining their two minds.

The dull ache continued to grow.

"You should be feeling the initial discomfort. Hold still. Keep focusing. Almost there. Almost..."

A spike of pure agony exploded within her skull.

Naero screamed, transfixed as if by lightning.

Through the torment, a voice awoke in her mind full-force.

Protocols unlocked and engaged. We...are.

Interface...partial.

Om awoke, reacting instinctively with fear and vast power.

Threat detected...Protect all access.

Neural net...INTRUSION. UNWARRANTED.

LEVEL 1.359 DEFENSIVE RESPONSE.

An intense blast wave of white-hot psyonic energy fanned out rapidly from the epicenter of her immolated mind.

Naero continued to scream.

As if far away in the distance, Klyne and his two adepts also shrieked.

*

Naero blinked, her eyes and mouth frozen open.

She lay with her head to one side, in a puddle of her own mixed blood and spittle.

More pain struck her when she attempted to move.

Blood continued to stream from her eyes, ears, nose, and mouth–a bloody mess.

It felt as if a fusion grenade had blown her head open.

She reached up with her hands, to make sure her skull was still intact.

Some kind of noise.

Warning alarms sounded.

A ship. Yes, they were on a ship. The Spacer Intel Ship *The Kathmandu*. She was...being tested, for the Mystics.

Something had gone terribly wrong.

Naero focused, getting to her hands and knees.

She heard other voices, groaning and whimpering.

Makita lay sprawled in a broken tangle, blasted across the room. His gray clothing had been shredded and scorched into tatters. He choked and coughed.

To the other side, Iselle fared little better. She lay convulsing, blasted, scorched, a yellow-white bone of her forearm sticking out of her wrenched flesh. One side of her face was blistered, her red hair burned, some of it still smoking. She trembled and shuddered in pain and terror.

Naero looked around for Klyne, and found the instructor in a burned, bloody heap, lying beneath a dark red smear on the far wall. His hands were charred black, and he was missing fingers.

Naero could not walk. She couldn't even stand. She crawled to Klyne as quickly as she could.

He still lived, just barely.

Then she noticed the intense effects of the blast, all around the room, less than a meter up.

A massive expanding ring of Cosmic force had sliced into the duranadium hull of the smartwalls, punching a deep crease right through them where they buckled, all along its full diameter.

The force of the strike disrupted all systems. The entire training room was compacted, crushed, and heavily damaged.

Rescuers struggled to force their way through the various ruined doors and access panels.

Naero's Gambit Amazon Link: *http://amzn.to/1lx5Tyy*

Please enjoy the following teaser from the next book in *The Citation Series, Book Two:*
The High Crusade

NAERO'S WAR:

THE HIGH CRUSADE

Amazong Link for The High Crusade: http://amzn.to/1DbFD5F

by Mason Elliott

General Walker's Marines from Bravo Command maneuvered into position under the cover of darkness using their stealth gear.

Naero agreed to slip in ahead and bait the trap, in her battlefield role as Shettana–*The Dark Angel of Death.*

Get ready, Om. The show's about to start.

I will need some time to prepare, concentrate, and focus enough of our energies in reserve, before you deplete them all.

Just get ready and keep us ready. I'm going to set our game plan in motion.

I will do all that I can to assist. Call upon me when you require me. Good hunting, Naero.

Thanks, Om.

The invaders would do anything to have a chance to destroy or capture her.

She was–in fact–the actual, literal bait, and the trap was being set for an entire invasion force of Ejjai elite, ravaging the Corps border world of Tholos-4.

No local planetary army, military, or militia had been able to stand before the horrific onslaught of the alien invaders.

The Ejjai hammered the local landers into submission with advanced artillery, orbital bombardment from Ejjai fleets, and close assault gunships and gravtanks.

Then the terrifying collection process began, and all the living, wounded, and dead were hurled into the shrieking, whining processing blades of the robotic meatships.

The horrible sounds of the meatships warred with the screams of their countless victims.

Given time, Ejjai mass cloning factories and robotic ship and weapon-building factories would also be established onworld.

The murdering bastards had already wiped three major cities and their mixed populations off the surface of the hapless planet, before Naero and the Marines could even deploy on world.

The enemy left those lost cities little more than red, blackened, burning scars and stains that could be viewed from orbit.

Nothing left alive.

Ejjai hyaenanoids loved carrion.

Every man, woman, and child of any kind, species, or age that the enemy captured was routinely tortured, killed, and processed into rotting ration blocks in the horrific, robotic meatships of the invading aliens. That included any sentients, pets, livestock—anything and everything that was meat.

The meatblock rations were only frozen to keep them from breaking down, and decaying completely.

Hatred was too gentle a word for what most humans felt for the Ejjai invaders and their extreme methods. Spacers, landers, and each of the other known races that encountered the Ejjai quickly learned to feel the same way.

This vile, uplifted, intrusive and opportunistic species needed to be completely exterminated, wherever it was encountered.

The invaders proved that they were incapable of co-existing with any other living things.

The Ejjai could only dominate, torture, and destroy all life that they encountered, anything they could sink their teeth and claws into. Uplifting them, and giving them advanced weapons and starships had only turned them into a galactic abomination, an interstellar menace, a virulent plague.

An utter nightmare.

One that needed to end for the poor people of Tholos-4.

Naero and her Marine allies were here to see to that.

It was amusing that the Ejjai always saw themselves as invincible, the supreme warriors.

Shettana and Bravo Command quickly intended to disavow the foe of such jaded notions, time and time again.

The Marines of Bravo Commander were the textbook picture of professional warriors. A legend among all the known systems.

Naero loved serving with the elite of the elite. Together they made a fantastic team.

Even the Ejjai had learned grudgingly to fear them from their initial engagements, and the proof was there.

Every invader force that came up against Bravo Command had been completely wiped out–in record time. And then Bravo quietly packed up and headed on to the next world, ready to do it all over again.

The enemy struggled to halt the Spacer advance and throw it back.

They tried everything they could think of.

Increased enemy numbers.

Different tactics.

New weapons–traps and tricks of many different kinds.

The Ejjai generals turned themselves inside out trying to find a solution–way to achieve victory against the Spacer advance.

Bravo Command slipped in and ruined the invaders' sick, twisted party, every single time.

And Shettana, The Dark Angel of Death, used all of her amazing, Mystic powers and abilities to help the Marines keep up the pressure, and drive the enemy to terror, madness, and distraction.

General Walker worked closely with Spacer Intel, always making sure his leathernecks had the latest high-tek toys, weapons, and armor that came online.

As a result, they landed an entire Marine Division on Tholos-4 and slipped into position, without the enemy even knowing they were there yet.

By the time the Spacer Fleets swept in to destroy the enemy naval forces–Bravo Command would already be implementing their plan to put the foe down hard and fast on the ground.

Three Marine infantry regiments, one artillery regiment, plus specialized units of meks, armor, and air-to-ground support.

The ghosts of Bravo Command spread the impending Shadow of Vengeance and Death over their foes like an unseen net, without any knowledge or awareness among the invaders themselves.

Bravo and Shettana prepared for another stunning series of lightning attacks.

All became poised and ready, while the heedless enemy celebrated their vile victories and atrocities.

Naero struggled to remain silent as she slipped in among the foe. Death and damnation to any invader who thought they could invade the human sectors with impunity, death, and Cosmicide.

On every world, the invader needed to be taught that bloody lesson.

Naero strode right into the belly of the beast.

Alone.

Defiant.

Confident in her skills and abilities and all of her comrades depending on her and backing her up.

Her cloaked combat armor made her virtually invisible. The Ejjai could not even smell her.

She used her gravwing to slip into the most heavily guarded command and control bunker the enemy possessed. With her skill and her tek, she could crawl upside down on the ceilings like an unseen insect.

Her miniature vidcams and audio collectors fed data to Intel in real time, covering everything she saw.

Naero's small contingent of cloaked Intel fixers and microdrones stayed close, ready to disrupt key enemy systems and communications when ready, planting microbombs and detonation devices as they went.

The Invader High Command celebrated their latest triumph with what one might expect from them—a huge, decadent, disgusting feast—held within a shielded bunker.

They set up their victory celebration within a huge underground arena, probably used by the Tholosians for some kind of urban or regional sporting event.

Ejjai got drunk on stinking, fermented grog made from human blood. They shipped it in from the meatships by the tankerful.

Under the bright lights of the hi-tek arena, tens of thousands of Ejjai feasted and celebrated their latest victories. The enemy generals praised their troops and used the huge arena vidscreens to plot out their next attacks on the three nearest Tolosian cities.

On the center of the playing field, Ejjai transports and appropriated trucks had also hauled in and dumped huge piles of human corpses from the local population for their undefeated troops to feed on.

Piles of fresh and not so fresh meat, diverted from the enemy meatships to help sate the troops in large numbers.

One of the piles was all dead children and infants.

Even worse, to Naero's horror, some of the bodies in the various meat piles were somehow still alive. They twitched or cried out in pain and terror. Some weakly attempted to crawl away, despite broken or missing limbs.

The Ejjai quickly seized them and began tormenting them even further, laughing hysterically at the sport. They stabbed, cut, and skinned them alive—or otherwise got creative.

As Ejjai were wont to do.

Ejjai were among the vilest, most disgusting creatures Naero had even encountered.

She resisted the very strong impulse to cut loose on them right then and there.

But she couldn't–not yet.

These monsters needed to die. Every single one of them.

And very soon, she would have a direct hand in launching the attack that would accomplish just that.

The timing had to be just right, so she steeled herself.

The generals. Reach the generals and stay ready.

Six Ejjai generals held court like warlords at huge tables overflowing with comconsoles, sensor stations, map screens, and piles of loot. And the bloody remains of horrific, eviscerated meals.

All Ejjai clone troops were female. Smaller male Ejjai concubines were kept around on leashes for fun, for the leaders. They even dressed them in human clothing and poorly fitting human lingerie.

As an oddity, one of the generals even had a human male dressed up as a concubine. But the poor guy apparently had to be kept in a heavily guarded pen off to one side–to keep all of the other Ejjai from devouring and murdering him, most likely in that order.

Naero circled around the generals and studied the arena, trying to devise the best way to take them all down.

She listened intently to the plans the enemy generals were making, feeding it all to Intel.

"So, are all of the atomics and genocide devices in place yet?"

Another general pulled up a mapscreen displaying all of their installation of such devices planet wide.

Naero instantly transmitted all of that data directly to Spacer Intel as well–priority alert.

Intel and Bravo Command were most likely already neutralizing the most vital elements of the enemy plot. These genocide devices could be scanned and located from orbit. But it was always good to be sure, and to know their exact locations.

The Ejjai generals scoffed. "We will be ready for anything the enemy can throw at us in less than a day," one of the other Ejjai generals boasted.

"They won't know what's going to hit them until it's too late."

"Good, very good. Speed things up if you can. Get it all up and ready."

"Don't worry, sir. We will be more than ready to deal with their so-called Bravo Command—and their spack witch."

All of the Ejjai generals had a good laugh and congratulated each other.

The lead general stepped up to a waiting podium and addressed the crowd.

"Great news, sisters! We have it on good authority that the spacks are sending their precious Bravo Command and their spack witch Shettana against us."

Lots of cursing and booing about that roared up.

Their lead general continued. "This time, we are more than ready for them!"

Huge rounds of applause to that.

"Let me just say that we have some heavy duty surprises of our own ready and waiting and in store for our enemies. We can't wait for them to get here—and have them all for dinner!"

That brought an even bigger round of cheering, cursing, and applause.

"We will engage the spacks in a matter of days, and with our increased numbers and new weapons—I say we're going to kick their asses and stomp them bloody. We will gut them! I want all my girls out there to feast on spack Marine flesh until you puke!"

Further rounds of cheering and vile responses.

"We will ferment their blood in our huge vats and get drunk on it!"

More horrendous rounds of cheering and applause.

"And once we have captured their filthy spack witch, all of you will watch as I personally cut her up and rape her with red-hot knives, and torture her to death over the course of an entire week. She'll sing to all of us with her screams. Then I myself will feast upon her guts, and eat her heart while the light in her eyes fades. I'll crack her skull open and eat her brains!"

The Ejjai went crazy.

"Wait until we post *that* on the webnets for the spacks and the skinners to watch! I promise you victory. We cannot be defeated. And we will sweep the human skinners and all the other inferior races into our meatships and out of all existence. They are our prey! Yet another galaxy that shall fall to us and our mighty masters!"

More about their mysterious masters. Interesting.

Furious cheering continued in waves.

"So my warriors. Feast on meat until you vomit, and then feast some more. Then prepare for battle as we crush our foes and ravage the rest of this world. We shall drown it all in blood and swim in it! Prepare for our ultimate victory! Our time has come. None can stand against us!"

They erupted in an orgy of celebration and vile gluttony.

Fights broke out among the meat piles, and the Ejjai fought with and murdered each other in their frenzy.

The lead general returned to the others, rubbing her claws together eagerly in the midst of the chaos.

"My sisters, I have a special treat that I've saved just for us, at this exact moment. Please, enjoy my precious gifts to you all." She motioned to a large knot of troops off to one side among some gravtanks.

A full squad of Ejjai in heavy battle armor led out six terrified human women, all of them naked, and extremely pregnant.

None of them had a mark on them. Yet.

But from the looks on their pale faces, they all knew very well what the enemy generals intended to do with them. Each of them was heavy with child in the later stages of pregnancy.

That they had remained unspoiled and unharmed up until now would quickly change for the worse–the worst fate imaginable.

Although they were unbound, there was no chance for any of these captives to break free or escape on their own against so many foes.

The generals each glared at them and gloated. The Ejjai generals slavered and drooled, snapping jaws and smacking lips.

Each general had a set of rusty, bloodstained butchering tools that they began to place out in front of them in heady, eager anticipation of their coming feast.

Then the squad of Ejjai troops guarding the six women suddenly staggered a few feet away as if drunk.

Some melted into slag where they stood.

Other Ejjai troops exploded.

The six human captives looked around in confusion.

The next instant, they all vanished.

The six Ejjai generals shot to their feet in stunned surprise.

They couldn't even speak, but a few flung cleavers and knives at the spot where the captives had stood.

Their weapons fell harmlessly to the ground.

All of this was captured and displayed on the big arena screens, and slowly attracted the attention of the astonished crowds.

Then Shettana appeared as if by magic, right before the lead Ejjai general, resplendent in her full Angel of Death mode. She was all dressed in black, shining black hair flowing in the wind, violet eyes burning above her mask.

Twin blood-red katanas crackled and hissed in the damp air, at the ready in either hand.

Every eye fixed on her–while the mini-gravpods from her fixers whisked the six cloaked, female captives away to safety.

Naero only had to buy few more seconds for them to make it out. Fierce Marines waited nearby to take charge of them and keep them safe.

With the six captives out of the way, at last Shettana could go to work.

"I have come for you, filthy Ejjai cowards. I am Shettana!" she cried.

She rammed both of her swords through the lead general's eyes and out the back of the Ejjai's scorched skull.

Two of the generals tried to run.

The other three tried to attack her.

It did not matter.

Bolts of scarlet lighting tore forth from both her blades, ripping and blasting the other five into charred pieces of meat and bone.

Naero cloaked and shot away, as the area around the tables was engulfed in torrents of enemy weapon fire the very next instant.

Then the gravtanks, gunships, transports and other vehicles lined up nearby began to explode.

Naero projected multiple holos of herself all over the arena and in the in the air, drawing fire in all directions.

She used *the voice*, her words booming and echoing from several directions.

"EJJAI FILTH. PREPARE TO MEET DEATH. FOR SHETTANA IS THE DARK ANGEL OF DEATH, AND HAS NO FEAR OF MURDERING COWARDS."

The Ejjai fired in panic from so many angles that they cut down each other by the hundreds–just as Naero planned.

Fear began to infect them.

Gouts of red lightning lashed into the arena stands from several directions like gigantic whips of destruction. The devastation flung dead and dying Ejjai everywhere in a cyclone of slaughter, adding to the total chaos and confusion.

"NO MERCY, EJJAI SCUM. NO ESCAPE. FEAR IS MY MOTHER, DEATH MY SIRE, AND I THEIR DAUGHTER! YOU CANNOT HARM ME. THERE IS NO ESCAPE FOR YOU!"

Just as the enemy started to figure out they were shooting at holos and murdering each other wholesale, Naero merged with one in her mirror images in the midst of hundreds of Ejjai in the arena stands.

Multiple thin rods of red Chaos energy shot out from her, fanning in a diameter of thirty meters.

First she impaled hundreds of the shocked invaders.

When she spun, the red blades chopped them all into smaller gory chunks and pieces.

Torrents of unleashed Ejjai blood suddenly gathered and swept down the arena, carrying others away in a sudden red rushing tide of gore.

Naero cloaked and flashed away again.

More enemy fire stormed and tore at her former position.

She took the place of another holo, and sent forth a sweeping hurricane of of Chaos bubbles and orbs of every shape and size into another section of the stands.

The explosions collapsed that entire section. Wreckage toppled inward.

Next she appeared on the field before the horrendous meat piles, in the midst of hundreds of more frantic enemies.

Half of them flung their weapons away and ran in terror before her as she raced toward them. So much for the valiant Ejjai.

"STAND AND FIGHT, SCUM!"

Naero surged and fought with the mob of foes, sweeping one way and then the other, cutting them down by dozens, by scores.

She moved among them so fast they could not focus their attacks.

Then she would abruptly change direction and sweep another way before they could hem her in.

She unleashed more scarlet lightening strikes.

She sent random Chaos blasts into packed pockets of foes.

At times she just whirled and passed through them with her swords fully extended, mowing them down in lines and bunches.

Once she had shattered them completely, she merely turned her back on them and began walking away quickly and with determination, toward the nearest exit.

Naero set her shield pod full on.

Three enemy tanks roared at her, cannons blazing.

Naero dodged and deflected their blasts into the stands.

Two gravtanks she exploded with Chaos bombs.

The last she sliced the last in half with her swords and kept walking calmly, straight through the burning wreckage as the gravtank exploded directly behind her to either side.

She ignored all enemy fire directed at her, kept walking, and cut down anything stupid enough to attempt to stand before her.

She crackled with destroying red lightning as she passed into one of the exit tunnels, laying waste to anything before her.

The enemy regrouped and poured into the tunnel in hot pursuit.

Just as Naero hoped they would.

Another kill zone. How convenient of them to all bunch up for her.

She turned at bay, just before exiting, and focused all of her energies in an intense Chaos blast cone.

The massive detonation tore the tunnel apart and blasted shredded pieces of the packed invaders out the other end, right before a massive fireball that followed hard thereafter.

Naero cloaked, and called out over her secure link.

"You guys ready? I've got them primed, but I'm also almost out of juice."

"We're in place and ready to join the show, Shettana. You okay? Do you need us to extract you?"

"Negative. I can finish my part. It just takes a lot of energy to sustain attacks at this level. You guys know that. Did Intel take care of those genocide devices?"

"Almost all accounted for."

"All right, I'm setting up for my final show. They'll take the bait, all right. You guys hit them hard when they do."

"Hard as we can, Shettana. You know us."

"I sure do, and I can't wait to watch it all go down–right from the front row. Copy that. Make the legends proud, Bravo."

She took up her position in the center of the fallen city nearby, just outside of the shattered arena.

She formed a Chaos construct around her that duplicated her and her every move.

Her construct became a scarlet, giant version of herself, semi-transparent and fifteen meters tall, red and glowing with huge blazing swords.

She stomped on a meat ship and slashed at it until it exploded.

Then she attacked the clone ship factory next to it.

"FACE ME, COWARDS. SHETTANA SHOWS YOU HER MIGHT. SHOW ME YOURS. FACE ME AND PERISH!"

Yet in actuality, her energies waned with each passing second.

It wasn't like being back on Janosha where there was limitless Cosmic energy to tap into. Away from the Mystic Homeworlds, Naero's energy levels and her abilities were not infinite or limitless. She made a good show of it, but even she could not sustain these levels of attacks for very long.

The entire enemy invasion roared to life , and locked on, bunching and sweeping her way, to engage her from all directions.

The Ejjai went insane with fury.

Up in the skies above and beyond Tholos-4, the Spacer navy sent the invader fleets spinning down in flames.

Thousands of Spacer Marines suddenly materialized out of the black at key points and positions.

Phantoms who owned the night.

The black was their domain, their element, and they surrendered it to no one.

Bravo Command unleashed a torrent of concentrated, interlocking fire against the bunched up invaders. Veils of destroying fire, artillery, and ordnance–a deluge of precisely timed destruction that no living thing could possibly survive.

Within a matter of minutes, a quarter of a million Ejjai invaders flashed and flared into a sweeping typhoon of white-hot death that overtook them.

Naero had done her job.

Completely drained of all her mystic energies for the moment, she could barely stand.

Even as she staggered away, a full platoon of gigantic Sterodans in phaze armor appeared all around her.

They piled on and overwhelmed her with their greater mass, and several shock charges that hit and rippled through both them and her. The shock charges rattled Naero's teeth in her skull.

The Ejjai and their mysterious masters still wanted her and the KDM alive and intact, apparently.

Naero grinned.

Yet another trap, and she had stumbled right into it.

This time, the enemy thought they had her at last.

Yet Naero knew something they did not, and called out into her own mind.

Om–you're up. They've got me.

Take these bastards down hard and fast!

Amazon Link for The High Crusade: http://amzn.to/1DbFD5F

Please enjoy the following teaser...and excerpt, from the next Spacer Clans Adventure, Book 3:

NAERO'S FURY

NAERO'S FURY

MASON ELLIOTT

NAERO'S FURY

Amazon Link to Naero's Fury: http://amzn.to/1hLrPpO

by Mason Elliott

Naero still hadn't done it much, but going into a direct trance to enter the Astral Plane shouldn't be all that difficult. Master Vane had shown her how once. And she had gone there lots of times in her sleep, in her mind, to speak with Khai, using their astral crystals.

Before her friend Khai had vanished without a trace.

Yet she had never been completely trained in astral travel, and didn't know that much about exploring or moving around. Master Vane had taken her there once, just to teach her the basics and give her his marker. Many other times later to spar with her.

If nothing else, she could probably focus on his marker and locate him.

Zhen had roused Naero and reminded her it was time. And that she and Shalaen would monitor her while she was in the astral trance.

Naero focused her mind and abilities, controlling her breathing. Remembering the little she had recently learned.

Within several minutes of focused meditation, she open her eyes and found herself floating in the Astral Miasma, the nebulae of energy. She hugged her knees to her chest in her astral form.

Om spoke to her, even more easily here than in her own mind before.

I have accessed some of the Kexxian Matrix's data files on The Astral Plane. Like everything else, they explored it quite extensively.

Om, I'm naked here. I'm not complaining–but just tell me–how do I put astral clothing on again?

You control everything here by imagination, and force of will. Concentrate on your favorite clothing and they'll appear.

That's easy.

She looked down and saw her favorite Nytex flight togs, programmed just the way she liked them.

Naero blinked, spinning and twirling in one spot, turning upside down.

Why can't I move more than a meter at a time in front of us?

You're not used to this reality. So it's not clear to you.

The air around her looked opaque. Not mist. Not smoke or vapor. And it glowed slightly with its own bluish-gray light.

In the twilight she glowed softly blue-white with her own light. From within.

"I once heard rumors that the Mystics could travel and send messages this way, but I thought it was all just a myth."

Since the other planes are entire universes within themselves, it is said, they are all nearly infinite. Thus, it is difficult to pin point any kind of location or person unless you already know them.

Naero instinctively tried to stand up, but there was nothing to stand on.

Then she recalled Master Vane's Marker, and it appeared right before her. Where she found him, she would find the other High Masters.

At least she deserved a chance to be heard by them all. To try to explain herself and her actions. What happened with the obelisk was clearly not her fault.

But they would still blame her for it–especially Mater Vane, who seemed to blame her for everything since Hashiko's death.

Naero could not simply stand by and let the High Masters decide her fate without herself being present at her trial, in some way at least.

She focused on the crimson and black star more and swept forward, seemingly at great speed.

She came to an abrupt halt, like a starship coming out of jump at its destination.

The opacity around her partially melted away. She proceeded forward, opening her visual field far wider. She made out the area around her as the miasma peeled back.

Slightly below her, she saw spheres within glowing spheres, all spinning within greater spheres.

Her own sphere, glowing white-blue, suddenly surrounded her like a glittering soap bubble.

Yet it did not pop when she poked at it.

One sphere in particular, the largest, glowed and pulsed blood red, containing a withered old man with a long beard, pacing impatiently.

Burning eyes vanished and re-appeared at random all over his bald head. The red sphere absorbed Master Vane's marker.

Was this his true form? What he really looked like?

His scarlet sphere was also flanked by two smaller spheres with figures inside them.

Om made a calculated guess.

His current guardian adepts, no doubt. The ones you rescued from the enemy Darkforce generators on Janosha.

I think so, Om.

At most times, every High Master had at least two champion adepts protecting him or her, each of them very close to mastery themselves. Just as Hashiko had been.

Naero studied Vane's new guardians for the very first time, and tried to see into their spheres.

Something about each of them did seem strangely familiar.

One of Vane's adepts, the male, appeared to be so deep dark black, he could be a singularity. This adept's sphere was flat black on the surface and barely transparent.

If Naero had been able to breathe, she would have gasped.

Instead she simply raised her hand to her mouth.

She recalled that she had seen many of these adepts long before.

In her dreams, nightmares, and crazed visions. Perhaps even on the Astral Plane somehow.

Vane's other adept was the white female, the exact opposite of the other. So brilliant and blindingly radiant, she could be a pulsar. Her orb was like a high intensity bulb, blinding and almost completely crystal clear.

It occurred to Naero that during her initial testing, Klyne had male and female assistants as well.

She couldn't guess what the significance of that pattern was all about. Perhaps just some weird Mystic, egalitarian tradition.

Then why weren't any of the High Masters female?

Everyone seemed to ignore her where she floated.

The next larger sphere, farther away, glowed silver-blue.

If she focused intently on it, she discovered she could zoom in with her third eye–her mind's eye.

Within that silver-blue sphere, a silver man sat serenely, neither young nor old. Master Tree, in his purest form of order.

Two smaller guardian spheres flanked him.

Master Tree's female adept glowed with intense blue energy in a deep blue sphere.

The male likewise glowed with vibrant green force within a green sphere, a shining sword sheathed down his broad, athletic back. He seemed very familiar somehow.

Naero did a double-take. Long blond hair. Green skin. Big glowing sword.

Yep. In the flesh–or–astral form at least.

It was Khai! She was sure of it. He was alive.

Had he actually succeeded in his great task of forging his mystic sword in the heart of a gigantic pulsar? Was that it on his back?

Naero gasped again. Now that she knew what he looked like, Khai was also the dreamy green hunk from many past, pent up nightmares. The one who kept sticking his astral sword through her head.

What did it all mean? She wasn't nuts enough yet?

Now she knew for certain she needed serious help.

And to do some serious dating at some point, once-and-for-all.

If the Mystics continued to let her live.

Khai must have sensed her inner turmoil, or thoughts, or maybe just her concentration on him.

Mr. Green-god even glanced her way for a second, looking just as confused and puzzled by her sudden appearance.

Neither of them had ever met the other in person.

Naero covered her face with one hand and looked aside, withdrawing her sphere suddenly further away.

How fricking embarrassing.

She crept forward again. Slowly.

The third and final sphere glowed golden, and contained an equally golden child within, energetic and bristling with lightning. He bounced back and forth inside like a gigantic electron.

Master Jo of course.

Two flanking spheres.

One of his adepts had no clear form, eyes gleaming within a shifting, flickering miasma like the Astral Plane itself. His female counterpart shifted shape from one fantastic creature to another.

When she suddenly made out their voices, she could sense that an intense debate had been doing on. One that still continued.

"We cannot be certain in this matter," the golden child insisted. "We do not dare act in any rash way."

"Agreed, High Master Jo," the serene silver man added. "She might yet be another Trickster from what I can tell."

"Yes. Quite possible, High Master Tree."

The old man in the blood red sphere blustered impatiently. "Fools! Always conspiring against me. Taking positions opposite of mine for no reason but to anger me. I've been telling you all along, this child is clearly the Great Destroyer—long foretold. Our duty is clear. She is a threat to all existence. To multiple dimensions. She must be eliminated, at once, before she can grow even more powerful."

"High Master Vane," Tree said. "None of us can be sure of that fact. Including you."

"I am."

"You are always certain when it comes to destroying someone," Jo added. "Your pure Chaos answer to everything. Destruction or Creation."

"It works."

"No. It doesn't. It only delays and worsens the inevitable," Tree said. "The Universe shall have its way. We all know this. You were mistaken with the last savant when he appeared, and now he remains at large–a renegade beyond even our control."

Baeven? We're they referring to her uncle?

Vane rolled his eyes. "Idiots! The Renegade is the Trickster, I say. This child must in fact be the Great Destroyer. Just look at the powers roiling within her. They will surely corrupt and overwhelm her entirely and drive her mad in the end. She will go berserk on a scale that makes her recent outbursts feeble and puny by comparison. She must perish now, while we have a chance to put an end to her. While the only crimes she has committed include destroying an entire planet, and another of the vital obelisks!"

"We still don't understand the purpose of the ancient obelisks. And we've studied the mysterious disappearance of Janosha, and we still cannot be certain in any conclusive way, that she had anything to do with it."

"Really? Who else could it be then? Planets like Janosha aren't in the habit of just obliterating themselves suddenly for no reason at all. Everywhere she goes, destruction follows!"

I cannot allow this.

Quiet, Om. Don't do anything. I'm trying to listen.

Naero...they're discussing our destruction. The Chaos Master means to destroy us.

Master Jo continued to protest. "You can't just kill off every entity that manifests Cosmic Abilities such as these. Our universe is peppered with them. We must continue to locate and guide them–not find excuses to execute them. Like the Others have told us, Tricksters often appear to oppose Great Destroyers. Without the former, final victory is never possible. "

"High Masters," Tree said. "This young woman also possesses the Kexxian Data Matrix. We cannot destroy her without destroying it. Intel and The Spacer Council of Elders value our wisdom, but even they would not agree to such action."

"Regrettable," Vane said. "Yet I cannot take the risk. I have decided this matter on my own."

"You have no such authority on your own," Tree insisted.

"Idiots! I cannot stand by and allow our galaxy–perhaps our entire universe to be destroyed–just to satisfy your foolish, philosophical, and theoretical whims."

Master Vane turned to his adepts. "My finest students, obey me. Delay these fools. Keep them occupied whilst I act for the good of all existence."

More rapid than thought, the male dark ensnared the blue sphere and its satellites in coils and tendrils of darkness. While the bright female enveloped the golden sphere and its companions in waves of of pure light.

Naero tried to pull away, but in her panic she did not know where to go.

High Master Vane sped straight at her with impossible speed.

I must act, Naero.

No, Om. Please, this is already bad enough. Don't do anything.

I cannot comply. I must defend us!

Naero went down on her hands and knees before Master Vane. She called out, using *the voice* to project her words.

"Please, Master Vane. Do not attack me. I only wish to be trained to control my abilities. I have struggled hard to do so. I still don't understand what happened with the obelisk."

Vane bore down on her, arcs of pure scarlet energy bristling around him.

"Far too late for that, monster. Nothing is ever your fault, is it? Now, you must perish for the good of all. I told you this hour would come."

Instinctively, Naero drew back again, trying to evade his attack. She rose within her receding sphere.

Vane closed in once more, gathering his powers.

"Don't do this," Naero begged. "Please. Help me. I know I can't fully control all of my abilities yet. I'm trying as hard as I can. I can't be responsible for what will happen if you attack me. I can't control myself."

"Yes, and look at the results? Countless lives crushed and eradicated. Janosha vaporized–an entire planet. You must never be allowed to reach your full potential. Now–monster–hold still and embrace your fate."

Naero put her hands out before her, holding her palms out defensively. Pleading.

"No. Don't. I can't–"

"I know, Maeris. You can't help yourself. That is why you are *an abomination*!"

Vane smashed into her, piercing all of her defenses as if they were shattering glass.

In the distance, she sensed that Master Jo and Master Tree finally broke free.

Too late.

Master Vane attacked, trying to overwhelm her with raw power.

He pummeled her with impossible blows.

In the end, he beat her up badly, but only succeeded in knocking her around once more.

Om roared in their mind.

Kexxian defense protocols unlocked and on line.

An energized, glowing armor of some advanced origin formed around Naero like a hi-tek battle suit.

Naero saw out of her third eye as it awoke and burst into radiance like a blue-white star.

Master Vane came at her once more, all of his powers focused through his primary scarlet, burning eye, centered in his forehead.

All of his other flaming eyes closed as he concentrated, his skull wreathed in weird cosmic flames like a mane of cosmic fire.

"See how powerful you have already become? No adept could have withstood those lethal attacks. We must finish this now, before the others can interfere."

"Please, Master Vane. Please–I'm begging you–please, don't do this."

"Maeris, just as I foretold–you shall fall before the greatest of all Cosmic attack techniques. And I am one of the few who have ever learned to master it: The Eye of Annihilation!"

The same Chaos technique that had destroyed Hashiko–even she couldn't control it properly.

A massive blood red beam of destroying Cosmic force shot straight at her.

It all happened so fast. Naero heard Om screaming.

Reflection defense. Analyze incoming cosmic assault. Duplicate and reflect attack tenfold!

Just before the incoming blast vaporized her, a blue-white beam shot out of her own third eye to war against Master Vane's powers.

The Cosmic flows flared intensely.

Naero screamed as if her body and soul were being sucked through the eye of a black hole's needle.

The wide blue beam quickly drove the red beam back to its source.

At the last instant, High Master Vane cried out in terror.

"Impossible! There can be no such–"

The destroying energy ignited on contact.

A massive detonation on the Astral Plane blinded the area within a few light years.

High Masters Jo and Tree barely managed to withdraw and shield the others. All of their spheres shattered.

Pure cosmic energy punched into High Master Vane right before Naero's eyes.

It drove him back like a white-hot comet.

He struggled against it with all his might.

To no avail.

The reflected attack obliterated High Master Vane to glowing ash and dust, screaming in the wake of his own annihilation.

Vane's dying force of will echoed off into the universe.

Naero would have caught her breath if she had any.

The outcome left her completely stunned for a shuddering instant.

Om…what did we just do?

We had no choice, Naero. My sole purpose is to defend our current form.

Naero stared down at her hands in terror. Tendrils of Cosmic energy rippled and still curled off of her body and her sphere like smoke.

Om…*Haisha!* We just killed a High Master of the Spacer Mystics!

Amazon Link to Naero's Fury: http://amzn.to/1hLrPpO

Please enjoy this teaser for The Citation Series, Book 3:

Naero's Trial Amazon Link : http://amzn.to/1oaMNE3

NAERO'S WAR:

NAERO'S TRIAL

Naero's Trial Amazon Link: http://amzn.to/1oaMNE3

by Mason Elliott

On the third day of Naero's trial, the Prosecution and the Defense made their final, closing statements.

Master Jo spoke first, for the Defense.

"In the final analysis, I would both conclude and insist that Naero Amashin Maeris has proven herself time and time again to be an honorable Spacer, and that her word is without question. She is also vital to the survival of her people in many important ways. Naero Amashin Maeris is a noble, invaluable warrior and a proven leader who has served the Clans and the Alliance well, in both peacetime and war. A Mystic Champion who is now part of the great and mysterious Cosmic Prophecy, long foretold. There is still so little that we do not know about those prophecies; who can say what her role will be in the end?"

Master Jo paced a bit. "And on a very basic level, she is a Spacer. As such, she has the right of all Spacers and all sentients to defend herself, to the death, against anyone who attempts to kill her. Reluctantly, she only resorted to lethal force when High Master Vane attacked her with the intent to destroy her, and take her life. Even after she had tried to get away from him, and begged him repeatedly not to attack her.

"She cannot not be convicted of murder for defending her own life against someone trying to kill her. Those are all many good reasons why you must see fit to exonerate her of these erroneous charges. We cannot take the life of this hero."

The Defense finally rested.

Master Tree was given the final word in the trial for the prosecution.

"Hero? First, let me also revisit the reckless side of this renegade, outlaw Spacer, who fled from justice and had to be brought back by force to face her crimes in shackles, in order to keep her from getting away once again. On several occasions, Naero Amashin Maeris has proven herself to be dangerous, unpredictable, and out of control. By her own words, she has more than once declared that if she ever lost control and became a threat to any of her people, that she herself agreed that she should be put down–and destroyed.

"The cold blooded murder of a High Mystic Master has not demonstrated this fact readily enough? Beyond all doubt? If she can slay a High Master of the Mystics so easily, how much more is she a danger to all? And she even admits that she cannot control her abilities. Her very existence has become such a clear and present threat that it cannot be ignored and must be dealt with. I repeat, she has admitted on several occasions that her powers can go out of control and be very dangerous.

"Next, she also clearly admits that she killed Master Vane. Now, of her own accord, she claims that she killed him in self defense. But she has thus far presented no single shred of proof of that. She claims that Master Vane attacked her, attempted to kill her, and that she killed him, as she now conveniently claims–in so-called self defense. And I remind everyone in this court, once again. It does not matter who she is, what she is, or whatever else she has done. No one is above Spacer Law.

"Not even the infamous, Naero Amashin Maeris."

Tree took in a breath and clasped his hands behind his back. "What are the facts, therefore? A High Mystic Master lies dead, murdered by his own student, who openly stated that she could not stand him. Who openly admitted that she killed him. Nothing else can be proven, beyond those facts. Nothing else exists as fact. And this case must only be decided, based solely upon the facts. Nothing else.

"A Spacer on trial for her life could readily claim and say anything. Merely stating something does not make it true. That does not prove it to be fact. According to the facts of what is known, Naero Amashin Maeris is clearly guilty of murder, and will undoubtedly say and do anything possible in order to get away with her crime. As anyone logically would, in order to escape punishment, justice, and execution."

Naero fumed. Haisha! What the hell did they expect her to say? Yes, I offed the asshole, I loved it, and I'm a fricking monster. Go ahead and kill me?

I wish that weren't so painfully funny, Naero.
Me too, Om.

Master Tree went on to demand that the jury uphold one of the key tenets of Spacer Law and Spacer society:

"Spacers do not murder other Spacers and take their lives! Naero Amashin Maeris is not above that law. Naero Amashin Maeris broke that solemn law. And like it or not, the law demands justice. There is no way around that law and no way to escape it. That law demands that she face the ultimate punishment for her being guilty of committing the ultimate crime!"

Tree emphasized his final point with a single, upraised index finger. "That punishment is immediate Death, by execution. To be carried out by beheading, at the hands and the blade of the Mystic Enforcer!"

The Prosecution rested its case.

Admiral Klyne looked slightly pale as he instructed the jury of Mystic Elders to decide the case and announce their decision after their period of deliberation.

Naero went back to her cell in silence feeling sick, unable to meet Khai's utterly heartbroken glance. She felt stunned and numb. She didn't know what to think. All that she could do was await the jury's decision, along with everyone else.

Yet it was her fate alone that was being decided.

But when she thought about it further it wasn't just her fate.

Everyone waited for eight long hours.

Naero could neither rest nor sleep.

Then everyone was summoned back to the court room.

A decision had been made. The jury had arrived at a verdict in her case.

Admiral Klyne announced, "All rise for the verdict to be read." They did so.

The jury leader stood up and read their decision.

"According to Spacer Law, and based upon all of the facts and evidence presented, we the jury find the defendant, Naero Amashin Maeris, of Clan Maeris…guilty of murder in the death of another Spacer."

Naero gasped, nailed to the bedrock of the planet itself in almost complete shock.

Guilty meant…

Master Tree rose up. "This Mystic trial has ended; it is over. A verdict has been reached. Without question, this grim crime is punishable among our people by death. Under the circumstances, the sentence is to be carried out immediately and without delay."

Naero, I can–

Shut up, Om.

Naero gasped and covered her mouth with both hands as she sobbed and went down on one knee.

Then she dropped her hands to her abdomen and her eyes met Khai's in explosive waves of desperate horror and regret.

Their child from their love within that distant star barely grew within her. Now, no time remained to tell Khai all that she needed to before he performed his duty as the Mystic Enforcer.

Before he took her head…ended her life, and the lives of his own family.

Naero Amashin Maeris clenched her fists, and rose up with her head held high to meet her fate with her eyes clear and wide open, if that was what must be.

Amazon Link for *Naero's Trial*: http://amzn.to/1oaMNE3

Edition Notes

If you do not see this edition note here in this spot on the copyright page and on the very last page of your ebook or print version of this title, then you are not getting the final, polished version of this novel that the publisher, editors, and author intended for you to receive. Please contact either the publisher or the author via their emails or websites if you do not see the following update code:

High Mark Publishing Update Code K2428E